P9-ELQ-196

THE

FRIEND

ALSO BY JOAKIM ZANDER

The Swimmer

The Believer

THE FRIEND

A NOVEL

JOAKIM ZANDER

TRANSLATED BY

ELIZABETH CLARK WESSEL

HARPER
An Imprint of HarperCollins*Publishers*

Originally published as *Vännen* in Sweden in 2018 by Wahlström & Widstrand.

FIRST U.S. EDITION PUBLISHED 2019.

Library of Congress Cataloging-in-Publication Data

Names: Zander, Joakim, author. | Wessel, Elizabeth Clark, translator.

Title: The friend: a novel / Joakim Zander; translated by Elizabeth Clark Wessel.

Other titles: Vannen. English

Description: New York: Harper, [2019]

Identifiers: LCCN 2018059008 (print) | LCCN 2019000392 (ebook) | ISBN 9780062859426 (E-book) | ISBN 9780062859358 (paperback)

Subjects: | BISAC: FICTION / Espionage. | FICTION / Action & Adventure. | GSAFD: Suspense fiction. | Spy stories.

Classification: LCC PT9877.36.A65 (ebook) | LCC PT9877.36.A65 V3613 2019 (print) | DDC 839.73/8—dc23 LC record available at https://lccn.loc.gov/2018059008

ISBN 978-0-06-291499-6 (library edition)

19 20 21 22 23 LSC 10 9 8 7 6 5 4 3 2 1

To Lukas and Milla, always

THE FRIEND

1

AUGUST 5—BEIRUT

SOME THINGS HAPPEN so fast. Jacob Seger lands in Beirut, confused. He slept on the plane, so perhaps he's still half asleep as he follows a stream of travelers headed to border control, to the heavily armed policemen or soldiers or whatever they are, who ask him why he's visiting Beirut, how long he plans to stay, why he doesn't have diplomatic status if he's going to be working at the Swedish embassy.

"Intern," he says. "I'm just an intern. Not a diplomat."

Not yet, he wants to add, slowly starting to wake up. *I'm not a diplomat yet*. This is just the first step. This and getting his degree in political science at Uppsala. All he has to do is pass that grueling statistics exam and complete this internship, then write his thesis. After that he'll get a real job at the Ministry for Foreign Affairs. That's his goal. He's been dreaming about it for the four years he's been in Uppsala, buying *The Economist*, studying up on heads of state in obscure Asian countries, Swedish exports, and Nobel laureates so he can pass the Foreign Service entrance exam. A blue diplomatic passport and a calfskin leather briefcase, that's the goal. He just needs to get a handle on his French and Arabic. A tiny, familiar squirt of anxiety shoots through him there at the counter, while a man in uniform with a tired, neutral expression looks him over. Languages are his Achilles' heel, and unfortunately they're key in a diplomatic career. He tenses up at just the thought of sitting in a classroom, memorizing vocabulary. It doesn't even help that his Arabic teacher, Hassan Aziz, an Iraqi man in his sixties with thick gray hair and a knitted tie, has offered to give him private lessons at his apartment outside Stockholm.

"I can see how much you want to learn, Jacob," Hassan often tells him, patiently, after class. "But you have to practice at home too. You're welcome to come to my home once a week, and we'll work on it together if you like."

But Jacob feels ill just thinking about studying at home. He can't stand the thought of hours spent on a train and a subway getting to and from Hassan's suburban apartment. He doesn't have the energy for that struggle. He just wants to be able to do it. Like in *The Matrix*: "I know kung fu."

He shakes off the thought. It doesn't matter. He'll take care of French and Arabic later. He surely can't be stopped by that; it would be too unfair. He's meant for this life, meant for airports and important missions.

His spirits lift again when the police officer or soldier or whoever he is hands him back his passport, his anticipation increasing as he passes by border control and follows the green signs toward the exit.

The arrival hall is full of a stifling Mediterranean humidity, automobile exhaust, cigarette smoke, and taxi drivers holding handwritten signs in Arabic, which Jacob should be able to read after his half-year course in the language, but he dejectedly realizes he can't. His pulse starts to race again. Will they test him on his Arabic at the embassy? He got this internship by claiming upper-intermediate proficiency in Arabic. Was that a lie? He decides to consider it a question of definition. Travelers push and jostle their way out toward the parking lots and taxi queues, while Jacob stops and looks around.

Someone was supposed to meet him here. Someone from the embassy. He was expecting to see a sign for "Seger" there among the taxi drivers, and he scans them again with the same distressing result. He'd hoped a black Mercedes or a Volvo would be waiting for him, the embassy's second-in-command sitting in the back seat with a briefing on Jacob's first mission. Some negotiation or a meeting with the Lebanese government, or maybe he'd be sent out directly on a fact-finding mission to a refugee camp or straight to a cocktail party at the French embassy. Childish, of course: he knew it wouldn't be like that right away, not on the first day, but he'd expected something, some indication. A task. The opportunity to show them he was a man with a future ahead of him. Someone to remember. Somebody to bet on.

But no one is here. Nobody has his name on a sign. No stressed-out European is scanning the arrival hall. Jacob takes out his phone. He made sure his cell phone would work here, just one small detail in his preparation. It's expensive to call—he knows that—and if there's one thing he doesn't have, it's money. But he looks up the number he received a few weeks ago for an Agneta Adelheim, while taking a seat on a bench.

It's important to be quick-witted, resourceful. Never end up the victim of circumstances; take control of the situation and handle it. It makes him happy to see the Adelheim name again. Not just some boring old Andersson. He even looked it up, and it is indeed aristocratic. That feels good. That's where he's headed, a world of diplomats with aristocratic last names. A small rush of satisfaction tingles up his spine as he pushes on her name in his contacts list, and the phone starts to ring.

But Agneta doesn't answer, and his call isn't forwarded to an answering machine. After fifteen rings, he stops trying, closes his eyes, and leans back on the bench. The concrete is cool against the short blond hair of his neck. He's sitting in the airport in Beirut. His first time in the Middle East. His first time outside of Europe. For a moment it feels like he's drowning; he gasps for breath, opens his eyes wide.

"No, no, no," he says out loud to himself.

He calms himself down. Time to be resourceful.

He calls Agneta Adelheim again. When she answers on the second ring, relief washes over him.

"Oh no," she says when Jacob introduces himself. "I'm so sorry. I was sure it was next week you were coming. I'll be there in half an hour."

Jacob hangs up, shaking off his disappointment. They forgot about him. It's a setback, but things like that happen. They have a lot on their plate. Of course things fall through the cracks. A person can't keep track of every little detail. It doesn't mean he won't be able to amaze them.

He pulls a copy of *Dagens Nyheter* out of his newly purchased brown leather briefcase. He's been carrying the newspaper since boarding the flight in Stockholm, but only now does he open it. *Might as well get up to speed on the latest news*, he thinks, skimming the front page. He's mainly looking for anything related to Beirut. He read online about the demonstrations taking place at the government headquarters. About garbage not being picked up, filling the streets with stench and disease because the government is so corrupt and dysfunctional. But none of that is in this newspaper. Instead, there is some Swedish Security Service scandal breaking in Sweden. He remembers hearing about it on the news yesterday, but he was too preoccupied to make much sense of it.

Now he has time. A half hour at least, and as he unfolds the newspaper, he sees a photo of a red-haired woman in her thirties, dressed professionally, taking up half the first page. Green eyes and a resolute expression, she's standing at some kind of press conference.

The headline reads:

RUSSIA BEHIND RIOTS IN THE SUBURBS

Jacob devours the article in just a few minutes, then reads the editorial and all the follow-up articles. Apparently, a Russian company with direct links to the Kremlin paid a Swedish professor to write a report for the Council of the European Union to persuade them to increase the privatization of European police forces. In the meantime, that same company helped to organize riots in several suburbs to coincide with the presentation of that report to the EU ministers during a meeting in Stockholm last week. Their goal was to destabilize the police and increase opportunities for private companies with Russian ties to take over some policing duties. And Säpo, the Swedish Security Service, knew about the whole plot and allowed it to happen.

Jacob flips back to the front page again, to the picture of the attractive red-haired woman. Gabriella Seichelmann. An attorney at one of Sweden's most prestigious firms. She was the whistleblower on all of this. Apparently, there were other people involved, but she's the public face. She's the one who presented the witness statements and documentation to journalists, who were allowed to read them only if they promised not to publish anything classified. The documents were verified by the journalists, but Säpo is still refusing to comment.

Jacob puts down the newspaper with his heart pounding in his chest. It's like a spy movie. So exciting, and yet the more he reads about it, the more jealous he gets.

That lawyer. She can't be that much older than him? Five, six years at the most? He sighs deeply. Can you imagine being in the middle of something like that? Standing up to powerful people. Your face and name splashed across every newspaper. It makes him feel so small. His internship, his unfinished statistics exam. His inability to master the languages he needs for a career that still won't be nearly as dazzling as what this Seichelmann has already achieved. Maybe he should have gone into law instead?

His phone beeps. Maybe Agneta is finally here. But he takes it out, and it's only Simon. Of course.

Have you landed yet, babe?

Babe. It annoys Jacob. How long is it going to take Simon to understand what they had this spring is over? They've barely seen each other all summer. Does Jacob really have to spell it out?

Sure, it was exciting. And it meant a lot more to Jacob than he'd let on to Simon. And maybe there could have been something more, something that made the word *babe* seem like a good fit. If Jacob had given in and let go. If he'd abandoned himself to the whole thing. But it moved too fast. Simon started talking about moving in together after just three weeks. Jacob felt the urge to be together all the time too. Felt like he never wanted to leave their bed. But he forced himself, refused to give in to the *flesh*. That wasn't what he'd gone to Uppsala for. It wasn't part of the plan. Not at all. And pretty soon Simon started talking about meeting Jacob's parents.

"You could at least tell me about them," he'd said. "I bet your mother is so glamorous and your father so strict. I bet their sex life is hot."

That's when Jacob couldn't take any more. He couldn't tell Simon about his parents. He'd left them far, far behind the person he'd become after leaving Eskilstuna, the small town where he grew up. They weren't a part of who he was, who he was going to be. They didn't fit into the Uppsala version of Jacob Seger. The diplomat version.

"Jacob?"

A voice startles him out of this line of thought, and when he looks up he sees a woman in her fifties with gray hair, wearing a thin navy-blue dress, standing in front of him.

"I'm Agneta Adelheim," she says. "I'm so sorry to make you wait."

Finally, Jacob is sitting in the back seat of a black Volvo, peering out the window as they drive through the suburbs on their way to central Beirut. At first it's just highways and Hezbollah's yellow-and-green flags, then slums and blindingly bright sun. As they get closer to the center, he sees bullet holes and shining glass. Construction cranes rising out of history. In the inner city, it's all traffic and rotting garbage on the corner of every street.

They get out of the car, go through the front door, climb the stairs. Enter some kind of conference room. Agneta starts talking about the embassy and how chaotic the situation is. They sit down among the blond wood tables and steel chairs, which glide silently across the floor when Jacob adjusts his position. They sit across from each other, drinking lukewarm water from bottles with peeling labels.

"You know this embassy is only temporary?" she asks. "We had to move the Syrian embassy here when the situation in Damascus got too dangerous."

Jacob nods. He knows all about that, he read up.

"And I don't really know . . ." Agneta continues. "I don't really know what they were thinking sending an intern into the middle of all this. The situation isn't normal right now. To say the least."

Jacob swallows. Is it his lack of Arabic skills? Is now when they'll be exposed?

"But what do I know?" Agneta sighs. "I'm just an assistant here. It's not my decision. Besides, we thought you were coming next week, so I'm afraid we don't have much for you to do right now. I managed to arrange an apartment in eastern Beirut for you. A colleague at the French embassy will be gone all through the autumn, so we're renting it for you. I suggest we put your documents in order and get you set up there. Then you start next week."

They go through a bunch of papers together, Jacob receives a security card to enter the embassy, and before he knows it they're back in the Volvo again, headed east, crossing over the green line Jacob read about during his summer vacation. The one that divides Muslim Beirut from Christian Beirut, the area he'll be living in. During the civil war it was the frontline. Now it's a throughway, nothing more.

Agneta asks the driver to stop outside Saliba Market.

"That's the address," she says. "They don't really use street numbers here. Just say Armenia Street, near Saliba Market to your taxi drivers, okay?"

Agneta unlocks the door to a stunning art deco apartment with mosaic flooring and a small balcony, facing out onto the street and the bullet holes and then finally the harbor and the sea.

"I'm sure you can take care of yourself from here," she says. "You seem like a resourceful young man."

Jacob's chest swells when she says that; it almost feels like he might float right off the ground with pride. Resourceful. Sure, despite her promising, impressive name, she's only an assistant. But if she sees it, won't the others see it too?

NOVEMBER 21—SANKT ANNA

THE SNOW IS heavier now, the flakes no longer fluffy and light, but small, hard, and mean. They don't melt where they land on the gray grass, the gray rocks, the gray fields that surround Sankt Anna's old church in the Östergötland archipelago. Instead, they form drifts and layers, small slopes against stone fences and tree trunks, windswept embankments leaning on the stone walls of the small church.

Klara Walldéen is squatting with her back to that church, and she turns up her face now to the snow, closes her eyes, lets it fall on her, lets it melt on her eyelids and forehead. It flows down her temples and cheeks, in under the collar of her navy-blue coat, down along her neck and collarbone, under her black dress. She lets the snow be the tears she can't cry.

"Your grandma said you were out here."

Klara is startled, opens her eyes, and almost loses her balance. She puts her hand down on the cold, muddy grass to keep from falling. Gabriella stands in front of her, thick red hair in a tight braid, wearing a dark coat, dark tights, funeral attire down to the minutest detail. With some effort, Klara straightens up, gets to her feet; she can feel the cold, sticky mud on the palm of her hand.

"Damn, you scared me," she says. "I didn't hear you."

Gabriella's arms are around her now, pressing her in toward the scent of jasmine and citrus.

I want to smell like a garden by the Nile, Gabriella had said when she bought this perfume for the first time at NK in Stockholm many years ago, back when they were students. Klara still remembers how she laughed at Gabriella's ironic, somewhat irritated facial expression.

Now Klara lets her arms hang down by her sides, doesn't have the energy to lift them, doesn't want to put her dirty hand on Gabriella, so she lets herself be held, lets herself be enveloped by Gabriella's warmth.

"I'm so sorry, Klara," Gabriella whispers.

Gabriella's lips are cold against Klara's ear. Klara presses herself closer to Gabriella, pushing her face past the collar of Gabriella's coat until it's resting against Gabriella's soft, warm neck. And Gabriella just pulls her closer.

And then, at last, Klara begins to weep.

Ten days since Grandpa died. Two months since he took her out on his boat with a thermos and a net, fished his flask out of his pocket, and poured a large splash of his homebrew into his cup of coffee while insisting that Klara do the same.

"Just this once, Klara," he said. "I know you don't drink anymore, but today we'll both need it."

She'd already seen the glances passed between grandparents when she'd visited a few months before, right before summer. Noticed he'd lost weight, his cheeks looking sunken, and they kept mentioning trips to Norrköping or Linköping for "errands." But these were errands she didn't ask about, signs she didn't want to interpret, an all-too-simple puzzle she refused to solve. It would have been easy to disappear into the chaos of London, to bury herself in work at the university. To just focus on her job, finding a way back to a normal life, and not drinking. But when they asked her to come home for a weekend in September, she knew.

There was no wind that Saturday morning; the boat was still, and Klara took a sip of her coffee, grimaced, then swallowed the whole cup, burning her tongue and the roof of her mouth in the process. And while the liquor flowed through her like a wave, she met her grandfather's eyes.

"How long?" she said. "How long do you have?"

But she didn't cry. Not when he told her the cancer had spread and was aggressive and they found it too late, though that probably didn't matter, and it would have ended up the same. She didn't cry when he told her he'd refused treatment, because it was useless anyway, would only buy him a few months of vomiting and pain at the most. She didn't even cry when he sat on the bench next to her and held her close just like when she was a child, when he and Grandma were raising her on the outskirts of the archipelago.

"My time has come, Klara sweetie," he said. "What do I have to complain about? I've had a long life with your grandmother. And when we lost your mother, we got you. Sorrow and joy."

He grabbed her chin and looked at her intensely with those bright blue eyes.

"Don't be afraid of any of it," he said. "Not sorrow, not joy. You have to learn that, my heart. Do you promise? Will you remember?"

Klara hadn't understood what he meant, could barely even hear his voice at the time. But at last, she does. Now, standing here in the snow, in the arms of her very best friend, she knows.

"You can't hide," she whispers. "You can't hide from it."

And then she starts to weep. No words, almost silently, against Gabriella's neck.

She doesn't know how long they stand there, in silence, the snow falling hard and fast around them.

"I should have gotten here sooner," Gabriella murmurs after a while. "I can't even imagine . . . You grew up with them, with him. Out here. And now he's gone. It . . ."

"Shhh," Klara says, and pulls back, freeing herself from Gabriella's arms. She puts a finger on Gabriella's lips and cradles her cheek; her palm still caked with cold, stiff mud.

"You came," she says quietly. "You're here now. You're always here, Gabi, even when you're not."

Gabriella turns her face to Klara. "He was like a father, your father," she says.

Klara nods. "Perhaps more," she says. "Grandpa and Grandma. I didn't get to have any parents, but what they gave me . . ." Klara shakes her head and closes her eyes. "I can't even say what I mean," she says. "And now he's gone. . . ."

She turns to Gabriella again, opening her eyes.

"But there's relief as well. He wasn't made for the life he led in his final month. He was meant for wind and boats and seabirds. Not for hospitals. He hated it all so much, Gabi. So damn much."

Gabriella nods. "Your grandma seemed to be doing well when I saw her," she says. "Like you. I mean, under the circumstances. Composed."

Klara nods. "They've known about it since last spring," she says. "She's grieving, but I think she's also relieved."

"They knew about the cancer? But they didn't tell you?"

Klara nods once more, feels snowflakes melting and flowing down her cheeks. "They always knew there was no cure," she says quietly, barely more than a whisper. "But, well, you know. They didn't want to burden me. They probably thought I wouldn't be able to bear it. And maybe they were right. I wasn't doing so well. As you know. Last summer. Or before that."

She shakes her head, and Gabriella pushes Klara's long black bangs to the side and tucks them behind an ear. "I like this new, shorter hair on you," she says quietly. "If I wore my hair like that I'd look like an old lady. But you look so glamorous, like a movie star. Very Natalie Portman."

They stand in silence after that, facing the stone fences and gray fields, the bare trees, and in the distance, not visible from the church but somehow ever-present, the sea. Eventually, Klara turns back to Gabriella again and lays her head on her shoulder, her nose brushing against the cold skin just below her ear. "I'm feeling better now," she whispers. "Despite Grandpa. Despite the grief, I feel better than I have in years. Everything that happened in the summer with the riots and the Russians and Säpo. I thought I was going to collapse, Gabi."

"But you didn't," Gabriella says, leaning her head against Klara's.

"I didn't because you stepped in," Klara says. "Because you took care of everything. The journalists and morning shows and all that attention. That's why I didn't collapse."

"Ah," Gabriella says, shrugging her shoulder a little. "You know what? I thought it was kinda fun." She glances down at Klara. "Maybe I shouldn't say that out loud? I mean, what happened was terrible. The riots in the suburbs. The Russians. Säpo just letting it happen. The whole thing. Sickening. But revealing it all, being there telling the world about it indignantly and fighting for what's right . . . I loved it."

Klara smiles and meets her eyes. "I know. I always knew you'd be good at that kind of thing. You love being the center of attention, you little drama queen."

Gabriella pushes her gently. "Weren't you the one who was just thanking me? And now you're gonna give me crap?"

"You're always saving me," Klara says quietly. "You always show up and take care of everything."

Gabriella throws a quick glance at her before turning back to the fields. There is something in that movement that surprises Klara, something that doesn't quite match the usual, solid Gabi, who mumbles something that's almost drowned out by the wind.

"What did you say?" Klara says.

Gabriella turns to her again with a quick smile, but only on her mouth, not in her eyes. "We should go in," she says, looking away. "You don't want to have to sit through the service completely soaking wet."

But Klara knows that wasn't what she had said. Slowly fragments of words penetrate Klara's consciousness: *Maybe you'll have to save me soon.*

Is that what Gabi said? But before Klara can ask, the first car arrives in the snowy parking lot. Gabriella turns to her with a strained smile on her lips.

"Come," she says. "We have a grandfather to bury." And immediately she freezes with panic in her eyes. "God, that's terrible, I'm sorry, I didn't mean to be so . . ."

"Literal?" Klara says.

She giggles. Gabriella laughs quietly behind her hand.

"Such bad taste," she says softly. "I'm sorry. Seriously, so sorry."

But Klara takes her by the arm and leans against her shoulder.

"You're right," she says. "We have a grandfather to bury."

AUGUST 5—BEIRUT

AGNETA HAS OTHER tasks to deal with and no time to babysit a new intern, so she excuses herself and disappears with echoing steps down the stairwell toward the street. It leaves Jacob feeling a mixture of disappointment and relief.

None of this is turning out like his fantasies this summer, but at least his apartment is beyond anything he could have hoped for.

Besides, it feels good to be on his own. He opens the double doors to the noise of Armenia Street and sees Agneta climbing into the Volvo. She turns up to him and waves.

"I forgot to tell you to talk to your upstairs neighbor about the generator," she yells. "There's a note on the table in the living room. Electricity can be a problem. Call me if you can't figure it out."

And then she's gone. Jacob sits down on one of the plastic chairs on the balcony, lets the heat and smog and the cacophony of honking traffic and loud voices wash over him. This is his home until Christmas. This city. This apartment. For a moment he feels no joy or satisfaction at all, just a sense of rootlessness that steals over him, empties him until he's gasping for breath with his eyes closed.

He's alone. As alone as he felt in Uppsala in his shabby sublet room on Rackarberget during the first few weeks of his new life there. After everything he's gone through to get here. And for what? For this emptiness and futility? He takes out his phone and finds Simon's text message.

It would be so easy to answer. To write: *Yes, babe! When are you coming to visit?* To just let go and let everything he still feels for Simon bubble up. Maybe it would grow? Maybe it's enough to live a life in a tasteful one-bedroom in the inner city of Stockholm. Simon would get a job at some museum or art auction house. Jacob would work as an analyst at a PR agency. Or maybe he could build a career at a ministry that would include short trips to Brussels. Maybe he would even tell Simon the truth about himself.

Maybe, maybe, maybe.

But he knows that's impossible, that's not the life he's striving for. There's more out there. Bigger missions. His heart pounds.

He swallows heavily and forces the emptiness down deep inside. With a few quick clicks, he deletes Simon's message. And with a few more, he deletes Simon from his phone.

It's dark by the time he realizes he forgot to ask the neighbor about the electricity, which is just as unreliable as Agneta indicated. When he does reach Alexa, which is apparently her name, using the number the French diplomat left on the kitchen table, she tells him nobody will be able to fix the generator until tomorrow morning.

"But come up to the roof," she says. "There's a terrace. And wine."

The lights don't work in the stairwell either, so Jacob fumbles forward using just faint light spilling in through the open windows on each landing. It gets dark so fast, not at all like Sweden. He didn't even notice the dusk, and it's no later than six.

Light suddenly returns to the staircase with a burst of yellow and a humming light bulb, just as he's pushing a wrought iron gate onto what has to be the shared roof terrace.

"Ah," says the voice from the phone somewhere in the darkness. "Praise be to the utility company! The power is back on."

Jacob takes a couple of hesitant steps onto the roof. In front of him the neighborhood of Mar Mikhael stretches out and down toward the harbor. Dim lights in windows, broken walls, and loading cranes and then a vast darkness that has to be the Mediterranean.

"You must be Jacob," Alexa says. "Welcome to Beirut."

She steps out of the shadows, and before Jacob can say a word she's kissed him on both cheeks and put a glass of red wine in his hand.

"Is this your first visit?"

Jacob nods slowly and looks at her. She's probably ten years older than him and about his height. She's not exactly overweight, more like solidly built, with a halo of dark curly hair that she has pulled back from her face with a wide reddish scarf. She's wearing a long green dress and sandals.

"Let me guess," she says. "This is your first time in the Middle East? You're shocked and just a little worried about all this mess?"

She laughs and tilts her head to the side. Jacob's mouth goes dry, and he can feel his face flush. She's treating him like a child, like some raw, naive newcomer. This is not what he imagined for his first evening. He expected an embassy, not electricity flickering on and off, not some rooftop with this woman.

Alexa laughs and puts an arm around him.

"Drink, *habibi*," she says. "It'll pass. When you're done drinking, you can help me carry up the food. It's better not to think."

Jacob drinks a glass, then one more and then another, while helping Alexa transport plates and dishes up from her apartment. It's her farewell party apparently. She's going to start working at a youth center in the Palestinian refugee camp of Shatila in southern Beirut next week. While they set the table, she tells him she's from France and Morocco and that she's lived in Beirut for almost five years.

"I started as an intern at the Red Cross," she says. "*Putain*, what a bunch of whores. Watch out for diplomats, baby."

She stops and puts her hand to her mouth.

"Sorry, I didn't mean . . . Well, you're just an intern? You still have some time to reconsider."

But Jacob laughs. He doesn't care, he just wants her to keep talking in an English that blends Arabic and French and flows like a wild river of swear words and strong opinions. Every word she speaks lessens the emptiness inside him. With every glass he drinks, he feels more inspired.

The terrace slowly fills up with people in jeans and dresses speaking a hundred different languages. Alexa lights the candles standing in empty wine bottles from the Beqaa Valley, and they flicker in the breeze. Somebody manages to get a small generator running, and a string of naked incandescent bulbs are strung along one wall. A stereo is plugged in and Arabic pop mixes with the Weeknd and Rihanna. Jacob fills his glass, and his body starts to feel lighter even though he's so confused, he barely even remembers how to speak English anymore.

But for once, it doesn't matter. For once he might just be able to let go and fall into or rise up to something he doesn't totally understand but which makes his head feel lighter, his heart beat harder, makes him move faster, with greater intention and direction.

This, this is why he left everything he knew behind. This is why he went to Uppsala. This is why he reads foreign newspapers and studies political science, and this is why he has to take that damn statistics exam and learn Arabic.

This roof is the kind of place he's longed for, searched for without even knowing it. This is the adventure. This is where it happens. This is where one becomes someone else. He's so close to blurting out this ridiculous idea that he decides to drink a glass of water and sober up. It's only his first night, he has to keep it together, not be seduced by cosmopolitan magic; he has to keep his eyes on the prize, the embassy, make a good impression there.

But right now he feels so happy in the company of the foreigners here, the anonymity, maybe even the safety of it, secure in the insecurity, in the uncertainty. So instead of water he grabs a beer out of a barrel, where it is lying on ice, just like in a movie. He thinks: *Fuck it. That's just how this night will be. One night. Then focus.*

He walks to the edge of the terrace and looks out over the city, run-down, broken, missing walls, bullet holes, the injustice and chaos and confusion, and beyond that the Mediterranean lying in the darkness. He can't see it, but he knows it's there.

He feels like he could put his beer down on the ground next to him, climb onto the concrete ledge in front of him, take aim at one of the ten towering cranes down below, stretch his arms out like wings and fly.

And then he hears a voice close beside him. First he lurches in surprise. He can barely hear the party anymore, barely hear someone strumming "Redemption Song" on a guitar. Has almost forgotten there is a party, that there are other people here at all.

"You look like you're about to take off."

He turns to the voice. And somehow he knows before even turning, before seeing the face that belongs to that voice, from this moment on everything will change. There's no going back, no past, only future. Nothing will ever be the same again.

Then he sees those eyes, the smile in them, and more than that, Jacob feels like he's seen them before. And he says as much: "Have we met?"

His English feels shaky, his accent so Swedish despite struggling for a cool British sound. But those eyes just smile at him. He knows they haven't met—he's just dreamed about this moment, what it would be like to look into eyes like those. He almost falls backward, not smoothly like a bird but clumsily, like a badly trained clown, and if the hand that belonged to that voice hadn't grabbed his left arm maybe he would have stumbled over the ledge and down into a coal-black Lebanese night.

"Careful," the voice says. "Don't disappear, we haven't even met yet."

NOVEMBER 21—SANKT ANNA

When Klara finally starts to cry, she can't stop. She cries like a child, shuddering, sobbing, in the church pew. She cries for Grandpa and Grandma. For everything they've done for her, because it's incomprehensible that she'll never sit with Grandpa in his boat again, unimaginable that she'll never hear him sigh or see him shake his head in disappointment when she doesn't recognize some distant birdcall. She cries through a veil of tears when she catches sight of Grandma's resolute face and realizes she doesn't know what her life will be like now. But most of all she cries for herself.

"I'm sorry," she whispers, and looks up at her grandmother. "I don't know what's gotten into me. I can't control it."

Grandma turns to her and caresses her cheek; there's warmth and something almost like relief in those eyes.

"Crying is the best thing you could do for me," she whispers back. "You've kept too much inside for too long, little love."

Klara knows it's true. She knows that for the last few years she's been carrying a weight inside her. Ever since Mahmoud died on the dirty floor of a Parisian supermarket, ever since a man who turned out to be her father died in the snow out here in the archipelago. A father she was never able to meet or get to know. She hasn't cried, hasn't grieved, not really. Didn't know she deserved to; didn't know she was entitled to relief and the atonement grief would bring. And she hasn't wanted to let go, hasn't dared to let go, to move on. Instead, she's buried herself in work and wine, late nights and short, empty relationships, pushing things deep inside and keeping a stiff upper lip. That's called living. That's called keeping it together, bucking up, doing what's got to be done.

But now, in the church, with the sound of the organ and the priest's dry, monotonous voice, surrounded by ritual and candlelight, with Grandma and Gabriella and her relatives, she realizes it was always impossible, not everything will fit inside, she has to let go of something. She has to find a way to reconcile with herself.

Afterward, Klara stands in the darkness, in blowing snow in front of the church, receiving hugs and condolences and pointing people in the direction of the reception at the parish house near the newer, bigger church. The wind is blowing faster now, and heavy snow drifts across the fields, through birches and firs. She feels Gabriella's hand around her elbow.

"How's it going?" she asks gently. "Keeping it together?"

Klara turns to her and smiles weakly. The tears have finally stopped, but she still takes sobbing breaths, like a little child whose crying fit just ended. She shakes her head. "No," she says. "I'm not holding it together at all."

Gabriella smiles back. "Good," she says. "We've all been waiting for you to stop doing that."

It's just them now. Klara, Gabriella, and Grandma, who exits the front door of the church and squints her eyes at the wind and the snow, while pulling her hat lower over her ears and forehead.

"He gets his way to the very end," she says. "There was nothing he was so fond of as a nasty autumn storm. Right, Klara, my love?"

Klara smiles cautiously and nods. "He would have liked this," she says. "No doubt."

"Come on," Grandma says, walking firmly past them toward the parking lot. "They can't very well have a funeral reception without us."

Klara feels Gabriella lean toward her ear, feels her breath.

"She can handle this," she whispers. "You know that, right?"

Klara turns to her and feels something like the contours of a distant calm inside, the promise of a feeling she's almost forgotten. She nods. "Yes," she says. "She can."

Klara peers into the gloom, searching for Grandma's slender figure through sheets of snow. She still moves smoothly, surely, and quickly across the uneven surface. It'll be some time before Klara has to convince her to leave Aspöja, where she and Grandpa have lived all their lives, and where Klara herself grew up. Grandma is well over seventy, but for a few more years she'll manage the everyday hardships that come with living on an island in the archipelago. And then? Klara doesn't even want to think about it. Not yet. Not today.

Klara thought only Grandma's and Gabriella's cars were still in the parking lot. But something slightly farther down the road catches her eye. In the darkness it's hard to make out, but Klara thinks it looks like a shadow jumping into a car. Then the dull thud of a door closing and a motor starting, dampened by the snow and the wind. No headlights are turned on. But Klara could swear a car backs out and disappears down the road. With a couple of quick steps she catches up with Grandma.

"Who was that?" she says, pointing to the spot the car just left. "I thought everyone was already at the parish house by now."

Grandma turns around and follows her finger, but there is only darkness there now. She shrugs. "Maybe somebody couldn't find their car keys." She turns and smiles at Klara. "We're not so young anymore, you know."

Klara turns around and sees Gabriella coming down to the parking lot, a few yards behind them, with a phone in her hand and a worried look in her eyes. She gestures that she'll follow them in her own car.

"Maybe," Klara says. But something gnaws at her. Maybe it's

just habit after what she's been through in the past few years, just the aftereffects of suspicion and fear from twice landing in the middle of strange and dangerous circumstances. But when they cross Highway 210 driving to the parish house, Klara throws a glance westward, toward the mainland. Halfway up the hill she thinks she sees two red taillights in the snow. A car parked by the road? She lingers on the sight while Grandma drives them to the parish house. Someone lost in the snow? But it's unusual to see unfamiliar cars here at this time of year. She feels a tingle run down her spine. Something doesn't seem right.

AUGUST 5—BEIRUT

IT ALL HAPPENS fast; maybe it's the alcohol, or the trip, or the party. But it's not just that, it's something more, something else. Something about those eyes, that look. Some gleam of adventure in them.

"I'll be by the stairs," the voice says quite close to Jacob's ear. "It's better if we aren't seen leaving together."

He nods, but he doesn't know which stairs the voice is referring to. The stairs in this building? Some other stairs? But the man has already turned around and is heading toward the door.

"Wait!" Jacob says, and grabs his shoulder. "Which stairs?"

The man turns around, his expression still warm, but he's no longer smiling, and something flashes in those eyes when he glances down to where Jacob is holding his shoulder. Jacob feels guilty, as if he's committed some inexcusable mistake, and perhaps he has. He read that it's illegal here, what the two of them are obviously up to. The police usually ignore it, but if you're unlucky or if they want to hurt you, you can be arrested for being gay. Thrown in prison, deported, subjected to humiliating medical exams. Jacob pulls his hand back.

"Sorry," he mumbles.

The man smiles again, just a little, and bends toward him. "You're new to Beirut," he says. "I understand. Take a left on Armenia Street, go fifty yards, it will be on your left side. The colorful stairs that lead up to Ashrafieh. Hurry."

And with that, he's gone.

It doesn't take Jacob long to find Alexa and thank her for the wine and the party. She smiles and kisses him on both cheeks.

"Just promise me you won't turn into a real diplomat," she says.

That *real* stings a bit, but Jacob lets it pass. He doesn't want to be seen as somebody who's not "real." And besides, what does Alexa know? She's just a hippie, right? But he promises to try, smiles indulgently, and feels like the naturalness of his smile is proof of an innate talent for diplomacy that will take him far.

"Here," Alexa says, pushing a business card into his hand. "In case I don't have time to say goodbye tomorrow. If you ever want to visit me. Just call first, *habibi*. Shatila is a labyrinth. You'll disappear there if you don't know what you're doing."

She kisses him on the cheek again, and Jacob smells wine and garlic and also a sort of natural self-confidence on her breath. She steps back and looks deep into his eyes.

"Beirut is not Sweden, *habibi*," she says. "Be careful. About everything."

A few minutes later he's stumbling over the broken cobblestones and concrete of Armenia Street, past the bars on the narrow sidewalks where parties spill out into stationary traffic. Honking and revving motorcycles. Calvin Harris and Arabic pop music, which sounds like nothing he's ever heard before. He feels confused and exhilarated and exhausted—like he might never sleep again.

The man from the terrace was right: the stairs are only fifty yards farther down the street, each step painted in red, green, blue, black, yellow, forming an abstract pattern that leads straight up into the darkness and another part of town. Ashrafieh. Mar Mikhael, where he lives, is a working-class neighborhood; Ashrafieh is for the rich, Christian elite.

Jacob sees the man, standing halfway up the stairs, and raises a hand in an eager, childish greeting. The man smiles and calmly waves him up. Jacob stops for a moment. He shouldn't be doing this. Not on his first night in Beirut. He should say, *We'll talk some other day*. He should sleep and focus on his career and his new life. What he's dreamed about ever since he started dreaming. Call Agneta early and ask if he can go in to the embassy, show them his resourcefulness, his sense of duty, his abilities.

He should, he should, he should.

But he knows he won't do that, and as soon as he takes the first step onto the staircase he has to hold himself back from running up to the man.

They walk in darkness down the street above the stairs. Jacob is still winded; the stairs were longer than they looked. It's unusually quiet up here in the middle of the night—not even the honking on Armenia Street makes it all the way up here. They walk in the middle of the street, because here among the crumbling art deco houses there's no traffic, not now—this isn't the Beirut Jacob saw earlier in the day: this is another city. Still chaotic, but calmer, with empty streets and alleys. Abandoned perhaps, a city after an evacuation or an apocalypse.

At first they say nothing to each other. Jacob feels like he's lost his voice, or has aphasia, or has suddenly forgotten how to formulate words and sentences. There's so much he'd like to say, so much he'd like to ask or discuss, but he's giddy and excited and tired, and this moment is so crisp and brittle that language might destroy it, words and sentences and subject matter might ruin it, change it, shift it up or down, or just cause it to disappear completely.

So he stays silent, and they walk side by side in the same direction, even though Jacob has no idea where they're headed. He doesn't even know where they are. They zigzag between the hundreds of dusty cars parked on the sidewalks, glancing at each other now and then, while avoiding each other's eyes. Jacob's thoughts dart back and forth, searching desperately for the right words to begin. There should be a thousand things, but his brain is too fast, and it stumbles over every idea, never able to focus on just one. Finally, he gives up completely, just lets things be as they are, realizes he has no control over anything now, nothing at all, just has to follow. It's an unfamiliar feeling. He never loses control of himself. One night in Beirut, and he's already fallen. Suddenly they stop at a garden hidden behind a rusty iron fence. Jacob can just make out a large house behind it, a palace in the darkness. He bends forward to peer between the rails of the fence. Gardens and parks are apparently quite rare in Beirut. He read that the American University campus is the closest thing to a park that Beirut has. He clears his throat.

"What is this place?" he asks.

He regrets it immediately, because his English sounds so Swedish and childish in his ears, the question so flat and silly, and he wishes he could take it back, had stuck to saying nothing at all.

But the man standing next to him, the man who has eyes Jacob recognizes though he's never seen them before, just laughs and shrugs his shoulders and follows the fence, drumming his fingers along it.

"I don't know," he says. "Some rich family who fled during the war?" He turns and looks at Jacob. "It doesn't matter. Tonight it's ours, *habibi*."

They stand in front of a warped, high gate locked with a chain. The man bends down, pulls the gate, and succeeds in creating a small opening near the ground.

"See if you can squeeze in there," he says.

Jacob doesn't say a word or even hesitate, just falls down on his knees and crawls through the little gap into the garden. Right now he doesn't care what the consequences are; he doesn't care about anything except making sure this continues.

As soon as he's through, he grabs on to the bottom of the gate, bending it up so that the man can crawl in over the broken cobblestones, between which yellow grass is sticking up.

Then they're both in the garden. The man points to a lopsided wooden bench under a magnolia tree weighed down by heavy flowers that almost glow in the dark. They sit down there. They both open their mouths at the same time, then laugh, fall silent, then try again.

"My name is Jacob," Jacob says.

He turns to the man next to him, who is finally looking straight into his eyes. "My name is Yassim," he says.

Jacob has never snuck into parks late at night or sought out many hookups on Grindr. How could he have? His ambitions have been higher and more narrowly defined. It's not that he hasn't fantasized about it; in high school it was the only thing he thought about while surfing restlessly on his phone in bed, the sound of his own blood rushing in his ears. All the sites and images and films dampened it, allowing him to temporarily find release and some imitation of satisfaction. But to seek it out for real? Back then? It would have been impossible. It wasn't until Uppsala and Simon that it actually . . . became real? And it wasn't what he'd thought it would be. Not like this, whatever this is.

He looks around. He's never been in a place like this one. He's never seen a darkness that crackles and shivers and trembles like this. He breathes shallowly, cautiously, barely at all. He doesn't really know why, but it's as if a single deep breath might disrupt something fundamental, some law of nature, that has turned the world upside down.

He glances at the man sitting next to him, whose name is apparently Yassim. He has stubble on his chin; black, medium-length, wavy hair; a white T-shirt, well-worn jeans. He looks like a thousand other people, Jacob thinks. Why is this happening? What is it about Yassim? What is it about his gaze and voice that brought Jacob here, that makes him lose control and follow after a feeling he's never experienced before?

When Yassim turns to him, Jacob doesn't turn away like he did earlier. He meets his eyes. He holds his breath, and it's as if blood no longer pumps through his body, as if everything is completely still. He clears his throat, tries to smile.

"Those flowers are odd," Yassim says, and it's barely more than a whisper. "Magnolias usually bloom in the spring."

A gentle breeze Jacob didn't notice before rustles through the top of the tree, and a few white petals, soft as silk, land on his hand. There's a swish as bats dive in under the high branches and disappear.

Something loosens inside him, a lock silently opens, and it's as if a part of him is now free and rising up to the top of the tree with the bats. He's staring down at himself on the bench, his thin body in a pressed, baby-blue button-down shirt, slim chinos and brown dress shoes, and in the gap between his trousers and shoes a flash of colorful socks. He looks so young from up here. So stiff and naive and restrained. Why has he never been in a garden like this before? Why hasn't he lived a life of chaos and risk and pounding, rushing blood?

He knows why. Choosing chaos and risk is a privilege, and it costs. And where he comes from, there are no extra resources. But tonight, what's happening right now, is not a choice, nothing he sought out. It's just happening, and he's letting it happen.

"Jacob," Yassim begins to speak quietly in his American-accented English. "Who are you, Jacob? How do you make the trees bloom in August?"

It should sound cheesy, overly sweet, like something from a B movie. It should make him giggle, break the spell. But it doesn't. Quite the opposite. This is a night where magnolia trees bloom in August, and every sentence has been set free from history. Jacob opens his mouth, closes it again. Yassim stares at him calmly, neither restless nor impatient.

"Or don't tell me," Yassim says. "Let me guess."

Jacob feels himself falling down from the treetop again, landing in his own body, in his own head. He doesn't feel calmer, not at all, but he does feel braver. Ready to go all the way, no matter where it leads.

"Okay," Jacob says, and smiles, he hopes seductively. "Tell me who I am, Yassim."

He scoots closer to his new friend, so close that their shoulders touch, and leans toward him so that their noses almost brush each other. If they are going to kiss, they should do it now. Jacob's whole body tenses up. How much more obvious can he be? He's gone further than ever before. He's going to do it now. Going to kiss Yassim. Let Yassim kiss him and caress him and put his hand under his shirt, unbutton his trousers. He'll let Yassim lie him flat on this bench, here in the darkness, and do whatever he wants to him. There's a kind of freedom in yielding.

But Yassim just looks at him with eyes that are half amused or arrogant, half filled with warmth. He doesn't kiss Jacob; he doesn't put his hand on his neck or against his chest. Instead, he pulls back and smiles again.

"You're a Scandinavian diplomat," he says.

Jacob quivers with pride. Yassim may not have kissed him, but he sees Jacob the way he wants to be seen, and it's such a confirmation.

"You're very new," he continues. "This is your first international posting, and you're a bit confused. You're used to being in control. Good at school, best grades all the way through. You probably speak perfect Arabic, but don't know any slang."

Yassim's smile widens; he's really getting going now.

"You play squash and tennis and like German white wines, and when you've had a couple glasses you let go of that polished surface and dance on the table to ABBA."

Jacob blushes a little. He doesn't know if what he feels is pride because Yassim sees him as he wants to be seen, or if he thinks Yassim might be teasing him, thinks he's a stereotype.

"What do you think so far?" Yassim says. "Looks to me like you're blushing, so I can't be too far off?"

"Go on," Jacob whispers. "I want to hear more."

Yassim nods and moves a little closer, so Jacob has to stop himself from gasping. He wants to close his eyes and open his mouth, pull Yassim close, but he knows that's not his role. It's Yassim who decides—that much is clear—and Jacob allows it to be that way.

"You come from a good family," Yassim continues, hushed now, as if he were telling a story, and he is, in a way. "A penthouse in Stockholm, perhaps? Your father is a politician, maybe an ambassador? You know which fork to use at the embassy's dinners, anyway. Your mother has money, maybe an estate in the country. You have a fancy last name, maybe even two."

Now Jacob is no longer blushing; instead he's just letting confirmation wash over him. It's working. This is the first time he's tested out his persona, and it's working. Everything he constructed so carefully and planned and studied while he was growing up. Everything he learned to imitate to the most minute detail in order to succeed at escaping, heading for something else, something bigger and better.

At the same time, it feels so insignificant now, completely irrelevant. It feels like he made the wrong bet, as if he's misunderstood something fundamental. He remembers the picture of that young lawyer in *Dagens Nyheter*, her obvious determination and conviction. He can feel his blood burning, here in the garden. Can feel chaos and risk trembling around him. Everything he believed about the world. One day in Beirut, one night in a garden, and all the old stuff feels meaningless. For the first time, he wants to tell someone who he really is. And he opens his mouth.

But before he can say anything, Yassim's face is so close to his that the tips of their noses touch, and Jacob almost laughs from nervousness, but Yassim's lips are already on his and instead he gasps and forgets everything Yassim said, forgets the garden, forgets his own story, what's true and what he created.

There's nothing but this, he thinks. *Nothing else matters.*

It's not until Yassim pulls back that Jacob opens his eyes and sees how the light in the garden has changed, how everything around him is suddenly sharper. The night will soon be over, the dawn is creeping over the uncut grass, through the wild tangle of the treetops, and climbing up the pink walls of the abandoned palace. Jacob shivers and tries to smile while Yassim caresses his chest, inside his unbuttoned shirt.

"You're freezing," he says, pulling back his hands, fiddling with the buttons of Jacob's shirt. "I don't want you to get a cold."

Jacob leans against him, puts his hand around his shoulder and his head tenderly against his neck just below his jaw. He kisses his skin lightly, nibbles and sucks.

"So keep me warm," he whispers.

He lets his hand slide over Yassim's T-shirt again, over his hard, flat stomach, down over his hip, toward his groin and cock. He feels Yassim's breathing quicken and pulls him closer. Feels Yassim press against his hand, put his hand on top of Jacob's, then pull it away, just as he did several times already. But his desire is so fierce now, the chemistry so powerful that he instead pulls Jacob's hand close and rubs himself against it.

"Let me," Jacob whispers. "Let me feel you."

He's surprised by a kind of happiness. That he got him here, even though Yassim for some reason stopped him whenever he tried to do anything more than kiss or caress him. The power he feels now that Yassim can't hold back is intoxicating, and Jacob moans deeply into his ear. And for a moment, he thinks Yassim might give in, but it's as if Yassim steels himself and gains strength as he pushes Jacob's hand away.

"Not now," he whispers. "Not here."

Frustration and disappointment sting inside Jacob. *Well, why not?* he wants to scream. *We're alone here, in a garden. You want this too!*

But before he can, Yassim quiets him with a kiss.

"Soon," he says. "But not now, not tonight."

He kisses him again and finishes buttoning Jacob's shirt, then pulls his lips away, scoots back, and stands up.

"I'm sorry," Yassim says. "I didn't mean to get you excited in this way. I didn't think I'd . . ." He falls silent and glances around at the outlines that are getting sharper around them.

"You'd what?" Jacob says, frustrated.

Yassim looks at him again, the arrogance almost gone from his eyes now. In its place is just a straightforward warmth. "I didn't think I'd feel like this," he says. "And I don't want it to end before it even starts. Do you understand?"

No! Jacob wants to say. *I don't understand anything. You have me here, I'll do whatever you want. Just don't stop now!*

But instead he nods, unwilling to reveal how horny and confused and desperate he really is. A slight headache has snuck up on him now as his drunkenness and excitement slowly recede.

"But you could at least sit down again," he says quietly. "Can't we talk? I never told you if I'm really the person you described."

Yassim smiles. "*Habibi*," he says. "Does it matter who you really are? I want you as you are, right here, right now, this morning. But I don't have time. I'm already late."

He glances over at the gate that leads to the street, then throws what looks like a camera bag over his shoulder. Did he have that with him earlier in the night? Jacob doesn't even remember; he only remembers lips and skin and eyes.

"Do you have to go now?" he says. Disappointment clawing inside him.

Yassim just shrugs his shoulders and fishes his phone out of the pocket of his worn jeans. "How do I reach you?" he says. "Before we forget."

Jacob rattles off his Facebook and Instagram, but Yassim just shakes his head. "Just a phone number," he says. "That's enough."

Jacob gives him his Swedish number; he doesn't have a Lebanese SIM card yet.

"You really are new here," Yassim says, taking a step toward him, and caresses his cheek. "I like it."

Jacob laughs but feels a stitch of annoyance. He may be new here, but it still hurts that Yassim views him that way, like a novice, naive and fresh.

"And how can I get a hold of you?" Jacob says.

Yassim doesn't answer; he just sits down again, puts his hands on the back of Jacob's neck, pulls him close and puts his mouth to his, presses his tongue into Jacob's mouth. This kiss is different, not tender and tentative like earlier in the night, but hard and knowing, full of intention and a kind of restrained violence that leaves Jacob breathless. If he ever thought he had any kind of initiative here, that thought vanishes now. The excitement in that insight drives him almost crazy, and he pushes himself against Yassim. But Yassim ends the kiss.

"You can't just leave me," Jacob whispers. "Not after this."

Yassim stands up again with a slight smile on his lips. "I'm sorry," he says. "But I can't stay. Believe me, there's nothing else I'd rather do. But I'm going on a trip, and I'm already late."

Jacob shakes his head. "Now? You're taking a trip today, this morning?"

Yassim nods. "I wasn't expecting this," he says. "With you. And I'm late. Very, very late."

He takes a step over to the sparse grass and slowly backs away through the dawn light, backs toward the gate they entered through, toward the world they came from.

Jacob stands up too. He wants to follow, he wants to say, *Wait! I'm coming with you. We can take a taxi, a flight, whatever you want.*

But instead, he just asks hollowly: "But you'll call, right?"

Now it's almost completely light in the garden, and he watches as the sun's rays make their way over the grass, toward the palace and up above the dark branches of the trees. Yassim smiles at him again and nods calmly. "I'll call," he says. "When I get back, I promise."

Jacob wants to believe him, wants to think that what Yassim says is true, that the fairy tale of this night was real. At the same time, he can't help feeling like this is the end. Not every fairy tale has a happy ending.

NOVEMBER 21—SANKT ANNA

SNOW WHIRLS IN through the doors of the parish house as Klara and Grandma send the funeral guests out into the darkness one by one—after two hours of coffee and sandwiches, halting speeches and anecdotes.

As Klara turns around to find a jacket for one of her grandfather's older cousins, she catches a glimpse of her face in the small mirror above the hall table. For a moment she doesn't recognize herself with her new haircut. She looks younger than her thirty-two years, she thinks. Thinner. She kept it in a longish bob for so long. It felt like a relief to cut it off the day after Grandpa told her about the cancer. It was time to move forward, time to lift her eyes, time to become herself again.

She closes the door and looks at the melting gray slush on the hall floor. "I'll clean it up before we leave," she says.

"Maj will do the cleaning later," Grandma says. "Don't think about it now." She pats Klara on the cheek and narrows her bright blue eyes. "You don't have to take care of me. And I wouldn't accept it if you tried. Do you understand?"

The last guests have gone now. They're alone in the dim hall. Grandma's pulled on her coat, waiting for her sister and her sister's husband, who just went to pick up their car. Klara nods. She knows, has known since watching her grandmother walk across the parking lot after the funeral, so calm and balanced, just like usual.

"Yes," she says. "I understand."

Grandma takes a half step back, leans her head up, and cups Klara's face in her hands. "Rock and salt," she says, patting Klara's cheek. "That's what your grandpa used to say. I know he wanted you to be like that too. Hard as rock and salt, as you become out here on these islands. And I can't just lie down and die, can I?"

She gives Klara a hug before cracking the door to see a car rolling forward.

"If you want, you can come with me and Maj and Roland, you know," she says. "But why would you want to sit with us old folks? You've done enough for us. For me, Klara. It's time to do something for yourself."

All through her childhood. Every summer and Christmas. Every cold morning in the kitchen with Grandma with the pipes frozen. Every afternoon with Grandpa in his boat on the choppy sea. Everything Klara had become was given to her by them.

"I haven't done anything for you," she whispers.

But her grandmother just looks at her calmly, with eyes shining in the dark, young and alert, almost like Klara remembers them from before that terrible autumn.

"We got you, Klara," Grandma answers calmly. "We lost your mother. But we got you. It's more than anyone could have hoped for."

Now Maj and Roland's car is pulling up outside; she can hear Grandma's sister opening the car door.

"You know, your grandpa would never forgive himself if he knew it was his fault you ended up playing gin rummy with a bunch of old fogeys in Bottna."

Klara smiles weakly. "Maybe," she says.

"Maybe?" Grandma laughs. "All he wanted was for you to live your own life, Klara. Just like you always did. You have no idea how proud he was, how much he bragged about you. Go to Stockholm with Gabriella. We'll talk soon."

She opens the door while Klara carries her bags to the car for her.

"You're not driving to Stockholm in this weather, are you?" Roland says, while gently placing Grandma's bag in the trunk of his ancient Audi.

"I think that's the plan," Klara says.

"It's out of the question," Maj says. "I'll call the hostel, and they'll fix a room for you. It'll take twenty minutes just to get to Bottna in this sleet."

"Is the hostel even open this time of year?" Klara says.

"Believe me," Maj says. "If we ask Gertrud to fix a room for you, you can be sure she will."

Grandma gives Klara a final hug, then climbs into the back seat. "Promise me you won't drive to Stockholm tonight," she says. "We'll talk tomorrow."

Roland does a careful U-turn on the now completely snow-packed parking lot and slowly rolls on toward the highway. It's been snowing so heavily that Klara can only barely make out the tire tracks of the other cars. She turns around and looks up at the illuminated facade of the newer, bigger nineteenth-century church. She feels a kind of relief, something close to freedom. The funeral is over. Grandma is with her sister. Maybe Klara can go to Stockholm with Gabriella without feeling guilty.

She starts to go back to the parish house, but something in the twilight makes her start, freezes her in her tracks. Slowly, she turns back to the parking lot, not sure what exactly it is that stopped her. There's the church, quiet with a gentle creamy white in the slight illumination of its walls. The snow is falling down in sheets in the gray light in front of her. All the tire tracks she can still see lead out toward Highway 210, of course—it's the only way out of here.

All but one.

She turns her head toward the forest and the gravel road that leads down to the sea and a small campsite. And there they are, the tracks of a pair of tires heading around the curve and disappearing. They can't be old, or the snow would have covered them. Someone drove down there after the funeral. But who would drive to a closed campsite in a snowstorm?

Klara shrugs her shoulders and shakes off the snow, buries her paranoia, or whatever it is. This is Grandpa's funeral; she doesn't have the energy to think of more than that.

AUGUST 12—BEIRUT

A WEEK GOES BY. Jacob learns how to get to the temporary embassy using *service*, the confusing blend of taxi and bus that's the only cheap way to get around in Beirut. He stumbles through Arabic phrases, and after getting a few quick tips from Agneta, he won't be fooled by taxi drivers again.

For the most part, it's just him and Agneta at the embassy. The rest of the small staff is in Stockholm or on other trips or at meetings.

"It's so stressful and chaotic right now," Frida, a young deputy secretary, tells him one afternoon, sitting on the edge of her desk in the corner.

Her blond hair has dark roots that need dyeing, and the furrow on her forehead speaks to how stressful things have been for a while, maybe her whole life.

"It's not clear what's going to happen to this embassy anyway, and I'm sorry you ended up assigned here right now. But we'll find something useful for you to do, I'm sure." She nods encouragingly toward his desk. "In any case, you certainly seem quick and competent," she says, smiling tiredly, before taking off for the airport and a conference in Ankara.

Quick and competent! Jacob can live on that for almost twenty-four hours. There is hope. Everyone is busy right now, but his time will come when things calm down a little. Agneta has given him a couple of books about Lebanon, but he can hardly stay awake when he tries to read them. All he does is check his phone, waiting for Yassim's call and avoiding Simon's increasingly cold messages.

Yassim. The night in the garden won't leave him alone—his frustration and anticipation and the electricity of it all—and that's what he's thinking about as he sits at his Scandinavian-style desk of blond-colored wood, beneath a filthy window that overlooks a dirty, trash-filled backyard.

He's so absorbed by his daydreams and his indefinable longing that he doesn't notice someone standing beside him until he sees a hand pluck up one of the unread books about Lebanon that sit on his desk.

"*The Tragedy of Lebanon*," a soft, brisk voice reads aloud. "Still the only book you need to read on the civil war."

In front of Jacob, flipping amusedly through the book, there stands a tall, fit man in his forties, dressed in a perfectly tailored, dark-blue suit. He's wearing an expensive-looking light-blue tie that's tied in an intentionally sloppy way. The man looks up from the book and stares at Jacob with piercing eyes. Jacob has never seen anyone who looks more like a diplomat than this man.

"So," he says. "What do you think? Were the PLO trying to get Gemayel killed in the spring of 1975? Or was it some other militia? Maybe the Phalangists themselves?"

Jacob reddens immediately. Gemayel, Gemayel, Gemayel. Where has he heard that name? Why didn't he read the book?

"Gemayel?" he says, and his voice is so croaking, weak, and uncertain that he wishes he'd just kept his mouth shut.

"Yes," the man says. "Pierre Gemayel? The attack that led to the bus massacre on the afternoon of April thirteenth, which caused the whole bloody thing to explode? The PLO were suspected, but that always seemed a little too obvious. Don't you think?"

"Well . . ." Jacob begins, searching feverishly through his memory for anything he might have learned over the summer, anything at all.

But his mind is completely blank.

"It was a terrible war," Jacob says instead. "All those factions that . . ."

The man just looks at him as if completely indifferent to Jacob's dodges. Jacob doesn't know who Gemayel is, and now he's worthless.

"That what?" the man says.

"That were fighting," Jacob says.

He wants to die now, just sink into the ground and disappear. His career is going up in flames faced with a man whose name he doesn't even know but who is probably a diplomat and therefore influential, exactly the kind of person he needs to impress.

"It was a terrible war because so many different groups were fighting?" the man says. "Yes, that's also one way of summing up Lebanon itself."

At least he's smiling a little now. Not in a friendly way, but still. And he stretches out his hand. "Lars Vargander," he says. "I'm the ambassador here. Or in Damascus, but we're not there any longer."

Jacob jumps up, his whole body trembling. Vargander. The ambassador. This can't be happening. His hand trembles as he stretches it out. "Jacob Seger," he says in a wavering voice. "I haven't had time to read the book yet. Agneta just gave it to me."

The ambassador looks at him indifferently. But there's a twinkle in his eye and a smile beginning to spread on his lips. "I'm just screwing with you, Jacob," he says, and gives him a friendly punch on the shoulder. "I don't expect you to have read Randal's book or know all the details of the civil war on your first week, okay?"

Jacob is overcome by enormous relief. Then hit immediately by another wave of humiliation at being played like that, like he's a beginner. He knows he's blushing again. "Okay," he says. "I—" He stops himself, shakes his head.

"Yes?" Vargander says with a smile. "What is it?"

"You know, I did actually know that Gemayel was president. I just got flustered."

"Don't worry," Vargander says. He turns his wrist to check his watch, which is steel gray and compact. A Rolex Submariner, Jacob thinks, stifling a sigh. That's where he wants to go. That's where he's been heading.

"I apologize," he continues. "But I just got back from Stockholm last night, and I'm headed to a meeting in Ankara for the rest of the week. I think we'll have to catch up when I get back after the weekend. Agneta can take care of you, right?"

"Yes," says Jacob, and nods. "Of course."

"It's pretty dead around here right now, and it'll probably stay that way for a while. Everyone's busy. But you'll just have to amuse yourself, discover the city."

He looks around and when he realizes they're alone he bends over conspiratorially toward Jacob. "You don't have a girlfriend, right?" he says. "I mean . . . Well, you know what I mean?"

He stares calmly into Jacob's eyes. Jacob can feel himself blushing again, shocked by the turn in the conversation toward such a personal question. He's heard there's nothing unusual about his situation, being gay in the Foreign Service, and in fact it can even be an advantage, since it's easier to move if you don't have any children and it is the firm and ancient belief in the archconservative Foreign Service that gay men do not have children. But what is this about? Did he misunderstand?

"No," he says. "I don't have a girlfriend." He gathers his courage. Perhaps this is the moment to take some revenge on the ambassador for what just happened. He looks straight into Vargander's eyes. "I have no partner at all."

Vargander pulls back slightly and stares at him calmly. "A car will come and pick you up outside Saliba Market at nine p.m. on Friday," he says. "I think it's time for you to see a part of Beirut that you might not discover on your own. That is if you want to."

Jacob feels his excitement growing. Whatever this is, it's definitely not something one says no to. He's ready for anything. "Absolutely," he says. "Sounds exciting!"

NOVEMBER 21—SANKT ANNA

IT'S DARK BY the time Gabriella pulls her shiny, black, and practical company car into the parking lot in front of Båtsholm's hostel. Even though the wind's died down, the snow is still falling with undiminished intensity. Large, wet flakes of snow mixed with rain.

"Lucky we didn't drive to Stockholm tonight," Klara says when Gabriella stops the car. "Even if we have to stay at Bates Motel for a night."

She nods toward the run-down wooden hostel. The hostel is dark except for a weak yellow light streaming from the lobby window.

When Klara was little they ate lunch here sometimes in the summer, and she remembers the dusty old-fashioned interior, the creamy gravy, and the homemade strawberry juice. It must be ten years since she was here last, but not much has changed.

Gabriella nods absentmindedly and takes her phone out of her pocket, gives a stressed glance at it, and then pushes it into her pocket again.

"Are you waiting for something?" Klara says. "Did you have somewhere you needed to be tonight?"

"No," she says. "It's just the usual. You know." But she sounds somewhat hesitant and evasive.

"We'll leave as soon as we wake up tomorrow," Klara says.

Gabriella nods again and throws her a look with that stiff smile on her lips. "Of course," she says. "No problem."

Gabriella bends to open the door, but Klara stops her with a hand on her arm. "Gabi," she says. "What is it? Are you okay?"

They stare at each other for a moment as newly fallen, wet, thick snowflakes melt on the car's hood. Klara sees a gleam of something in her friend's eyes, something she's not used to seeing: a flash of irritation.

"Yes, Klara," she says. "Stop worrying. I came to the funeral, but I can't turn my whole life off for you, okay?"

Klara trembles a little, as if a tiny, tiny bomb has exploded in her chest and left a jagged crater behind.

"I'm sorry," Gabriella says quickly. "I didn't mean to sound so . . ."

"It's fine," Klara says. She turns away and opens the car door. The wet air hits her as she puts her feet into the slush.

"I really didn't mean for it to sound like that, Klara," says Gabriella, rounding the other side of the car hood. "Things are just kind of messy right now."

"How did you mean it to sound, then?" Klara says, as she walks around the car and up the stairs to the hostel. She immediately regrets her tone. She has no right to sound like that, to be so touchy. But she's too tired to hold back anymore. An incredible wave of exhaustion has flattened all of her defenses. She doesn't even have time to turn the doorknob before she hears Gabriella's quick steps behind her and feels her put a hand tenderly on her shoulder.

"Well, I definitely didn't mean it to sound like that," Gabriella says. "Please turn around, Klara."

Reluctantly, with a sigh, Klara turns around and looks at her friend from beneath her bangs. "I'm sorry," Klara says. "I'm just too tired for any bullshit tonight."

Gabriella nods and keeps her hand on her shoulder. "I get that," she says. "The thing is . . ." She falls silent.

"Yes?" Klara says. "What?"

"Well," Gabriella says. "This isn't the night to talk about it. But it's the job, Klara, not you. Come on, and let's go inside. I'm freezing."

Their adjoining rooms look exactly like Klara had imagined them. White walls, soft mattresses, thick blankets with starched duvets and bedside lamps with bulbs missing. The sea lies no more than fifty yards away, but the darkness and snowfall make it impossible to see anything through the windows.

"It's off-season," says Gertrud, the hostel's owner, while she turns on the radiators and checks to make sure all the faucets are working. If only she'd had a little more notice, she could have made it more comfortable, she complains. But Klara assures her that a bed is all they need. They're getting up early in the morning again. Gertrud continues to apologize while putting a couple of ready-made liver pâté sandwiches into the ancient refrigerator in the restaurant's kitchen and shows them how the coffeemaker works. Finally, she's done prepping, and as she turns on the last of the heaters and makes sure all the windows are shut tight, she tells them that payment is out of the question.

"Out here we take care of each other," she says, narrowing her eyes at Gabriella. "It's not like up in Stockholm, where people only think about themselves."

Klara notices Gabriella trying to catch her eye, sees the shadow of a smile on her lips. She smiles back, but the crater in her chest makes it hard for her to give in to their usual level of mutual understanding.

"I'm so unbelievably tired," she says. "I think I have to head to bed right away, Gabi."

Klara sits on the twin bed in her room, staring at her reflection in the dark window. Her blue eyes seem pale now, rather than intense as she sometimes hopes. The black eyeliner around her eyes, her sallow, autumn complexion. It's been a long and terrible day. At the same time, she feels like somehow things will get sorted out. Maybe they'll even get sorted out for her after all the shit she's been through these past few years.

She turns off the lamp, stands up and walks over to the window. Wet flakes swirl in the wind. She puts her forehead against the cold glass and tries to catch sight of the sea and the islands, with no success. But just as she's about to climb back into bed, she hears something that makes her stop cold. The muffled sound of an engine, dampened by snow and wind, almost imperceptible.

Someone is driving on the road out there, and it's getting louder. It sounds like someone is approaching the hostel.

AUGUST 14—BEIRUT

JUST A FEW minutes to nine and the evening is already in full swing on Armenia Street, just outside Jacob's apartment building. People are wandering around, dressed up, with drinks in their hands, through honking traffic, between restaurants and bars where the music is turned up to the max.

It's been a hot day, and the stink of garbage is as overwhelming as it is inescapable, no choice but to get used to it, then forget it. As Jacob exits into the somewhat cool evening air of the street in front of Saliba Market, the smell hits him again, forcing him to suppress his queasiness.

A car should be picking him up here in a few minutes. It feels so strange. Was Vargander really serious about this? On the other hand, what does Jacob have to lose if no car shows up? It's not as if he knows anyone here or made any plans.

It's been over a week since Alexa's rooftop party and his meeting with Yassim, and since then he's basically spent all his time at home, at the embassy, or at a few local restaurants. He's almost in shock from Beirut, its chaos and messiness, that indeterminate menace that seems to rise from the asphalt and ooze out of every bullet hole on the buildings' facades. He's attracted to it, wants nothing more than to throw himself straight into it. But he doesn't quite dare.

And then there's Yassim. Just the thought of his name, his hands, his mouth, makes Jacob almost pant with desire. How could he feel like this after just a few hours in a dark garden late at night?

Maybe this is good for him, to get out a little, focus on something other than his suffocating worry that Yassim might never get in touch with him again.

He's wearing jeans and a dark-green Ralph Lauren shirt with neatly rolled-up sleeves. One of three identical shirts in various colors that he bought on sale two years ago, which he now switches among for special occasions. He has a tote bag carrying his keys, phone, and wallet on his shoulder. He takes a deep breath and fishes out the wallet to flip through his confusing mix of dollars and Lebanese pounds. How much is this night going to cost? His student-loan money hasn't come in yet, and the little he managed to save from packing ulcer medicine in Fyrislund for two months at the beginning of the summer has to last him all the way to Christmas. So far Beirut has been much more expensive than he imagined. He needs to be frugal. Even if he's used to stretching to make ends meet, the thought of money always fills him with piercing anxiety.

"Mr. Seger?"

Jacob jumps a little, pushes his wallet back down into his tote, and turns in the direction of the voice that said his name. A midnight-blue Volvo SUV with blue diplomatic plates is sitting in traffic right in front of him, with the window of the passenger door rolled down. The driver is trying to get his attention. Jacob goes over to the car.

"I'm Jacob Seger," he says in English.

"Ambassador Vargander asked me to pick you up," the man says. "I'm a driver for the Swedish embassy."

Vargander has sent a diplomatic car. Jacob tries to hide his widening smile as he opens the back door, jumps in, and gets settled on the light leather seats. The air is cool and dry inside; it doesn't even smell like garbage.

"There are refreshments," the driver says. "Just help yourself to whatever you want."

The driver stretches a hand back between the seats and taps on what turns out to be a built-in refrigerator on the floor at Jacob's feet.

Jacob bends over and opens the door. Two bottles of white wine are cooling inside, along with a few bottles of beer and four wineglasses.

"I . . ." he begins. "I don't even know where we're going. I hope you do?"

The driver nods calmly. "Trust me. Also, the ambassador wanted me to tell you tonight is on him. He was very specific on that point. He's paying for everything. There's money in an envelope over there."

He points to the fridge again and Jacob opens it. Sure enough, a white envelope is tucked between the wineglasses. He plucks it out and opens it. A small bundle of twenty-dollar bills—he counts ten of them. In Beirut, he's learned, US dollars are as useful as Lebanese pounds.

He bends down and takes out one of the bottles of Lebanese wine. The traffic is almost completely still. He pours himself a glass and sinks down into his seat, watching the people and the lights and the chaos on the narrow sidewalks outside. Feeling equal parts calm and expectant as he takes his first big gulp of cold, dry wine.

They drive slowly eastward along Armenia Street, and the bars eventually become sparser and are replaced by stores selling lamps and wall clocks and refrigerators standing on the sidewalks. He sees older men in small holes-in-the-wall, sweating and welding in the dusk.

"Where are we going?" Jacob asks. He's on to his second glass of wine now, and he's enjoyed his ride in the diplomatic car so much that he completely forgot that he has no idea where they're going.

"Bourj Hammoud," the driver answers.

Jacob's heard of the Armenian district beyond Mar Mikhael, and his curiosity is piqued again, along with a gnawing nervousness. Bourj Hammoud is the neighborhood with the highest concentration of gay culture, though nothing happens openly there either. Apparently he didn't misunderstand Vargander's hints.

After they cross the highway the traffic lets up a little, and the character of the neighborhood becomes something completely different from his own. It looks poorer, more like he imagined Beirut. Run-down houses and dirty neon signs, power lines that turn and twist like spiderwebs over streets and buildings.

The car turns off the main street and stops at what must be one of the older houses in the area. A modest and worn brass sign hangs on the door: HAMMAM ORIENTAL.

"Well," the driver says, staying where he is, with his back to Jacob. "We've arrived. I'll wait close by and pick you up when you're ready."

A hammam? A bathhouse? Jacob knows what that means, and he can feel his pulse start to race. It was more than a little forward of Vargander to arrange this. He takes a deep breath, swallows hard, and opens the car door.

"Welcome," a boy says to him in Arabic when he rings the bell. The boy, who can't be older than fifteen, shows him into a hall with green, blue, and black mosaic tiles in intricate patterns on the walls and floor. On the benches lining the walls some men sit drinking tea from glasses. They study him with interest as he walks over to a small counter in the middle of the room, where a stout woman in her fifties asks him for twenty dollars and hands him a towel and some lavender soap in exchange. She says something in Arabic, but when Jacob stares at her doubtfully she switches to English.

"The locker rooms are that way," she says, pointing over her shoulder. "We have three saunas. Firas will show you."

The boy smiles at Jacob and gestures for him to follow. They go through the hall, deeper into the building, which is much bigger than it appeared to be from the street.

In the dressing room, Jacob puts his towel and soap on a bench and stares questioningly at the boy, who is standing in the door, looking at him invitingly.

"Massage?" he says in shaky English. "I make you feel good. Only fifty dollars."

He winks in an almost comical way, and Jacob feels suddenly very uncomfortable in this situation. It's obvious the boy is offering more than just a massage.

He's been in a state of constant agitation since that night in the garden with Yassim. But this feels wrong; the boy is far too young.

"No, thanks," he says. "I'm good."

The boy shrugs in disappointment and disappears through the door, leaving Jacob alone in the room.

Jacob settles in inside a steam room that he has to himself. Slowly he closes his eyes and leans back on the hot mosaic tiles while the steam hisses around him. A slight and pleasant intoxication makes him feel lighter and freer than usual.

He hears the glass door opening, and when he peers through the steam swirling in the draft, he can just make out the outlines of a fit young man. Jacob pretends to shut his eyes so the young man won't see Jacob checking him out as he walks by. But he takes a peek at those shoulders, the sculpted chest and arms. How old is he? A bit younger than himself? Twenty? Now he sits down next to him, and Jacob glances furtively at his straight, large nose, at his full lips, and then down at his skin, down to his waist where his towel sits.

Suddenly the man looks up and glances at him. Or not really a glance: he looks straight at him, and Jacob tries to turn away but doesn't quite manage, so their eyes meet for a moment.

There's something absolutely shameless about the look the young man gives him. Something that requires no interpretation or explanation. Jacob closes his eyes again and can feel his body start to tingle with excitement and anxiety.

Cautiously, he takes another peek and has to suppress a gasp when he sees that the man has opened his towel and is sitting naked next to him. His penis is completely smooth and hard and is standing straight up. He slowly turns toward Jacob.

"It's hot in here," he says in English.

Jacob nods weakly. "Definitely," he says.

Now the young man scoots a little closer. "Do you want to cool off with me?" he says. "There's a room where we can relax a little."

Jacob can't help staring at him, at his naked body, at his hard cock, and he can feel the attraction awakening inside him. All the frustration that's been brewing inside him since that night in the garden. This is so far from all his plans and goals and tightly controlled life. But this was what Vargander meant, he supposes. This is what he was offering him, and somehow that gives him permission to give in.

"Okay," he says. "Show me your little room then."

The young man has wrapped the towel around himself again, and he walks past Jacob toward a small pool, a few deep and low sinks, and showers where a few men are busy washing themselves. No one pays them much heed.

"Here," the young man finally says, opening a door next to a dry sauna.

Jacob takes a deep breath, but he knows he's already made his decision, and he can feel the excitement pulsing through his veins. He steps into a room with a leather-covered massage table at its center and a small sofa on the short-sided wall. The man locks the door behind them and walks slowly toward Jacob while letting his towel fall.

"I want you to fuck me," he says. "I want you to be brutal. Do you dare?"

Jacob's heart is pounding in his chest. Simon was tender and careful, excessively aware that Jacob was inexperienced. It felt safe in the beginning, then boring. Now something awakens inside him, and for once he lets it.

"Get down on your knees," he says, trying to sound brusque, but he can hear how insecure and inexperienced his voice sounds. The man smiles provocatively.

"You'll have to be harder on me than that," he says, taking a step toward him.

The young man bends forward and bites him lightly on his earlobe.

"I wanna be your little whore, do you understand?" he whispers.

It feels crude and a little dangerous, and it scares him, but that's not the only thing Jacob feels. He stops, hesitates, and for a moment considers turning around, going back to the locker room, getting dressed, and leaving. But there's something in all this that he finds alluring. It's not sexual excitement, or not only that. It's the adventure.

He takes a step closer to the man and looks straight into his eyes.

"Get down on your knees, whore," he says.

The man obeys immediately, gets on his knees in front of Jacob, whose towel falls to the floor. Now he's standing in front of a nameless man, completely naked. And the man stares up at him with pleading eyes.

"Hit me, hit me in the face," he says in a low voice.

Jacob reacts; this is another step toward the unknown. "Are you . . ." he says. "Are you sure?"

The man gives him an almost scornful look. "Don't be a little pussy; hit me now!" he hisses.

And Jacob gives in and slaps him across the face, which makes him look up with an almost contemptuous expression.

"That was nothing," he says. "You should be embarrassed. Hit me for real."

Jacob looks at him and hesitates again. But then he raises his hand and strikes him with full force across the cheek.

The young man turns his head up again and smiles weakly. Redness spreads across his cheek. "There we go," he says. "Pull my hair now. Force me."

Afterward, Jacob sits in the back of the Volvo, unable to speak to the driver beyond monosyllables, completely unable to think. The lights and traffic, the people outside the windows of the car seem blurred.

"Just drive me home," he says, opening the fridge, pouring himself a glass of wine, bringing it to his lips.

What exactly happened at the bathhouse? Who did he become in there?

He shakes his head and closes his eyes. Everything he did, everything the man wanted him to do. It was exciting, but now he feels only anxiety. Not about the young man; he wanted what happened, and they had a brief, almost friendly talk afterward. But he feels uneasy about the role he played. Dominant, brutal. Would he rather have had the other role? He knows that's true. He would rather be on his knees in front of Yassim.

For a short while in the massage room he thought that might be enough, enough to let go of that night in the garden and move on. But sitting in the back seat of the embassy car on his way home through eastern Beirut, he realizes Yassim planted something inside of him that Jacob can't let go of.

He takes another gulp of the wine, and his phone vibrates in his bag. He almost spills his wine in his eagerness to read the message. Four words from a blocked number, no sender name, as if it dropped straight into his phone from space. Still, it's enough for the world to regain its sharpness, enough for his brain to come back to life:

Next Saturday. I'll call.

Yassim.

NOVEMBER 21—SANKT ANNA

SHE HOLDS HER breath to listen again. The sound of a car's motor is getting louder. Is Gertrud on her way back? Did she forget something?

Klara looks up along the road. A pair of headlights bounces over gravel on their way to the hostel. Suddenly the lights disappear, but the sound of the engine is still there—as if the headlights were turned off in order not to be seen.

What the hell is going on? she manages to think just before the sound stops completely.

She stands at the window, her senses fully alert, staring into the darkness and the melting snow on the window. All she hears is wind.

She slowly backs away from the window, turns around, and heads out into the narrow hall. It's so cold that the skin on her arms turns to gooseflesh, despite the fact that she's wearing a thick wool sweater that Grandma brought her from Aspöja.

Klara hesitates a moment before knocking on Gabriella's door. Maybe it's unnecessary to disturb her? Maybe she's just being oversensitive? Maybe she's overanalyzing everything?

But Gabi is her friend, and just as she's about to knock, she hears Gabriella's muted voice inside her room.

"I don't think we should talk any more about this on the phone, better if we discuss it on Tuesday. And as I've said several times now, I can't do it any sooner. I'm so sorry, but—"

It sounds like she's being interrupted.

"We can't risk that you're being bugged."

She falls silent again.

"I'm hanging up now," she says emphatically. "We'll meet in Brussels like we planned. Don't call again unless you have to change the time. This is serious."

And with that, her conversation seems to be over. *Is this the reason? Is this the demanding client who made Gabi seem so distant all day?*

Klara knocks on her door, and it takes no more than a second before she hears Gabi's voice from inside. "Klara?" she says, opening the door. "I thought you were going to sleep."

Klara shakes her head, shrugs while looking at her friend. "I thought I heard something," she says.

"Was I disturbing you?" Gabi says, then falls silent, irritation springing into her eyes. "Were you eavesdropping?"

Klara shakes her head. Now she's annoyed too. What the hell's the matter with Gabi?

"No," she says, giving her a chilly look. "I wasn't standing here eavesdropping on your fucking conversation. Believe it or not, I have bigger things than your phone calls to worry about today."

They stand there staring at each other for a moment, both unused to any discord. Finally, Gabi takes a step toward her and hugs her. "Damn it," she says. "Forgive me, I'm so sorry, Klara."

Klara awkwardly returns her hug.

"I'm just so fucking stressed," Gabi continues. "There's something very sensitive going on, or so it seems. And I can't risk dragging anyone else into it, least of all you."

"But you know you can tell me everything, Gabi," she says. "Whenever you want."

"Not now," Gabi sighs, and pulls away from Klara's arms. "Not today. I don't even know if it is something . . ." She falls silent again, hesitates. "But," she says after a short pause. "If something were to go wrong in the future I've . . ."

Klara waits, tensely, while Gabi searches for words.

"Aww," she says at last. "Fuck it. I'm so dramatic. I'll tell you when I know more." She looks up at Klara. "What was it you wanted?"

Klara looks at her. She should nag Gabi to tell her what's going on, but she knows it's futile. When Gabi makes up her mind there's nothing anyone can do to change it, especially if it has to do with her job. But it's still a relief that this is job-related, Klara thinks, that Gabi's irritation isn't because she's tired of Klara.

"No, I just thought I heard something," Klara says. "A car outside." She points over her shoulder to her own room. "It was headed here with its headlights turned off."

"Out on the road?" Gabi says.

"Headed down toward us, toward the hostel," Klara says.

Without a word, Gabi goes past her, into the hall and then into Klara's room. The lights inside are turned off, and Gabi goes over to the window, stares intensely out into the darkness. The only sound is the radiator knocking, the wind whining around the house. No engine. No lights.

Gabi turns around and puts a hand on her cheek.

"It's been a long day for both of us," she says. "It's time for us to go to bed."

"But there was something," Klara says. "I saw a car earlier that seemed a little off . . . after the funeral. It drove down to the campsite. There's nothing there at this time of year. . . ."

She looks at Gabi, but at the same time she hesitates. What was off about it anyway? Maybe it was just someone taking a driving lesson. But in this weather? Of course, it could have been anything—maybe someone got lost—and right now she's not even sure if she really heard that engine, saw the lights.

"Okay, okay," Gabi says, holding up her hands. "If it makes you feel better, we'll look."

Klara sees it. Gabi is trying to calm her by making it seem like it's ridiculous that some mysterious car would be out here. Which of course it is. But at the same time there's something in Gabriella's eyes that's not totally convincing.

It takes a few minutes to find a couple of flashlights, and then they spend a half hour in the snow and wind searching the parking lot in front of the hostel, but they don't find anything. Not even any tire tracks.

Now they're back in the living room of the hostel, wet and frozen.

"You've been through a lot," Gabi says. "You've been through the wringer, friend."

Klara nods and stands up from the sofa she was sitting on. She doesn't know if she should feel relieved not to have found a mysterious car, or worried that she's imagining things. But it's true: she's been through so much in the last few years.

"I know," she says. "But hopefully I can get some sleep now."

She smiles at Gabi, who also stands up.

"One can always hope," she says.

The bed is so warm and soft and sleep so incredibly near that for the first time in a long time Klara almost feels content. Despite the funeral. Despite everything. Going to sleep with Gabi in the room next door has a calming effect, and she can feel herself falling, falling into the deep, soothing hole of sleep.

But just before she's drifting away she hears it again. A sound, barely audible through the wind.

A motor.

She immediately sits up in bed, puts her feet on the floor, and walks to the window. The sound is constant. She cups her hands and peers out into the night. A small light flashes for a moment and disappears halfway between the hostel and the road. Just for a moment. As if someone were lighting a cigarette. Then it's quiet again.

Quiet and dark. As if nothing happened.

AUGUST 17–22—BEIRUT

EVERYONE SAYS IT'S a stressful time, but for Jacob, the week crawls with unbearable slowness. At the embassy it's mostly just him, Agneta, and Frida, who greets him hastily every morning, but doesn't stop by his desk until midweek.

"So sorry, Johan," she says, "I promise we'll figure out something more for you to do, but do you think you could sort these receipts for now? I can't really ask Agneta; she's so busy."

She puts down a small cardboard box filled to the brim with wrinkled slips of paper onto his desk and looks at him apologetically, her forehead imprinted with a deep furrow. He feels his own motivation sinking even lower; they don't seem to care at all. And Vargander, who let him borrow the embassy's car and arranged that strange excursion? Didn't that mean anything at all?

"*Jacob*," he says, with emphasis. "You mean Jacob."

She looks at him uncomprehendingly at first. Then she makes the connection. "Did I say something else? Please forgive me if that was the case. I didn't mean to. I've just got so much on my plate right now."

He nods.

"You know, the political situation?" she begins. "You've read about the demonstrations, right? So far they have been centered downtown and mainly taken place on the weekends, but it feels like it is building up. If the government doesn't sort out the mess with the trash collection, there could be a late iteration of Arab Spring here too. We have to be prepared for that."

His interest and excitement are piqued by this. He can see it himself on the streets. Both the trash and discontent are spreading. More and more groups are joining in and airing their grievances at the corruption of the state. Soon it will be only the army defending it. And maybe not even that. He sees the graffiti and hears the slogans echoing when he heads home from the office in the evening. At the same time, a couple of streets over from where the demonstrations take place, life continues as normal. Maybe that is how revolutions start, he thinks. Maybe you hardly even notice them at first. Or maybe the Lebanese are just so used to turmoil that for them this is nothing.

"I'd love to help you." He straightens up. "If you need someone to go to the demonstrations or meetings and report back, I can—"

Frida holds up a hand to interrupt him. "Stay away from the government district," she says. "I'm being serious, we cannot afford to have our intern get caught up in something." She sighs. "That's the last thing I need now. Please, just focus on the receipts."

The air rushes out of him again, and he nods in defeat. Frida returns the nod and disappears into her office, a phone already pressed to her ear.

At least the box of receipts offers him something to do. He deciphers the smudged print on the thin slips of paper and sorts them chronologically before attaching them to letter-size paper. There's no use thinking about how this task is something for an assistant and miles away from what he thought he'd be doing here. Better to see it as one assignment among others, and do it to the best of his ability. One day they'll notice him and let him prove what he can do.

And on Saturday . . . On Saturday, Yassim will be back.

His evenings have started to fall into a pattern. He leaves the embassy around six and heads on foot back to Mar Mikhael. He can kill an hour that way. On his way home he buys two small shawarmas or a falafel, which he eats while walking. Sometimes he stops at a café or bar, orders a beer, and tries to read a few pages of *The Tragedy of Lebanon*, but usually he heads straight home to his apartment and sits on the balcony watching something on Netflix until it's time to go to bed. He's counting the days until the weekend.

Three days left. Two. One.

On Friday, all of Beirut is full of rumors of an uprising. They say the demonstrations will be even bigger this weekend. Everyone will be there; the discontent is shared by every group now: Christians, Shia, Sunni, Palestinians, Armenians, and Syrian refugees. It's not just the middle class anymore: everyone is tired of it.

On his way to the office that morning he walks by the mosque and the government buildings that are wrapped in barbed wire, guarded by nervous young police officers and soldiers in helmets and riot shields. Something's afoot, of that there's no doubt.

He avoids the government district that evening, even though he can feel the vibration of the demonstrations all the way to his balcony on the other side of the city. He doesn't avoid it because they told him to but because he's waiting for Yassim to come back.

But Saturday goes by without a word from him, and Jacob reads the text from last weekend over and over again, weighing every possible scenario. Maybe it wasn't even Yassim who sent that text. Why did he take that for granted? It was from an anonymous number. When he analyzes it more closely he realizes it doesn't say it's from Yassim anywhere.

He can't believe he's been so stupid, so terribly naive that he allowed such empty hope to dictate how he lives his life. At half past seven he feels completely dejected. He drinks half a bottle of wine on the balcony with disappointment pounding inside him. He considers taking a taxi, but by this time it's just as fast to walk. If he can't have Yassim, at least he can have the uprising.

He's almost to Martyrs' Square when the extent of the protests, the extent of the rally, becomes clear to him. Thousands of people pouring into the square in front of the mosque: students, families with children, masked men with their upper bodies bare and stones in their hands. And everywhere armed police officers dressed in black. Barbed wire and smoke. He moves toward it, feeling as if nothing matters now, and he just wants to be part of something, feel something, finally see something.

He walks straight into the crowd, moving with them across the square. Notices families with children becoming more rare, until finally the crowd consists of only young people with angry faces chanting slogans. The masked faces become more frequent, as do the hands holding rocks. He feels his pulse start to race, but he wants to follow through, wants to see what this is, what it will lead to. So he lets the crowd sweep him toward the government district; he can feel himself becoming a part of it, can feel the sweat running down his neck and mixing with other people's sweat. Everywhere are flags, posters, slogans, songs, drums. It's so deafening that he doesn't hear his phone ringing in his pocket. But he feels it vibrating. And he manages to free an arm despite the press of people, gets a hand into his pocket, takes out the phone, and pushes it to his ear.

"Where are you?"

He can barely hear, but it's a voice he'd recognize anywhere. Yassim.

"At the demonstration!" he screams into the phone. "You didn't call. I didn't know. Where are you?"

"Listen to me," Yassim says. "Get out of there. I'm taking a taxi to the Four Seasons on the Corniche, the boardwalk, in about twenty minutes. Repeat what I just said."

"Four Seasons!" Jacob shouts. "In twenty minutes."

And with that Yassim is gone. And everything else too. Jacob stops in the middle of the crowd, which is flowing like a river around him. He doesn't notice it at all.

Later the two of them are walking westward along Charles Helou, past the Four Seasons and the new skyscrapers, and the darkness around them feels gentle and alive, full of holes, not even darkness really. The traffic is sparse here, when they get away from the protests and chaos down near the border between East and West Beirut.

Jacob coughs; his throat is dry like always after a day spent breathing in the smog and the stench of trash. It's hard to really take in that he's actually walking beside Yassim again; it feels more like a memory. He glances at his friend, who smiles at him, amused.

"You didn't think you'd hear from me again," Yassim says. "You thought I'd disappeared?"

Jacob shrugs and turns his eyes to the blackness above the ocean. "Where were you?" he says, too quietly. His voice is drowned out by a motorcycle weaving in and out of traffic. "Your trip?" he says again, more loudly now. "Where were you?"

Yassim turns to him and says nothing at first, just looks at him with those sad, curious eyes. "Syria," he says finally. "Near Aleppo."

Jacob stops, gets goose bumps on his arms. "What?" he says. "Aleppo? What . . . Oh my God, what were you doing there? How did you even get there? I don't know what to say."

Yassim holds up the camera hanging across his chest. "Taking photos," he says. "That's what I do. I'm a photographer."

"I didn't know that," Jacob says.

He's speculated about what Yassim does for a living, imagined a thousand scenarios for why he disappeared, trying to avoid the suspicion that Yassim just didn't want to be with him.

"How could you know?" Yassim says. "We barely spoke last time."

Jacob blushes, and they slowly start walking again. Yassim guides them away from Charles Helou and the sea and in between the new skyscrapers, in toward the chaos, toward the city.

"I don't know anything about you," Jacob says.

Yassim laughs again. "There's not much to know. I'm a photographer. And right now, you know, with the war, there's a lot of work in Syria. That's the only good thing you can say about it. A lot of work in the area."

It doesn't sound cynical when he says it, more resigned, like a reflection.

"Aren't you afraid?" Jacob asks. "I mean . . . My God."

Yassim shrugs and leads them farther into the city, toward the financial district, where it's calm and quiet this time of the day. Here there are only glass facades and building cranes, Persian Gulf money and black BMWs.

"You get used to it," he says. "Don't think about it much."

They've arrived at a newly built high-rise that shoots upward for at least twenty irregular floors, with white terraces and glass windows from floor to ceiling. It doesn't look like it has any exterior walls, and you can see straight into the apartments on the lower floors wherever they're lit up. It's a completely transparent building, and Jacob wonders where the bedrooms are, if they too are fully open to the city.

To his surprise Yassim goes to the entrance, where a bored security guard stands smoking, a machine gun leaning against his chair. Yassim greets the guard and walks past him toward the entrance, then turns to Jacob. "Are you coming?"

They ride upward in a sleek elevator of gleaming steel. It's like traveling through water: silent and almost no resistance. Finally, the elevator stops gently, and Yassim smiles at him and carefully pushes past him, out onto the eighth floor. Three doors, three apartments, no names on any of them, only numbers. Yassim goes over to number 801, the left door, holds a small card against the handle and opens it.

"Like a hotel," Jacob says.

It's the first thing he's said since they entered the building, but Yassim doesn't answer, maybe he didn't even hear, he just goes inside.

The apartment is large—over one thousand square feet—and sits in one corner of the building with two glass walls facing the city. Concrete floors, a kitchen island in an open floor plan, it looks completely unused, like a set, like a showroom. In the middle of the floor there's a large table and a laptop. Two chairs, one on each side. No paper, no clothes, nothing.

Yassim stops and turns to Jacob, his eyes now somewhat nervous and apologetic. "I would love to offer you something," he says. "But I only have water at home."

"It doesn't matter," Jacob says. He doesn't want to drink anything. The images from the protest he was just in the middle of linger, and he can feel his legs start to tremble; a wave of exhaustion rolls over him.

He goes to the window and looks out over the other newly built skyscrapers, the empty lots between them, the cranes and the traffic. He can't even hear the cars up here.

Yassim walks over to an almost invisible door in the glass wall and opens it. "There's a terrace," he says.

The warm, humid night tumbles into the dry, air-conditioned apartment as they head out onto the terrace. Outside it still feels like Beirut, the trash and exhaust and the traffic, albeit muted. It feels safe, and Jacob leans over the railing and stares down onto the streets below.

"Do you live here?" he says. "You don't have much furniture."

Yassim is standing next to him now, close enough to catch a whiff of his fragrance and some kind of crackling, leaping electricity. But not close enough to touch him.

"I don't need much," Yassim says. "I'm not here very often."

"How . . ." Jacob begins, but he's unsure what's allowed, what he's entitled to ask.

"What?" Yassim says.

"Well," Jacob begins again. "How can you afford to live here? I heard that only Dubai businessmen live in these newly built condos."

Yassim says nothing at first. Then he turns around, takes Jacob by the hand, and leads him back into the apartment.

"How do you know I'm not from Dubai?" he says quietly.

Jacob sits on one of the chairs at the table in the big room, and Yassim asks him to wait there while he takes care of something farther into the apartment. The lights from the surrounding buildings glitter outside, and it occurs to Jacob that he's completely unprotected here, anyone can see inside. He looks around, and it's hard to imagine anyone living in such an open and clean and completely transparent way.

He spins around in his chair, clicks restlessly and curiously at the computer, which quietly wakes up, the screen turning on. He doesn't know anything about Yassim. Just that he speaks English with an American accent and that the little he's heard of his Arabic doesn't sound like he's from the Gulf. More like he's from Lebanon or Syria. Should he suggest that they speak Arabic instead? He'd like to get better at Arabic, but it takes so much goddamn effort, and it makes him tired just thinking about it.

The computer is password protected, but he can just make out a blurry background image behind the dialogue box. Jacob squints. It's a picture of a big family, ten, maybe twelve people. Adults and children dressed in nice clothes. Suits with colorful shirts and ties. Shimmering silk dresses and a lot of makeup. One of the women has red flowers in her arms, a veil, a white dress. It's a bride, and this is a wedding photo with her entire family. Is it Yassim's family?

Jacob looks up and sees Yassim on the other side of the room with a large, framed painting in one hand. He puts it down with its subject against the wall.

"Come here," he says.

They end up on the bed, of course, and Jacob doesn't even know how it happens, how all of a sudden he doesn't have a shirt on, how Yassim's warm, dry hands are caressing his chest. He feels Yassim's hand in his hair; the other one is on his cock, unbuttoning his jeans, eager, searching, and unruly. And so Jacob puts his own hand down there to help with the buttons, pulls off his trousers, and suddenly he's naked.

He's panting and pressing himself against Yassim's hand, which is around him now, steady, almost firm, and it feels so unbelievably good that Jacob thinks it might already be over for him, but Yassim just holds on, doesn't move his hand, even with Jacob pressing against it.

Instead, Yassim pushes him back on the bed and lets go, gets up on his knees. He's still dressed, and Jacob is completely naked, completely at his mercy, and it's so exciting he can barely contain himself. He would do anything right now, anything to feel Yassim on him, in him.

Yassim laughs and pulls his T-shirt over his head, throws it on the floor behind him. He slowly unbuttons his trousers and stands up.

"Do you want this?" he says.

"There's nothing I want more," Jacob says.

His voice is hoarse, almost unrecognizable. This is unlike anything he's experienced before. Not like his tense and predictable nights with Simon in Uppsala after a bottle of wine. Definitely not like the dirty and frightening thing that happened at the bathhouse. This room, the sight of Yassim, his scent, the very thought of his skin, his hands, his mouth, give Jacob goose bumps.

Yassim has his trousers off now, and he's standing on the floor in front of Jacob. He's bigger than Jacob imagined, and when he lies down on top of him, when he pushes Jacob's thighs up toward his chest and pushes inside him without any warning, without asking for permission, it's as if nothing in the world exists other than this.

It hurts, but it's a pain he never wants to end, a pain he'd stop time for if he could. Yassim covers his mouth as he sobs. Holds it hard and moves deep and sure inside of him, pushing Jacob's hand above his head and pressing it down toward the mattress. Jacob is held tight beneath Yassim's body, couldn't move if he wanted to.

He can feel his eyes filling with tears from the pain, but he doesn't want to close them. He has to see Yassim, has to look into his eyes. And when he does, it's as if he can see straight into him, as if he forgets he doesn't know anything about him, that they just met, that he disappeared for over two weeks and then just as suddenly came back. None of that matters, because he sees something in Yassim's eyes, feels it in the desperation with which he's being forced down onto the mattress, knows this is more than sex: it's something elemental, something that's more than lust, so much bigger, infinitely more risky. Something you can't resist, no matter how much you might want to.

Afterward they lie on their backs in bed in the empty room. Jacob stares straight up at the ceiling, doesn't dare glance at Yassim, afraid this fragile bubble of something like happiness might burst. Finally, Yassim breaks the silence.

"I have no room for this," he says. His voice is thin, barely more than a whisper.

"No room for what?" Jacob asks as quietly as he can.

Yassim takes a breath and turns his face toward him. "For what we just did," he says. "For you. I have no room for us."

"And yet you let it happen," Jacob says. "And yet you were the one who contacted me. You could have left me alone."

Yassim nods. "I should have," he says. "But I couldn't. After that night in the garden, I couldn't stop thinking about you." He sits up halfway, resting on his elbows. "But my life," he continues. "My life is not simple. I travel, take off on short notice. And what I do . . ."

He falls silent for a moment, as if thinking of how to put this.

"It's necessary that I don't draw any attention to myself," he says. "What I photograph and the contacts I need to maintain in order to do my work, if they knew this about me it would be over. This isn't Europe. What we're doing is a liability, you know? A risk I can't really afford to take."

Jacob nods. He knows how it is in Beirut. He's heard the stories of sudden crackdowns on the bathhouses in Bourj Hammoud, on doctors who perform anal exams, about the humiliation and harassment. And still Beirut is the most open place in the Middle East. He can only imagine what it must be like in Syria, in the war zones. He suddenly feels so selfish, that he didn't think about this more, didn't think about anything but himself.

"I understand," Jacob says. "I really do."

Yassim nods. "I want us to meet again. But I'm going to Aleppo tomorrow for a couple of days and coming back in the middle of the week. And that's how it will be. Just so you understand. You can't talk about this. I can't be your boyfriend; I have to be kind of like a ghost."

He smiles a little, and Jacob sits up and takes his face in his hands, kisses him gently.

"Yes," he says. "I understand. You can be my ghost."

Later, Jacob is sitting on the edge of the bed, listening to Yassim's now heavy and rhythmic breathing, until Yassim rolls over onto his side, curls up like a child, all the while still holding Jacob's hand.

Cautiously, Jacob pulls his hand free and stands up. The room is silent as he tiptoes over the floor, except for the quiet buzz of the air conditioner.

The corridor and living room are just as empty as they were a couple of hours ago, and the light from the city falls through the huge windows. He looks for the door, momentarily disoriented. There's the table with the computer, the open kitchen. His glance falls on the painting that's leaning against one of the walls, still with its back side facing out.

Why did Yassim come out of the bedroom with the painting? Why did he leave it here? Doesn't he want Jacob to see it, or was he planning to show him later?

He goes over to the painting, hesitates for a moment, listening for Yassim before turning it around.

It's an enlarged photograph, almost a yard wide and half as high. The light in the room is so dim that he has to lean the picture against the wall and hold up his cell phone with the flashlight on. The bright light falls onto the photograph, and he takes a step back to get an overview. But it takes a moment for him to make sense of what he's looking at.

The photo is taken from above, blurry and out of focus, not something you'd expect to see framed. Nor is its subject, he realizes as his eyes adjust to it.

The photograph shows a courtyard at a large country house, a farm where some wealthy family probably lived for generations. But the inner courtyard and the buildings around it are in ruins, as if a bomb has exploded in the middle of it. As he leans closer and lets the light fall in different angles, he starts to understand that's exactly what happened. In the gravel and the pits of the farm you can make out what could only be dead bodies, or parts of bodies.

Jacob gasps. He can see a child on his back, apparently untouched, in dirty but fancy clothes and shiny shoes, his dead eyes staring straight up. He sees the upper body of a woman in a purple dress lying face-down, but he can't see her legs. He sees something that might be an arm lying bloody and by itself in a crater in the middle of the picture.

"I guess you understand why I didn't want that on the bedroom wall tonight," Yassim says from somewhere behind him.

Jacob jumps, frightened and guilty; he didn't hear Yassim coming out of the bedroom.

He manages to put the picture back in its place against the wall before standing up; the flashlight on his phone is still shining.

"I'm sorry," he begins. "I was just headed home, didn't mean to . . ."

"It's not a problem," Yassim says calmly. "It's the first picture I took of a drone attack. A wedding near the beginning of the air campaign against ISIS."

Yassim stands there, his face dimly lit by the light coming through the big windows.

"I have it on the wall so I don't forget what it is I'm doing. It's hard to explain." He shrugs his shoulders and smiles sadly. "But tonight I didn't want it to be watching over us."

Jacob nods and walks toward him. "I understand," Jacob says. "I didn't mean to snoop. I was just heading for the door and saw it. Forgive me."

He's now reached Yassim and kisses him on the cheek. Yassim looks tired, but something flashes in his eyes as he deliberately pushes Jacob's hand away from his cheek.

"I hide my secrets better than that," he says evenly. There's something hard and indifferent in his expression now, something that feels almost like a blow. They stand there, facing each other for a second that never wants to end. "*If* I have any secrets, that is," he adds.

He smiles again, and his eyes are as warm as before; the change is so quick it leaves Jacob confused, with no idea what to say.

"But you have to go now, my friend," Yassim says. "I have to get up early."

He takes Jacob's hand again, leads him to the elevator door and opens it.

Jacob turns around. "Again, I'm sorry," he says. "It really wasn't my intention to snoop, I don't know what got into me."

"It's no problem," Yassim says, and caresses his cheek gently. "It's just a photo."

Jacob nods. "Will you call when you get back?" he says. "Or can I get your number?"

Yassim pushes him gently out the door, laughs, and shakes his head. "Jacob, you really have to go now," he says. "Don't worry, I'll call you in the middle of the week when I'm back. It may be hard for you to understand, but I actually want to see you too."

When he says that, it's as if something sticks in Jacob's chest, a little nub of hope, a tiny shard of reciprocity. "Yes, it is hard to understand," he whispers.

Yassim leans forward and kisses him on his lips, pushes him into the hallway. "But so it is," he says. "Perhaps unfortunately. But so it is."

NOVEMBER 22—STOCKHOLM

THEY ROLL OVER the bridge into Stockholm just before eleven. Below them, the city sparkles in the autumn morning sun.

Klara is in the passenger seat, and Gabriella has just finished a phone call with her boss, Göran Wiman, who asked her to go by the office on Skeppsbron. Immediately.

Gabriella puts up a good show during the call, says things like "of course" and "no problem," maintaining an attitude that Klara recognizes quite well from her own past life as an ambitious political adviser in the European Parliament. It's not a life that she misses.

"Back to the salt mines?" Klara says now, looking at Gabriella, who smiles tiredly without taking her eyes off the road.

"What the hell choice do I have?" she mutters.

"I thought you'd have it easier once you made partner," Klara continues.

Gabriella sighs again. "I'm the most junior partner," she says. "Apparently there's a fucking hierarchy among us as well. You can't win at this game."

"Doesn't it help that you're famous now?" Klara says. "After last summer, I mean?"

"Fame," Gabriella mutters. "Seems to create more problems than it solves."

"Why?"

But she doesn't answer, just keeps driving in silence.

"One strange thing . . ." Klara begins when she finally tires of the silence in the car.

"Yes?"

"You promise not to give me shit now?" she says. "And please remember, I buried my grandfather yesterday, so I'm obviously a basket case."

"Now I'm curious," Gabriella says, glancing at her. "Tell me."

"You know George Lööw?" As soon as she says his name her face gets warm. Why is she even bringing this up?

"George from Brussels, the PR guy?" Gabriella says. "Who somehow managed to first represent a client that was a front for the CIA and then another that was a front for the Kremlin?"

"Forget it," Klara says. "It's nothing." She leans back in her seat.

"Not a chance!" Gabriella says, glancing over again. "What about George?"

"I know he's a douchebag; you don't have to tell me that, okay?" Klara takes a deep breath. "But . . ."

"Stop it!" Gabriella turns away from the road completely to stare at Klara with her eyes wide. "I knew it! I knew it this summer! Have you been in touch? Met? Tell me everything!"

Klara's cheeks still feel hot; her mouth is dry. "Please stop!" she says. "And no, we haven't met or even been in touch. We're friends on Facebook; that's it. And it's so stupid, he's . . . Well, you know what he's like. But still. I think of him pretty often. Too often."

Gabriella drums her fists on the wheel. "Yes!" she says. "Finally back in the game." Then she stops, puts a hand on Klara's thigh. "I'm sorry.

"It's not the right day to tease you about this. And honestly"—she turns to Klara again—"it's a good thing. He's hot, and he'll grow into himself. You two are going to have the most beautiful little babies."

"I barely know him, Gabi. And I have no idea where this comes from. It'll pass. I hope."

Gabriella glances at her again. "We'll see," she says. "We'll see."

"Ha ha," Klara says. "I don't think we'll see anything at all."

She turns her head and looks out over Stockholm. She asked Gabriella to take this route via Essingeleden, even though it's a bit longer and more complicated, just for this very view. The city looks so grand from here, so promising and undeniably beautiful. The silver, sparkling water of Riddarfjärden contrasting with Kungsholmen's yellow and pink buildings.

She runs her eyes along Söder Mälarstrand, past the brick walls of Münchenbryggeriet and toward Mariaberget, where Gabriella lives. The bare trees seem so lonely in the bright morning light.

Klara leans back in her seat, allowing herself to feel this blend of calm and expectation that Stockholm always evokes in her, pushing away the sadness and emptiness of the past few months. Even though she's never lived in Stockholm, she feels at home here. In Stockholm and on Aspöja. In East London sometimes. In the Brussels municipalities of Ixelles and Saint-Gilles. *Home can be many places*, she thinks, gently turning her head back, glancing over her shoulder.

There's another reason she asked Gabriella to take this way. On Sunday mornings the traffic here is sparse, and the bridge feels extra long and straight. It's a good place to check if someone is following you. She thought she saw a Volvo take off from the rest stop at Sillekrog right behind them. Thought the driver was a man she saw smoking outside the kiosk.

Now there's a truck behind them blocking her view, and before she can get a good look they're on Kungsholmen, making their way toward the inner city and Gamla Stan. On these city streets it's impossible to see if you're being followed.

Gabriella gives her a furtive glance. "Klara," she begins exhaustedly. "Are you looking for that car again?"

Klara turns back toward the front, looks out at the cream-colored buildings instead. She shrugs. "Just wanted to check," she mumbles.

"Paranoia," Gabriella says, but her smile isn't convincing, and it quickly dies on her lips.

Gabriella slows outside the law firm Lindblad and Wiman on Skeppsbron 28. Klara looks up at the art nouveau building. A flag with the company's logo hangs above the entrance, flapping in the wind.

"When are they going to add Seichelmann to the company name?" she asks.

"One thing at a time, Klara," Gabriella warns her. "I have to start with partnership."

"I'm serious," Klara says. "You should push them a little. By the way, you can't park your car here, you know that, right?"

Gabriella gives her a tired look. "Sunday morning, and I'm working? The company can pay the fine. I'd say it's the least they can do if they won't put my name on the flag."

"Hell yes, girl," Klara says.

She smiles and glances down the street in search of mysterious cars but sees nothing. The Volvo seems to be gone now. All she sees is a police car and a black Volkswagen van slowly driving past them and turning onto one of the narrow side streets of the Gamla Stan. Klara points to them through the windshield.

"Listen," she says. "I can drive around the block. Doesn't it feel a little provocative to park here right in front of the police, when they're circling the block? I can take a few laps and wait."

Gabriella looks up, following the short motorcade with worried eyes and a furrow on her brow.

"What the hell?" she mutters. "A SWAT van? At Skeppsbron on a Sunday?"

She puts the car keys in Klara's lap.

"Okay, I'll call you. I think he just wants to give me a few documents. Shouldn't take long."

She jumps out onto the street, her eyes on the police cars. Klara follows her example and walks around the car to sit in the driver's seat. She turns the key, then makes a slow turn onto a deserted street.

A SWAT van, she thinks with a crooked smile. It just takes one glance, and Gabriella knows what's up. Klara often forgets how many years she spent as a defense attorney and all the knowledge that entails.

It's a little tricky to make her way around this neighborhood. She can't remember if she's ever driven through the narrow, cobblestone streets of the old town before, and it takes her at least ten minutes to find her way back to Gabi's office, though she enters at a point much closer to the city, near the royal palace.

The traffic is still sparse, so she finds it puzzling when the cars in front of her slow down and then stop completely. She stretches up in her seat, trying to see what's happening. There are only two cars in front of her, and in front of them stands a police officer in a black helmet with an automatic weapon hanging across his chest.

Her heart starts to pound. The SWAT team she saw earlier. Some kind of crackdown. The other drivers open their doors and step out to get a better look, and Klara does the same.

Farther down the street she sees a black Volkswagen van and at least two regular police vehicles. Around them stand dozens of police officers, all heavily armed. They don't have their weapons raised yet, but they're dressed in black, with helmets and Kevlar, and they seem prepared for a face-off at one of the buildings. Klara raises her eyes slightly and sees the Lindblad and Wiman flag they just joked about waving outside Gabriella's office.

It takes a moment to make the connection, but when she does, her blood runs cold. No, it's too surreal, too crazy. The police are at the door of the Lindblad and Wiman office.

AUGUST 24—BEIRUT

SUNDAY WAS EMPTY and endless, so it's a relief when Jacob's workweek starts again. A release to step into the room with the safe buzzing of the air conditioner, to pour himself a cup of coffee in the small, windowless kitchenette.

"You've been following the news, right?" Agneta asks.

She spreads cottage cheese on crispbread and looks at him in her friendly way. He thought diplomats would be different, more exotic and cosmopolitan. Or at least they'd eat Lebanese snacks. He does his best to hide his disappointment that they're more like gray bureaucrats, that they usually do their best to re-create a Swedish work environment, complete with caviar, cottage cheese, and crispbread. He nods, almost tells her he was there, at the protests on Saturday, about Yassim, and everything. But he stops himself. He was told not to go anywhere near the government district, and Yassim isn't his boyfriend—he's a ghost.

What if he really is? What if Jacob just made him up?

"Yes," he says. "It's crazy. What are the others saying? And where are they?"

It's usually only Agneta who gets to the office before him, but it's almost half past ten, and he hasn't seen Frida or Vargander.

"Meetings with the other EU ambassadors all day." Agneta sighs. "They're at full capacity after the riots this weekend. They're talking about an Arab Spring here too, you know. It's typical that you'd end up in the middle of all this, Johan. As if it weren't messy enough after the move from Damascus and all that."

He feels his heart sink in his chest again. "Jacob," he says quietly.

"Excuse me?"

"My name isn't Johan. It's Jacob."

Agneta looks at him with embarrassment and puts a hand on his arm. "Oh dear. Did I say Johan? I'm so sorry, I didn't mean to. I know what your name is. It's just a lot right now, you know."

"It's no problem," Jacob says, smiling slightly. "And I think it's exciting that so much is happening right now. Please tell me if I can help you with writing background material or anything at all."

He's not really sure what *background material* means or what it's supposed to contain, but he heard Frida use the word the other day and it sounds like a reasonable task for an intern. Something he could do so at least they'd remember that his name is Jacob.

"Of course." Agneta nods. "Are you done with the receipts Frida gave you?"

"Almost," he says. "They'll be ready this afternoon. I'd better get to it." He lifts his coffee cup like a small salute and goes back to the corridor and to his own little office.

"I'm really sorry about that thing with your name," he can hear Agneta saying behind him before he turns the corner.

With a sigh he takes down the box of receipts from a bookshelf and starts again. "Almost done" was an exaggeration. He's done about a third. But today, in his current state, he feels a kind of reluctant appreciation that he's only sorting and stapling papers. The work is monotonous, almost automatic, and he can do it while his head and body are still in Yassim's apartment. He feels his pulse start to race whenever his thoughts touch on what happened. Yassim's mouth and hands. How he surrendered to Yassim, how he was willing to do anything for him. He stifles a gasp—so physical is the memory. He's never felt anything like it.

At five o'clock he puts the final receipt on a shiny white piece of paper and is filled with pride when he looks down at three thick packets of chronologically arranged receipts.

But he's also restless. He doesn't feel like staying here at the embassy and doing nothing. It's not as if anyone would miss him, he thinks as he stands up and heads toward Agneta's room. He knocks softly and Agneta turns from her screen.

"I'm done with the receipts," he says. "Is there something else you need me to do?"

He looks at her, hoping for something else, something more. There are riots and a revolution brewing no more than a few blocks away. There must be something bigger for him to do. Something more meaningful and noble than sorting through receipts.

Agneta smiles at him. She looks stressed and like she hasn't slept properly.

"Good work, Jacob," she says. "You see? Got the name right."

He smiles back. "Bravo!"

"Go home, you," she says. "You've done your duty for today."

It's dark by the time he reaches Mar Mikhael, and the lights of the traffic and restaurants dance around him. He stops outside his front door and gazes up the street, toward the sidewalk outside the bars where people are gathered for drinks, buzzing with laughter. Here the riots downtown seem to be just gossip and fodder for conversation, hardly even real. But this is how Beirut is, they say. Even during the wars people gathered in bars in calmer neighborhoods. Life goes on, even under difficult circumstances. For a moment he considers crossing the street to get a cocktail at Internazionale. But he's hungry and tired. With a sigh he turns around and walks up the stairs to his apartment.

It takes a while to find his key and even longer to realize he can't turn it because the door is already unlocked.

He freezes. Did he really forget to lock it this morning? That's unlike him.

Cautiously, he pushes the door open to the dark apartment. The curtains on the windows and the balcony door are pulled open; the light from the neon signs and an unusually bright moon falls across the mosaic floor. Everything is as he left it, and he lets out a small sigh of relief. He just forgot to lock up.

He walks into the kitchen and takes a bottle of water from the fridge, unscrews the top, and he's just lifting a glass out of the dish rack when he hears a woman's voice behind him.

"You're late, Matti," she says. "I almost started to despair."

He drops the glass, and it feels as if ten seconds pass before it reaches the floor and explodes into a thousand shards, before his life explodes into just as many shards, which will never, ever be put back together again.

The woman is standing in the darkness next to the door to the living room, just a few yards away. A sharp, thin stripe of light from the street illuminates the left side of her face, making her look ghostly, almost as if she glows. She's in her midthirties, looks Middle Eastern. Thin, with short, dark hair. Slowly she takes a step closer to him, and he sees she's wearing tight jeans, a black tank top, and a red-striped, button-down shirt.

"Who are you?" he whispers.

"Come on, Matti," she says, cocking her head to the side. "We have a lot to talk about."

She holds out a hand to him and gestures toward the living room. He stands frozen in place and just shakes his head. "I want you to leave," he says clumsily.

She smiles at him again, as one smiles at a child whose demands one has no intention of giving in to. "That's not going to happen, Matti. Like I said, we have a lot to talk about, you and me."

Jacob swallows hard. "Don't call me that," he says. "That's not my name anymore."

"Your name's not Matti Johansson anymore," she says. "Well, that is indeed true. You're Jacob Seger now. It's a much grander name, you might say. Fits the person you want to be."

"Please," he says. "Leave me alone. I haven't done anything wrong."

But the woman isn't listening to him, doesn't hear him. "It wasn't good enough for you to grow up with a lonely, alcoholic mother in Eskilstuna," she begins. "That's understandable. Welfare and evictions. You have big dreams, Matti. Your background must feel like a handicap. You're made for embassies and elegant dinner parties. Castles, perhaps? Surely you didn't grow up in such miserable conditions?"

He shakes his head. It can't be true. Everything he put behind him, everything he worked so hard to escape. Why now? Now when he's so close?

His mouth is dry; his head is spinning.

"I need water," he whispers.

But the woman's already passed by him, found a glass, and is filling it from the tap that is still running. She hands it to him.

"There you go," she says. "Now let's sit down in the living room."

"I don't know who you are," Jacob says when they finally sit down at the table in front of the closed balcony door. "But there's nothing illegal or suspicious about changing one's name."

Jacob has to raise his voice to be heard over the traffic and baseline thumping from the bars.

"Illegal?" the woman says. "No, definitely not. Suspicious? Well . . ." She holds up her hands like scales.

"How do you know about this?" he says. "Why did you investigate me? Why are you here?"

The woman leans back in her chair and stares calmly at him. "When are you planning to meet Yassim Al-Abbas again?" she says.

"I . . ." he says. "I don't know what you're talking about."

He takes a gulp of water. Al-Abbas. Is that Yassim's last name?

Slowly the woman leans over the table, her dark, expressionless eyes boring into his own. "My name is Myriam Awad," she says. "Officially, I work with cultural affairs at the Swedish Institute in Alexandria."

"And unofficially?" Jacob whispers, his lungs tightening in his chest, the whole room shrinking around him.

"*Unofficially* I work for something called the Office for Special Acquisition," she says calmly. "It's part of MUST, the Swedish military's intelligence service."

Now the whole room is spinning around him. Is this woman in his apartment some kind of spy?

"You're in over your fucking head, Matti," she says. "What did your new fella tell you about his job?"

"Don't call me Matti," Jacob says.

Myriam smiles slightly, and Jacob can see what she might be like outside of this sick, terrifying situation. She's almost beautiful, with her soft, clear features and smooth, olive skin. Her symmetrical mouth and determined nose. They don't fit her ruthless manner. Then her smile disappears, and she's coldly menacing again.

"Okay, *Jacob*," she says, with air quotes. "Let me guess: he told you he's a photographer?"

Jacob nods reluctantly. She seems pleased.

"Ask to see some of his photographs," she says. "Ask him where they're published. If you doubt the truth of what I'm about to tell you this evening."

"What do you think he's done?" he says.

"Your boyfriend is a terrorist," she says. "Or worse than that. He doesn't do the deed himself. He's what they call a 'lighter.' That means he doesn't carry out or even plan terror attacks. But he's the one who transports the plan. Do you understand?"

Jacob shakes his head. "Excuse me?" he says, convinced he misheard or that she's joking.

She just looks at him with a blend of impatience and contempt. "Your boyfriend is a terrorist," she says again. "Is that so hard to take in, Matti? Maybe you didn't run into them very often in the housing projects of Eskilstuna?"

"It's impossible," Jacob whispers. *Terrorist*. The word echoes in his mind. "How do you know that?"

"We know because we keep an eye on these things, Matti. We put together puzzles with our colleagues in the other Western intelligence services. Trade information. I'm sure this is overwhelming for you, but you've landed in the middle of something much bigger than you can imagine."

He looks up at her. "What do you mean?" he whispers.

She doesn't answer, just stands up and walks with her hands behind her back over to the balcony door and looks out.

"Often a terrorist attack is planned in the Middle East by ISIS. But the perpetrators of the attack are already in place in Europe; it's too risky to fly people in. There's no shortage of willing brothers who want to kill the infidels already in place. But someone has to bring the plan to them, because often several different cells are involved and most of them don't even know about the others. Nowadays, terrorists don't use email for the most sensitive information—only human couriers will do. We've gotten too good at picking up any chatter online, and they know that."

Jacob rubs his hands over his face. *Lighter. Chatter online*.

"Something's up right now," she continues. "Something big is being planned in Europe; I can't say more than that. And your new boyfriend is mixed up in it."

Jacob thinks of Yassim's eyes, his voice and hands, of his wrists. "You're wrong," he says. "Yassim is gay. ISIS hates gay people."

Myriam shrugs and turns to him. "They're very pragmatic, just like everyone else," she says. "He's westernized and can easily pass back and forth over borders. The fact that he's gay is probably even good cover. Or has been until now, when we got him in our sights."

"Why don't you just take him in then, if you're so sure?"

His shock is starting to pass, and in its place he's started to feel pissed off. Why the hell should he get pulled into this?

"Because he's just a little cog," Myriam says. "Because we want to know more about his network. Where his orders are coming from and where he's taking them. We want to know what the plan is and how it's being carried out. One person is just one person—we want to know it all."

She falls silent and then says slowly: "And you're going to help us with that."

She turns and looks at Jacob.

"The information about Al-Abbas was shared with us by another country. They've known about him for a long time and were waiting for the right moment. When you showed up a few weeks ago they found out who you were and contacted us." She smiles and throws her arms wide as if she were presenting a magic trick. "And voilà, here we are."

Jacob meets her eyes. His shock is now a crushing headache, and he feels unfathomably tired. "I'm not interested," he says.

Myriam nods and settles down at the table again. "I know everything about you. I know exactly how hard it must have been for you to rise out of the environment you grew up in, to get to where you're headed now. A career. A foreign post. After studying you, I know it wasn't easy to go from Matti Johansson to Jacob Seger. But this is where we are now. And you now have a unique opportunity to make a real contribution."

Jacob massages his temples with his fingertips. He doesn't want to make a real contribution. He just wants to live his life, become what he always wanted to be. And be left in peace.

Myriam takes a computer out of the bag she brought with her and puts it on the table in front of him. She also fishes a thumb drive out and puts it on the table. "The next time you meet Yassim, put this in his USB jack. It's preprogrammed with mobile broadband. It'll take care of the installation on its own, and it's lightning fast. Through that program we'll get access to whatever's on his computer. Piece of cake."

Jacob doesn't move, he just stares straight ahead. "No," he says. "I'm not interested." Slowly he lifts his head and looks at Myriam. "Go ahead and tell them I'm from a fucking working-class background if you want. It'll be embarrassing for me. And tough. But I've been through worse."

His rage is growing. Why did he change his name anyway? Because the whole time he was growing up he wanted to escape the stigma of being poor. Escape his mother. Escape where he came from.

Becoming Jacob Seger was a big part of his metamorphosis, and he's been terrified for a long time that someone would find out who he used to be. But now, in this apartment in Beirut, he feels like it doesn't matter. He has finally become who he wanted to be. And he won't let anyone force him to do anything anymore.

Myriam doesn't say a word, just opens the computer and runs a hand over the track pad until a video window opens. When she presses play, Jacob knows there's nothing he can do. Escape is impossible.

He can watch only a few seconds of the video—it's too naked and raw and disgusting. His hands tremble when he slams the screen shut. He falls forward and buries his head in his hands. "What have you done?" he sobs. "Why?"

"What have *we* done?" Myriam's voice is ice-cold. "Isn't that you in this video? Aren't you the one raping that kid? Tarik is his name, by the way. And he's fifteen years old."

His world is collapsing. That's Jacob on the video. Jacob and the guy from the bathhouse. Before he closed the screen, he saw himself hit the boy across the cheek and pull his hair. Call him a whore.

"It's not what it looks like," he whispers. "He asked for it. He wanted me to do it."

"*Really?*" Myriam says. "Is that your defense? That he *wanted* to be raped?"

"If you replay it you'll hear that he wants it." His panic has awoken again in a kind of delayed reaction and sends a fever through him as he realizes the consequences of that video. Homosexual rape in Lebanon, where homosexuality itself is illegal. And even if he managed to explain it in a convincing way . . . His career is over. Long before it even started. Everything he struggled for. Everything he dreamed about. Over.

"I've watched it more times than anyone should ever have to watch such a thing," Myriam says. "And all I see is a Swedish brat brutally raping a poor, underage boy."

"That's not what happened!" he screams. "He came on to me, and I didn't even want to go to the bathhouse! It was Vargander who arranged a car and . . ."

He falls silent when the pieces finally fall into place. Myriam says nothing. She just sits on the other side of the table, staring at him with those dark, icy eyes.

"It was a trap," he whispers. "The car, the bathhouse, the guy who hit on me. Vargander arranged everything."

Myriam shakes her head in frustration. "Vargander is just a useful idiot," she says. "He loaned the car out to you because we asked him to. He doesn't know anything about this, and you shouldn't tell him either."

"This can't be happening," Jacob mumbles. It's not happening, it's not happening, it's not happening. . . .

He doesn't stop his mantra until Myriam takes him by the chin and forces him to look deep into her eyes, her face less than an inch from his. "It's happening, Jacob," she says. "The sooner you accept it, the better things will be for you. None of this will matter if you just do what I ask you to do. It's fucking ridiculous that I would have to go to these lengths to get you to do what's right. You're dating a terrorist, for fuck's sake. Wake up!"

Her eyes are so intense that Jacob has to look away.

She stands up and slams a piece of paper onto the table. "My number. You call me when your boyfriend's back in town. Or we'll let the law take care of this matter."

When Jacob finally looks up again, Myriam is gone. It could have been a dream. If it weren't for the thumb drive and the phone number on the table in front of him.

NOVEMBER 22—STOCKHOLM

KLARA TAKES A step out from behind the car door and heads to one of three heavily armed police officers blocking traffic. Something's happening farther down the street, and the police officer turns around to see it. The SWAT team is making its move: two of them are heading slowly toward the doors of Lindblad and Wiman, one of them has a machine gun in his arms, and the other seems to be taking out handcuffs from a pocket in his belt.

They open the building's door with caution. Klara catches a glimpse of Gabriella's red hair and jacket. Then the police scream something she can't make out. But now she's almost to the barricade, staring beyond it, her pulse pounding at her temples.

"I said: Get back in your car!"

Suddenly there's an officer in a black helmet right in front of her, his eyes black with adrenaline and authority. She didn't hear him, barely even saw him; now she stops midstep.

Gabriella is out on the stairs of the office, and the police are moving toward her. Klara can hear her surprised, incredulous voice, despite the distance.

"What the hell is this?" she shouts.

They're around her now, the police officer with handcuffs and two more. It's so fast, so surreal, Klara can't even take in the details, can barely distinguish them. She hears Gabriella shout again and sees the police change their tactics; they no longer appear as individuals, just fast and violent movements. They scream: "Get down! Don't move!"

They grab hold of Gabriella, two of them at least, forcing her down to her knees and then pushing her entire body onto the sidewalk. Onto her stomach with her face to the street. They sit on top of her, pressing her to the ground.

Klara opens her mouth, takes another step toward the barricade, feels her whole body pulsing, shaking with doubt and adrenaline.

"I'm not gonna tell you again: go back to your car!" The officer in front of her is screaming now. He's in her face, and she stops. She looks at him with her eyes wide, then takes a step back, then another, holding up her hands.

"What . . ." she begins. "What's going on?"

"I'll arrest you if you don't get in your car immediately!" the officer says.

He's young, Klara notes as she stumbles backward. Probably no older than twenty-five. Her hands tremble. What does that matter? She can feel the car door against her back, see one police officer sitting on Gabriella and forcing her arms behind her back to handcuff them. She hears Gabriella shout and scream, hears her upset and confused voice.

"That's my friend!" Klara screams at the police officer forcing her away. "What are you doing to her?"

The officer doesn't say anything, just stares at her with those dark, nervous eyes.

"She's a fucking lawyer!" Klara continues. "You can't just do whatever the fuck you want, do you understand? There are rules and laws and . . ."

The policeman's fingers move to the handcuffs hanging from his belt. It's clear he won't tolerate much more from her, and she reconsiders, holds up her hands again, and backs around the car door.

Behind the barricades, the policemen are lifting Gabriella to her feet and putting her into a waiting black van. It slowly rolls away down Skeppsbron.

Klara sits down in the car, her head pounding, the whole world vibrating around her.

What the hell is going on? She dropped off Gabriella ten minutes ago, and now she's been arrested at her own office?

Behind the barricades, the police have started to relax and take off their helmets; a police car is slowly rolling away in the same direction as the van, toward Slussen. Another van rolls out from one of the side streets and stops in front of the entrance to the law firm. Two people in white overalls jump out. They wait on the street outside the door, chatting with the police.

The policeman with the black eyes at the barricade takes a step to the side, onto one of the wide sidewalks. He says something into his headset and waves his arm to a car at the back of the queue that's now formed on Skeppsbron. The black Volvo pulls away from the line of cars and slowly drives up onto the sidewalk, toward the police officer, then stops. One of the tinted windows rolls down halfway and what looks like a driver's license is stuck out. Klara can't see inside the car from this angle, but she can see the police officer return the card and wave the Volvo toward the waiting police.

The car stops behind the newly arrived van, and a man in his sixties with messy gray hair jumps out, dressed in a cardigan, leather jacket, and sturdy boots. He goes over to one of the uniformed police officers and grabs him before he can disappear into the building. The two men in white overalls follow him into the foyer.

There's no doubt who it is.

Anton Bronzelius.

The Säpo officer she and Gabriella have encountered a few times in recent years. Bronzelius, who this summer threatened them when they were planning to reveal that Säpo knew a Russian company was planning to infiltrate European police forces. Säpo even gave the Russians more or less free rein to foment riots in the suburbs of Stockholm.

Klara and Gabriella ignored Bronzelius's threats and instead went to the media and exposed the entire scandal. Klara was convinced that Bronzelius was bluffing when he said he'd get his revenge.

You don't want me as an enemy, believe me, he said.

But now it's obvious Bronzelius has led a SWAT team to arrest Gabriella. Klara's been naive. Bronzelius meant every word.

SEPTEMBER 7–OCTOBER 16—BEIRUT

Y*OU CALL ME when your boyfriend's back in town*, Myriam had said.

And Yassim was supposed to be back after just a few days. But two weeks go by, and Jacob still hasn't heard anything from him. Jacob passes his time at the embassy letting his mind wander back and forth between the memory of Yassim's smooth body and the terrible meeting he had with Myriam Awad.

Her indifferent expression is burned onto his retinas, and his mind is filled with what she told him about Yassim. That he's a terrorist.

But he knows it can't be true. She doesn't know Yassim; she knows nothing at all about who he is, what he is.

Or does she?

It's as if there are too many variables, too much contradictory information, too many emotions, and it makes it impossible for him to find any calm right now.

In addition, he can't get those few seconds of the video she showed him out of his head. The bare room, the man on his knees in front of him. Fifteen years old. He couldn't have been fifteen years old; it's impossible. Besides, the whole thing was a setup. But it doesn't matter. He's a rapist now.

"Did you eat something that was off? You look very pale, Jacob," Agneta says. She's realized that not everything is as it should be with him, and she suggests he take a few days off to rest up.

But even though he doesn't feel like being there, especially whenever he sees Vargander's fit body striding down the corridor outside of his office, headed to meetings in Beirut and the rest of the Middle East, he knows it would be even worse if he stayed home.

Instead, he catches Frida in the kitchenette and nags her to let him write a background memo on protests still raging into September, though they are slowly starting to ease up a bit now.

"Okay," she says. "But I don't have time to supervise you. You'll have to take care of yourself. Does that work?"

She gives him a pile of books and articles from a few English-language newspapers and a few names of researchers at American University who he can contact, and he finds it helpful to bury himself in Lebanon's endlessly complex system of shifting alliances and sectarian groups. He reads about Shia-Phalangists, Sunni Muslims, and Maronite Christians, and about the civil war and the shaky, ineffective compromise that allows Lebanese state power to be shared between religious groups. He reads about corruption and nepotism, violence and war. He reads about how dissatisfaction had been boiling and that it finally bubbled over when the government couldn't even manage garbage collection anymore. People overlooked the bad electricity, the unreliable postal service, the nonexistent public transport, and the chaotic traffic. But stinking garbage in hot streets was apparently the breaking point for the young people from the various cultural groups, who joined together in protest for the first time. And then not just young people. And not just Western-educated elites, but also the ones who couldn't imagine an alternative before. It all stands in the balance now. The protests are growing. Will it turn out like Egypt? Or Syria? Or will this suffocating compromise win in the end after all? Nobody seems to know. And Jacob doesn't really know why he's writing this memo or for whom or even how long it should be. He suspects it's to keep himself occupied. But it doesn't matter right now, because it gives him a temporary respite from the near constant anxiety pulsing inside him.

It has been more than two weeks, and he's stopped manically checking his phone, when the text finally arrives:

I haven't forgotten you.

The Ghost

That's all, but it's enough to reawaken everything he's tried so hard to forget. Both Yassim and Myriam.

He sits with the phone in his hand, reading the message over and over again. How should he answer? What does one say to a ghost?

He writes and rewrites; the words feel too big, as if they won't fit on the screen. Finally, he sends only a red heart emoji. Nothing else is needed. Yassim knows. Jacob knows he knows.

The feeling settles in, it's there when he wakes up the next morning, all through the day, even when he leaves the office after the sun sets. He buys a bottle of red wine in the small shop beneath his apartment. He needs peace and escape. He has to stop thinking about this dilemma, about who Yassim is. The risk he's taking. If he's not a terrorist, then who is he?

The key to the door doesn't work, and he's just about to put the wine bottle on the mosaic floor and grab hold of it with both hands when he hears a voice from within the shadows of the stairwell.

"When were you planning to tell me he contacted you?"

Jacob turns around and sees Myriam in the shadows leaning against the wall.

"Don't think you can play both sides, Matti," she says. "You're surely not so naive you thought we weren't watching your phone?" She moves toward him with those icy eyes flashing.

"You landed yourself in the middle of this shit, *habibi*," she continues.

"I know your head is spinning now. How can you have your cake and eat it too? Let me answer that question for you: you already ate it. The only things left are the crumbs of your life. Scrape them up and do what you can with them."

He looks at her, shocked, confused. "I haven't met with him," he says.

"You will be crushed if you continue to waver on this," she says. "You have to understand that now."

He nods slowly. All he wants to really do is disappear.

"The second he contacts you, you contact me, do you understand? If you wait any longer, I promise you your life as you've known it will end."

He understands nothing, and she already knows everything. But before he can ask, she's disappeared into the shadows.

Everything is quiet. A month goes by and Jacob starts to think Yassim might never contact him again. He's sat with his phone in hand writing text messages over and over again. But never pressed send on them. He already knows that if he does meet Yassim he can't break the rules, can't force Yassim to be anything more than a ghost.

Maybe this is how it ends? Maybe it's for the best? Or not *maybe*. It *is* for the best. If Yassim never comes back, everything returns to the way it was before. No Myriam. No videos. No threats. No doubts about who Yassim is, no weighing attraction against risk, no gnawing suspicion that Yassim might be who Myriam says he is: A terrorist. A murderer.

Finally, the summer is over and an early-autumn sun shines down at a new angle on the traffic and bullet holes and sidewalk cafés, and the only thing left from the protests are the graffiti, the memories, and the conversations. Compromise won over the chaos. Maybe they've seen too much war here to have the stomach for a revolution? Jacob keeps working on his memo and has started meeting researchers at the university who are so friendly and interesting that sometimes he's almost able to forget Yassim.

One day he's walking over the pedestrian bridge from the Zaha Hadid concrete colossus that houses the Issam Fares Institute for Public Policy and International Affairs at the American University when his phone vibrates in his pocket. He just met a very helpful Palestinian professor and for once is feeling calm.

Around him darkness has fallen, but the campus is still bustling with students on their way to their final lectures of the day and with crickets on the slope that leads down to the soccer field and the sea. It's early October, the air is still warm and soft against Jacob's cheek, but when he steps out onto the gravel that surrounds the Green Oval, a breeze moves between the trees and buildings. The students feel it too; they close an extra button on their shirts and move closer to one another, as if seeking shelter from what's coming. It's as though they all feel it at the same time: it's not autumn yet, but not summer either, and a kind of melancholy falls over the city.

When he takes out his phone he sees the caller has a blocked number, and whatever calm he felt is obliterated. As he answers, every detail surfaces, and he stops and leans against a low wall, listening. The chaos and stress make it almost impossible for him to breathe. But that's not all. There's something else, and it scares him even more. Is it love?

After the conversation, he can barely walk, almost stumbles over to a bench, sinks down with his eyes closed, the phone still warm in his hand. The breeze makes the pine trees behind him sway and the students quicken their steps. But Jacob could stay here forever, in this moment of expectation and fulfillment, hopeless dreams he's been carrying inside him for almost two months. His skin feels electric; he's surprised his clothes don't catch fire.

Slowly he stands up and walks past the stairs by West Hall and the pillars, up toward the main gate. He remembers every syllable Yassim said in that short conversation.

"I missed you. Can we meet in an hour? You remember where I live?"

Does he remember? He remembers everything, every nuance, every insignificant detail.

Yassim hangs up before Jacob even has time to respond. The wind is rising again, and he lets it carry him across the campus, take him all the way to the traffic on Bliss Street.

He's halfway down the slope to the sea when he remembers Myriam Awad, and doubt overtakes him. But everything is so insignificant now that he's heard Yassim's voice. So weightless. So small in comparison.

He hurries. Whoever Yassim might be, whatever happens to Jacob, it doesn't matter. The only thing that matters is that he's about to see Yassim again.

NOVEMBER 22—STOCKHOLM

IT TAKES JUST a few more minutes for the traffic to get going again. The black van and a couple of uniformed police officers standing outside the entrance of Lindblad and Wiman are the only ones still there by the time Klara drives by. It has started snowing, first just a few lonely snowflakes, but it picks up quickly and soon a thin layer is covering the ground.

She squeezes the steering wheel with both hands and turns and looks up at Gabriella's office. If only she could see what was going on inside.

What should she do now? She has to gather her thoughts and she lets the car roll on for a while, until she finds herself passing Gamla Stan again, taking the same street she did before.

It's incomprehensible. Gabriella, arrested on the street. Handcuffed, forced into a SWAT van.

Klara turns off at Munkbroleden and pulls into a disabled parking spot outside the Trattoria Romana restaurant. She leans forward, rests her forehead against the cool plastic of the steering wheel. The Volvo out on Sankt Anna. The same Volvo at the gas station on their way here. Gabriella's being arrested.

She takes a deep breath, leans back in the seat, and closes her eyes for a second before opening the car door and jumps out into the chilly air. Throws a glance at the disabled icon. Fuck it.

She starts to jog at an easy pace back down toward Skeppsbron. The cold, fresh air clears her head. The only logical place to start is by asking the police officers outside the law firm what the hell is going on. And where they took Gabriella. She'll see about the rest. One thing at a time. Rock and salt.

A police car is still parked on the sidewalk outside Skeppsbron 28, and from a distance Klara sees two uniformed police officers on the stairs. She slows her pace, walks slowly down the wide sidewalk. The traffic is flowing as usual now. If she hadn't been here just ten minutes ago, she'd have a hard time believing a SWAT team arrested someone in the middle of the street.

Fifty yards before reaching the office, she stops. What should she say when she gets there? If Säpo wants revenge on Gabriella for what she exposed this summer, isn't Klara also in danger? Sure, Gabriella became a very visible and committed critic of Säpo's methods, and even though Säpo refused to make any comment on the whole affair, there's no doubt it had an impact on the public's trust in the organization. But the idea that they would actually seek revenge? It sounds insane.

She's on the stairs now and goes over to two police officers, a young woman with a blond ponytail and a middle-aged man with a shaved head.

"Excuse me. What's going on here?" Klara says. "I drove by and saw someone being arrested."

Both police officers turn around and look at her. "Nothing," the male officer says. "Just routine."

"But it looked so dramatic," Klara tries. "You blocked off traffic; there was even a SWAT team, right?"

"Like I said. Routine."

Klara turns her attention to the young woman instead, trying to find a way through that cool look. "Where did you take her after you arrested her?" she says. "To the city jail?"

"The person who was arrested is being taken in for questioning.

Not sure exactly where," the woman says. "We have no more information for you regarding this."

"But this is a law firm," Klara says. "It surely can't be routine to arrest a criminal lawyer?"

"How do you know we arrested a lawyer?" the woman says. "Do you have some connection to the person we arrested?"

"No. I was just driving by, like I said. Just curious."

The woman exchanges a look with her partner; obviously Klara has piqued their interest. "Were you the one driving the car that the suspect got out of?" the man asks.

Klara instinctively knows this is no longer a good idea, she shouldn't have asked them anything, and she takes a few steps back on the sidewalk. The female officer takes half a step toward her and holds up her hands to show she's harmless. "We'd like to ask you a couple of questions," she says.

But Klara has already turned around and started running as fast as she can. Blood pounding through her body. They took Gabriella; they can't take her too.

It's just ten yards to a tiny alley that leads farther into Gamla Stan, and she turns so abruptly that she almost loses her balance on the cobblestones, but somehow she manages to stay upright.

Just a few yards behind her, she can hear them shouting for her, knows they've started hunting her.

The narrow alleys of the old part of town are like a maze, and they twist and turn until Klara barely knows what direction she's running in. All she can think is that she has to keep moving forward and not to end up at a dead end.

She runs faster than she ever has before and rounds a corner where a couple of bikes lean against the building. She runs by them, throws them behind her to slow her pursuers, like she's seen people do in the movies. The bikes clatter behind her and someone shouts, "Stop!"

But she doesn't stop. She just keeps running and turning into tiny, deserted streets. Gaffelgränd, Pelikansgränd. Suddenly she's out on the somewhat wider Österlånggatan. Shops, cafés, tourists. She runs a few yards before bounding under a low archway and arriving in an inner courtyard.

A dead end.

Panic seizes her. She twists her head, looking for somewhere to hide, anywhere. A cargo bike is parked just to the left inside the archway, with a fabric cover over the cargo box.

She pulls the cover, frees a corner, throws herself into the box, and zips it up quickly.

Someone is already in the courtyard—she can hear footsteps. They move farther away from her hiding place, then stop and head back in her direction across the snow-covered cobblestones, closer and closer. Until they're just on the other side of the fabric, not more than a foot away, only thin plastic between her and her pursuers. She can hear the male police officer on his radio. She closes her eyes, holds her breath.

OCTOBER 16—BEIRUT

One hour, Yassim said, but it takes only twenty minutes for Jacob to make his way through the traffic on the streets that lead to the Corniche and the sea. His mouth is dry from exhaustion and nervousness, and he stops at a small kiosk to buy himself a Coke Zero. Forty minutes until Yassim said they should meet, but Jacob's already there, can see the glass walls of his building between construction sites and building cranes.

He meanders down the street, stopping at a bank across from his destination. He opens his drink, takes a couple of deep gulps, and leans back, letting his eyes wander up the side of the building. The apartments are dark and empty, no more than items of expenditure on a spreadsheet in an open office somewhere in Dubai, bought by investors with oil money, never intended for habitation.

He counts the floors to number eight, follows the terraces to the corner, until his eyes hit a silhouette standing in the corner. He almost loses his breath.

Yassim.

He knows immediately, would recognize that body anywhere, from any distance. Yassim has a phone pressed to his ear, and he's standing in the corner of his terrace looking down at the Corniche and the sea. Jacob feels guilty, like he's a spy. He has no right to stand here in the shadows like some kind of stalker, but he can't stop looking at him. Then Yassim finally takes the phone from his ear, puts it in his pocket, and goes back into the apartment.

Then Jacob's phone vibrates again. Blocked number.

"Hello?" he answers in English. "I'm already outside."

"I'm sure you are," says Myriam's hard voice. "Do you remember what I said last time, Matti?"

Jacob closes his eyes and waits for her to continue.

"I told you to call the second he contacted you. But you didn't."

"I just . . ." he starts. "I got so stressed."

"There's no room for stress. You know what you're supposed to do. You call me on the number I gave you as soon as you hear from him. Is that clear?"

"Yes," Jacob whispers. "It is."

He cuts the call and looks up toward Yassim's apartment again. The terrace is empty, but he follows the windows until he catches sight of two people in the shadows of Yassim's apartment. One is Yassim, the other is nearly as tall but looks older. They seem to be having a serious discussion. Yassim seems to be listening, as if the one talking is an authority figure.

Jacob checks the time on his phone again. Twenty minutes until he said he'd be there. He heads toward the entrance. Should he just take the elevator and ring the doorbell? But Yassim has a visitor.

He sits down on a low wall, out of sight of the armed guard in front of Yassim's building, but still with a view of the entrance.

It doesn't take more than a few minutes until a man exits. He looks stressed and hands some cash to the guard, says a few words. The guard nods, looks pleased, and the man looks up and down the street as if making sure nobody sees him. Then he crosses the street with a phone pressed to his ear and heads straight toward the wall where Jacob is sitting.

It's the man from Yassim's apartment, Jacob is sure of it despite the distance. He has an innate authority in the way he moves, a commanding presence. He appears to be in his fifties and is wearing an expensive, dark-blue suit. His thick white hair is carefully combed back over his head. When he turns and looks up the street Jacob flinches. It feels as if the man is looking straight into him, as if he knows who Jacob is, what he's waiting for. A shiny black Mercedes with blue diplomatic plates stops. The man lowers his phone, jumps into the back seat, and disappears into the throbbing stream of Beirut traffic.

Jacob stays on the wall, slowly drinking his Coke. He thinks about Myriam and the first time he saw Yassim on the terrace in Mar Mikhael. He thinks of the photograph that was leaning against the wall of Yassim's room, and he thinks of Yassim's naked body. He thinks about the man he just saw, his remarkably white hair, and how nothing is simple here in Beirut, nothing is what it seems.

He puts his drink on the wall next to him and stands up, restless and suddenly afraid. It's as if he's looking at himself and his situation from the outside: a naive Swede falls in love with somebody he doesn't know. He's neither experienced nor gifted enough to handle the situation with Yassim and Myriam.

He pushes his fingers through his hair and turns away from Yassim's building, takes a step up toward Hamra, back to his normal life, away from folly and risk.

Then his phone rings again.

"Where are you?" Yassim asks.

Jacob stops. He gulps, closes his eyes, feels his blood become light, lighter than air, lifting him, his whole body, up above traffic and conflict and confusion, up above Beirut, out above everything that's impossible to understand, up to something that's only emotion, only instinct, lust, and trembling excitement.

"I'm here," Jacob replies. "I'm coming. I'm coming."

Afterward, they lie naked in Yassim's white sheets on his low bed in his empty bedroom. Jacob feels Yassim's arm around his shoulders, feels himself being pulled close and kissed. Lightly this time, not rough and relentless like a few moments ago.

"Have you missed me?" Yassim asks, his lips still against Jacob's.

Jacob presses closer to Yassim, lets his tongue wander inside his mouth again. He's getting hard, even though it's been just minutes since he emptied himself into Yassim's hot, waiting mouth.

"Yes," he moans. "I thought you were never coming back."

Yassim pulls away and holds Jacob's hand in his own. The regretful sadness that Jacob saw last time—which feels like an eternity ago—is back.

"But I did," he says. "It's impossible to stay away from you."

"Is that what you want?" says Jacob. "Do you want to stay away from me?"

He's not just seeking confirmation, not just waiting to hear Yassim say: "No, of course not. I want to be with you forever." He says it because he doesn't know what this is, who Yassim is.

But his friend rolls onto his side and puts on his white briefs and his shirt.

"Come," he says. "Let's eat something."

By the time Jacob pulls on his jeans and T-shirt and goes out into the large living room, Yassim has cleared the computer from the table and arranged takeout boxes of salads and spreads. He opens a bag of pita bread and tears it into pieces.

"I picked up some food on my way," he says, smiling at Jacob. "Thought you might be hungry."

Jacob nods, moved by this thoughtfulness, and keeps his eyes on Yassim's face, though Yassim never looks directly at him. Jacob watches as he fills up bowls, puts the bread in a basket. Jacob wants nothing more than to go and put his arms around him. The doubts he felt seem negligible now. That Yassim is what Myriam says he is seems only laughable. He suddenly wants to tell him everything. About Myriam and the bathhouse and the threats and accusations.

But something holds him back, and he turns his eyes away. A little sliver of suspicion.

"Were you in Aleppo?" he asks quietly. "This whole time?"

Yassim puts tabbouleh on Jacob's plate and drizzles olive oil over a container of grainy baba ghanoush.

"I've been just about everywhere," he says cautiously. "I go where they want me."

Jacob nods. Why would he lie? And yet he can't let go of Myriam's words. All these conflicting agendas.

"I got here a bit early," Jacob begins doubtfully. "So I was waiting outside."

He gestures toward the window where the city's yellow light streams onto the gray concrete floor. "You had a visitor right before I arrived?"

Yassim takes a bite and looks up at him questioningly. He shakes his head slightly. "Excuse me? I don't quite follow you."

"I thought I saw someone in the window," Jacob says, looking away. "But I must have been wrong."

Wasn't that Yassim's apartment he was looking up at? Wasn't that Yassim he saw? He'd been so sure. But now Yassim just smiles at him.

"You must have been spying on the wrong apartment, Jacob," he says, taking another bite of the bread. "I'm not the only one who lives here."

Jacob shrugs. "I guess so. Sorry."

But it does seem to be only Yassim's apartment that's inhabited. And he's absolutely sure he'd recognize Yassim's silhouette anywhere. But he doesn't say anything. Just eats his hummus Beiruti and takes a gulp of water.

"Can you tell me about life at the embassy?" Yassim says. "I want to hear something that's not war or misery."

NOVEMBER 22—STOCKHOLM

EVERY HEARTBEAT FEELS like a tiny explosion, every single beat seems like more than enough to draw their attention, Klara thinks, huddled in the fetal position beneath the cover. She holds her breath as the legs of the police officer brush against the cover that forms her only defense. He's unbearably close to her.

Then she hears more steps enter the courtyard. A breathless voice. "Berg!"

A woman's voice. The other officer.

"Witnesses say she disappeared to the left, up Svartmangatan."

"Svartmangatan?" Berg answers. "I could swear that I saw her sneak in here."

"Well, she's not here," the woman replies impatiently. "We'll lose her if we waste any more time."

"But you can't trust eyewitnesses," he mutters. "I know what I saw." He runs a hand over the cover.

"Forget it," the woman says impatiently. "If she was the one driving, I don't know why they didn't take her in immediately during the crack-down."

The bike shakes as Berg accidentally hits it with his hip. "Oh, damn!" he mutters.

"We don't even know if she's got anything to do with this," the woman continues.

"But you know how it is," Berg says. "You don't run if you've got nothing to hide."

"That's not our problem right now anyway," the woman says.

“They want us back at our post. Anttila is covering for us now, but he goes off duty in three minutes.”

The man sighs. “A terrorism crackdown on a law firm, and we decide to leave loose ends. Fucking amateur hour.”

“Save it for the break room,” the woman sighs, exhausted. “No one else wants to hear it.”

Their boots crunch across the snow that covers the inner courtyard as they slowly head out through the archway onto Österlånggatan again.

Klara stays there until she loses all track of time and starts to shake violently from the cold. Finally, she slowly gets up on her hands and knees. She’s lost all feeling in her fingers and struggles to take off the cover so she can stumble out of the cargo bike.

Terrorism crackdown. The words echo in her head.

Has Gabriella been arrested in a terrorism crackdown?

Klara remembers the phone call last night, the one she heard from outside Gabriella’s door. She was going to meet someone in Brussels. A little skeptical, but still willing to fly to Brussels. After the terrible slaughter at the Bataclan in central Paris just a week ago, it feels like the whole world is on edge.

If this isn’t Bronzelius’s way of making good on his threat, then it must be a huge misunderstanding. What else could it be?

She’s out on Österlånggatan now but soon turns off again onto one of the smaller streets. She can slowly feel the warmth returning to her limbs. Does she dare go back to Gabriella’s car? The police could have it under surveillance. But how would they even know where it was parked?

She continues down toward Kornhamnstorg, where she abandoned it before her failed attempt to talk to the police.

When she arrives at Mälartorget, the car is still standing on the disabled spot at Trattoria Romana. She stops fifty yards from it and scans the street. No police officers. Nothing unusual at all. Just a normal, sleepy winter Sunday in central Stockholm.

Not so much as a parking ticket, she discovers when she reaches the car. Her hands tremble after the events of the past few hours, and she glances at the Italian restaurant she parked at, feels that familiar desire for a glass of wine. Just one. To calm down, to think clearly.

But she steels herself, unlocks the car, and hops in. It would be too ironic if she were to hide for twenty minutes from the police and then end up arrested for drunk driving. She presses the start button and puts it into gear. From the corner of her eye she sees a bag on the passenger side. Gabriella didn't take it with her.

Klara stops, turns off the engine, and puts on the handbrake, then bends down and grabs the bag, a spacious leather tote, decorated with a familiar golden monogram pattern. She takes out a sweater, a vanity case, and the clothes Gabriella wore yesterday, and puts them on the passenger seat. She was only going to Sankt Anna archipelago for a night, so she packed light.

No computer, no phone either—she must have had it on her—only a charger in the bottom of the bag, a hairbrush, an old pack of chewing gum, a pot of expensive face powder, and a half-full bottle of water.

Something jingles, and Klara grabs hold of the keys to Gabriella's apartment. But that's all. Nothing of value. Nothing that gives the slightest clue as to what Gabriella was up to, the reason for her arrest.

Klara notices something curious on the face powder's label, and deeper in the bag she feels the contours of something else. She grabs hold of a thin black notebook she didn't notice at first. She takes it out, puts the rest of Gabriella's things back into the bag, then opens the notebook to the first page.

OCTOBER 20—BEIRUT

JACOB WAKES UP next to Yassim in a dark room, the only room in the apartment that doesn't have translucent walls. In fact it's the opposite of transparent thanks to thick blackout curtains. Despite the darkness, he can still make out Yassim's face, eyes closed, mouth half-open. He's so still right now, unlike earlier in the night when he tossed and turned in his sleep so much that Jacob woke up and turned toward his stern face. Yassim's mouth was moving in his sleep, as if he were speaking or praying, but without words, and Jacob gently pressed close and waited for him to calm down.

This is the fourth night in a row he's slept here. The fourth day he's come here directly from work, and they've collided in desire in the hallway, could barely make it to the bedroom, the fourth night they've eaten among the lights of the city in the living room, while Yassim insisted that they stay away from windows and balconies.

"We're ghosts, darling," he said. "We can't let anyone see us. This is only happening between you and me."

And then he pulled Jacob deeper into the apartment and kissed him until no thoughts were in his head, no other need except for him. Until the memory of his betrayal faded almost completely.

Because this is happening only between them.

Every morning on his way to the embassy, Jacob calls Myriam to report while betrayal burns in his throat and chest. Just to keep her at a distance, he thinks, just to save the crumbs of his life. And every morning he hears her frustration growing.

"Jesus Christ, you can't just spend all your time fucking," she says. "You have to get the password to his computer so you can load the thumb drive. Do you understand? You have one task here. Focus."

Each call forces him to confront and conquer himself, his doubts, his worries. Every conversation with Myriam forces him to harden himself to what she's saying. It can't be true; Yassim can't be who she says he is.

But what if it is true?

What proof does he have that Yassim isn't a terrorist? What proof does Jacob have that Yassim couldn't be both the person Myriam says he is and the person Jacob knows?

The thumb drive burns inside his pocket. He knows he has to do what Myriam says. There's no other way out of this. He has to because she's forcing him to, but also because he can't be sure. Because there are limits even for him, even for his naivety, his desire, and his infatuation. Because no matter how much he doesn't want to face it, no matter how wrong it feels: he doesn't know who Yassim is.

Jacob sits up, careful not to wake Yassim. He pulls on a pair of underwear and tiptoes barefoot over the cool concrete floor into the living room, where he's dazzled by the morning light falling through the huge windows.

He fills the moka pot with coffee from a jar in the cabinet and turns on the gas stove. While waiting for the coffee to brew, he sits down at the table in front of the computer. He bends forward hesitantly. With trembling hands he pushes the screen up and is met by the blurry photo overlaid by a dialogue box asking for a password.

He sighs, closes the computer again and pulls his phone out of his pocket to check his messages and the news, but it gets stuck and drops onto the floor. He throws a foot out reflexively to soften the fall, and somehow manages to kick it under the table.

He swears silently and crawls under the table. He hits his head against something cold and angular, and stifles a moan of pain as he turns his head.

It takes him a moment to understand what he's looking at. Duct-taped to the underside of the table, there is a large, black gun. He gapes at it and runs his fingers along the barrel.

He can hear Yassim moving around. He turns around, grabs hold of the phone and backs out from under the table. When Yassim comes out of the bedroom, he's back on the chair again.

"Did you sleep well?" Yassim says, going over to the stove. "Ah, you already put on the coffee!"

There's a gun under the table; it's the only thing Jacob can think of. He knows it's not unusual for people to be armed here; it's not like Sweden. But still, how could there be a gun under the table?

"Yes," he says. "I slept great."

Yassim pours coffee into two small cups and puts one on the table next to Jacob before bending down and kissing him on the cheek. "What is it, my darling?" he says. "You look like you've seen a ghost."

Jacob clears his throat, tries to collect himself, takes a small sip of the strong, black coffee. What do you say when you've just discovered a gun under the table of someone who you're inexorably drawn to, but who you suspect might be a terrorist?

"Didn't I?" Jacob says. "You're my ghost."

He takes Yassim's hand and kisses it with Myriam's message ringing in his ears: *He's not who he says he is.*

But who does he say he is? Jacob doesn't know anything about Yassim. Just that he's more attracted to him than anyone else he's ever met. And that it's mutual. Yassim can't keep his hands off Jacob either, can't be without him. What exactly have they been up to the last four nights?

Jacob has come here late, straight from work, where he stayed as late as possible despite a near complete lack of tasks, because Yassim supposedly had meetings with clients into the evening. They've eaten and slept with each other. It doesn't sound like much when he puts it like that. But there's so much more to it than just sex and takeout. But what has Yassim actually told him about himself? His family is from Syria but lives in England. He's a photographer.

Myriam's voice is in Jacob's ear. The gun's cold against his fingers. Doubt and worry and confusion.

"Sometimes I think you really are a ghost," Jacob says. "It feels like I don't know anything about you at all."

Yassim laughs and takes a sip of coffee. But Jacob thinks he hears some sadness there, something more than just amusement at how adorable Jacob is. "What do you want to know? I'm an open book."

Jacob shrugs. Then he pushes up the screen of the computer in front of him. "I'd like to see the pictures from your Syria trip. You're so far away sometimes. I want to see what you see."

Yassim takes another sip of coffee and sits down at the short side of the table. "There's nothing to see yet. They're not ready. I have to go through them and edit them. They're for a magazine, and I don't need to turn them in for a few more days."

This is how it's been every time he brought up something about Yassim or his job. There's always an excuse. He hears Myriam's voice in his head again.

"I don't care if they're not ready," he says, frustrated now. "I know we can't be a couple outside these walls. But I'm interested, Yassim. I want to know what you're working on, what you experience, where you come from." He pushes the computer toward him. "Just a couple of pictures, okay? Just something?"

Yassim doesn't move, just stares at Jacob without saying a word. It's a test. Both of them feel it. Jacob didn't mean it like that, but that's how it turned out.

But he doesn't have the strength to hold out, doesn't want a confrontation, doesn't want to upset this fragile magic.

"Forget it," Jacob says, sliding the computer back. "It's not important. If you don't want to tell me, then . . ."

But Yassim leans over, and grabs the computer out of Jacob's hands. "Okay, okay," he says. "If you're so fucking curious then you might as well see. But only a few."

Jacob nods and moves his chair closer to him. For a moment he thought there were no pictures. That there was only this blinding passion, Myriam's version, and guns taped under tables.

Yassim's fingers fly over the keyboard, putting in his password, and Jacob focuses on memorizing what he types. Just numbers: 201207 . . . He doesn't see the last two. Fuck!

The background is a solid blue. There's only one nameless folder on the desktop. Yassim quickly clicks on a Photoshop icon in the dock, and the screen fills with tiny pictures. He also finds a folder on the left side that Jacob didn't see at first and clicks on it. Eight thumbnail images appear on the screen, and he clicks on the first one. It's of a small, dirty boy sitting in the back of a truck with a blank stare. Around him is only rubble and ruins.

"Western Aleppo," Yassim says, and clicks on the next picture.

A house that's lost its whole front wall so that the viewer can see straight into people's apartments, like a dollhouse. Armchairs and sofas and beds. Yassim enlarges the image.

"The table was still set," he says.

He shows a few more pictures of civilians, ordinary people in the midst of indescribable destruction and misery. Then he stands up and shares the rest of the coffee between them.

Jacob takes out his phone and takes a picture of what's on the screen. "Terrible," he says. "I honestly don't understand how you have the strength to face it. Or the bravery to go there."

"What are you doing?" Yassim says, and turns around. "Stop taking fucking pictures of the screen, okay?" His voice is suddenly empty again, like the first time Jacob was here. Like when he said if he had secrets he'd hide them better.

"I'm sorry," Jacob says. "I'm deleting them. I didn't know I couldn't, just wanted something of yours." Was that the reason he was photographing them?

"Delete them," Yassim says. "The resolution is shitty, and they haven't been published yet."

Jacob opens the Photos app on his phone, marks the pictures and holds his thumb above the trash icon. But he doesn't press. "Okay," he says. "I'm sorry."

"You have to ask me first," Yassim says. He's at Jacob's side now, staring into his eyes. He slowly bends forward and grabs Jacob's chin hard. "We're not married, no matter how much you like me. Do you understand?"

Jacob nods. He feels stupid and naive again. At the same time it makes him horny to be reprimanded by Yassim. He's attracted to his violence, for better or worse. And he hasn't deleted the pictures.

"I'm just impressed by you," he says quietly. "I can't understand how you can go back and forth to Aleppo, that you can do the things you're doing."

Yassim lets go of his chin and laughs weakly. He shrugs and drinks his coffee.

"You do what you have to do," he says. "I know the city now. Have my contacts. I just don't have the energy to discuss it when I get home. It's two different worlds. Sometimes it feels like even more than that." Yassim bites his lower lip and looks at him with those eyes Jacob has never been able to hide from. Then he stands up and walks over to the kitchen area.

"There's so much . . ." Yassim begins again with his back to Jacob. "So much I can't share with you. Especially not here in Beirut."

He turns around and looks at Jacob with bottomless eyes. Their expression equal parts tragic and terrifying. Jacob wishes he hadn't pushed him to the limit, wishes they could just have gone on like before, without any of this, without forcing them here. But this is where they have ended up.

"What kind of things?" Jacob asks. "What do you feel like you can't share?"

But the moment has passed, Yassim has covered the abyss in his eyes, forced it away again, and replaced it with a slanted, somewhat annoyed smile. "Don't you have to work today?" he says, moving toward Jacob. "Say no."

Jacob shakes off the feeling he had a few seconds ago. He thinks of the pictures on Yassim's computer. Of the interviews he should transcribe. But nobody cares, of course. It's just an activity to fill the time.

"No," he says. "There's nothing I can't reschedule."

Yassim grabs his cheeks and kisses him on his mouth. "Good!" he says. "You know what people who want to see each other without being seen in Beirut do, don't you?"

Jacob shakes his head. "What?"

"They go to Byblos."

They take off in Yassim's VW Golf, head north over the uneven highway under the autumn sun, and make their way out of Beirut, past the beaches and the casino in Jounieh, in between the mountains and the sea.

"They say it's the oldest city in the world," Jacob says. "That people have been living there for seven thousand years."

Yassim just nods and puts a hand on his thigh. Jacob has been reading about Byblos, and he remembers Agneta saying that Byblos was a place to get away from the watchful eye of one's family, a temporary retreat for a date or affair. Nevertheless, it feels strange to be with Yassim outside the apartment.

It takes only half an hour to get there in such light traffic, and Yassim has a completely Lebanese attitude to parking—he has no problem leaving the car halfway on a sidewalk close to an intersection.

A short walk between historical ruins among a few school field trips and tourists, and they're sitting down at Pepe's, close to the harbor, with the sea in front of them shining like brass in the afternoon sun. Jacob orders a glass of white wine, Yassim only water, and then they go to the refrigerated counter to point out what fish they want grilled up. It's expensive, more expensive than Jacob was expecting, but Yassim just waves off his attempts to object.

"My treat," he says. "Don't worry about it."

They're in the middle of their appetizer—hummus and bread, always hummus and bread—when Yassim's phone rings and he apologetically rises and heads for the stairs that lead to the fishing boats in the marina. Jacob watches him go. Yassim's face is tense again. That abyss in his eyes is back; he can see it even from this distance. Jacob takes a gulp of cold wine when he hears a voice he recognizes all too well right behind him.

"It's lovely here at Pepe's, isn't it?"

Jacob swallows the wine far too fast and starts to cough. When he turns around, Myriam's leaning back comfortably in one of the plastic chairs at the table behind him. Black jeans and sneakers. A pair of large black sunglasses. He fumbles for a napkin, his hands trembling. He didn't call her this morning.

"What are you doing here?" he whispers.

"You didn't tell me you were coming here," she says.

"I don't know what you want me to say," Jacob whispers. "I mean, I'm with him. Please . . . Leave me alone."

She nods calmly and lifts her glasses, looks into his eyes. "It's all about trust," Myriam says, shaking her head. "Such an unreliable friend. You'd better not forget that I see everything. That we see everything. It's not just me, Jacob. Not just Swedish interests involved in this. There are many people waiting for you to do what you're supposed to."

Down at the harbor, Yassim's call seems to be over. He nods and gestures. Myriam stands up and takes a step toward Jacob. "It's time now, you get me?" she says. "You've had days to take care of this. If I didn't know better, I'd almost think you were trying to avoid your job."

"But how the hell should I do it?" Jacob has raised his voice in desperation. "His computer has a fucking password!"

He anxiously turns back to the harbor again and sees Yassim take the phone from his ear and turn back toward the restaurant. He raises his hand in an apologetic greeting. Jacob waves back before turning to Myriam again.

But she's disappeared as if she were never there. There's just a napkin lying on the table next to a half-eaten plate of hummus. He turns it over.

YOU HAVE UNTIL TOMORROW.

That's it.

"Who were you talking to?" Yassim asks, and sits down on the chair opposite him.

Jacob grabs his glass of wine, his thoughts racing, the whole restaurant shaking around him.

"Nobody," he says. "Just some British lady who wanted to know how to get a taxi back to Beirut."

"Maybe she thought you were cute," Yassim says with a smile. "Not so strange."

Jacob forces out a smile. "Maybe," he says. "I'm popular with women."

Yassim leans over and grabs his hand, stares deep into his eyes. "I have to go back to Syria," he says. "Soon."

Jacob is so relieved that there are no more questions about Myriam that he doesn't even understand what Yassim is saying at first. When he does, the air rushes out of him. "Okay," he says stoically. "But you just got back."

Yassim nods calmly. "But after that," he says. "Do you want to go to Europe with me? In a few weeks."

Jacob shakes his head and lets go of Yassim's hand. "What?" he says. "What do you mean?"

"A job," Yassim says. "I just got asked to do a job in Europe in about a month and I don't want to go without you."

The napkin with Myriam's command is turning damp in Jacob's hand. He looks at the face in front of him, remembers the cool of the pistol beneath the table against his fingers.

"Yes," he says. "Yes, I want to go."

NOVEMBER 22—STOCKHOLM

IT'S NOT YET two in the afternoon, but it feels like a gray twilight is settling in around Klara as she sits in the car in front of Trattoria Romana and opens the black notebook to the first page. She holds it close to her eyes, trying to make out Gabriella's messy handwriting.

Cucumber. Yogurt. Garlic. Bread.

A grocery list.

Besides the insight that Gabriella was probably planning on making tzatziki, this doesn't give her much, and Klara keeps flipping forward.

Gabriella seems to use the notebook for all sorts of scribbling. Most notes are lists, a couple about work, a few sentences about a meeting or a conversation with a client.

Klara flips quickly until she gets to the middle of the book, where the notes end abruptly. With a sigh she starts from the beginning, reading each page a bit more carefully. But there's nothing, as far as she can see, that seems to be linked to what happened earlier.

Disappointed, she flips even faster through the notebook until something stops her. She thinks she might have seen something, some note, some numbers. She goes back until she finds the page again. Holds the book at another angle trying to get more light on its pages. There are a few words dashed down. Just a few lines.

Palais de Justice. In front of the elevator, she reads. 11/24, *16:00.* Then a name. *Karl.* Then no more.

November 24? That's in two days, Tuesday.

Klara recalls Gabi's phone call yesterday at the hostel. Tuesday in Brussels, she said. *Terrorism crackdown*, the police said.

She puts the notebook back in Gabriella's bag and takes out her phone. First, she needs to figure out where they've taken Gabriella.

She looks up the number for the city jail, and a young woman answers almost immediately. She can confirm only what Klara vaguely remembers from studying criminal law in Uppsala.

"The police have seventy-two hours to decide if they want to detain your friend," the girl says. "The detention will be decided by one of the Stockholm district courts, and all you can do is wait for a detention order to be established. You'll have to contact the district court this week. That's all the advice I can give you for now."

Klara hangs up and leans back. Seventy-two hours. Three days. Gabriella is unreachable until Wednesday unless they release her early.

It takes less than fifteen minutes to drive to Bastugatan on Södermalm and find a parking spot. She grabs Gabriella's bag and locks the car, then walks shivering through the early-evening light toward her friend's apartment.

The weather has shifted quickly, and heavy clouds are rolling in above the rooftops. She can already see tiny, fleeting raindrops shining in the streetlights. She's not quite sure what she's going to do in the apartment, but it feels like the natural place to start.

She unlocks the front door with one of the keys on Gabriella's key chain and turns the light on in the stairs. The apartment is on the third floor, with French doors that open onto a stunning view of Stockholm. Gabriella bought the small one-bedroom when she became a partner at the firm, and the price made Klara almost faint. But Gabriella just shrugged.

"I don't have anything else to spend my money on right now," Gabriella told her.

There were many who'd dreamed of a life like this when they were studying in Uppsala. Partner in a law firm. A beautiful apartment in central Stockholm. But Gabi and Klara used to consider it a prison. They wanted to be free. Be creative. The law was just a starting point for them, a foundation while they figured out what they were going to do to change the world. Gabriella as a defense attorney and Klara in international relations. But then they ended up with those ten-hour days just like everyone else. Gabriella at a prestigious law firm, Klara as a political adviser in Brussels. Or not Klara anymore. Not after everything that's happened.

On the second floor she stops to listen. It occurs to her that since the police have arrested Gabriella, they might search her apartment, or at least have it under surveillance. Why didn't she think of that until now? She feels so stupid.

She cocks her ear but can't hear anything besides her own breath echoing between the stone walls of the staircase.

As quietly as she can, she starts up the final flight of stairs to the third floor. She can see it's empty when she peers around the corner. She exhales and takes the last steps two at a time.

But when she gets to the landing, she freezes. Slowly she lowers the bag onto the stone floor and approaches Gabriella's door. Police tape crisscrosses the doorframe. The lock seems broken, like someone drilled into the mechanism itself, leaving it completely unusable.

She's not surprised, but it still feels like an assault, almost worse than the arrest itself. That somebody would go into her friend's home, rifle through it, paw at her most private possessions.

She presses down on the handle to test it and feels the door start to open. The only thing keeping it closed is the tape. Couldn't they at least have replaced the lock? Do they really intend to leave Gabriella's door unlocked, protected only by just a few strips of tape?

Not caring about the implications, she carefully pulls away just enough police tape to be able to open the door and go inside.

She's barely set one foot inside when she hears someone behind her on the staircase.

"Stop!" a muffled voice says. "Not another step."

OCTOBER 20–NOVEMBER 13—BEIRUT

Yassim is unusually quiet during their lunch at Byblos and also during their walk down by the small marina. When they're finally back in the car again, he seems to hesitate before turning the key. He turns to Jacob.

"I like being with you so much," he says. "It's like everything else disappears, like we're in a bubble." He falls silent, turns away, staring out through the windshield.

"But?" Jacob says.

Slowly, Yassim turns back to him again. "I thought things would work out in some way, thought I'd be able to stay here longer. But the call I just got . . . It's impossible. I have to leave sooner than I thought."

"But what about Europe?" Jacob asks quietly. "Surely you're coming back?"

Yassim smiles and leans over to him, kisses him gently on the cheek. "I'll always come back," he says. "And we'll go to Europe together, later. I promise."

For Jacob, October still feels summery, but in comparison to the suffocating heat they had before, it feels cool. He no longer feels like he's going to die every time he's forced out into the sun.

Two weeks without Yassim go by, and Jacob can hardly remember what he looks like. But he remembers Yassim's smell, his voice—

especially the strict one, the one that makes Jacob blush and do whatever Yassim wants. Almost anything he wants.

Myriam is furious, of course, when he calls and informs her that Yassim has disappeared again and that he still hasn't managed to install the flash drive. Her voice terrifies him, and it scares him even more when he realizes he's not going to tell her about their planned European trip. She expects him to tell her stuff like that, to tell her everything. So why doesn't he?

To protect Yassim, to gain some time. Because he doesn't feel sure about her, and because he's slowly starting to realize that Myriam needs him. He does have a few cards to play in the middle of all this hopelessness. If she exposes him, she'll also lose him, so she'll just have to understand that this will take some time. That insight reduces the intensity of her threat.

"This isn't a fucking game, Jacob," she says. "You're hanging out with a terrorist. When will you get that through your thick skull?"

When she says that, it sounds so convincing, so obvious. Why else would she do all this? The weight of that insight threatens to drown him completely. He's somehow become an accessory, living close to a terrorist, sleeping with a terrorist, in love with a terrorist. There is no context that can justify it—not if he knows.

At the same time he's seen the photographs Yassim took in Syria, heard him talk about them. He's looked more deeply into Yassim's eyes than into anyone else's; has felt his hands on him, his skin against his own, and what Jacob saw and felt is not consistent with what Myriam tells him. For one moment, he believes it can't possibly be true; it's impossible that Yassim is lying, and the assurance of that calms him, decreases the pressure around his chest.

Then he remembers the gun beneath the table and he's back at square one again.

At the embassy, Jacob looks at the pictures Yassim took again. They're blurry, naturally, since they're photos of a computer screen snapped in haste. But they're all he has, so he opens the browser on his computer and starts to search for images from Aleppo. He limits the search to the last few weeks. They may have been published by now.

It doesn't take long to find the pictures. First, the one of the boy on the truck. Then one of the razed house where the table is still set. They're not iconic images of Aleppo, not images that define the conflict for the general public, but they've appeared in articles in a French magazine and also been reprinted on a few blogs and web pages. How did they manage to spread so fast? Yassim said they weren't ready for publication just a couple of weeks ago.

He clicks on the image and is directed to an article in a French magazine. It's behind a paywall, but the photo can be glimpsed behind it. He goes back again and clicks on one of the blogs. The blog is also in French, but the photo of the little boy on the truck appears in full. Jacob clicks on it. It's a good picture, of that there's no doubt. Yassim has talent. He closes the picture and scrolls through the article even though he's not very good in French.

But something gnaws at him, something's not right. Slowly he scrolls up to the top of the post.

The date. The blog post is almost a year old.

He goes back to the French magazine. Despite the paywall, it's the same there. November 2014. The picture wasn't taken a month ago. It was taken at least a year ago.

With trembling fingers he returns to the blog and sees that the image is attributed to a large photo agency. And as he scrolls farther down the blog, he sees the image of the house with no front wall, and several other pictures he remembers vaguely.

Why did Yassim lie about taking the pictures just a few weeks ago if he actually took them a year ago?

Jacob suddenly feels very cold. Something's not right, and despite all his defenses, he has to give it up now, admit to himself that what Myriam says is probably true. There's no longer any way to hide from it.

Another week goes by before Myriam hunts him down again, even though she calls every other day to make sure he hasn't forgotten about her. He's close to telling her about the pictures, about Yassim's lies, but he lets it be. It's as if Yassim's betrayal will only become real if he says it out loud, and he's not sure he can handle that right now.

He sees Myriam everywhere, feels his paranoia growing, thinks he sees cars waiting outside his front door. Thinks he sees men on the street who quickly avert their eyes when he looks at them. He no longer knows what's real and what's just in his head. His only wish is that this had never happened, that he never would have met Yassim, never gone to that party on the roof. That Myriam was just a fantasy, just air, nothing more.

At the embassy, Frida asks absentmindedly and without much interest how it's going with his memo, and he answers evasively that he's waiting to meet someone for an interview.

"I can send you what I have," he says.

"Finish writing it first," she says. "I'll read it when everything's done. There's no hurry."

Then she's gone, and Jacob is left alone with the certainty that the work he's doing will never be finished.

He spends his days at his desk thinking it surely can't be possible to miss someone he barely knows this much. He hardly leaves his phone for a moment for fear of missing a call. He needs to let go. Especially now that everything indicates that Yassim is nothing but trouble and destruction. Now when a happy ending seems impossible.

He should sleep. He should eat. But he tosses and turns, thoughts racing, until he wakes up one morning and autumn is outside his window: gray rain, gray seas, and only sixty degrees. Now is the moment to finally shake this all off and say, *Enough*.

And he almost gets there, almost convinces himself he can put his foot down. Then one day he goes to the American University campus to have a cup of coffee with a young professor he's become friendly with. He turns toward the sea and takes a deep breath. Looks at the trees and grass and water. For the first time in a long time, he feels something close to peace. In the distance he can almost sense something like freedom.

And at that very moment a soft hand closes around his elbow, and he turns and sees who it is, and freedom vanishes before his eyes, and he forgets all of his longing, his yearning, and his worries. In the blink of an eye, it all becomes meaningless. And he's only here, in the present.

"Come," Yassim whispers in his ear. "I need you in my arms."

NOVEMBER 22—STOCKHOLM

SHE FREEZES IN the doorway—obviously entering a cordoned-off apartment was a bad idea, she should have known—and slowly she turns around.

But behind her is no police officer, as she'd expected, but a stately woman in her sixties, wearing a flowing piece of colorful fabric, a kaftan or some kind of dress. She's tall, a bit heavy. Her hair is short and blond, her eyes liberally painted, her cheekbones rouged. She has a kitchen knife in her hand.

Klara holds up her hands. The woman doesn't seem threatening, more eccentric, but a knife is a knife.

"Who are you?" the woman asks.

Klara takes a step back into the apartment to get out of the radius of the knife, and swallows, trying to sound as calm as possible. "I'm a friend of Gabriella, the woman who lives here," she says. "I was supposed to stay with her tonight, but . . ."

She lets the sentence ebb away, holding up Gabriella's key chain as if to prove something. The woman's face changes, her aggression or fear gives way to something softer and more open. She lowers the knife slightly, angling it more toward the floor.

"What's your name?" she asks.

"Klara. Klara Walldéen is my name."

Now, the last of her suspicion and indignation drains away and is replaced by a crooked and somewhat confused smile. "Oh, forgive me. I didn't mean to scare you. I"—she looks down at the knife in her hand—"I don't usually run around with knives."

Klara relaxes and takes a deep breath. The woman takes a step closer to her and into the doorway, glancing back at the staircase. She pulls the door shut behind her again.

"I know who you are, Klara," she whispers. "Gabi has told me about you." She lowers her voice further. "Did something happen to her? Gabriella has seemed to have a lot on her plate lately."

"What do you mean?" Klara says.

"It doesn't feel safe here," the woman says, shaking her head. "Not safe at all. Come with me. We have a lot to talk about, I think."

Klara follows the woman to her apartment, which is twice as big as Gabriella's and just one floor up. She's led through a hall with a green marble floor into a large living room that's dominated by an enormous emerald sofa and a black baby grand piano. Through the windows she can see Gamla Stan and Kungsholmen spread out behind Riddarfjärden in the twilight. The snow is falling more heavily outside, and the snowflakes swirl in front of the French windows. The woman lights a couple of low table lamps before disappearing farther inside the apartment. In that warm light, Klara can see the walls are covered with framed posters from the Royal Swedish Opera.

Then the woman appears in the doorway with two wineglasses and a bottle of white wine so cold it has condensation on it. Klara has to hide the tiny wave of relief and euphoria that hits her at the sight of it. She's hardly touched a drop all through the autumn. But now she really wants a glass. No, not *wants*—she *needs* a glass.

"My name's Maria, by the way," the woman says. "Maria Wittman. I'd say it's about time I introduce myself."

"Are you an opera singer, ma'am?" Klara asks, gesturing toward the framed posters.

Why did she say *ma'am*? But there's something about this woman that demands a certain level of respect, so it just popped out.

Maria laughs and invites Klara to sit down on the green couch. "You're not the first to make that assumption," she says. "I suppose I fit the part. No, my husband played the French horn in the orchestra at the royal opera house and liked collecting souvenirs. As for me, I'm afraid I'm quite talentless. I was forced to make do with a job in finance."

While Klara looks around at the large, tastefully decorated apartment, Maria pours wine into the two glasses.

"You can't be completely talentless," Klara says. "I mean, it's quite an outstanding apartment."

Maria shrugs and sits down on the sofa beside her. She takes a little sip of the wine and smiles at her guest. "There are various kinds of talents," she says. "What are yours?"

Klara picks up the glass and has to resist the temptation to down it in one gulp. After all, she's barely drunk anything for almost six months. But she manages to take a cautious sip instead, feels the warmth and the calm spreading through her body.

"Always ending up in some kind of trouble," she says. "I'd say that's my most outstanding talent."

"It's a talent you certainly shouldn't take too lightly," Maria says. "Gabriella seems to share it with you."

Klara takes another sip, a bit bigger now. The wine is dry and earthy, full of life. It tastes like someone's glory days.

"She was arrested this afternoon," Klara says. "Outside of her office on Skeppsbron, in some sort of terror crackdown. I sat in the car and could only watch while a SWAT team dragged her into a van."

To Klara's surprise Maria seems neither shocked nor upset. She just listens quietly, spinning the glass between her fingertips. A single large emerald glitters on one of her ring fingers.

"She made a lot of people angry this autumn," Maria says. "A very brave young woman, our Gabi, you have to admit that."

Our Gabi, Klara thinks. There aren't many besides Klara who call her Gabi. Why has Gabriella never told her about this Maria if they were so close?

"I guess you were also mixed up in what happened last summer?" Maria continues.

Klara nods. "You can definitely say that. I"—she takes another gulp of wine—"I wasn't doing very well."

Maria just looks at her calmly. "A person can't always be doing well," she says. "Sometimes you need your friends."

Klara can feel tears fill her eyes. There's something so warm and genuinely empathetic about Maria, something that makes her think Maria knows what she's talking about.

"Gabi needs me now," Klara says quietly. "She's done so much for me. And now she needs me."

Maria places her wineglass on top of an enormous book about Dutch architecture that lies, along with several other books about design, on the low coffee table. She stands up and walks over to the baby grand. She lifts the lid carefully and sticks her hand inside.

"Dramatic," she says. "I know. But I have a gift for drama, as you may have noticed."

Slowly she pulls out her hand with a small envelope dangling between her fingers.

"Since Alf passed, nobody plays the piano. A good place to hide mysterious messages, don't you think?"

Maria puts the envelope on the coffee table. Klara can feel her skin pucker with goose bumps as she takes a deep breath. The envelope is addressed to her.

NOVEMBER 13–14—BEIRUT

YASSIM'S HAND ON Jacob's elbow almost doesn't feel real, and Jacob keeps glancing over at him to make sure as they walk down the steps and along the footpaths that lead through the campus down to the sea.

"Where are we going?" Jacob says.

He realizes it's the first thing he's said. Yassim smiles and turns to him, looks into his eyes.

"A tunnel down to the beach," he says. "Not so many people there."

Jacob nods. The American University's own enclosed beach club, on the other side of the Corniche, the ultimate, exaggerated triumph of the privileged. Nothing summarizes Beirut better than the bullet holes in the locker rooms at the private, insanely expensive beach clubs. Hedonism, privilege, and violence locked in an eternal dance along the privatized coastal strip.

He feels relieved that they're headed in that direction, away from the main gate and Hamra, where there's a risk that Myriam or one of her companions might be waiting with their threats.

"You were gone for so long," Jacob says.

They're in the tunnel now, and the calm of the campus is replaced by the roar of the cars on the Corniche. Yassim tries to smile, but it's a half-hearted attempt; there's no joy there, just the other look, hard and bottomless, which sometimes appears in his eyes.

"I'm a ghost," he says. "You know that."

"But you could have said something so I had some idea when you were coming back."

Jacob's voice echoes in the tunnel, and Yassim doesn't answer, just pushes them farther through the tunnel and then out into the drizzle coming down on the concrete and cliffs.

The locker rooms are empty; the showers are turned off. It's abandoned down here by the water in the autumn. A breeze cools them, and the sea is gray-green and choppy in the twilight. Yassim grabs his shoulders and turns him around, stares deeply into his eyes.

"This is how it is," he says. "You knew that from the beginning."

"I knew I couldn't be your boyfriend," Jacob says. "Not that you'd disappear without telling me whether you were coming back."

He realizes he's almost shouting; he must be more upset than he thought. Maybe he's being dramatic, but it's bubbled up inside him now. His worry that Yassim might have left him mingles with a vague, now dashed, and completely contradictory hope that he would never come back. Jacob doesn't want to feel this happiness pulsing inside him now, doesn't want to be helpless in Yassim's hands anymore. The photographs from Syria, the gun, the lies. But it doesn't matter, with Yassim he has no defenses.

"I know," he says. "But I can't do anything about that. When someone needs my camera, I have to go. It's not easy to call from the front, darling."

Jacob looks at him. "Aleppo again?" he asks and receives a calm nod in reply.

"Where else?"

Jacob wants to grab Yassim's shoulders and shake him. *Were you really there?* he wants to scream at the top of his lungs. Or: *Who are you?* But he says nothing, just nods back calmly.

"But forget it," Yassim says. "I'm going to Europe soon. I have to get away. And you are coming with me."

Jacob's face is becoming wet in the drizzle, and he turns into the strengthening wind. It won't be hard to get away; no one will miss him at the embassy. Right now, here at the pier by the sea, he doesn't care about any of it.

"Yes," he says. "I will come with you."

It's dark by the time they leave the beach club; the headlights of taxis and SUVs glitter in the rain. Jacob's shirt is damp, and he's freezing for the first time since he got to Beirut, but Yassim doesn't take them directly to the apartment. Instead, he takes them down side streets and winds through packed parking lots. Yassim looks at him, and they chat, but Jacob feels like there's something off, as if his friend is more cautious than usual.

"This way," he says, leading Jacob past a sleepy security guard, down a ramp into a parking garage. "A shortcut."

It feels as if they walk more than half a mile underground, but finally they arrive at an elevator that takes them right up to Yassim's place.

"That's not what I would call a shortcut," Jacob says as they step into the empty apartment.

But Yassim doesn't answer; he just pushes him against the wall and kisses him so hard that Jacob thinks the wall might tumble down, the whole house might fall over, that the world will start collapsing into tiny pieces all around them.

Eight numbers keep Jacob awake in the middle of the night in Yassim's low bed. He's barely slept, mostly he's just lain there waiting for his friend's breathing to turn deep and even. The last two digits. He saw them tonight over Yassim's shoulder, even though he was trying to protect the keyboard with his body. If Jacob hadn't caught the first numbers several weeks ago, he never would have gotten all of it.

20120714.

Now Yassim is sleeping quietly on his back among the white sheets. Not troubled like last time, but calm. For now.

Jacob sits up carefully, still naked. His heart is pounding in his chest. He finds his underwear and tank top and pulls them on before putting his feet onto the cool concrete floor.

Is he really going to do this? He tiptoes cautiously across the floor. He needs a drink, still can't sleep. Nothing strange about going to the living room in the middle of the night.

20120714.

The computer stands on the table in the middle of the room, bathed in the artificial light that shines in through the high windows. He walks to the kitchen area and takes a glass from the shelf, fills it with ice-cold water, then takes only one sip before pouring it into the sink as quietly as he can. Slowly he walks over to the computer.

He sits down on the chair. The only sounds are the gentle buzz of the air conditioner and a few cars accelerating and honking on the street below. It's just past two o'clock.

It's as if he has no control over himself. His hands follow their own logic, pushing down on the spacebar and waking up the computer. The dialogue box asks for a password. He looks down at the softly lit keyboard and pushes the eight numbers. A moment of hesitation before pressing enter. A moment of anticipation before the computer logs him in.

His first instinct is to shut the computer immediately. To ignore it all; what will be, will be. But it's not Myriam and her threats that stop him. It's himself. It's that little nudge that won't leave him alone, no matter how hard he tries to convince himself that Myriam couldn't possibly be right about Yassim. That nagging uncertainty makes him lean over the computer and see that the desktop now has two folders.

One is called "Pictures." The other is called "20120714." Just like the password. He clicks the latter without hesitation.

The folder contains dozens of videos and PDFs. He clicks on the first, which is a scanned article from Beirut's English-language newspaper, the *Daily Star.* The headline reads:

SUNNI MEDIATOR KILLED IN BOMBING

He skims the article, dated July 15, 2012. It's about a Sheikh Yussuf, described as a possible unifying force for the Syrian rebels. According to the article, he and many of his family members died in a gas explosion at a wedding the day before.

Jacob clicks one of the video files. He recognizes the setting from somewhere, but can't quite place where he's seen it before. It's an inner courtyard, decorated for a wedding. People in fancy clothes are greeting an older man, a sort of patriarch. Sheikh Yussuf himself? Jacob freezes the video and leans forward. Next to Yussuf stands a person Jacob recognizes.

Yassim.

He's younger, of course. He has longer hair, traditional clothes. But that's Yassim, no doubt about it. And he doesn't seem to be there as a photographer. He looks like he's part of the celebration. Part of the wedding party.

Part of the family.

Then Jacob hears a voice in the room behind him, and it's as if the whole world stops.

"You won't find what you're looking for on that computer."

Jacob raises his eyes.

Yassim is standing in the corridor that leads to the bedroom. Behind him is the big photograph leaning against the wall, and Jacob remembers where he saw that inner courtyard. It's the same place. The video from before the explosion. The photo from afterward. Yassim didn't photograph the party; he was one of the guests.

Yassim has lied to him, he isn't who he claims to be at all, and Jacob doesn't know how it happens but suddenly he's pushing his hand up under the table, grabbing on to the black gun and pulling it free. The tape comes loose, and he almost falls backward under the table but regains his balance.

Yassim is coming toward him. His eyes are black now. Completely black, only anger and destruction inside. Everything he keeps hidden.

"Who are you?" Jacob hisses, scrambling backward over the concrete floor.

Without even knowing how, he suddenly raises the gun with both hands; his finger is on the trigger, his fear is almost blinding.

Yassim stops in the middle of the floor, holds up his hands.

"Who are you?" Jacob screams as loudly as he can. "Who the fuck are you?"

NOVEMBER 22—STOCKHOLM

KLARA TAKES AN even bigger gulp of wine and lifts the envelope.

"What is this?" she asks. "Why do you have an envelope that's addressed to me?"

Maria sits down next to her on the sofa again. "Gabriella gave it to me last week. She asked me to keep it hidden and only mail it if something happened to her."

Klara looks up and meets Maria's eyes. "So she thought something might happen to her?" she asks.

"Recently she believed she was being followed. When she told me that, I didn't know what to think. We didn't know each other that well before, mostly just short chats in the stairwell. I recognized her, of course, from the news. She's hard to miss with all that fabulous red hair."

Klara nods.

"But to believe you're being followed," Maria continues. "Alf was . . ." She pauses, takes a sip of wine to gather her strength. "My husband was manic depressive. Sometimes his manias led to paranoia. When Gabi talked about being followed, I'll admit I was mostly worried about her mental health."

"I understand," Klara says. "It must have been terribly hard. With your husband, I mean."

Maria nods slowly, staring out the window at the snow and the water. Then she shakes it off and turns to Klara again. "But Gabriella wasn't paranoid. I quickly understood that, though she didn't want to tell me what she was involved with."

"But why did she tell only you she felt she was being followed?" Klara asks.

Why didn't Gabriella tell *her* anything this autumn? After everything they'd been through in the past few years? Didn't Gabi trust her anymore? She can't make sense of it.

Klara takes another gulp of wine and leans back on the couch with the still-unopened envelope on her knee.

"She probably wasn't sure," Maria says. "And maybe she didn't want to worry you. But she came up here and rang my door about a week ago. She pulled me to the kitchen window, which looks out on to the street, and pointed to one of the stairwells on the other side. A man stood there, talking on a phone. She asked me to check again the next night. And I did, and sure enough there he was again. And the night after that.

"Before she left that night, she gave me this envelope and asked me to send it to you if anything happened. I thought it all seemed a bit dramatic. But, well, I'm drawn to such things too. We have too little excitement in our lives, Klara. Well, not you and Gabriella. But I do."

Maria leans back in the sofa, staring thoughtfully down at her glass. "But I didn't think it would turn out like this. As I said, at first I thought she was a bit paranoid, that what she'd been through with Säpo had left its mark. But now I understand that she knew what was going on. Or what was about to happen."

"Gabi is many things," Klara says. "But paranoid is not one of them."

"You're only paranoid if it never happens," Maria says.

"Did she tell you anything else?" Klara says. "Anything about why she was being followed, or why someone would follow her?"

"No, she just gave me the envelope. I'm not one to snoop."

Klara takes a drink and turns the envelope, hoping that the contents will in some way explain what happened to Gabriella this afternoon.

"I told her she should go to the police if she was worried," Maria says. "But she didn't want to."

Klara nods, and without putting it off anymore she slides her finger under the flap and rips open the envelope. She puts in two fingers and grabs on to a folded piece of paper and pulls it out.

Maria rises from the sofa with the wineglass in her hand and walks over to the window. She stands with her back to Klara, looking out over the darkness and the rain and the lights from Kungsholmen on the other side of the water.

Eagerly, Klara unfolds the paper.

There's a short handwritten message.

Klara,

I guess if you're reading this something has happened to me. You know I hate melodrama, but I guess you'll never see this if I'm wrong. And after everything we've seen and gone through, it feels like we can only really trust each other.

Anyway: I'm pretty sure someone is following me. Several different men, who don't seem like cops—maybe Eastern Europeans. I've seen them outside my door and outside work. I don't know what they want, but I noticed them after I received a few phone calls on November 15 from a Swedish guy calling himself Karl. He's quite young and seems totally in over his head. He claims he's come into possession of some important information, and he believes he's being followed. It's possible that he has some Snowden complex, but the more we talk, the more I trust him. And he's very scared.

I set up a meeting with him in Brussels on November 24 at 4:00 p.m. at the glass elevator outside the Palais de Justice, but he's incredibly nervous, so I'm not quite sure how it will turn out.

As of now, this is all I know. But if something happens to me, it's good to start there. Maybe you could meet Karl if I don't manage it?

But I hope you never have to read this.

Love, Gabi

PS. I'm leaving you one of my credit cards. Not sure how much cash you have, and I don't want you to have to abandon your best friend for financial reasons.

NOVEMBER 14—BEIRUT

THE GUN IS heavy—Jacob can barely hold it, his hands are trembling, and it's a surprise he's even holding it at all.

Yassim stands in the middle of the floor. He has his hands at his sides now, and slowly he raises an arm toward him. He says something, but Jacob doesn't hear him, there's a roar in his ears.

"Who are you?" he screams again.

Then Yassim is in front of him. The gun is ripped out of his hands and thrown onto the floor. Through the roar in his ears he can just make out the sound of it clattering onto the hard floor. Yassim is on top of him now, and Jacob holds up his hands to defend himself, but Yassim is too strong, and Jacob falls back onto the floor, as if in slow motion, with his friend above him.

Yassim's thin body feels heavy as it pins Jacob onto the cold floor; his hands are strong, relentless around his wrists. That is how he holds them when they fuck. But their sex is a game, or that's how Jacob thought of it. Yassim's domination, his own submission, each to stimulate the other. He's thought of his submission as a choice, as roles they assumed and could break out of at any time. But this is serious, and it scares him for real.

Yassim turns him so that Jacob is lying with his stomach on the floor. And Jacob can feel Yassim's weight, his breath, his hips, his cock. It's humiliating. Not just getting caught snooping on the computer, but also that he is unable to defend himself physically. But the most humiliating thing of all is how horny this makes him. That he can't resist this or defend himself against Yassim on any level. This is neither fucking nor a game. This is being steamrolled.

"Fuck me," Jacob hisses against the cold floor. "Fuck me as hard as you fucking can."

Yassim tears off his underwear, and then he's moving inside him. The world explodes in pain and a raw, terrible pleasure, and for a moment Jacob thinks he's going to die, that the world is ending.

Afterward, Yassim pulls out and collapses with his back against one of the table legs. Jacob is still lying with his face against the floor, eyes closed. It's too much. This is just way too much.

"It was a Saturday," Yassim begins quietly. "My sister's wedding was on a Saturday."

Jacob lies completely still.

"My whole family was there, of course. Everyone. My father was an important man. Influential. Powerful in his way. But most of all, he was very good at keeping everyone happy, understanding what people needed the most. That's why they listened to him. That's why the Americans listened to him too. Everyone was there for the wedding. Secular rebels, al-Nusra representatives, al-Qaeda. Even Abu Bakr was on his way, but he was late. He wasn't the caliph yet—just Ibrahim, an ambitious nobody."

Yassim falls silent. It's hard for him to tell this story, but Jacob knows that all he can do is lie still, act like he's not even here.

"It was a mistake, they said afterward. The drone attack. An order that went awry. A drone pilot in fucking Virginia, or wherever they are, received the wrong coordinates. Who the hell knows? But instead of a wedding there were twelve funerals. My father. My mother. My cousins. My sister . . ."

Yassim pauses.

"On her wedding day. She didn't even have time to get married before they killed her."

Jacob's mouth is dry; he has the floor against his lips as he moves them. "But why did you lie?" he whispers. "Why didn't you tell me the truth from the beginning?"

He turns over so he can look at Yassim, leaning against the leg of the table with his eyes closed. "I couldn't put that on you," Yassim says. "I don't know you. Or . . . didn't know you."

Jacob rolls over on his side, leaning on an elbow. "I'm so sorry. If I'd known . . ."

Yassim waves his hand, embarrassed, self-deprecating. "Stop. How could you have known?"

They stay on the concrete floor for a while without speaking.

"Where do you go when you disappear?" Jacob finally asks.

Yassim doesn't answer, but he opens his eyes and looks at him. He puts a finger to his lips to hush him. Then he stands up and stretches out a hand.

"Come," he says. "Let's take a walk."

The city is quiet as they exit the parking garage in the middle of the night. A bass line is thumping from some roof terrace where the party hasn't stopped despite the drizzle. A few cars roll by over the wet, bumpy asphalt. They don't speak, and Yassim leads him across a makeshift parking lot, into a late-night café that consists of just a few tarps over the ruins of a building that no one has bothered to tear down or rebuild. They buy Sprites and a bag of chips and sit beneath the tarp on dirty plastic chairs, sheltered from the rain. Yassim leans over toward Jacob and looks him in his eyes. The threat is gone now—there's only warmth and sincerity.

"Has anybody contacted you?" he asks calmly. "Has anyone asked you to keep an eye on me?"

Jacob drinks the soda and looks into the parking lot and the rain through the dirty, transparent plastic. It's cold and he pulls Yassim's cardigan tighter around him.

"I thought we'd been careful," Yassim says. "I'm sorry. I didn't mean to drag you into this. I swear."

"They say you're a terrorist," Jacob says. "That you're planning an attack."

His mouth is very dry. Saying it out loud makes it feel real. But Yassim just nods calmly.

"Do you believe them?" he asks.

Jacob turns and looks straight into his eyes for the first time since they left the apartment.

"I don't know," he says. "You disappear to Syria. You lie. You tell me you're a photographer and show me pictures I don't think you've taken. You have a gun under the table in an apartment that's far too big and expensive."

He looks out into the rain again.

"What the hell am I supposed to think?"

Yassim just looks at him steadily. "Who's contacted you? The Americans?"

Jacob looks back at him, ignoring the question. "Are you a terrorist?" he asks. "Are you, Yassim?"

NOVEMBER 22—STOCKHOLM

KLARA SHAKES THE envelope, and a gold American Express card falls out onto Maria's coffee table. She can't help but smile. Gabi thought of everything.

Maria is still standing with her back to Klara, staring out the window, and Klara downs the last of the wine in her glass before standing up. "Thank you so much. You've been incredibly helpful."

Maria turns around and smiles at her. "Where are you off to now?"

"Thought I'd go get myself a hotel room. I can't exactly stay in Gabi's taped-off apartment."

"That's out of the question," Maria says in a voice that leaves no room for any protest. "I live alone and have two guest rooms. You'll stay here, end of discussion."

Then she goes and grabs sheets and towels out of a linen closet. Puts the small stack in Klara's arms and points to the end of the corridor where the guest rooms are located. As she does it she looks deep into Klara's eyes.

"How are you doing?" she says. "Have you sought out any help? Gabi's told me how rough you've had it."

Maria's warm eyes and pressed, fragrant sheets. Her thoughtfulness and steadiness. Klara feels her eyes fill with tears. She's been feeling better this autumn, but she still wakes up in the night. Can't remember when it hasn't been a struggle to get out of bed in the morning.

"I don't know," she says, surprised by how thin and small her voice sounds. "I'm not drinking as much as I did anymore."

Why did she say that? She knows she drank too much last year, until what happened in the summer. She knows she craves wine too much right now. But she never talked to anyone about it, hardly even admitted it to herself.

"That's good," Maria says quietly. "But maybe you need some real help? We can't handle everything on our own, no matter how strong we think we are."

Klara shrugs and turns around. She doesn't have the energy to think about it more now. Doesn't have room to care about herself. Gabriella is the one who needs help now. Besides, she is feeling better.

"Should I take the room on the right?" she asks as she heads toward the guest rooms.

Maria finds some fish fillets in the freezer and throws together a béchamel sauce, which she pours over the fish and some spinach and puts it all in the oven and then, much to Klara's hidden delight, opens another bottle of wine.

Klara knows the wine calms her and makes the struggle a little easier, keeps her from falling back into that dark hole again. For a moment, she succeeds in pushing away her thoughts about Grandpa and what happened to Gabriella, and instead can focus on just sitting in this beautiful kitchen with Maria, while the smell of fish in the oven starts to fill the air.

"Sogliole alla Casanova," Maria says finally, as she serves up fish to Klara. "A good recipe for when you receive an unexpected guest."

It's not until they've cleared the table, Maria has headed for her bed, and Klara is smoking a cigarette on the balcony outside the guest room that those thoughts wash over her again. She feels snow swirling in the darkness, melting against her skin. Sees Grandpa's face in his casket and can almost feel Grandma's dry hand in her own.

She hasn't called her yet. She was supposed to call as soon as she got to Stockholm. But then all of this happened. Gabriella pushed onto the ground outside her office. Her own escape from the police. Maria's kindness. Gabi's letter.

Klara sneaks back into the kitchen. Just one more glass of wine. Tomorrow she won't drink at all.

She opens the fridge door and helps herself to the already-open bottle. Tomorrow she'll book tickets to Brussels.

It's been a long time since she was there. She shivers at the thought of what happened before she left the city that she called home for many years, at the thought of what happened to her father and Mahmoud.

Her pulse starts to race; her chest tightens. She swallows half the glass in one gulp. Brussels. It's as if she feels a purely physical resistance to returning to the city that she'd once been so fond of.

She has only one friend left there now. One she's thought about an absurd amount lately, and who she can't seem to avoid, even if she wanted to. It must be more than a coincidence.

George. Is she really going to contact George Lööw again?

A little flutter somewhere in her stomach, a little buzz in her ears. How is it possible for an asshole like George Lööw to cause these feelings inside her? Someone who's all surface and talk and quick success.

Or maybe he's more than that? He did save her life. And last summer, when they met, she saw another side of him, a calm behind the expensive shirts and the jargon.

She walks over to the window, takes another gulp of cold wine, and lets her eyes wander down to the yellow shine on the street below. She almost drops her glass on the floor. Just a little bit down the street she sees a man in a doorway sheltering from the snow. Maybe it's a coincidence, someone out for a late-night walk surprised by the intensity of the snow, waiting for it to let up. But somehow, she knows that's not the case. Her hand trembles slightly as she pours the last of the wine into her glass. She's sure. Whoever was watching Gabriella has found a new target. And it's her.

NOVEMBER 14—BEIRUT

THE RAIN HAS started falling harder, and Jacob can hear it drumming on the roofs of the cars parked outside.

The question hovers like a cloud above them. He should have asked it a long time ago.

"They definitely think so," Yassim answers evenly. "To them, I'm a terrorist."

The air trembles around them as Jacob turns to Yassim. Myriam's story is true. There's no way to deny it anymore. He should stand up and just run away, don't look back, never go back again. But he can't move.

"But it's not black-and-white, Jacob," Yassim continues. "A person is many things. And I'm a terrorist in the same way Snowden is a terrorist. In the same way Assange is a terrorist."

Jacob shakes his head. "What do you mean?" he says. "What the hell are you talking about now?"

"My trips," Yassim says. "You're right. I'm not a photographer. Or I *am* one, but that's not all. Recently that's not why I've been going to Syria. I'm working on a project compiling information about drone strikes and the West's other military efforts in Syria and Iraq."

Yassim pauses, drinks from his can, and puts it down again. He places a hand on Jacob's shoulder, but Jacob pulls away.

"I don't understand what you're talking about," he says. "What project?"

"Statements from witnesses," Yassim says. "Videos, photographs.

Any information that might help us map their attacks on civilians and children. To prove who the real terrorists are. I'm close now. We're close. We'll soon be handing over the information to someone who can publish it."

Jacob shakes his head again. The rain sneaks in through a gap in the tarp and a small drop runs down from his head to his cheek. He shivers. "Someone is following me," he says. "A Swedish woman. She calls herself Myriam Awad and works for the Swedish Institute in Alexandria. But she's a spy."

"You've spoken with her?"

Jacob stares out into the rain. "She showed up a few weeks after our first meeting. She has a video. Of me and a guy I . . . in one of the bathhouses in Bourj Hammoud. It was right after I met you, before I knew whether you were coming back. It was a trap, something my boss apparently planned at her request. A guy picked me up and wanted to hook up with me. It was . . . violent. On the video, it looks like I'm raping him. I've never done anything like that before. I mean, I've never had sex with strangers . . ." He sighs and forces back tears. "But I was lonely and confused . . ."

A cold wind ripples the tarp around them. Jacob looks up and sees deep irritation in Yassim's eyes.

"You should have told me," Yassim says. "This changes things."

Jacob looks at him, then turns his eyes toward the parking lot. "Maybe you should have told me what you're doing."

Yassim looks at him, and then he just nods silently. "It's not easy, all this."

"Myriam has information on you. She says you're a 'lighter.' That you're planning to carry instructions for a terrorist attack to Europe, where some jihadist cells are going to carry it out."

Yassim looks at him without a hint of surprise. "What does she want you to do?"

"She wants me to tell her when you're back in Beirut. And she wants me to install some fucking program on your computer."

"So you've been watching for my password . . . that's how you got into the computer."

Jacob nods without looking at him, still staring out at the wet cars in the darkness. "She pops up sometimes to remind me if I don't contact her. When we were in Byblos and someone called you, she was there, at Pepe's. And sometimes she's been waiting for me in my apartment."

Jacob feels a lump in his throat, it's hard to swallow, and he buries his face in his hands.

"But I haven't done anything," he says. "I haven't told her anything. And I didn't do anything to your computer tonight before you woke up. I don't even know if I would have. But I had to know who you were." He sobs, everything is welling up inside him. Stress, frustration. Love. "I'm sorry. I should have said something. I should have told you."

Yassim sighs deeply and shakes his head. "You didn't know. I should have told you who I was, of course. But what I'm doing is dangerous, Jacob. I didn't want to drag you into it. Not before I knew you better. Mostly for your own sake. I felt I could trust you right from the start."

Yassim leans in and kisses him lightly near his temple, and Jacob puts his hands on Yassim's knee.

"You are so innocent, Jacob," he whispers. "That's your strength here, where nobody is innocent. Don't forget that."

They sit for a while listening to the rain. They're alone, apart from the old woman who runs the café who's sitting behind the counter watching reruns of an old Syrian soap. Yassim pushes him away, holds his head in his hands, stares deeply into his eyes. He's preparing for something, collecting strength to say something.

"I like you so much, Jacob," he says quietly.

And it's as if the whole café with its dirty plastic chairs and bleached and tattered tarp fades away, as if the rain stops and night turns to saga and myth. It's like that first night in the garden, as if the only real thing is the two of them.

"I like *you*," Jacob says.

His mouth is dry, but he doesn't want to free himself to take a drink, doesn't want Yassim to let go of his face, doesn't want this to end.

"You'll come with me to Europe, promise me," Yassim says.

"Yes," he says, nodding his head in Yassim's hands. "Anywhere. I'll follow you wherever you want."

"I have to go back soon," Yassim continues. "After what you told me . . . I can't risk staying here now."

His voice breaks suddenly, and he has to clear his throat. "I can't risk you either, Jacob. It's dangerous. They're dangerous. It's better if I'm not here."

Jacob nods, he understands but feels empty at the thought of Yassim disappearing again.

"I'll wait for you in Europe, in Brussels, darling," he says, and smiles weakly. "Don't be sad."

"I'm not sad," Jacob says. "Not when I know I have you."

"You do," Yassim says, stroking his cheek. "You know you do."

He finally lets go of Jacob's face and then takes a drink of his soda. He seems to be preparing himself again. Maybe to say what he tried to say before. It feels solemn; Jacob can feel it in the air, a glimmer of something large, something important.

"The information we've collected . . ." he begins. "We've been immensely careful about it. We don't save it on computers that are connected to the Internet; we don't send emails, don't make calls. We always meet face-to-face, never use any intermediaries."

"I've noticed that," Jacob says, smiling cautiously. "You just disappear. Even from me."

Yassim nods. "It's necessary. They see everything. There are no secrets unless you're very strict and share them only with those you trust."

Jacob doesn't look away. *Am I one of them now?* he thinks. *Am I one of the people Yassim trusts?*

"That includes you and me, too," Yassim says. "I said from the beginning that it's too dangerous, we have to be ghosts, that you were far too big a risk. But when we met . . . When we sat there in the garden . . . every time since then. We're human—how could we deny ourselves everything?"

"We can't," Jacob whispers. He runs a hand over Yassim's stubble, feels him leaning into that hand.

"I thought we'd been so careful," Yassim continues. "But they must have been following me from the beginning. And now . . ."

"What?" Jacob whispers.

"Now I have to disappear again," Yassim says. "And I have to find a way to get the material out."

He takes his phone from his pocket and opens the *Guardian*'s website. Jacob looks at the screen.

Hundreds have been injured in a series of terrorist attacks in Paris, the article reads.

The shock comes in a new wave and he grabs the phone. There were separate terrorist attacks at the French national arena and in a rock club in central Paris. The situation is unclear and still ongoing. He totally missed it because he was with Yassim and didn't look at his own phone once during the night.

"Did you know . . ." he begins. "Did you know about this?"

Yassim looks at him with those hard, black eyes. "She's really done a number on you, that spy." But Yassim turns his face away, as if he can't meet his eyes, and Jacob sets down his phone and puts his hands on Yassim's face.

"I don't know what to believe," he says. "I don't fucking know anything anymore."

"Of course I'm as disturbed by this as anyone else," Yassim says quietly and unambiguously. "I saw a news flash about it on my phone earlier, but I didn't want to ruin our evening. I . . . didn't realize how big it was."

Jacob looks at him again, tears in his eyes. There's something in Yassim's eyes, something else. Something darker and deeper.

"I can't explain it now," he says. "But it's more important than ever to get this information out of the Middle East as soon as possible. I don't trust anyone here. Not in the media or the diplomats. Everyone is a spy. Everyone has their own agenda, their own angle."

He falls silent, looks out at the rain. He seems furious, and Jacob would like to ask if it's the Paris attacks that have upset him, or if it's something else entirely. At the same time it's so clear to him now. So obvious what he has to do. He looks at Yassim, at his tired eyes and wavy hair falling onto the collar of his shirt.

"Give it to *me*," Jacob says calmly.

Yassim turns away from the rain slowly and looks at Jacob with a question in his eyes, as if he hadn't really heard or understood what Jacob meant. "Give *what* to you?" he says.

"What you've collected. Give it to me. I can get it out easier. I'm European. The rules are different for me."

Yassim says nothing, just stares at him, then turns away, shaking his head. "I can't let you do that. It's too much. Too dangerous. This is not your fight, Jacob. Besides . . . You're already marked, because the Swedish intelligence service thinks you're working for them."

But Jacob pulls him close and turns his face to look into his eyes. He doesn't look away for a second. He's calm now, not shaky or nervous anymore.

He sees Myriam's icy eyes in front of him, her threatening expression. He has never been surer of anything.

"Don't you understand?" he says. "That's the whole point. They think I'm working for them, so they won't suspect me."

"The risk is too big," Yassim says. "They'll see through it, believe me."

"But I want to do it," he says, almost desperate now. "After what happened in Paris tonight, it will be impossible for you as a Middle Easterner. Everyone will be checked and treated with suspicion. I mean it, Yassim. I can do it; let me do it."

Yassim looks down and pulls away.

"Don't you trust me?" Jacob says. "You think I'm trying to persuade you because . . ."

He falls silent because Yassim has turned to him again, placed a gentle hand to his mouth. "I trust you," he says. "If you wanted to fool me, you wouldn't have seemed so eager." He smiles crookedly. "They would have coached you better if they wanted you to fool me. It's not that. I know you're honest. But you don't know what you're getting into. You don't know what I know. . . ."

"Just give me the information," Jacob says. "I'll bring it for you."

The rain has finally let up as they leave the café. Just a fine mist now. It feels like they're moving in unison, as if their hearts are beating the same rhythm, as if they're welded together, a single unit, strong as titanium, diamond, tougher than anything.

"What do we do now?" Jacob asks.

Yassim takes his hand in his own, presses gently. "First we give them what they want," he says. "You do what Myriam asked and install the program on my computer. We'll act normal. Who knows if they're listening to us?"

"What?" Jacob says. "I don't understand."

Yassim shakes his head. "If they contacted you, they've certainly bugged the apartment as well."

Jacob just nods. There's something about Yassim's competence and calm that makes him feel so safe, that makes him go along without asking questions.

"The next time Myriam contacts you, you have to tell her that I caught you, but that you pretended to be convinced that I was a photographer. Promise me that. There can't be any gaps."

Jacob nods. "But if I install the software, won't she be able to see the information on your computer?"

Something flashes in Yassim's eyes. A shadow of implacability. "Didn't I tell you I'm better at hiding my secrets than that?" he says.

NOVEMBER 23—STOCKHOLM

At some point Klara finally gives up any attempt to fall asleep, and she finds Maria already in the kitchen with *Dagens Nyheter* open in front of her, a cup of coffee on the table beside it.

"You're up early," she says, standing up. "There's coffee." She pours a cup and hands it to Klara. "You don't look like someone who uses milk," she says with a smile.

Klara takes the cup and sits down hesitantly by the table. She shakes her head and can feel it pounding weakly from lack of sleep and yesterday's wine. "No, that's not my thing."

Maria sits down and looks at Klara with worry in her eyes. "What are you going to do now? You don't look like you slept much."

"I'm going to Brussels," she says quietly. "But it's probably best if I don't say more than that." She shivers when she says *Brussels*. It's going to take an incredible effort to book those tickets.

Maria suddenly stands up again and goes over to the kitchen cupboard. She takes down a small white jar and puts it on the table in front of her.

"I went through some difficult times a few years ago," she says. "And sometimes medication is the only thing that works. Especially if you have to keep going."

She gives Klara a small, gentle smile.

"You have to get some sleep," she says. "And I don't think I can prevail on you to go to a doctor."

Klara smiles faintly back and shakes her head. "I'm going to help

Gabriella," she says. "That's the only thing I care about right now."

"I understand that," Maria says. "I'm not saying you should take any of these pills right now. But I can see you're not feeling good." She pushes the bottle over the table toward Klara. "This is all I have."

Klara lifts up the bottle. *Flunitrazepam Mylan*, she reads on the label. "Rohypnol," Maria says with a shrug. "Bad reputation, but it works if you need to keep going."

There's something so unexpected about the well-to-do lady in her sixties on the other side of the table giving her this bottle of Rohypnol that Klara just has to smile. She meets Maria's eyes.

"So I'm headed back to Brussels for an anonymous meeting armed with nothing more than a bottle of roofies," she says.

Maria drinks her coffee and shrugs her shoulders. "You do what you need to make it through the day," she says. "But you seem to have come to terms with that."

Right after lunch Klara jumps into a taxi waiting about a block from Gabriella's front door. Maria's shown her a way out of the house through the laundry room, which takes her to another door farther down the street, so she can slip past anyone who might be following her.

"Bromma Airport," she says to the driver, leaning back in her seat.

The temperature has fallen during the night and the snow drags on. The streets are black and slippery. She looks up at the roof, but the sky is such a bright blue and the autumn light so unusually bright that she has to close her eyes.

She turns around and looks out the back window. The street seems empty, but just as the taxi turns the corner, a pair of headlights on a parked Volvo light up, and she flinches. Before she can see if it's following them, the taxi has turned the corner and the Volvo has disappeared from sight.

Brussels, she thinks with a sigh. She shakes her head to get rid of that suffocating feeling, but it doesn't help. Her pulse quickens, her temples are pounding, and her breath has become quick and shallow.

"Is everything okay?"

She opens her eyes and sees the taxi driver's worried look in the rearview mirror. She nods as calmly as she can.

"Didn't sleep well," she manages to get out.

She looks through the window, trying to avoid the driver's gaze. They're driving across Central Bridge, and Klara can see the parliament towering up on one side and Norstedt's blue neon sign on the other.

And in between those iconic buildings, on the road, just a few cars behind her taxi: a black Volvo. She can't be sure, but somehow she knows it's the same car that was parked outside Gabriella's front door.

When the taxi stops outside Bromma's only terminal, the anxiety, loneliness, and vulnerability are replaced by obstinacy. Who are these assholes following her and Gabriella? Why can't they just leave them alone?

She jumps out of the taxi and grabs the little black backpack of clothes she'd originally packed to spend a couple of days at Gabriella's. She peers past the airport buses, over toward short-term parking. Hesitates a moment. Then she turns her back to the terminal and heads toward the parking lot.

She's gone only a couple of steps when she sees the Volvo parked just behind the airport buses, its engine running. It's cold, probably fourteen degrees, and she pulls her coat more tightly around her, finds a stocking cap in her pack that she pulls down over her ears. She can feel her heart pounding again, but this time it's from anger, not a panic attack. What the hell do they want from her?

A short, fit man wearing jeans and a black beanie is standing next to the black Volvo, as if he just jumped out of it. He has a short beard and a blue puffy jacket, brown leather gloves. When he catches sight of

Klara, who has started to walk toward the car, he bends down, opens the door, and hops in the passenger seat. The Volvo's engine revs and the tires skid in the snow as the car pulls away from the curb, does a hasty U-turn, and then speeds away from the airport.

Klara runs after it, despite knowing it's a lost cause. She has no idea what she'd do if she caught up to them.

After a hundred yards she gives up, almost falling on the slippery asphalt. She leans forward, panting as the Volvo disappears. The adrenaline and anxiety rush through her, and she screams out loud in frustration. A man in a coat, pulling a bouncing suitcase behind him as he heads toward the terminal, turns and stares at her. But he makes no effort to approach, and Klara wants to scream at him too: *What the hell are you staring at, you asshole?*

But she stops herself and forces herself to regain control over her feelings.

Her head pounds as she straightens up. JNK 314. At least she got the license plate number.

With her hands still trembling from excitement and physical exertion, she pulls out her phone and looks up the number. The Volvo is registered to a car rental company.

She closes her eyes and squats down. She thinks back to Gabi's letter—she was right. The man pursuing her didn't look Swedish, more like Eastern European. A rental car. It wasn't the police. She's sure of that now.

NOVEMBER 14—BEIRUT

He can't have slept more than a couple of hours when he feels Yassim stroking his hair. In the darkness of the bedroom he can make out only Yassim's profile and that he's holding a finger to his lips. Carefully he bends over Jacob and whispers in his ear: "Put on your clothes as quietly as you can and come with me."

Jacob's eyes adjust to the darkness, and he can see Yassim is already dressed.

He obeys without making a sound, rolls over on his side, puts his feet on the floor, grabs his underwear, shirt, and trousers.

Barefoot, carrying their shoes, they sneak across the concrete floor, open and close the door to the apartment soundlessly. Yassim pulls him away from the elevator and toward the stairs. His lips tight against Jacob's ear. "Like ghosts," he whispers, and smiles quickly.

Then they're down in the garage again and Jacob sees three yellow taxis waiting by the ramp that leads up to the street. "What's this?" he says.

But Yassim doesn't slow, just pulls him into one of the cars. The cabin smells like smoke and old plastic.

"Lie down," Yassim says, gently pushing his head onto the seat and sinking down beside him.

The cars start rolling up the ramp.

"The people watching us can't follow all three," Yassim says. "And they don't know which one we're in. I've arranged for the two other cars to take off in different directions."

Jacob says nothing, just feels the warm vinyl against his cheek. Slowly they roll along the still-almost-empty streets.

"Now . . ." Yassim says finally, patting him on his shoulder. "I think we're okay."

Jacob sits up and looks at him, at his tired face, the tiny wrinkles around his eyes. Yassim has his large black backpack on his knee. They both slip their shoes on.

"Are you leaving already?" he whispers. Fatigue is pounding at his temples. What did he think? That they'd have a few more hours, a few days?

Rays of morning sun stream in through the dirty taxi windows, shining on the worn vinyl between them. Yassim puts a fist on the seat between their thighs and turns to him.

"I can't take the risk," he says. "Not after yesterday. After Paris. Even if we avoid the worst of their attention and maybe even manage to make them think you're playing along. It's too dangerous."

He lifts his hand from the seat and opens it. Jacob sees that there's a small, flat memory card in his palm, like from inside a camera.

"Everything we have," he says. "All the information we collected." He puts the memory card into Jacob's hand and closes his fingers around it. "Are you sure? You know you can still pull out."

Jacob nods. He has never been surer of anything in his life. "I'm sure."

Yassim strokes his cheek. "Then there are many people depending on you now, Jacob," he says. "You don't know how much depends on you not losing this little card."

It feels like the memory card is burning in his hand, and he wants to drop it onto the floor of the taxi and stamp it out before it burns a hole through his palm. He feels instantly anxious. Not because of the risk the card entails, but because he's afraid he won't be able to fulfill his task.

"But what if they stop me?" he says.

Suddenly he is overcome with the magnitude of the situation.

"What if I lose the card? What if I do something wrong?"

But Yassim puts a gentle hand on his knee and it calms him. "You won't lose it," he says. "We'll take care of that now."

"What do you mean?"

Jacob looks out the window. It must not have taken long to get through Beirut's morning streets because he doesn't know where they are now. The buildings here are far from the expensive shops downtown and the newly built skyscrapers. Instead, there are winding alleys and bullet holes, dirty laundry and tarps for windows, electrical lines in a tangled spiderweb just above the roof of the taxi.

Yassim bends over to the taxi driver: "Wait here."

Then he takes Jacob by the hand and pulls him out into the dusty street. "Come," he says. "Time to make sure you don't lose your little chip."

They're waiting. The door is opened up by a young, shy woman in a hijab and white hospital clothes before Yassim even rings the bell. She says something in Arabic that Jacob doesn't catch, but she looks stressed and nervous that they're here, and she hurries them inside and closes the door carefully.

It's not a hall they enter: the door leads directly to a staircase, and they follow the woman as she goes up it.

"Is she a nurse?" Jacob asks. "Where are we?"

Yassim just turns around and gives him a quick, strained smile. "I'll explain. Soon."

The stairs lead up to a shabby waiting room. Old steel-tube furniture, a rickety table; the blinds are drawn on the window that looks out over the street. The woman leading them opens a door on the opposite end of the waiting room and gestures for them to enter. Yassim turns to Jacob and looks at him in a piercing, solemn way again. He doesn't pull him close. They're just friends here. Nothing more.

"Where are we?" Jacob says again. "At a doctor's office?"

But before Yassim can answer, a short man in green surgeon's scrubs is standing in the door. He is wearing a protective cap and mask, and only his dark, tense eyes are visible.

"What are you waiting for?" he says. "I don't want you here any longer than absolutely necessary. Come on!"

It happens fast. Suddenly Jacob is on an exam table, can feel the stiff, crisp paper scratching and scraping beneath his bare chest, paper sliding against the worn vinyl. Someone, probably the woman, smears cold gel between his shoulder blades. He senses Yassim somewhere behind him.

"It was supposed to be me," he says. "This is how we transport information when it's particularly sensitive."

Jacob swallows and nods. Adrenaline pumping. No turning back.

"They'll place the chip just beneath your skin," Yassim continues. "Between your shoulder blades. It takes two minutes, no more. Just a quick cut and three stitches."

He says something in Arabic that Jacob doesn't catch, and the nurse backs away, as he squats down by Jacob's face.

"Last chance, Jacob," he says. "Once we do this, there's no going back."

Jacob takes a deep breath. He doesn't hesitate for a second. "Just do it," he says.

Yassim rises and nods to the doctor. Then Jacob feels the quick prick of a needle.

Fifteen minutes later they're back in the taxi. Yassim holds his hand and turns to him. The sun is brighter now, flashing off the windows of the buildings that line the streets.

"Does it hurt?" he says.

"Not yet," Jacob says. "Can't feel it at all. The anesthesia is definitely working."

Yassim nods. "You're brave," he says.

"I'm not so brave," Jacob says. "But I like you. A lot."

Yassim squeezes his hand and turns his face away, looks into the morning sunlight.

By the time the taxi stops outside Urbanista on Gemmayzeh Street, the anesthesia has started to wear off, and Jacob can feel the small incision between his shoulder blades starting to sting and tighten. Three stitches. "You'll hardly notice it," the stressed doctor said before shooing them back out to the taxi again. "Like a wasp sting."

"I wish I could have taken you all the way home," Yassim says now. "But I think it's for the best if you go the rest of the way by yourself. It's just a few hundred yards from here."

Jacob nods. "What happens now?"

"Now you live your life as usual, darling. You stick to the story we talked about when Myriam contacts you. In just two weeks you'll be on a flight to Brussels. I'll meet you there."

"It feels so surreal," Jacob says.

Yassim stares deep into his eyes. "I know it's too much," he whispers. "I know I have no right to ask this of you." Yassim kisses him gently on the mouth.

Jacob almost pulls back, shocked by this sudden open display of intimacy. Then he pushes Yassim away and shakes his head. "I'm doing this because I want to," he says. "For you. And because it's what's right."

When he says it, he knows it's true. This is what he longed for, and almost lost in his wish to do right, to move forward. This is who he really is. Yassim has given him the chance to be someone who can make a difference, who is not afraid, not exploited, not just grateful.

"You know the international bookstore at Gefinor Center in Hamra?" Yassim says.

Jacob nods. "Why?"

"This happened so fast," Yassim says. "You'll need tickets and other things. Lie low today and go there tomorrow after lunch. The owner is an old Armenian who likes his cigars."

"I know," Jacob says. They suggested it to him at the embassy, and he had spent several hours there going through the selection of English paperbacks.

"Good. Ask him if he's received any new deliveries in the last twenty-four hours. He'll give you what you need. Use what's in the envelope. Promise me that. Don't improvise."

Jacob nods.

Yassim reaches over him to open the taxi door. He kisses him quickly on the cheek before nudging him to jump out. Then Jacob is standing on the sidewalk, leaning over the car door.

"I have to go," Yassim says. "There's no turning back. See you in two weeks. I'll miss you."

Yassim waves to him through the car window as the taxi turns around and heads back west. Jacob holds up a hand in reply. Then he's alone on a narrow sidewalk in eastern Beirut with a small memory card embedded beneath his skin.

What should he do now?

What is he supposed to do when he's landed in the middle of something so much bigger than he ever imagined? *Live your life as usual*, Yassim told him. He should go to the embassy and call Myriam. He should pretend everything is normal, that nothing has happened.

Yassim and the chip and the mission, he feels the weight of it all now. Confusion and euphoria, fear and love and longing. He stumbles into Urbanista and orders a coffee. Drinks it with trembling hands.

His mind is on Yassim's hands, Yassim's mouth. And how he's going to manage this. If he will possibly be strong enough.

As he stands up, the small wound tightens on his back, and he feels dizzy. He leans forward, supporting himself with the table, then finally is able to make his way out into the sun again. The phone buzzes in his pocket just as he's about to cross the street, and he fishes it out of his pocket. *Yassim!*

But it's not Yassim. It's Myriam.

15:00 Sursock Museum. Last chance.

2

NOVEMBER 23—BRUSSELS

At the very moment the plane bounces onto the runway at Brussels Zaventem Airport just outside Brussels, she opens her eyes. She must have fallen asleep as soon as she sat down because she has no memory of the flight itself.

Klara looks out through the cabin window and thinks of all the times she's landed here in the rain. For more than three years, whenever she landed at Zaventem, followed all the people dressed in business attire pulling carry-ons up the passenger bridge and into the larger terminal, past juice bars, tax-free and chocolate shops, and then into the arrival hall, she felt like she was going home.

Now as she rises from her seat and follows that stream of people, all she feels is a weight in her chest and a headache coming on. At one of the small Lavazza kiosks she buys a double espresso and burns her mouth as she knocks it back in two gulps. The sleep on the plane didn't help: on the contrary—she's not used to sleeping during the day, and her head feels groggy and heavy.

Halfway through the terminal, she takes off her backpack, throws the cardboard cup into the trash, and sits down on a bench near one of the gates. She pulls her phone out of her jacket pocket, scrolls down to George Lööw's name, and sits for a long time with her thumb hovering above the phone, struggling with contradictory impulses.

With a sigh, she locks her phone and puts it back in her pocket. It'll have to wait. Instead, she raises her eyes and looks out over the crowd of stressed travelers. And that's when she sees him. On the other side of the hall, about fifty yards away, a cap pulled down over his eyes and a jacket draped over his knees, a man is looking in her direction. When she looks at him, he turns his eyes away. Under normal circumstances, she wouldn't think more about it. But now, after Gabi and Bromma, it makes the hair on the back of her neck stand up. She recognizes him from the plane ride here.

Her legs tremble as she turns around and walks the last stretch through the terminal building, into the arrivals hall. She stops at regular intervals to turn back, and every time she does, the man with the cap is behind her. Did she really think she'd scared them away at Bromma?

She starts to hurry, and when she reaches the arrivals hall she turns again. There is only one exit. The man in the cap has to come this way.

The sudden flash of energy she felt before, which made her want to confront them, has disappeared completely during the flight.

Now she looks around at the people waiting here for travelers: taxi drivers in ties with handwritten signs. Parents waiting for teenagers, friends and spouses and a Muslim family with balloons and a long banner in Arabic. The stream of people is swift, and minutes pass by with no sight of her pursuer.

She feels a blend of relief and disappointment. What was she going to do if he did come out here?

Maybe she was wrong. Perhaps Bromma just made her hypervigilant about anyone with a vaguely Eastern European look and shifty eyes.

Full of doubt now, she turns and walks through the automatic doors toward the taxis. It's four in the afternoon. She doesn't even know where to go, just knows she needs a glass of wine as soon as possible.

The taxi queue takes less than five minutes.

"Place Sablon," she says to the driver. It surprises her that she's requested that flashy and touristy square, with its chocolate and antiques shops, rather than the neighborhood of Ixelles, where she lived for three years. But the thought of her old neighborhood just makes her anxiety worse. Better to stick to the tourist areas; better if she doesn't let the city really sink in. Better to have a soft landing.

She stares worriedly out the rear window as the taxi rolls past the parking lots and airport hotels. Suddenly it hits her that in one of those cars behind her slowly gliding through the afternoon rain there could be a person who's following her. She shudders as she turns forward again.

They take the Brussels Ring in, past NATO headquarters, the gray and gritty streets on the outskirts of the Schaerbeek district, and then past Square Ambiorix. She bends forward to get a view of the apartment building at this small park's southeastern corner, where she sublet a furnished one-bedroom for the first three months she lived in Brussels. The taxi swings away from the square and over toward the EU institutions. It feels like another life now, among the restaurants and bars of Rue Archimede. Everything looks familiar; she knows everything about this life, the lunches and the smiles, the suits, the dresses. Nevertheless, it's impossible to imagine that she was ever a part of it, that the person who experienced all that is the same person sitting in this taxi.

Then they're at the very heart of the EU—the Schuman roundabout with the European Council headquarters and the commission's star-shaped building, the Berlaymont, on the right. She feels a little ache in her stomach when the traffic stops just in front of the roundabout, and she sees all the stressed-out people in suits on the sidewalks with their hands full of folders and binders, phones pressed to their ears.

That could have been her. That was her. Until Mahmoud contacted her two years ago. Before Paris and London and last summer. That was her before the anxiety and the sleepless nights and the grief.

Now a pit opens inside her again, and she can feel herself falling and fast. She bends forward between the seats toward the driver.

"Drive to Place du Luxembourg instead," she says.

It's closer. She needs a drink right now if she's ever going to be able to handle all this. She knew it would be difficult to come back here, has been worried since yesterday. But this? It's worse than she expected. She shouldn't be alone. She needs someone to talk to.

She takes out her phone and finds George Lööw's number again. This wasn't how she thought she'd contact him again, not under these circumstances. But what choice does she have?

I'm in Brussels. At Ralph's in half an hour. Can we meet?

NOVEMBER 14—BEIRUT

JACOB WALKS ALMOST the whole way home with his phone in his hand. *Last chance*, Myriam wrote. But he doesn't need a last chance; he's made his decision. He's left everything behind now.

He's in front of the apartment, and he should go up and at least grab some clothes. Why? Where should he go? They decided that he was going to live life like usual, not draw any unnecessary attention. Now he realizes he'll have to meet Myriam too, play along. Go to the embassy every day so as not to draw attention. And then just disappear.

He takes out the business card he's kept in his pocket the whole time.

ALEXA TAYEB
DIRECTOR
PALESTINIAN RECREATIONAL YOUTH CENTER, PRYC
SHATILA, BEIRUT

Shatila is a labyrinth, she told him. You'll disappear there if you don't know what you're doing.

Disappearing is exactly what he'd like to do. He sighs and puts the business card back again, feels discomfort and fear at the thought of meeting Myriam. But he doesn't have much of a choice.

It's so cool out now that Jacob barely breaks a sweat in the autumn sun as he climbs up the colorful staircase from Mar Mikhael to Ashrafieh, even with his backpack of extra clothes. He doesn't know if he'll go back to the apartment. He doesn't know anything right now.

The time is ten to three. And he feels like he has no control over his own steps. But when he looks down at his phone, he's put the Sursock Museum into his map app so as not to get lost among the run-down, bullet-ridden art deco houses. He only has to deny everything, stick to his story, get her to leave him alone for a little while. Buy some time.

It was here, under these twisting power lines, over this uneven asphalt, that he and Yassim walked on that first night just three months ago. That was another world: Beirut looked different; he'd been confused and fragile, a stranger. Who was he now?

He feels like he recognizes balconies and flaking shutters. But he can't find the garden, doesn't see the palace or the bench where they sat. It's as if that night was a dream.

The Sursock Museum's newly renovated; its white facade shines like mother-of-pearl, like a mirage in the midst of all that gray decay. He stops and takes a deep breath of clear autumn air. He should probably just leave. He's already chosen Yassim. Love and truth.

But he takes a deep breath and walks through the gate, turns to the left, heading toward the newly built café and the small boutique. Myriam is already sitting there with a small cup of coffee in front of her, nothing else. Besides Byblos, Jacob's never seen her in daylight, and he's struck by how attractive she is. Just a cool, local girl spending her afternoon off at the museum. That's what he'd think if he'd never spoken to her, didn't know how ruthless she is.

He walks slowly toward her, across the polished sandstone slabs, squinting against the pale autumn sun.

She doesn't even look up from her phone when he sits down across from her. "What is your friend going to do?" she asks.

Jacob feels that familiar powerlessness creep over him. He has to get back his strength, his power. "What do you mean?"

Myriam puts the phone on the table in front of him and stares at him with empty eyes. "You still don't understand how serious this is," she says slowly with suppressed rage. "You think it's a fucking game, don't you? A novel? Are you aware of what just happened in Europe? In Paris yesterday?"

Jacob's leg starts to tremble and hop, the sore on his back starts to pound.

"Your boyfriend disappeared again," she continues. "This time he's on his way to Europe. Answer the question: What is he going to do there?"

"I did what you asked me to," Jacob whispers. "I installed the program on his computer."

"What do you want? A medal?"

"What do you want me to do then?" he says. "I've done what you asked me and all you do is question me."

"Do you think I'm an idiot?" She's raised her voice now and is leaning over the table. "You disappeared from his apartment sometime in the early-morning hours. Again: Do you think I'm a fucking idiot? Well?"

Jacob shrugs; he wasn't prepared for this after all. "I don't know where he is. You seem to know more than me."

Myriam sits comfortably in her chair staring at him. Rage burning in her eyes. "Come on," she says.

Jacob shakes his head and leans over the table, looking her in the eyes. "Come on with what? What the hell do you want me to say? That I know where he is when I don't?"

Myriam leans over the table, and with unexpected speed grabs his forearm, squeezing so hard it brings tears to his eyes. Their faces are no more than a foot apart now. "It's time for you to stop fucking around," she hisses. "Do you plan to meet him in Brussels? When are you going to meet him? Don't you realize this is a whole new game since yesterday, you fucking idiot?"

Jacob pulls his hand away, and she reluctantly lets go in order to avoid a scene, even though the outdoor seating is almost empty.

His arm is an angry red where she held on, and he rubs it with his other hand. "What the hell," he says. "Are you fucking crazy?"

"Am I?" Myriam asks. "Am I crazy? Or am I just frustrated that you don't understand what the hell you're mixed up in? You're protecting a fucking terrorist, Jacob. You're making it harder for us to stop more terrorist attacks."

He shakes his head again, his arm still hurting, and he continues rubbing it. "But I did what you asked me to do," he repeats. "I did everything."

She looks at him with the same irritated contempt as before, just more intensely now. "I think you know as well as me that his computer didn't help us."

He just looks at her coldly. "How would I know that?" He feels like a child repeating the same transparent apology over and over again.

"When are you going to Brussels?" she asks again.

"I don't know what the hell you're talking about. Why would I go to Brussels?"

They sit there, eyes locked, without saying anything else for a while, then she bends over the table again.

"Listen to me right now," she says. "And really fucking think about it before you answer me, okay? Has Yassim given you something that he wants you to pass on to someone else, or that he wants you to take to him in Brussels? Take your time now, Jacob. Really think about it. Did you receive anything from Yassim that he wants you to take care of in any way?"

His head pounds. The wound on his back. Last chance.

"Do you have it here?" she asks.

Her voice sounds different now, not threatening; on the contrary, it sounds understanding and almost friendly.

"I know it's hard," she says. "He made you believe he's in love with you, that you have something together. But you have to understand that he doesn't care about you. He only cares about one thing: his mission. And that mission is terror, Jacob."

He looks around at the restaurant, suddenly aware of their surroundings. It's as if the world is more intensely colored, clearer, than just a second ago. Two men sit at the table closest to the museum building itself. There's something about their short hairstyles and wide shoulders and how they don't speak to each other at all. Jacob's heart pounds, and he glances over toward the souvenir shop. A man stands flipping through some art books with an earpiece in his ear. These aren't visitors to the museum. None of them. It was a mistake to come here; he knew it. His chest tightens.

"Think about it," Myriam says at last. "Why would I be interested in Yassim if he wasn't a terrorist? Why would I care at all?"

Because he's collecting information about Western war crimes, Jacob wants to scream. *Because you're all working against Assange and Snowden, all of them. That's why!*

He says nothing, only sits up straight in his chair. What would happen if he just stood up and left? Would they let him go? If not, where would they take him? What would they do to him? And how can they be so sure he's received something from Yassim?

What if she's right about Yassim? What if Yassim is just using him?

Myriam puts a phone on the table in front of him. On the screen is a picture of a man with a deep tan, very white and meticulously cut hair.

"Have you seen this man?" she asks.

He has seen him. He saw him leaving Yassim's apartment and hopping into a car with diplomatic plates a month ago. Jacob remembers his eyes and his authority, how even through the window he saw how Yassim listened to him.

"Who is that?" Jacob asks quietly.

"Gregorij Korolov," Myriam says. "A Russian spy. Somewhat of a legend, actually. We think he met with your boyfriend. And we want to know what the hell that's all about."

Jacob thinks about that night in the garden. About Yassim's eyes, how he listened to him yesterday at the late-night café. About how he still doesn't really know anything at all.

"No," he says, looking straight into Myriam's eyes. "I have never seen him."

He doesn't know where he finds the strength or courage to do it, but he stands up before he even realizes it, as if his spine has reacted without the help of his brain.

And suddenly he turns over the table with great force. It's easier than he imagined, and he heaves it toward Myriam. Glasses and ashtrays shatter against the floor of the terrace. She tries to get away, but she's too slow and the table falls onto her. From the corner of his eye he sees, as if in slow motion, the men at the table by the museum stand up. He can hear their distorted voices as he turns around. And he moves faster than he ever has before, is already down in the courtyard, has already covered half the distance to the gate out of the garden. He hears them screaming behind him as he turns right, onto the cracked concrete and asphalt.

They're running fast now, no longer in slow motion, quite the opposite, and Jacob knows he isn't in shape for this and his pursuers probably are. They're not screaming now, but their footsteps are getting closer.

He's on something that feels like a sidewalk now, and he knows he has no margin for error, that they'll catch up to him any second.

A high iron fence. An overgrown garden. A gate.

He bends down. The gap in the gate. Which Yassim bent up for him on that very first night. This is where he crawled through.

He's down on his knees now, and he hears them approaching, hears that they're almost to the intersection behind him. He bends and pulls and pushes his shoulders sideways through the gate.

Then he's through, with bruises and scratches, and the palace towers in front of him in the cool afternoon sun. He runs into the garden, in among the green bushes and the uncut grass. Sits down on the bench where they sat.

Outside the gate he hears his pursuers heading farther down the street, and he realizes he's escaped.

He hunches down in the grass, but his legs won't hold him, so he collapses into a small, lonely heap and cries his heart out like a child.

NOVEMBER 23—BRUSSELS

IT'S A MISTAKE asking the taxi to drop her off at Ralph's. Klara realizes it as soon as she pays and steps onto the cobblestones with her bag over her shoulder. She tries to keep her eyes on the door, and her thoughts focused on the wine in order to avoid looking to the right, where the European Parliament stands with its blue glass and memories of her former life.

Ralph's is remarkably empty on a Monday afternoon. It was always bursting to the limit when she was here in the past, full of lobbyists with an extra button undone on their pink dress shirts and gold cards at the ready, and red-cheeked interns from EU institutions with their badges dangling around their necks.

She orders herself a glass of white wine, sits down on one of the colorful plastic chairs at the far end of the long room and feels her anxiety grow. Maybe it's the depressing, deserted bar with Adele's soft voice streaming over the speakers above her, filling the bar with empty nostalgia, but her breath becomes more shallow, and the pressure in her chest starts to spread to her left arm with acute and intense pain. For a moment, she's afraid she might fall off her chair. She closes her eyes and grabs the table so hard her knuckles turn white.

"Miss?"

Klara can barely hear; her ears are ringing so loudly it sounds like she's standing in a waterfall.

"Are you okay, miss?"

She turns her head to the bar and sees, as if through a haze, a worried bartender leaning over the counter. She tries to nod and give him some kind of smile, but answering is beyond her capabilities. She manages to loosen her grip on the marble table and grab on to the stem of her wineglass. The noise just increases in her ears; she can barely hear Adele anymore, and she can see the bartender's lips move, but his mouth isn't making any sound. He leaves the bar and starts to move toward her, but it's as if he's in another world, as if she's in a bubble all by herself. The pit is wide-open inside her now, and if she had the strength, any strength at all, she would scream or start to weep.

She feels the bartender's hand on her shoulder—he's shaking her gently, but she can't do anything other than keep her eyes shut and try to hold it together as best she can.

"Miss? Miss? Are you on something? Are you on any medication?"

The roar in her ears. The pain in her chest.

And then suddenly something else. A voice she recognizes. A voice that cuts through it all.

"Klara?" the voice says. "What the hell? What's going on?"

She opens her eyes and the noise starts to diminish until it's no longer deafening, more like the slight buzz of a bee or a wasp. The pain is just a strip across her chest, and she takes a breath, forcing herself to suck the oxygen as deep into her lungs as she can.

"It's fine," the man says to the bartender. "I'll take care of it; she's my friend."

She recognizes the man leaning over her, despite the round, tortoiseshell glasses, even though the blond hair isn't slicked back with gel anymore but is product-free, tousled, and longer. Even though he has on a denim shirt instead of a neatly pressed, tailored pink one, even though he's not wearing a pin-striped suit jacket, but a navy-blue bomber jacket.

"Everything's okay, Klara," George Lööw says. "Just breathe. We're gonna take care of this, okay?"

She senses him sitting down on the chair next to her, putting his arm around her and pulling her close. Something releases inside her, and she lets it float away. She lets her head fall onto his shoulder.

"George," she mumbles. "I meant to contact you, I was going to call, I was . . ."

"Shh," he says, stroking her hair. "It's fine, Klara. Just breathe now."

He lets go of her for a moment, fumbling in his pocket for something, and then he lifts her weak arm with one hand and pushes something small and dry into her palm with the other.

"Take this," he says. "Beta-blockers. Nothing dangerous, but it'll help you slow your pulse, okay?"

She looks at him. The buzzing in her ears has almost completely disappeared now. She's almost out of the bubble. He looks so different. Not like the slick lobbyist she met a couple of years ago. This George is softer, his eyes not shifting and impatient but warm and worried.

"You got glasses," she whispers.

He smiles and pats her cheek. "Always had 'em. Just stopped using contacts. Take the pill now." He holds up the wineglass to her.

"You're giving me wine to wash down the medicine?" she asks. "Haven't changed that much, I see."

He shrugs. "Just do what I say. Believe me, I know exactly how you feel right now."

They walk slowly and quietly toward Matonge, the Congolese part of the Ixelles neighborhood, which borders on the EU district, and Klara remembers these contrasts were exactly what she loved about Brussels: privilege never more than a block away from poverty, the future never disconnected from the past.

She feels better, almost functional, after downing her wine and George's pill. She can feel George glancing over at her as they cross Rue du Trône, continue past small, dusty shops full of wigs and phone cards, dried fish in wooden crates on the sidewalk.

"You've changed," she says. She runs a hand over his jacket. "What happened to the Wall Street look?"

George was really the quintessential lobbyist when Klara first met him. Flashy job at a big American PR firm. The suits, a glass of champagne in his hand at Ralph's, big talk, high stress, and shady customers.

"Laid off after last summer," he says. He takes her arm gently and pulls her close to keep her from being run over by a teenager on a Vespa tearing around the corner.

Klara nods. Her pulse isn't racing anymore. She glances up at him. The panic attack has started to give way to something else, something warmer, something bigger. It feels so good to be walking side by side with George. Too good.

"What are you up to now?" she asks.

"You won't believe it," he says.

"You started working for the Social Democrats in the European Parliament?" she says with a smile.

"Worse," George says. "I'm moving home."

"What? Moving back to Stockholm?"

Klara thinks she must have heard wrong. George is so much a part of Brussels for her that she never imagined his leaving; it feels like the city itself wouldn't be the same.

"But what will you do there?"

He looks so uncomfortable that Klara almost starts to laugh, despite her condition. "I got a job as an official at the Ministry of Enterprise," he says.

Now she does start to laugh. "You're becoming a bureaucrat?" she says. "Well, I don't know what to say."

He shrugs. "It's a good job," he says quietly. "And I haven't felt so great lately either. Been through a lot."

She turns to him and looks into his eyes. "Seriously, it is a good job. A dream job for a lot of people. Just odd to think of you . . ."

"I know," he says. "Seriously, I don't want to talk about it, okay?"

She hesitantly puts her arm around him and can feel herself getting goose bumps. He looks so different in his grown-up glasses and tousled hair.

"Damn it, George," she says. "I'm proud of you."

They end up at Ultime Atome on Saint-Boniface, at a table in a large, bright room. George orders some kind of complicated and potent amber beer for them. This is apparently also part of his new persona; Klara never pegged him as a beer drinker. Champagne and cocaine were more his style.

She looks around at the other tables in the room, which are slowly filling up as darkness falls. Ultime Atome is a modern *grande café*, a classic place where she used to go for a beer on Sunday or a drink before dinner along with all the other newcomers in Brussels. She'd almost forgotten it, but it feels homey and safe to be back. With every gulp of beer, every minute spent with George, she feels better.

"But you haven't told me why you're here," George says.

Klara takes another gulp and realizes she's almost drunk it all. George is barely halfway through his. After Ralph's and the intense anxiety she felt there, she almost managed to suppress her reason for being here, but now she hears that slight buzz in her ears again. She downs the rest of the beer and stands up.

"Do you have a smoke?" she asks.

They're standing outside the bar in the dark, cold drizzle, and George lights her cigarette with a silver lighter. The facade of the church on the short side of the square is illuminated, and above it hangs the Christmas lights the city puts up every year.

"Gabriella was arrested yesterday," she says.

"Excuse me?" he says. "But she's a . . ."

"Lawyer, yes," Klara says. "But that doesn't seem to matter to a national SWAT team."

It takes her a whole cigarette to tell him what happened yesterday, and George listens without interrupting. They stand in the gray twilight while Klara tells him everything she knows. About the letter Gabriella wrote to her, and the men who were following her and who now seem to be following Klara.

"We need another beer," is the only thing he says when she's done. "At least one more."

They have two more beers, then three, and Klara can feel herself almost floating out of her chair, her head finally empty and manageable, her breathing easy.

"Shall we have one more?" she says.

But George just stretches a hand over the table and carefully, unexpectedly, takes her hand.

"You're gonna meet this guy Karl tomorrow," he says gently. "Tomorrow is the twenty-fourth. You have to be sharp for that. No more beer for you now."

She pulls her hand away and leans back in her chair. "Who the hell do you think you are?" she says, barely slurring. "I drink as much beer as I want."

His eyes seem worried now, and it makes her furious. Where did she put her bag? She looks around. There, on the floor. She bends down and gets her wallet, heads over to the bar. George can do whatever the hell he wants; she's having another drink.

"Where are you staying?" he asks before she's made it to the bar. "What hotel?"

She stops. Staying? The pleasant, blurry feeling in her head scatters and gives way to something else lurking beneath, something sharp and stinging. She hasn't even thought about where she's going to stay tonight.

"I . . ." she begins.

"Come on," he says. "You're staying with me. We'll have another drink when we get there. I promise."

NOVEMBER 14–15—BEIRUT

HOW LONG DOES he lie in the garden without moving a muscle? He doesn't know, just notes that darkness has fallen by the time his strength starts to return, and he realizes he's next to the bench that he and Yassim sat on that night in August. The temperature is falling fast as the sun goes down, and he grabs his backpack off the sparse grass next to the bench. He grabs a sweatshirt and pulls it on. He takes his phone out of his pocket, mostly to check what time it is. But it's turned off at Yassim's request.

Always off and throw it away if anything strange happens, he told Jacob. *They can track everything.*

If anything strange happens. He takes a last look at the phone and throws it into the bushes. He can't describe the last twelve hours as anything other than strange.

He sits up straight on the bench, but then has to lean forward with his head between his knees as a wave of dizziness hits him.

What has he done? Yassim's face flickers by. His warm, deep eyes. Myriam's indifferent expression. The man with the white hair. The sting of the wound on his back. He can't think about it anymore. He has to trust that Yassim has a plan. And he has to stay alive until they're together again.

Slowly, he lies down on the bench and adjusts his shirt. Tomorrow he has to go to the Gefinor Center, to the bookstore. A wave of exhaustion hits him. Even if he had a plan or knew where to go, he wouldn't have the strength to leave this garden now. He closes his eyes and falls asleep instantly.

It's light out when he opens them again. He shivers a little and stretches, stands up, and steps out into the sunshine on the yellow, scraggly lawn. He hears a single car out on the street; it's still early. He takes a few deep breaths and walks over to the gate.

The street is deserted, but his legs tremble as he presses his way through the opening in the gate and out into reality again. Myriam's men are gone. He drags his backpack out behind him and grimaces when he puts it on. The wound on his back aches—if it weren't for that, this might all seem like a dream, too blurry and terrifying to be real.

He wanders around for hours, walks toward the center of the city from eastern Beirut, down toward the sea. Buys a coffee and a croissant, constantly glancing over his shoulder.

He has almost no memories of the morning, barely any of yesterday either, and he doesn't know how he got here, but suddenly he's in Hamra, near the main entrance of the American University.

Why is he here? He doesn't know where else to go, and maybe the university offers some sense of security, stability, and order in the midst of this chaos.

His legs ache from walking. He flinches and looks around. It feels as if he's been walking in his sleep, as if he hasn't been conscious, but his legs have carried him here of their own accord. He looks up toward the tops of pine trees peeking out above the university's gray wall and still feels drowsy. He runs his eyes along the wall up the street, the traffic noise washing over him, and then overwhelming sadness settles on him, and for a second he's dizzy again.

He's standing on the street just fifty yards from the entrance. He never hesitated for a second, he realizes. Not when Yassim asked him. Not at the museum with Myriam. Not in the garden. But now he feels like he's looking at himself from the outside: just a confused, naive Scandinavian lingering on a street in Beirut.

He starts to walk slowly toward the main entrance. The university feels like a sanctuary. The green tranquility inside those walls, away from Beirut's frenzied energy, replaces the chaos of the Middle East with an atmosphere of learning and sober conversations. He wants so badly to be inside there again, to catch his breath; he doesn't know if he can stand to just be swept along. He can't go to the embassy—Vargander is involved in this somehow. He knows he's completely alone there. But maybe he could talk to Rafi, the teacher he interviewed and got a coffee with sometimes? Maybe he has a contact after all? A *wasta* as it's called here, a connection to some influential person who can help him.

Everyone has a *wasta* in Beirut, Rafi told him, and Jacob needs help; he can't handle this on his own. In fact he probably should have reached out for help a long time ago, before he ended up in this insane situation. But he knows it's too late now, and he sinks against the wall with his head in his hands. There is no one, no matter how influential, who can help him with what he's landed in.

He stands up again, hesitantly heading toward the main entrance, without even knowing exactly why. He's almost reached the security guards at the entrance when he stops midstep.

He doesn't exactly know what it is about the black SUV across the street from the entrance—Beirut is full of black SUVs—but there's something about how carefully it's been parked with a proper distance in front and behind it, while every other car is squeezed in bumper to bumper. And there's something about the European-looking man on the street ten feet away from him, in jeans and a windbreaker. Something about how still he is while everyone else around him is on the move.

It has to be one of Myriam's men, there's no other explanation. No way to hide from him, the sidewalks are full of people, but not enough for him to disappear into the crowd. The man's eyes pan over the entrance to the university, then out over the dense, sluggish traffic and the sidewalk, on their way to where Jacob stands. It's only a matter of time before he sees him. The sound of the traffic blurs together into a roar in Jacob's ears.

The man lights a cigarette and turns his head in the opposite direction from Jacob, then he pauses and quickly looks back. Their eyes meet, and Jacob's heart stops. The man looks surprised, as if he never thought he'd be the one to find who they're looking for.

His lips move quickly, as if he's rattling something into a headset. At the same time he starts to move through the crowd of students on the sidewalk toward Jacob.

Jacob runs. The sidewalk is narrow and uneven, and he stumbles and weaves with his arms out in search of something to catch hold of. He grabs a man walking in front of him and manages to stay upright. The man says something, but Jacob has already run by.

The street branches, and he turns to the right, toward the American hospital and Hamra Street. He crosses between honking cars and people on their way home or headed to restaurants and shops. The hill is steeper than he remembers and he goes as fast as he can while panic threatens to paralyze him. He looks back over his shoulder and sees the man is only fifty yards behind him.

The man is faster. Just like yesterday, but now there's nowhere to hide. This will soon be over.

Jacob's up by the gray concrete hospital now, panic pounding inside him. The street is full of honking cars trying to make their way into the hospital's improvised parking lot. He's passed by here before, amazed by the chaos allowed to reign even here, outside the hospital.

Like everywhere where crowds gather in Beirut, there are several makeshift guard posts. Sandbags, rolls of barbed wire and rusty bars. Tired soldiers and police officers carrying heavy automatic weapons and caps around their necks. He feels his fear rising. What if the guards are looking for him too? What if he's heading straight into the lion's den?

The man is close to him now; Jacob doesn't dare to turn around. It's as if he can hear the man's steps even through the street noise, as if he can feel his breath on his neck. In any case, the soldiers in their worn camouflage uniforms just follow him listlessly with empty eyes as Jacob heads up the street.

That's when the idea hits him. He doesn't know where it comes from, maybe it's just the lack of any other options. Jacob heads for a couple of young soldiers standing and smoking at their post. He opens his mouth and screams as loudly as he can in Arabic: "Bomb! He has a bomb!"

It's as if his words cast a spell that makes the whole world freeze. The flow of people between the hospital and the parking lots halts. This is Beirut. They know all about bombs here, and it takes no more than a millisecond for the world to switch to a whole other tempo.

The soldiers are on alert now, cigarettes thrown to the ground, the automatic weapons raised, stress flashing in their eyes.

"He has a bomb!" Jacob screams again and points to the man behind him.

He lets all the pent-up terror erupt in those words, and they sound believable and genuine.

The man has stopped. He has his hands up, and he's backing away slowly. The people on the street are taking their children by the hand, lifting them up, and running away from the threat of terror as fast as they can go.

The soldiers have their rifles on their shoulders, screaming at his pursuer. The last thing he sees over his shoulder as he joins the rest of the terrified crowd that's moving away, down toward the Gefinor Center, is the man kneeling with his hands on his head, one of the soldiers putting a foot on his back and pushing his head down against the cracked concrete.

Jacob continues running until he's at the cool concrete of the Gefinor complex. The polished stone floor is slippery under his rubber soles as he finally slows down. His whole body aches. He looks around. He's ended up very close to the Armenian's bookstore. He must have headed in this direction unconsciously when the panic took hold of him.

He looks around at the enormous complex. The Gefinor Center feels so clean and clear and modernist, not at all like the rest of Beirut, and it fills him with immediate relief. Straight lines, glass. No hidden agendas or lies.

He turns around and scans the direction he just came from. Everything is calm again, as if nothing happened. Drama is close at hand all the time in Beirut. Bombs and weapons are a part of everyday life, part of the city's DNA. Tragedy flares up, like now, then dies out again. No one has time to ponder on it; everyone just wants to get home after work.

He wonders what happened to his pursuer, if the soldiers released him immediately when they discovered there was no bomb. Did he contact his colleagues?

Jacob hurries toward the international bookstore. With determined steps he walks over to the store and opens the door. An electronic chime rings when he steps inside.

The little Armenian who owns the place is standing at the counter, smoking a cigar, just as Jacob remembers, just as Yassim promised, and Jacob nods to him and walks by the paperbacks and the shelves with Middle Eastern history and politics, into the dim interior of the boutique where the art books are hidden, while he gathers his courage to approach the owner.

He randomly flips through a heavy volume, waiting for his breathing to return to something resembling normal. The door chime rings as the only other customer in the shop disappears out into the sunshine. Jacob sees that he's alone in the shop with its owner, who's now headed up the aisle toward him.

"Can I help you with something?" he asks in English.

The man's question is completely neutral, an offer he makes fifty times a day. But there's something in his eyes, something hidden, a secret.

Jacob clears his throat. "Did you receive any new deliveries?"

The man studies him calmly. "You're the Swede," he says. "We have a common friend."

Jacob nods, then raises his gaze slightly, looks through the display window above the man's shoulder, out toward the big, empty, dark space outside. But the square isn't empty anymore. A gray van with tinted windows has pulled into the middle of it. Four men jump out in short jackets and bulky khaki trousers or jeans. Earpieces in their ears. He tries to swallow, but his mouth is very dry. He thought he'd escaped.

The men don't even look at one another, just move quietly in formation toward the entrance of the bookstore, as if following some perfectly obvious and straightforward choreography.

Jacob freezes. The wound on his back aches, he feels pressure in his chest.

Is this as far as he goes?

NOVEMBER 23—BRUSSELS

THEY WALK IN silence past the bars and small Pakistani grocery stores that are open late, up toward the wide Avenue de la Toison d'Or, which leads to the luxury stores near Place Louise. The drizzle is constant but barely noticeable.

"Should we grab a taxi? I live just behind Place Stéphanie," George says, stopping outside the cinema at Toison d'Or.

Klara looks around. Her head has cleared a bit. George was right, of course—she didn't need another drink.

"Let's walk," she says, and starts down the street again.

Even though it's not much past eight thirty, the sidewalks are almost empty. Monday and the weather has kept the flaneurs at home.

"How long have you been feeling like this?" George asks quietly outside the entrance to Marks & Spencer. The English department store wasn't here when Klara left Brussels, and she lets her eyes sweep across the display window.

"I don't feel any particular way," she says quietly. "Is it really so strange to end up a little shaky after your friend is rounded up in an anti-terrorism operation, and you realize you're being followed by the Russian mob or whoever the hell they are?"

George grabs hold of her elbow gently, and she pulls it away but regrets it immediately. It would have been so nice to be held by him.

"I don't mean *that*," he says. "It was like this in the summer too, right?"

Klara glances at him and starts walking again. "I feel better now," she says.

"You know what I mean." His voice is louder now and carries a touch of annoyance, and he's grabbed her elbow, turning her toward him. "You had a panic attack at Ralph's, Klara. You've been drinking like a fucking sponge. You think you can fool me?"

She turns her eyes away, but after what he saw at Ralph's she knows she can't hide from him. "Can we just go home?" she says. "I can't talk about this now. I'm sorry."

She turns her eyes up the street, in the direction they just came from, mostly to avoid looking at George. There are only a few people hurrying through the drizzle, maybe headed to the movies or to get a beer. But her eyes settle on a man leaning against a doorway next to a souvenir shop fifty yards farther up the street. He looks like he might be of Middle Eastern descent, has a short, neatly trimmed beard, is wearing tracksuit bottoms and a dark puffy jacket of some glossy material. He looks like he's waiting for somebody while staring at his phone. A completely unremarkable situation in other words. But something about him makes her heart beat faster, despite the alcohol and beta-blockers. There are a thousand strangers who look like him. But she can't help noticing he's dressed in the exact same style as the men in Bromma and Zaventem, and she starts to tremble.

"Come on," she says. "Let's get going."

George lives in a small one-bedroom on Rue Berckmans, just behind the legendary Hotel Conrad, which has been renamed something long and German-sounding since Klara left. They step into his hallway, and she's surprised by how ordinary and impersonal the apartment is. George's personality—or at least his former personality—promised something more spectacular.

"It's only temporary," he says apologetically, hanging up Klara's jacket. "I had a sweet place down by Place Lux, but I bought a two-bedroom in Stockholm to get ready for the move. Renovating the kitchen now. Gaggenau, a wine fridge. The works."

It's clear that his old, flashy personality isn't completely gone, and Klara smiles a little as she walks past him into a living room that looks out over the street. "Nice to know that deep down inside you're still the same superficial asshole I used to know."

"Oh, come on," George mutters behind her. "Am I supposed to live like a Social Democrat just 'cause I got a government job?"

Klara turns back to him and smiles more widely.

"No offense, of course," he adds, since Klara used to work for the Social Democrats in Brussels. "You know what I mean."

He walks over to the window and turns on a small lamp, and soft light fills the room, then he takes out his silver lighter again and lights a few candles on the coffee table.

"This place is nothing special," he says. "I just rented something furnished until I was ready to move. Just one month left."

Klara sits down on the sofa and looks at him. He's so much softer, she thinks. It's done him good to let go of his slick persona. He looks nice. His eyes used to seem so impatient and restless, but now she thinks they look mostly worried and a little nervous. It seems like his attention-seeking, childish self-confidence was only a mask, and he's let go of it. Not completely, but enough to see what's behind.

He settles down beside her on the sofa, so close that she catches a whiff of his cologne: citrus and wood. It smells expensive.

"Damn," he says, rising halfway. "We should eat. I can go out and grab something. Don't really have much at home. Cooking's not my thing."

Klara nods and leans back. She gently grabs his arm and pulls him back down. She feels so safe here, in his company. All of the stress of Brussels is flowing out of her on George's sofa, in George's company. It's confusing—she barely knows him, after all. But she didn't imagine it. Maybe there's always been something there, something that she has tried to ignore.

"Can't you wait a minute?" she says. "Can't we just sit here for a while?"

Without really knowing how it happens, she's leaning against his shoulder, and he's hesitantly putting an arm around her.

She turns her face cautiously up toward George's throat and lets her lips run along the skin just above his collar. She feels his skin tense under her lips, and he changes his position on the sofa, twisting toward her. Suddenly, his hand is beneath her chin and their faces are just millimeters apart. She raises her hands and runs her fingers through his thick hair. She gently takes hold of it and pulls him close.

His lips taste like beer and tobacco and peppermint chewing gum, and at first it feels almost too surreal to even register what's happening. She's kissing George Lööw! It would have made her laugh out loud if it didn't feel so natural, if it didn't feel like letting go of something she'd held in check far too hard, for far too long.

He runs a hand over her hair now, grabs the back of her neck and pulls her even closer, going from careful to hesitant to intentional. She pushes him back so that he's half lying on the couch, but she doesn't stop kissing him, she just straddles him. Now he moans into her mouth, and she can feel his hands on her back, running down toward her butt. She fumbles with the buttons of his shirt, without letting her lips leave his, without letting anything come between them. If she were to pull back for even a second it feels as if the magic would be broken and reality would flood over them again.

He has a hand on one of her breasts now, inside her bra, and she feels that he can't hold back either, that he's caressing it with a desperation that would hurt if she wasn't so unbelievably turned on.

"We should go to the bed," he gasps.

But Klara pushes him down on the sofa while pulling at his belt, unbuttoning and pushing down his trousers and suddenly he's in her hand. He's smooth and hard, and Klara pulls down her own trousers, her underwear, and then she pulls back for a second and looks deep into his eyes.

Afterward she lies with her cheek pressed against his warm chest, her hands still in his hair; he's still inside her. She can feel his chest falling and rising beneath her. Maybe she should say something, but she doesn't know what, and honestly doesn't know if her voice will hold.

Somewhere in the distance a siren is approaching, and when she opens her eyes she can see flashing blue lights shining on the wood floor as a police car drives by outside. Gently, she turns onto her back, lying next to him on the sofa. She glances at him as he stares up at the ceiling.

"Well, well," she says finally. "You sobered me up."

She turns toward him and sees a little smile on his lips. He glances at her, then turns his eyes away nervously. "This . . ." he begins. "I wasn't expecting this."

She laughs. "Really? I thought you were a player? A hawk among the sparrows down at Place Lux? Was I completely mistaken?"

She glances at him and can swear he's blushing. "This . . . is a little different."

She's sitting up now, has found her underpants between the cushions of the sofa. She fishes them out and pulls them on. "Is it?" she says, smiling provocatively. "How is it different, George? Do tell."

She sounds tougher than she feels. Or she doesn't know at all how she feels—just that she liked what just happened. That she likes George's lips and breath, his hands on her skin. That she feels so safe suddenly. And she doesn't want it to end.

George has pulled on his chinos now and is standing up. His hair is disheveled, almost wild, and Klara likes the way he runs his hands through it, trying to get it back in place.

"I don't know," he says quietly. "Just different." He looks at her and grins. "Well, are you hungry now?"

She nods. She actually is. The beer has given way to a weak headache. But the pressure in her chest is gone. When has she felt this light lately?

"There's a Lebanese restaurant down the street," he says. "I can go pick up some food. I think they have a lot of vegetarian stuff too."

"You know I'm not a vegetarian, right?" she says, looking at him with amusement.

"Really? Could have sworn you were." He holds out his arms. "You've got that kind of aura, you know."

She wants to take a shower, but she can't let go of what happened, so she settles down on the sofa again. What the hell is this? Did she really just have sex with George?

She stands up and walks over to the door of the balcony. Carefully draws the curtain and looks down onto the street.

He just left to get food, but she already feels a little empty and lonely and warm and raw. She misses him. It's crazy. George Lööw? The original Brussels playboy? She must be even more fucked-up than she knew.

She glances down at the street bathed in a hazy, yellow light. She'll just stand here and wait for him to come back.

The street is empty now, and she looks up toward the intersection where the restaurant is located.

And there, leaning against one of the leafless trees, a man stands in slacks and a dark, shiny, puffy jacket. With her heart pounding, she draws the curtains again.

Somebody is still watching her.

NOVEMBER 15—BEIRUT

JACOB SEES THE men through the window. One of them has stopped halfway to the bookstore; the other three move toward the door with their hands at their waistbands, which are partially covered by their short jackets. Who are they? Americans? Does it matter?

They're here for him. They'll find the chip beneath his skin. And then?

All he can imagine is orange overalls and small cells. That was what awaited Chelsea Manning after she gave information to WikiLeaks. At that very moment, the bookstore owner touches his elbow and startles him. He turns, and the small man is stretching out his hand, taking him by the elbow again, this time more brusquely. A cigar smolders under his mustache, his eyes narrow, and he nods toward the depths of the store.

"Come," he says in English. "You don't have much time."

He pulls Jacob between the tables and the shelves that sag under the weight of books, and farther through a jingling curtain of glass beads, into a small room with drawers stacked up to the ceiling, a vacuum cleaner in the corner.

"Wait," he says, placing the cigar on a plate on the floor. Then he bends down and starts to fiddle through one of the stacks. "Help me," he says roughly. "We have to move this." He has grabbed one of the boxes at the bottom and draws it outward, bringing the whole stack along.

Jacob sees a doorframe behind it. He squats down next to the bookstore owner to help him pull.

Behind them, the door chime rings in the store. He can hear several people rushing inside. Hear them making their way through the aisles toward the small room.

The boxes are heavy and the piles are unsteady, and for a second he thinks they might overturn, but the bookseller steadies the boxes.

They've shifted the stack enough that the small man can reach the knob and turn the lock. The door springs open into a dark and silent alley.

"Hurry now," he hisses, pushing Jacob out of the doorway.

Jacob steps out into the shaded, dirty alley and turns back toward the door, looking at the bookseller's face, sees him holding something through the gap. A thick, white envelope.

"Take this," he says, shaking the envelope urgently toward him.

Before Jacob can say more, the owner has closed the door, and Jacob's alone in the tiny alley.

He thinks he hears the boxes being pushed back in place on the other side of the door, then he runs off toward the alley's entrance. He hears traffic again, and that feels like his only salvation. A taxi. Somewhere to disappear.

He exits onto the street, turns back, and sees the alleyway door bursting open and one of the men in black storming out, followed closely by another.

They scream something, and he sees their hands at their waistbands, sees them stop and pull out black steel and hold their arms up in front of them. Aiming for him.

"Stop! Get down!" they scream in what sounds like American English.

They're twenty feet away from him now, and he holds up his hands to show he's unarmed, still with the thick, white envelope in one hand. He should lie down on the ground, should admit to himself he's not made for this. He should give up. But something inside him hardens. He feels a core now that wasn't there before.

And then it's as if time is standing still again. Like in the garden, as if the entire universe freezes. He turns his head and sees an empty taxi right behind him.

"Wait!" he shouts at the men farther down the street, and takes a short step toward them.

They seem surprised that he says anything at all, that he's making the first move, and they answer something that he can't hear. He turns around and tears open the door of a taxi that has just pulled up behind him and throws himself into the back seat.

"Just drive," he screams in English. "As fast as you can."

The driver turns around and looks at him, sees it's serious, and nods as if he understands. There's a gap in traffic ahead of them, and he steps on the gas and the twenty-year-old Mercedes roars in protest but finds some kind of power and speeds eastward as if it were brand-new.

Jacob turns around and sees the men are out on the street now. One of them stops and waves for a taxi, the other stands wide-legged, with his gun in front of him. The rear window of the taxi explodes into a thousand crystals. Jacob throws himself down on the worn vinyl of the back seat, feels glass falling all over him. He hears the driver screaming and turning onto a side street, away from the guns and bullets and violence, and then the car stops. The driver turns around with wild eyes.

"Leave!" he screams. "Out of my taxi!"

He's in shock, and Jacob already has the door open, jumping out. The shards of glass clatter around him, cutting him, but he takes out his wallet and throws three twenty-dollar bills into the back seat and runs as fast as he can over the uneven asphalt and gravel.

After twenty yards, he turns around, sees the taxi still there, the driver with a phone to his ear. But he doesn't see his pursuers.

Another taxi stops beside him. Jacob pulls open the door and jumps in for a moment of protection, security, and the taxi starts to roll forward anonymously, just one among a thousand others.

He feels dozens of tiny pieces of glass making their way under his collar, his hair still covered with dust. When he turns around he sees nothing but the normal chaos of traffic here. No guns or the men who wield them hunting him down.

"Just drive," he says. "Anywhere at all."

Beirut is a city to disappear in. People who are from here have their groups, their ethnicity, their religion; they can fall into Beirut as if it's a black hole and they will never be found again. But Jacob isn't from here. He's blond and terrified and foreign; he's exposed, a black swan, impossible not to notice.

Jacob sits on the honeycombed vinyl of the back seat of an ancient Mercedes, and the driver asks where he wants to go. As the taxi rolls eastward, he turns around and looks out the dirty rear window. Just row after row of cars flowing slowly, slowly through the city. No gray van. Not yet. He has to hide, has to catch his breath, get on his feet.

Suddenly he's back on the roof that very first night in Beirut. Alexa's warm eyes. *Shatila is a labyrinth.* He fumbles in his pocket and takes out her business card again. It's only a small chance, barely even that. But it's all he has.

"I want to go to Shatila," he says. "To a youth center there."

He sees the driver shake his head. "I don't drive to the refugee camps," he says in heavily accented English. "I can drive to the border, but you have to go the rest of the way yourself."

He turns and looks at Jacob.

"But that's no place for you."

Jacob just nods. "Well, it will have to be. Drive me as close as you can."

The driver shrugs and mutters something inaudible, but at least he speeds up.

The envelope is on Jacob's knee, and he fumbles to get a finger in one corner, under the tab. With a quick flick he opens it, grabs hold of the contents, and pulls them into the light.

NOVEMBER 23–24—BRUSSELS

KLARA JUMPS OFF the sofa as soon as she hears the key slide into the lock. She knows it's George, but still she's so tense, so close to the breaking point, that she runs into the kitchen. She's grabbing a large carving knife from out of the top drawer when he enters the kitchen bearing two plastic bags full of aluminum containers from the restaurant.

"Hey!" he says, and slowly lowers the bags onto the kitchen floor, then holds his hands up. "What the hell are you doing?"

She's holding the knife in front of her, pointing it at him. She points it downward, then drops it with a jangle onto the tile floor. Then she sinks down and looks up at him.

"I'm so fucking messed-up," she whispers, then lowers her eyes. "I don't know what the hell I'm doing anymore. I'm being followed; I see men on every street corner. . . ."

He also sinks down in front of her and puts a hand on her cheek. "I know," he says. "I know exactly what it's like."

"You know?" she says skeptically, and looks at him again. "I honestly don't think you can imagine how . . ."

But he's not listening; he's moved his hand from her face to somewhere behind his back and he seems to be pulling something from the waistband of his trousers. When he brings his hand forward again, he's holding something so big and black and terrifying that Klara scoots back and almost falls backward onto the floor.

"What the hell?" she says. "A gun? Are you crazy?"

He holds it in his palm and gently puts it down on the floor between them. “You’re not the only one with issues, Klara. Why do you think I’m moving home? Why do you think I’m leaving my fucking dream job? After everything we went through in the archipelago a couple of years ago, then this summer . . . I didn’t think I’d survive it. And I’m so tired of being afraid.”

She meets his naked, terrified eyes. “I didn’t know you . . .” she begins.

“You remember that Christmas in the archipelago two years ago? I was kidnapped by my clients who turned out to be a freaking CIA death squad, as you might remember?”

He smiles crookedly.

“I shot somebody. And it wasn’t exactly like I could talk about what happened to anyone—Säpo made that abundantly clear. If anyone understands keeping it together with alcohol and work and a little bump now and then, surely it’s you? But after what happened this summer . . . The Russians and those fucking riots in the suburbs? I haven’t been able to sleep. I think people are breaking into the apartment; I think I’m being followed and monitored. And do you know what the worst part is?”

Klara shakes her head.

“That I’m not even sure I’m paranoid. Because who the hell knows, right?”

Klara stretches out her hand and puts it on his cheek, caressing it gently. “Yes,” she says. “Who the hell knows?”

“So I bought a gun from a guy down in Anderlecht who my cocaine dealer knew.”

He lifts it up and turns it over, inspects it.

“It’s so damn big. But I didn’t know what else to do.”

“You bought a gun and applied for a job at the Ministry of Enterprise. Unusual strategy, I’d say.”

George laughs and stands slowly. He puts the gun on the kitchen counter. “I don’t know,” he says. “Maybe if I can get out of here, if I get away from my job at Stirling and Merchant and all the bullshit, maybe it will stop. Maybe I can start sleeping again, won't panic every time I hear a sound I can't quite place."

Klara stands up too. "You should get help. For real. You can't live like this, surely you know that."

George picks up the bags of food and puts them onto the small kitchen table. He looks at her ironically. "Good advice. How's that working out for you?"

It's five o'clock in the morning when Klara slips into the kitchen, opens the door to the fridge, and takes out an almost untouched tub of hummus. Neither of them ate much last night, despite being so hungry when they ordered that George bought basically the entire menu.

"You sleep about as well as I do."

She turns around and sees him standing in the doorway, in a tank top and a pair of striped boxers. He's squinting at her; without glasses his face looks so naked and clean-cut, and he's so . . . cute? Is George Lööw cute? She truly has lost control.

"I have some Rohypnol," she says. "To help me sleep. But I don't dare use it."

She has an important meeting in about twelve hours. After she got control of her drinking last night, she couldn't risk being affected in any other way. Better to be tired than chemically hungover.

"And here I gave you the bed," he continues, passing by her to the fridge. "You could have taken the sofa if you didn't want to sleep."

Klara dips a piece of bread, chews, and swallows while looking at him evenly. "Or you could come into the bed with me?" she says. Damn, that sounded more forward than she'd planned.

They haven't discussed what happened on the sofa before he picked up the food; they just let it be.

Now he turns around from the fridge, still squinting in the dark kitchen, but with something more confident and interested in his eyes. "Is that what you want?"

She doesn't say anything; she just dips another piece of bread and stares down into the food. Does she? Really?

Then she looks up and nods.

"Yes," she says. "I do."

NOVEMBER 15—BEIRUT

SHATILA IS FAR from the glittering downtown and the galleries of Mar Mikhael, far from the Corniche and the university. Shatila is poverty and permanent impermanence, a fifty-year-old refugee camp that's turned into a neighborhood.

The taxi drops him off at the embassy of Kuwait, near the edge of the camp, and Jacob stumbles on through winding, narrow alleys, between walls covered with flaking graffiti and spray-painted stencils of Arafat. As he looks up at the gritty, decaying buildings, he sees Hamas flags and Fatah emblems hanging out of the windows. The sun is setting, and he can feel eyes staring out at him from small, improvised kiosks and shops. He tightens the backpack around his shoulders.

Nobody will find him here, but he also knows he shouldn't be alone; he should have calmed down and waited to enter with a guide. Most of all, he should have called Alexa first, despite the risk, and asked her to meet him.

Reflexively, he puts his hand in his pocket and reaches for his phone, but then remembers that he doesn't have one anymore. He tossed it in the garden.

The alley he's walking down bends slightly to the left and narrows, and when he rounds the turn he sees two men in leather jackets staring at him without expression, and his mistake dawns on him with full force.

Jacob stops. He glances around and sees another man blocking the path behind him. He raises his hands with open palms to show that he's unarmed, that he's not a threat, that his intentions aren't bad.

The men say nothing at first—they just stand there with unreadable eyes. Jacob opens his mouth and closes it again, takes a step backward. He doesn't know what to say or what's required in a situation like this. Something flashes in the sunlight. A gun at one of the men's belts.

"I'm a friend," he says in his faltering Arabic. "I'm looking for the youth center."

It rings so hollow, and he can feel the man behind him getting closer. The two other men also move slowly toward him. Jacob swallows hard, panic pounding in his chest.

"I'm looking for the youth center," he tries again.

The men stop and look at him. The echo of stories of robberies, disappearances, and kidnappings bounce around inside his head. What is the actual name of the center where Alexa is working? Why did he come in here so unprepared? What the hell was he thinking? He should have gone to the Four Seasons or some other Western hotel, tried to disappear into the crowd. This is folly and naivety, nothing else.

"Who are you?" asks one of the men.

"My name is Jacob," he says, but his mouth is so dry the words barely make it over his lips. "I'm a Swedish diplomat."

It's not exactly the truth, but perhaps it might function as a shield of some kind. The expression of the man who asked doesn't change, but he nods almost imperceptibly to the man standing behind Jacob, who slowly closes a hand around Jacob's upper arm.

He gestures with one hand to the man behind him and then turns around and heads into the alley. Jacob is dragged in the same direction, his feet moving without choice, following the two men, deeper into the labyrinth of Shatila.

Is this a kidnapping? He tries to memorize the path they're taking; that's all he can do. Past some kind of workshop, a mural in the PLO's honor, a small opening between houses that are barely more than hovels; he sees four children kicking a ball in the shadows. But it's useless.

"Where are you taking me?" he says to the man holding him by the arm.

But the man just glances at him without answering and quickens his steps. Suddenly the two men in front of him head to the door of a concrete building, which seems more substantial than most. One knocks.

The other man turns to Jacob. He no longer seems threatening; he's almost friendly, almost harmless. He points to a sign above the door. It's slightly illuminated by a fluorescent lamp that sways in the chilly breeze.

PALESTINIAN RECREATIONAL YOUTH CENTER, PRYC, the sign reads. In English and Arabic.

"This was where you wanted to go?" the man asks. "The youth center?"

Jacob swallows again. He can't believe it's true. They've taken him where he wanted to go. This wasn't a kidnapping; they just wanted to help.

"Thank you," he says. "I didn't know . . ."

He doesn't get further before the door opens and he sees Alexa's worried eyes in the gap. She looks at him, trying to place who he is for a moment.

"Jacob?" she asks. "What are you doing here?"

They sit down at one of several long tables with linoleum tops in a room that's used as both a cafeteria and a classroom. A woman is wiping down another table on the other end of the hall. Alexa puts a cup of tea in front of him.

"So tell me," she says. "What made you come all the way out here without even calling first? You were lucky to run into those guys; you could have been robbed. You know that, right?"

Jacob nods and feels the wound on his back start to ache again. For a while he'd almost forgotten it.

"So much has happened," he begins. "I don't even know where to start."

Then the dam bursts, finally, and tears start coursing down his face. Everything washes over him: Yassim and Myriam and the gunshots at Hamra. The kidnapping that never was.

He's expecting Alexa to put her arm around him, try to comfort him, tell him everything will be okay, and that she'll take care of him. But she just puts her hand on his and stares deeply into his eyes.

"There, there," she says. "Pull it together now, Jacob. Men don't break down around here. Do you understand?"

It takes him fifteen minutes to tell his story. Alexa doesn't say anything, just sits there completely still, listening. Half the time she doesn't even look at him, just stares at the wall without expression. When he's done, he takes a deep breath and buries his face in his hands.

"I don't know what I got caught up in," he whispers.

Alexa turns her face to him and looks at him calmly: "Beirut," she says. "You got caught up in Beirut."

She stretches out a hand and puts it on his back, runs her hand slowly between his shoulder blades until she finds the little bandage that covers the stitches and the chip.

"You can almost feel it through the skin and the bandage," she says. "If you know it's there."

Jacob just nods.

"And what happens now?" Alexa says. "You have something under your skin that you've promised to get out of Beirut. You're being hunted by the Swedish and probably US intelligence services. You can't exactly buy a ticket and fly home. What are you going to do?"

Jacob removes the thick envelope the bookseller gave him and slides it across the table to Alexa. She opens it and extracts the contents. Flight tickets to Brussels via Istanbul. A MasterCard. And finally, the most shocking thing of all: a Swedish passport, for one Patrik Andersson.

"Lordy," Alexa whispers.

It's the first time she shows any kind of reaction. Apparently, her limit is at counterfeit passports.

"They're quite serious about all this," she says, flipping through the passport. "This Yassim—I don't know him. I know he was at my party, but he arrived with someone else. Do you trust him? Or are you so blinded by love that you'll do anything for him?"

"I don't know," he whispers. "I do think I love him."

"Blind it is," Alexa says dryly. "But it doesn't really matter." She sighs and leans toward him, puts the passport back in the envelope again, lowers her voice. "Either you have information about war crimes beneath your skin, which the Americans, or somebody else, don't want made public. Or you have instructions for a terrorist attack or network or something like that. Either way you're fair game, Jacob. Either way you'll be hunted and imprisoned."

He sobs and puts his forehead on the table. The extent of what he's gotten himself into is finally coming into focus. "I know," he whispers.

"In other words, there is no help for you," she says. "But you know that. There is no state or institution that you can trust."

Jacob tries to nod, still with his forehead to the desk. It doesn't matter what's on the chip, or if he trusts Yassim, or if what Yassim says is true. He will be on the run or locked up; he'll be in danger no matter what he does.

"Is there anyone else who can help you?" Alexa's voice sounds distant, barely able to penetrate his self-pity. He shakes his head so that his cheek lies against the table as he looks at her.

"What do you mean, anyone else?" he asks. "What do you mean?"

"Someone at the university? A politician. A journalist? Anyone really, just someone you trust who has the power and influence. *Wasta*. Do you understand?"

Wasta. Always this *wasta*, these patrons. Always someone you can call when the police stop you or when you're denied some permit, or when you want your daughter to get into one of the French schools. A distant relative who's the mayor of a small town. A godfather whose brother is chief of the police. The connections are complicated, and the paths between people often laughably long. But Jacob has nobody. No one at all. He just shakes his head.

"Not here," Alexa says. "I mean in Sweden."

"Sweden doesn't work like that," he mutters. "It doesn't matter who you know."

"I get that it's not like here," she says. A slight note of irritation in her voice now. She doesn't have time for the obvious. "But someone who's independent. Someone you trust and who trusts you?"

"I don't know anyone," he says. "I don't have those kinds of contacts."

As he sits up in his chair and opens his eyes again, he remembers something he caught a glimpse of. Someone he read about. It's not much. Almost nothing.

"Can I borrow your computer or phone?" he says. "I want to check something."

NOVEMBER 24—BRUSSELS

PALE SUNSHINE STREAMS in through the bedroom window, and Klara wakes up in a panic and sits straight up. Has she slept the whole day away and missed the meeting?

"Fuck, fuck, fuck," she says under her breath, and bends over the edge of the bed to find her phone.

"What is it?" George mumbles.

Klara twists around and sees his naked body beside her. They had sex again. And fell asleep in each other's arms.

"What's the time?" she says.

George turns to the bedside table and a grotesquely large watch. "Half past eight. Calm down, it can't be that much of a hurry, can it?"

Klara falls back against the pillows again, less panicked, but still not calm. He puts the watch on his wrist. "I got this after all the bullshit in the archipelago. From my boss. It's a limited-edition Panerai; it costs tens of thousands of dollars. Pretty sick, right?"

She looks at the huge black watch on his wrist and shakes her head. "What's sick is that you walk around with that on your wrist as if it's normal," she says. "I've honestly never seen anything more vulgar."

George snorts. "Don't hold back, please," he mutters. "Tell me what you really think."

She glances over at him in all his wounded ego, wondering for a moment how she could have slept with such a person.

But then he turns to her, and his face is serious. "You're going to meet the guy today. Who do you think he is?"

She shrugs, sits up, and starts searching for her underwear. "How should I know? Even Gabi didn't seem to know."

"And those men you think are following you?" he says. "It has to be related, right?"

She finds her underwear balled up next to the bed and pulls it on. "I can't imagine any other explanation. Did I tell you I got some kind of adrenaline rush in Stockholm and almost confronted them at Bromma?"

George nods. "You have to find a way to shake them off," he says. "Before you meet this Karl."

"I wanna know who they are," she says. "I'm so tired of being in the middle of things I don't understand." She gets out of bed and turns to George. "Don't you have a job to go to?" she says.

"Just a couple of weeks left," he says. "It's not like I'm irreplaceable at the moment, obviously."

"Well, there's nobody out there right now anyway," George says.

He's just come in from buying croissants from a small nearby bakery, and he's standing with a steaming espresso in each hand, half hidden behind the curtains at the window, peering down toward the crossing where he bought food yesterday. Klara sips her coffee and stretches to get a better look. He's right. The street is empty except for a few men and women in suits on their way to work at the EU Commission or maybe at some law firm down on Avenue Louise.

"Do you think they gave up?"

"Maybe," Klara mutters. "But if they bought a last-minute plane ticket just to keep an eye on me down here, it hardly seems likely that they're about to give up."

George takes a sip of his coffee, his eyes still on the street. She looks at him from the corner of her eye. He's so concentrated and unexpectedly protective of her, and her overheated brain slows down when she's near him. She doesn't feel the constant panic. She doesn't feel so alone.

"Over there?" he says. "In that old BMW?"

Klara leans toward the windowsill and peers down. She can just make out the silhouette of someone sitting behind the steering wheel. He seems to be drinking something out of a big cardboard cup.

"Maybe," she says with a shrug. "But it's not the same guy as yesterday."

"That's the guy," George says. "I'm one hundred percent sure of it. He was behind me at the bakery just now. Bought a large coffee." He nods down at him. "He's drinking it now. Seemed Middle Eastern. Had a beard. Jeans and some short bodybuilder-type jacket that made him look like a big guy. He kept glancing behind him all the time in the direction of the apartment. Wanted to make sure you didn't disappear while he was getting his coffee. It's him for sure. They've just changed the guy, realized that you know they're following you."

Klara sighs. For a moment she'd allowed herself to think they might have miraculously let her go.

"Where are your pills?" he asks, and turns to her with a smile tugging at the corner of his mouth.

"My sleeping pills?" Klara asks.

"Yeah, unless you have more drugs you'd like to mention to me? Grab them. I have an idea."

NOVEMBER 15–21—BEIRUT

THE CONNECTION IS slow and unreliable, and it's driving him crazy, but finally the browser loads.

He starts by reading through a few articles about the scandal in Sweden this summer. The riots in the suburbs that were subsidized and even partly organized by a Russian company with links to the Kremlin. And the woman who exposed it all, whose picture he could hardly escape throughout the autumn. The young Swedish lawyer with red hair and eyes so sincere and intense that they burned straight through every photograph and video clip.

Gabriella Seichelmann.

Now he skims through the story again, and it's still unimaginable. That Säpo knew all about the Russians stirring up things in the suburbs, that the Russians paid criminals to organize the riots among bored teenage boys rejected by society. The cynicism of it all. And Säpo just let the suburbs burn in order to achieve some political advantage.

And then this Gabriella Seichelmann ferreted it out and told everyone. In article after article, news show after news show, she talked about how Säpo threatened her and her clients to keep them silent. It ended with the justice minister promising an investigation, despite the fact that Säpo denied everything or refused to comment.

She'd become a kind of celebrity, a symbol for those who dare to stand up to the powerful. A truth teller in the most literal sense of the word. And she was a lawyer.

Jacob looks up the law firm where she works: Lindblad and Wiman.

A few clicks later and he has her profile in front of him: a tasteful, serious black-and-white picture. And the number to her cell phone.

He takes a deep breath. She took on the whole establishment this summer. She seems dedicated and convincing and knows what she's doing. Maybe she has some idea or thoughts about what a person in his position should do? It'll be expensive of course, but he has no other choice now.

"Did you find what you're looking for?" Alexa has entered the messy office, stands at the doorway behind him. He spins around in his chair, away from her cluttered desk, and looks at her where she stands, still with a cup of tea in her hand.

"Well, it's no *wasta*," he says. "But it might be something. Can I borrow your phone?"

Gabriella answers at the first ring, as if she'd been waiting with phone in hand.

"This is Seichelmann," she says briefly.

Jacob is startled; he didn't think she'd just answer the phone.

"The lawyer Gabriella Seichelmann?" he asks after a short pause.

"The same," she says briefly and formally. "To whom am I speaking?"

"I can't talk long," Jacob begins, nervous to actually have her on the line, nervous how much it's costing Alexa.

"Then I suggest you tell me what you want," she says dryly.

The phone connection crackles from atmosphere and distance. "I've come across some information. That is, I'm in Beirut. And someone's given me some information that they want me to bring to Europe."

He stops. It sounds so fucking crazy.

"What's your name?" she asks. She sounds distracted, as if she's not listening properly or as if she doesn't take him seriously.

"I'm not crazy," he says. "I can't say what my name is. Call me Karl, okay?"

"Okay, Karl. Tell me, then. What is this information and what can I do for you?"

"A few months ago in Beirut I met a guy who's a photographer in Syria," he begins. "But it turned out to be a cover story. In fact, he's been gathering information about drone attacks that the West are carrying out, and how they're killing civilians. But he has people after him, and he asked me to get the information out of Lebanon. A Swedish spy threatened me, and today I was shot at when . . ."

"Calm down," Gabriella says. There's something new in her voice now, interest rather than suspicion. "Don't give any more details over the phone, okay? But you have a passport and tickets to Europe? And you're being hunted?"

"Yes," he says.

"When are you flying out and to where?"

"Brussels," he says. "In about a week."

"Okay," she says. "I can be in Brussels on the twenty-fourth."

Gabriella seems to be writing something down on her end. "Don't tell me which date you're flying," she says. "Buy a burner phone when you land. Call me, and I'll tell you where to meet me. Do you understand?"

"Yes," he says. "I understand."

Her obvious competence is an immense relief to him. She's silent for a moment as if thinking. "It's your only chance, the way I see it, if you don't want to contact the Swedish embassy, and you don't want to, right? You fly according to plan."

"Okay," Jacob says. "Thank you."

"We'll fix this," she says. "Just one more thing. Make sure you copy the information on the card and put it in a safe place. Send it by mail or whatever."

"That could be . . . difficult," he says.

"Just figure it out," Gabriella says curtly. "That information is all you have. Call me when you're in Europe. I'll meet you there."

And then she hangs up. Jacob looks up at Alexa, who's leaning against the doorframe of her tiny office. She gestures for him to accompany her.

"Come on," she says. "I have a slightly unpleasant suggestion."

Over the next few days Alexa takes care of everything. A bed at a hostel, a meal in the youth center's dining room three times a day. Even some English books that former guests left behind and a shaky Internet connection that allows him to send half-hearted lies to his colleagues at the embassy about how sick he is and that he won't be into the office this coming week.

The days go by, and he leaves bed only to eat and go to the bathroom. He hears the serious voices of young European volunteers but doesn't participate in their conversations. Just eats and goes back to his room, opens up an American thriller, and reads until he falls asleep.

How long does he lie there before he starts believing it's all a dream? Two days? Three? The wound on his back has almost healed now, and the chip almost doesn't hurt at all.

Besides the chip there's nothing to remind him of what he's been through. It's so strange to live like this. No contact with anyone, besides Alexa, who looks at him with worry and eventually stops trying to include him in the center's various projects. He doesn't have it in him. Doesn't dare. Just says "maybe tomorrow" every day but doesn't mean it.

On the fourth day, doubt settles in again. He can barely even remember Yassim's face, how his lips tasted, how his hands felt on his skin. The only things that exist are his stress, the hole in his chest, his doubts, and a task he doesn't really understand. He asks Alexa to borrow the computer in her office, just to read news and see what's going on in the world. She's told him to stay away from email if he doesn't want to be discovered, and he trusts her and is relieved to follow orders.

But he hasn't read his embassy email since he sent his excuse and he has to see if someone has answered or commented. So he logs in.

He has two new messages. One "Okay. Feel better" from Agneta. And then one from an address he's never seen before. Just numbers and a Gmail message, sent a few days ago. That's all. He clicks on it.

The message consists of three words in English. Nothing more.

Hold on. Soon.

But it's enough. Jacob's heart stops when he reads it, and suddenly he can feel Yassim. He stares at the email for five minutes, then logs out, erases his search history, closes the browser, and stands up. Two days left. That's all.

He almost floats out of the office into the empty dining room. He's almost back to his bed when he hears Alexa's voice behind him. "Jacob, it's time."

He turns around and sees her standing there, her dark eyes, her thick hair in a braid that hangs over one shoulder. But all he can think about is Yassim's message, and Yassim. He slowly shakes his head. "I don't know," he says. "Is it really necessary?"

But Alexa just nods calmly. She looks so determined. "The car's waiting. Remember what the lawyer said? You can't afford to chance it, Jacob."

He knows she's right. He knows love is not enough, that nothing is ever what it seems to be. So he shrugs. "Okay, let's get it over with."

A clinic that's even smaller than the one Yassim took him to, a room full of worried faces and feverish eyes, but Alexa guides him straight across the waiting room and into the doctor's office, which is barely bigger than a closet. No windows, just a shabby bed covered with cracked vinyl, a round stool, and a small table of wrapped disposable instruments.

The door opens and Alexa turns around, greets a woman in green surgical scrubs with a green shawl over her hair. Her eyes seem tired—maybe she's worked all through the night, maybe longer than that. Alexa kisses her cheeks.

"Thank you, Aisha," she says. "I owe you."

But the woman just smiles and shakes her head and pushes past Alexa. "We're even," she says. "For now."

She sits down in front of Jacob and looks at him with eyes as exhausted as they are cold and indifferent. "So," she says. "Alexa is my friend, and she says you have something under the skin on your back that I need to take out. Which I will. But I've been up for thirty-six hours, and I have a waiting room full of people who need my help. That means I don't want to hear anything from you, okay? I don't want to know who you are, why you're in Shatila, or what you have under your skin. And I don't want to hear any whining about how much it hurts. Short and sweet. This will take fifteen minutes, and I want complete silence from you. Is that clear?"

Jacob nods. Her sternness and competence are soothing, and for the next fifteen minutes, he allows himself the temporary relief of surrendering completely to someone else's demands.

Then they're back in the car again—Alexa, Jacob, and the small chip in a plastic bag in his hand. He turns it over and over in the yellow, dusty afternoon light.

"It's probably password protected," Alexa says. "So you won't be able to see what's on it. But that's not the point."

"What is the point?" Jacob whispers.

Alexa turns to him in the back seat and grabs his face, draws it close, and looks deep into his eyes.

"The point is that now you're not just a shell, *habibi*," she says. "Not just a passive vehicle. Now you have some kind of power, some kind of control. If you need it."

And so the week passes by, and the time is here at last. Jacob stands in the hallway of the youth center with his backpack next to him on the floor, the wound on his back aching more than ever. Alexa opens the door to the dark drizzle falling like a haze over the alley. A motorcycle idles energetically beneath the small staircase. A black helmet with a black visor covers the driver's head. Jeans and a motorcycle jacket that match the bright-red paint on the gas tank.

"Well, then," says Alexa, putting an arm around Jacob. "Bashir will take you to the airport."

Jacob turns to her. He's scared and stressed. No doubt about that. But he also feels relief, almost joy that it's so close to being over now. Finally, it's moving forward. He nods seriously to her. "Yes," he says. "Thank you for—"

But he doesn't get further, because Alexa holds up a hand to stop him. "Don't thank me now," she says. "Thank me when it's over."

He leans over to kiss her cheeks, but she holds him at a distance. "Aren't you forgetting something?" she says, opening a hand.

Jacob looks down in confusion at an unopened condom package in her palm. He looks up at her, smiles uncomprehendingly. "Well," he says. "I'm not really in the mood. I don't even know where Yassim is."

She laughs and shakes her head. "Darling," she says. "Your little secret? The chip? Did you intend to take it out of Beirut in your pocket?"

"You mean . . ." he begins.

She nods. "I mean you're going to swallow it like a good little drug smuggler, is what I mean."

His mouth still tastes like rubber. It felt like the condom got stuck halfway down his throat, no matter how much water he drank, but swallow it he did. And now he jumps onto the motorcycle behind Bashir, doesn't even dare to look at him first, just inches closer to Bashir than seems comfortable. Holds his arms tightly around his stiff, red leather jacket and keeps his eyes shut as they speed through the labyrinth of Shatila and out to the real streets and roads.

Before he knows it, they're on the highway to the airport. When Jacob forces his eyes open, he can see them weaving between honking cars, and he senses the yellow-and-green flags whipping in the darkness above the Hezbollah-controlled suburbs, which are hardly more than shantytowns. *This is the last time I'll see this*, he thinks. *The last time I'll travel this stretch.* He's leaving Beirut behind him. And more than that, he's leaving his old life here. Everything is new. Now there is only insecurity and fear. And love. Most of all, there's love.

At the airport, Bashir finally slows and follows the normal rhythm of the traffic. Then stops at the sidewalk outside the terminal. Jacob loosens his grip around Bashir's upper body, his arms stiff from holding so tight. He can barely straighten them out. He should say something to Bashir, who's flipped up the visor of his black helmet and turned around. But Bashir looks past him, up the street, and there's something in his eyes that makes Jacob fall silent.

Slowly, he turns around and sees what Bashir sees.

Up at the entrance that connects the terminal building and the parking lot sits a gray van with tinted windows, slowly rolling past the roadblocks and security guards. Panic grips his chest, bouncing through his blood. He thinks of the men at the Armenian bookstore in Hamra. The gunshot through the rear window of the taxi. How did they find him?

Jacob lowers the visor on his helmet with trembling hands and grabs hold of Bashir's waist again.

"Drive!" he says. "Please drive away from here."

NOVEMBER 24—BRUSSELS

GEORGE TAKES FOUR pills from the bottle Gabriella's neighbor gave to Klara and puts them on a wooden cutting board in the kitchen.

"Google suggests you do this," he says, starting to hack the pills up with a sharp Japanese knife. "And you know you can always count on the sociopaths, right?"

"This is the craziest plan I've ever heard in my life," Klara says. "Wouldn't it be better if I just ran away as fast as I could and jumped onto the subway?"

"That's plan B," George says. He stops hacking and turns to her. "Don't you want to find out who's following you?"

"Yes," she says. "I just don't see how this will help me answer that."

George bends over the cutting board and chops the last of the pills into a fine powder that he gently brushes into a small plastic container.

"Stop nagging and just trust me. We don't have any time to lose if this is going to work. He'll be done with his coffee soon."

He throws on his coat and puts the bottle on the floor of the hall while he ties his shoes. "Give me three minutes," he says. "That's all, Klara. There are small margins in this brilliant plan."

Klara shakes her head skeptically. "You've fucking lost it."

"Come up with something better then," he says with an even stare.

"I just did," she says. "Run down into the subway."

George puts an arm on her shoulder. "What do we have to lose?"

he says. "If this works, we'll find out more about these people. If it doesn't work, we do your plan, okay?"

Klara sighs. "Just do it then."

It's a clear, cold morning as she steps out of George's building exactly three minutes after he disappeared up the street, heading toward the intersection, past the BMW where her suspected pursuer sits.

She pulls her coat more tightly around her, forcing herself not to look at the BMW. But after she passes, she can't help but glance back at the man sitting there. Just like George said: wide shoulders and short beard, the same style coat as the other men she's seen following her. He's still holding a coffee cup in his hand. That's good, at least.

She's about twenty yards past the car when she hears its door open and close. She resists the urge to turn around but can feel her pulse start to quicken.

She starts to hurry, just as they agreed upon. Almost jogging now, which will force her pursuer to do the same.

She comes to the corner and turns to the right, catches sight of George straight ahead, even though he has the collar of his coat turned upward and a dark stocking cap pulled low on his forehead. He's leaning against the door of a closed restaurant, and when he sees her, he starts walking in her direction at high speed. She nods quickly, and he nods back. Resolute and focused.

Then she stops at the entrance to the bakery, as they decided, and lights a cigarette. She glances back toward the corner.

She can't believe her eyes. It happens just like George planned it. The man following her barrels around the corner, and George is standing there ready. He takes a step toward him, and they collide.

The man is much bigger than George, and George almost bounces off him. But George grabs hold of his hand, bumps into the cup, and backs up.

"*Oh, pardon!*" she hears George shouting. "I didn't mean to. I—"

"What the hell!" the man hisses. "Watch out!"

He catches sight of Klara and calms down, relieved he hasn't lost her and obviously not wanting to expose himself.

"Forgive me, forgive me," George repeats in French. He's brushing the man's jacket where the coffee spilled. "Let me compensate you, that's the least I can do. Let me buy you a cup of coffee."

"It's not necessary," the man mutters in heavily accented French. "Just leave me alone."

"Out of the question," George continues. "I insist."

The man seems confused. He's trying not to look over at Klara, still standing by the bakery, while also wrapping up the situation with George. The last thing he wants is to draw attention to himself. George apologizes again and then walks past Klara into the bakery without acknowledging her.

It takes no more than a minute for him to come out again with a cardboard cup of hot coffee in his hand. The man is standing where he left him.

"I apologize again," George says, handing him the coffee. "I'm so clumsy."

The man looks annoyed, but he takes the cup and shoos George away, who heads back toward his building, farther down the street.

Klara finishes her cigarette, pretending that she didn't see what happened between the men. She stubs out her cigarette, goes into the bakery and buys a loaf of bread.

When she comes out again, she no longer sees the man.

"He's back in the car," is the first thing she hears when she enters George's apartment. "With the coffee. I'm a fucking genius!"

She walks through the hall and into the living room without taking off her shoes or coat.

"He's drinking it!" George says.

Klara reluctantly goes over to the window. She can see the BMW, see the man sitting behind the wheel again.

"What if you got the dose wrong?" she says. "What if you kill him?"

"The glass is always half empty with you," George mutters. "You don't die from a few roofies. He'll just get a little fuzzy and disoriented, that's all. Which means his friends will come and check on him. Focus on him drinking the coffee. This is a fucking triumph!"

George has completely abandoned the idea of going to work. They barely speak, just fiddle with their phones. Klara throws a glance over at him on a regular basis, and she can feel him doing the same. Last night and this morning linger in the room like a force field, but neither of them knows how to handle it.

After about forty-five minutes George turns his wrist and looks at his oversize watch. "Should have worked by now, I'd think," he says, standing up.

"Okay," Klara says. "This is what we do: I head out, and if he catches on, I try to get rid of him in the subway or something. Then I meet Karl myself."

George shakes his head.

"Not a chance," he says. "I'm coming with you."

"I don't want to have to think about you too, George. Stay here, I'll call you afterward."

"But what if something happens? You know, if something goes wrong?"

"*If something goes wrong?*" she says. "What would you do then? Grab another cup of coffee?"

She walks over to him and strokes his cheek. It's the first time she's touched him since they woke up in his bed this morning.

"This is my problem, George," she says. "I want to take care of it myself. For Gabriella. Do you have a hat I can borrow? Anything that might change my appearance would be good."

George roots around in a box in the hall and finds a light-gray hat in thin wool. He pushes it down over her ears.

"At least be careful," he says. "Promise me."

She nods. George's blue eyes. She can't look away from them. Slowly she rises up onto her tiptoes and kisses him on the mouth. "I promise," she says, disappearing through the door, toward whoever is following her, toward whoever it is who got Gabriella arrested.

NOVEMBER 21—BEIRUT/BRUSSELS

THE GRAY VAN drives slowly through the barriers, approaching where Jacob sits on the back of Bashir's motorcycle.

"Please drive!" Jacob begs, folding up the visor of his helmet. "I have to get out of here!"

Bashir turns around and folds down Jacob's visor. "Calm down," he says sternly. "If we drive away now, we attract their attention. Just sit still and shut up."

The van is getting closer, just twenty yards from them now. Every fiber of Jacob's being is urging him to jump off the motorcycle and run away as fast as he can. But even if he gathered the strength to act, he's not sure his legs would carry him. The van is just ten yards behind them, and it slows and stops just outside the entrance to the departure hall. Jacob watches as the back door glides up.

"Drive!" he screams. "Please drive!"

He doesn't get further before Bashir elbows him in the solar plexus, and he doubles over against Bashir's back, gasping for air. "Shut up," he hisses.

Jacob turns his head back despite the pain in his stomach. The door is completely open now and a middle-aged man in a suit steps out. Then a gray-haired man and a woman in a beige suit. The driver jumps out and starts unloading suitcases. The passengers grab them one by one and head en masse toward the departure hall.

"It's a hotel shuttle," Bashir says, folding up his visor. "You need to stop this. You need to take a deep breath, do you understand?"

Jacob nods cautiously.

"If I'd driven off in a panic, we would have attracted attention," Bashir says. He gestures toward the parking checkpoints and police and soldiers. "A motorcycle acting suspiciously is dangerous around here, you understand?"

Jacob nods again.

"I don't know what kind of shit you're involved in," he continues. "And I don't wanna know either. I'm just the guy driving the motorcycle. But I've lived here long enough to know you can't panic. Remember that. Ice in that gut." He knocks his fist against Jacob's helmet.

"Thank you," Jacob says, unbuckling the helmet's straps. He feels stupid, like some excitable novice. At the same time, Bashir is right: he doesn't have a clue about what Jacob is up to. "I'll think about it," he says, leaving the helmet behind.

Bashir and his motorcycle disappear. Jacob throws his backpack on his shoulder and heads toward the departure hall. His fake passport is burning a hole in his pocket. Stress is crackling beneath his skin. The wound between his shoulder blades aches.

There's no point in waiting: it won't get any easier, so he goes straight to passport control. He's flying from Beirut to Brussels using a fake passport, with tickets issued in someone else's name. What happens if it doesn't work, if he's discovered? He sees Myriam's indifferent eyes in front of him, the men in the bookstore—Guantanamo. But he has no other option now; he's made his choice.

With trembling fingers he pushes his passport over the counter to a tired man. Should he make eye contact? Or turn his eyes away? What is one supposed to do when he has something to hide?

The man takes the passport and flips to the first page. He looks up at Jacob and then down at the passport again. Flips through the pages and is just about to push it back to Jacob when he stops and holds it up again.

He looks back and forth from Jacob to the passport. Jacob swallows and tries not to blink. He can feel his armpits break out in a sweat.

The man doesn't release Jacob from his gaze, as if nailing him into place.

"Excuse me?" Jacob asks. His mouth is dry, his voice barely more than a whisper. "Is there a problem?"

The man doesn't answer; he just holds the passport in front of him, as if to get a better look. Then he meets Jacob's eyes again. "Mr. Andersson?" he says.

Is it better to admit it? Will it matter? "Yes?"

The man closes the passport and puts it on the counter. "Your passport expires in six months," he says. "Just so you know."

He pushes the passport over the scratched gray countertop. Jacob almost thinks he heard wrong, shakes his head in disbelief then grabs the passport.

"Th-thank you," he says. "I'll . . . make sure it gets renewed."

He's almost at the security check now when he feels someone take a hard grip on his shoulder. He spins around and sees a soldier in a beret, a small, efficient automatic rifle hanging across his chest.

Jacob instinctively holds his hands out so that the man won't perceive him as threatening; the panic is almost paralyzing. The man takes a step closer and holds up a backpack. "You forgot this," he says. "At passport control."

Jacob shakes his head to make all the pieces fall in place. It's his bag. In all that stress, he forgot it.

He stretches out a shaking hand and takes the bag. "Oh. Thank you."

"Keep track of your belongings," the soldier says. "Next time it will be confiscated."

Just after six in the evening, Jacob lands in Brussels, and he's convinced that his shaky hands and blurry eyes will make the woman at passport control look more closely at his passport, push some little button beneath her counter. But she just glances at him and the passport and waves him on. It's so easy—he can't believe it's really happening, that he managed to escape Lebanon alive.

As he walks through the terminal, he realizes there are even more soldiers here than in Beirut. The Paris attacks just last week have left their mark. It feels absurd, but he slept for most of the flight, exhausted and wiped out after the stress at the airport.

What should he do now? He received no further instructions, just the tickets. Will someone come meet him? And what should he do if not?

And then he starts to think about Gabriella Seichelmann. Was it a mistake to pull her into this? It didn't seem like it when he was in Shatila with Alexa. Then, he was so scared and confused, felt completely lost and abandoned. And now he doesn't know if there will be a Belgian SWAT team waiting for him in the arrivals hall.

"No, no, no," he whispers under his breath, and heads for an electronics store near the baggage claim area and arrivals hall.

He buys a burner phone with the MasterCard the bookseller gave him and takes out the piece of paper with Gabriella's number on it. She answers on the second ring.

"This is . . . Karl," he begins. "I called you—"

"I remember," she interrupts calmly. "It's important we keep this short, Karl."

He takes a deep breath. "I'm here now . . . and I'm afraid," he says.

He hasn't even considered it before, just swung back and forth between a hard-won calm and full-fledged panic. Now he realizes how scared he is. Completely terrified.

"I understand that. But you have to hold it together. We have our meeting on Tuesday, as we already agreed. The elevator outside the Palais de Justice at four p.m."

Tuesday? Three days. It feels like a year from now. "But . . ." he says. "What should I do until then? I'm in Brussels now. What if nobody meets me, what if—"

"I don't think we should talk anymore about this on the phone, better if we discuss it on Tuesday. And as I've said several times now, I can't do it any sooner. I'm so sorry, but—"

"You don't understand!" He's raised his voice now, but gets control of himself and lowers it so as not to be overheard in the airport. "I'm being hunted by so many people. I need your help. Why don't you want to talk to me?"

The frustration and fear claw up along his spine.

"Because if what you're saying is true, we can't risk that you're being listened to."

"But there's no way they could have bugged me, I just bought this phone—"

"I'm hanging up now," she says. "We'll meet in Brussels like we planned. Don't call again unless you have to change the time. This is serious."

Her firmness and her calmness have an effect on him, and fear loosens its grip somewhat. Just a few days. A backup plan if all else fails.

"Okay," he says. "I'll manage."

Jacob follows the stream of travelers heading toward the exit. What will happen when he exits into the arrivals hall? Will Yassim be waiting for him? Just the memory of his face, his body, makes Jacob's hands tremble. But if he's not there? If he's been arrested?

The arrivals hall is full of people waiting for family and friends. He stops and scans the motley crowd, turning his head toward the taxi drivers and their handwritten signs. He thinks he's mistaken at first, but one of them is holding up a name that makes him jump.

Patrik Andersson.

The driver in a leather jacket sees him at the same time—he must have been briefed on his appearance—and starts to approach. "Mr. Andersson," he says in accented English. "Come with me, please."

Jacob looks around and hesitates for a moment. He has to trust this will work out, that Yassim will make it work out. He follows the driver out of the building. They pass by taxis and cross the street into the darkness outside, toward the parking garage.

"My car is over here," the driver says, without turning.

Jacob follows him toward the dull yellow lights of the garage. They don't take the elevator, just stay on the street level, heading deeper and deeper into the building, toward one of the most remote corners.

"It's just over here, not far," the driver says.

Jacob thinks he hears a car door opening and closing again and footsteps echoing.

"There," says the driver, pointing to an old black Citroën.

The footsteps are approaching from behind. Something's not right. There is no taxi; it looks like a private car. And why is it parked out here, so far away, despite the fact that there are so many parking spots close to the terminal?

"Wait," he says, stopping. "Who sent you to pick me up?"

The man turns to him with his hand in his pocket. He's holding a gun; it's obvious, far too obvious.

"Your friend sent me," he says. "Yassim."

Just as he says it, Jacob hears footsteps right behind him. He doesn't have time to turn, just feels his jacket being lifted above his waist, feels a cold breeze on his bare skin.

A needle is stuck into his side. The garage spins around, his legs buckling beneath him, and everything goes black.

NOVEMBER 24—BRUSSELS

KLARA EXITS GEORGE'S building and turns right, heading in the opposite direction from the intersection and the bakery, to avoid passing by the man in the old BMW. She sticks close to the gray buildings; this residential street is empty and silent at this time of day—most people are at work.

She hasn't gone far when she hears a car door open and close behind her. Damn, that was too simple. She'd been convinced George's plan would prove useless. Just a few more steps to the Avenue Louise, as quickly as possible, then down to Place Stéphanie and the subway.

She throws a glance over her shoulder. The side street where George lives is almost empty, except for a dark-haired woman in jeans. She turns her head to get a better look farther up the street.

There he is—the man with the beard. But he doesn't look at all like before, not nearly so driven and focused. On the contrary, he seems drunk or sick, and he's leaning against the hood of his car, searching for her while struggling to take out his phone.

George's pills have had the desired effect after all; the man is too inebriated to follow her. He's fumbling with his phone now. Is he about to call a colleague? She'd better hurry before they find a replacement.

Then she sees another figure crossing the street, headed for the man. George. She turns around completely. George is there now and grabs the man's hand, the one holding the phone. The last thing she sees before turning right onto Avenue Louise is George pulling the phone out of his hand and then shoving him so he's lying over the hood of the car.

"Damn it," she mutters, and starts to jog back down the street, back toward George and whatever bullshit he's up to.

"Seriously!" she cries as she approaches. "What are you up to?"

George is just a dozen yards away, and he turns to her with astonishment. He raises his arm and makes a shooing movement, while staring down the street. "Get out of here," he hisses. "There could be more of them, for fuck's sake."

But Klara doesn't listen. "What the hell, George?" she says. She's in front of him now, looking at him with equal parts irritation and frustration. "What are you planning to do?"

The man who was following her turns toward her, his face lost and confused. He opens his mouth to say something but closes it again. George pushes him back into his car, and he falls onto the wheel with his eyes closed.

"I'm trying to find out who these guys are," he says. Triumphantly, he holds up a small, old phone.

"What are you gonna do with that?" she says, pulling him by the shoulder, away from the car, back toward his door.

"I haven't thought through every detail," he says.

"*Quelle surprise.*"

They're at his door now, and Klara enters before George, heading up toward his apartment.

"Why did you come back?" he complains. "The plan was for you to get away."

"That was before you started mugging people," she mutters. She turns to him and gives him an annoyed look. "And if his buddies call him, what do you do then?"

George's eyes dart back and forth, struck by the holes in his plan. "I'll figure it out," he says. "Just thought we might be able to use the phone. See who he is. His contacts."

Klara shakes her head. "You asked him for the password too, right?" she says.

She opens the door to the apartment and enters the living room, sits down on the sofa. “Give me that,” she says.

George throws her the phone and sits in the armchair opposite her.

“A burner,” she says.

She presses the home button and a small screen with poor resolution lights up. A PIN code is required to be able to use it. But that’s not primarily what Klara wants to check. The screen displays the current time in digital numbers. Beneath the time stands what Klara assumes must be the day and month. But she can’t read it, because the letters are Cyrillic. The phone is set to what looks like Russian.

She holds it up for George. “Something very fucking shady is going on here,” she says.

George takes the phone from her, looks at it, and stiffens. “What the hell is this? Russian?”

Klara nods. She feels a chill run down her spine.

“So that explains the Eastern Europeans Gabriella wrote about in the letter. They’re Russians?”

“Seems so,” she says. “I don’t like this, George.”

“Me neither,” he says. “I think we better leave right now. Before his friends show up.”

NOVEMBER 23—BRUSSELS

THE ROOM IS dark and dank; just a single strip of gray light penetrates a sloppily painted black window near the ceiling. The smell of mold and rancid cooking oil radiates from the walls, filling the musty room.

Jacob's temples are pounding, his head aches, and as he opens his eyes, he's so cold his teeth are chattering. The wound on his back burns.

Is he in a basement? On a floor? He can feel a thin mattress beneath him, hardly more than a rug. Apparently he's lying on his side. He should sit up, but when he tries to he can't make his hands move. He tries to send signals to them, but it's as if they're stuck. His wrists sting, and he turns his head and looks down. There they are, tied up with white plastic ties.

The memory comes back in flashes and fragments. Flying out of Beirut, the man waiting for him with a name on a sign, the gun in his belt. The footsteps. The pain of what seemed like a needle. The legs that wouldn't hold him. The darkness.

He's flown from Beirut under a false name. Using a fake passport. And now he's been shackled in a cold basement.

Only Yassim knew which flight he'd take and under which name.

Despair washes over him. There are only two options. Either Yassim has lost control of what's happening. Or Jacob has been completely duped.

Then comes the terror. He screams. No words, just a bottomless, empty roar that feels like it might never end.

But it does when two men in ski masks throw open the door and come into the room. The scream ends when one of them bends down and slaps him across the cheek with a gloved hand so hard that his lip bursts and blood runs down his face and onto the dirty mattress. The other man pushes a big white rag into his mouth so no sound can come out.

One of the men grabs his shoulders and forces him into a seated position. Then he pulls Jacob forward until he's kneeling on the floor. Hands behind his back. Rag in his mouth. Blood flowing down his chin. The man leans over him, and Jacob can smell his acrid breath.

"Be quiet," he says in heavily accented English. "Not a sound."

He takes a step back and pulls a small gun from the waistband of his cargoes. He puts it against Jacob's forehead, and Jacob feels tears flowing down his cheeks.

Then he pulls the trigger.

The gun clicks, and Jacob collapses onto his side on the mattress again, his whole body shaking.

"Exactly," the man says, laughing quietly. "Keep your mouth shut."

Jacob nods.

The two men turn around and disappear out the door. He can hear them locking it behind them.

It's impossible to say how long he's been there when he hears someone outside the door again. Maybe an hour. Maybe twelve. The cold is a part of him now. Like frost has buried itself in his brain and spine. He's so hungry. And unfathomably, indescribably afraid.

Slowly the door is pushed open. In the dark he can't see what's happening other than a dark figure entering the room and crossing the floor toward him. It's not until the figure steps into the dim, gray light falling from the small window that he realizes who it is. And his heart stops.

There in the middle of the room stands Yassim.

Jacob tries to say something, but the rag just sinks deeper into his mouth, almost suffocating him. He manages to push himself up into a semi-seated position with his shoulder against the wall.

Yassim is here.

He's here.

The two men in ski masks have stepped into the room, but they're standing at the door. It may be the same men as before, impossible to say. Yassim is almost in front of him now and stops and stares at him calmly, without emotion, as if he's never seen him before, as if Jacob didn't mean anything at all.

When Yassim's boot hits him a few inches beneath the ribs, it's not the pain that paralyzes him but how surprising and inexplicable it is. He rolls into a ball on the mattress as best he can with his hands behind his back. He pulls up his knees, pain radiating in his abdomen.

The second kick hits him in the back and he screams into the rag stuffed into his mouth. It comes out as no more than a stifled mumble. He should close his eyes, but he can't. Instead, he keeps them open wide, staring up at Yassim. Unable to believe that this is happening, that his friend would do this to him.

Now Yassim squats down. He slowly pulls the rag out of his mouth, grabbing hold of Jacob's throat.

"What the hell have you done?" he says. "What kind of worthless fucking idiot are you? Do you understand how fucking dead you are?"

Jacob just stares at him and shakes his head; he can't answer even if he knew what to say.

"You took the chip out," Yassim continues quietly. "How could you be so fucking stupid?"

He finally lets go of his throat, and Jacob gasps for breath, his mouth dry from the rag that's been stuffed inside it for hours. But before he can say anything at all, Yassim has punched his face. There's a flash before his eyes, and he cries out in pain, humiliation, and confusion.

"Now you're going to tell me where the chip is," Yassim says.

Jacob tries to swallow, tries to make his mouth work again. "W-why are you doing this?" he sobs.

Yassim grabs hold of his neck again and starts to strangle him.

"Did you think I ever cared about you?" he hisses, then a laugh that's both dry and joyless. "You're so much more naive than I ever could have hoped, you little faggot," he says. "You thought we had a relationship after only seeing each other three times? Don't you get it? You're a tool for me, nothing more."

Yassim loosens his grip on Jacob's throat slightly, and Jacob gulps for air and coughs and almost chokes on his own breath.

"Tell me where the chip is," he says. "Or, I swear to God, I'll strangle you right here."

Jacob sniffs, tears run down his cheeks. "Don't kill me," he whispers. "Why are you doing this? Don't kill me."

"Then tell me, you stupid little shit," Yassim says, leaning over his face again. "Tell me."

Jacob has no other alternative, so he tells him, with blood flowing from the reopened split on his lip, with his face and body aching from the blows and kicks. He tells him about Myriam at the museum and how her men hunted him, how they shot at him. He tells him about Alexa in Shatila and how she called a friend who ran a clinic for the Palestinians in the refugee camp. That she took the chip out of his back and gave it to him in a small plastic bag without asking any questions. That he tried to find out what was on the chip, but that it was password protected. About how he hesitated and didn't know what to do. And how, finally, he decided to trust Yassim and take the plane out of Beirut. When he gets to that point in the story he closes his eyes and sobs so hard he doesn't think Yassim can hear him anymore. But hands press around his neck again.

"So where is the chip now?" Yassim asks. "What the fuck did you do with it?"

Jacob's thoughts spin. There's nothing left, he won't survive this. But he has to keep a cool head; he has to win some time. "I hid it," he whispers.

Yassim lets go, and so he's able to speak.

"I had it removed," he says. "And then I gave it to someone to keep it safe."

"Who?" Yassim says.

"A friend from the Swedish embassy," Jacob whispers. "She doesn't know what is on it, only that it is mine. But if she doesn't hear from me she will hand it over to the authorities."

Yassim just looks at him and shakes his head quietly. Then he throws himself on top of Jacob, presses Jacob's belly against the mattress, puts a knee in his back, grabs him by the hair and pushes his head down. Then he leans over and whispers in his ear: "Then it's time to call this friend now."

He lets go, sits up, turns around, and says something in Arabic. One of the men by the door answers.

"You'd better be telling the truth," Yassim says. "You don't understand what kind of trouble you're in."

Jacob can't even gather the strength to turn his head, but he can hear Yassim's footsteps making their way out of the room. Hear him saying something to the other men, hear the door opening and closing and the lock start to move.

Only then does he turn on his side.

And that's when he notices it.

He's lying on something. Something hard and sharp.

Something that wasn't there before Yassim came into his cell.

Jacob lies there, immobile, until he's sure that Yassim and the others are gone. His whole body is throbbing and tender from the beatings, and the wound on his back is burning.

They must have cut him open when he was drugged. Like he was just a package they could treat however they want, and throw it aside when its function was over.

Was Myriam right the whole time?

Alexa was definitely right. If he hadn't done as she said, he'd be dead now.

It is impossible to understand. That's all he was for Yassim. A tool. A package.

He won some time by lying about leaving the chip in Beirut. But sooner or later his lie will be discovered. Sooner or later, the chip will come out. His backup plan goes no further than that.

He slowly rolls onto his back. What he has underneath him lies in a rolled-up plastic bag, narrow and about ten centimeters long.

He grabs on to it and manages to find the opening of the bag. Spinning the plastic until he can stick his hand into it.

Something cold and smooth meets his fingers, and he runs them along the bag's contents.

A knife.

Eagerly, he rummages it out of the bag and feels it glide out of his hands and onto the mattress. With his heart pounding, he runs his hands over the dirty fabric until he grabs hold of it again. Fumbling carefully, he tries to keep the sharp edge away from his body and hands. Tries to poke it between his wrists and the taut zip ties.

It's easier than he expected. As soon as he finds the right place, the plastic falls off.

He can hardly believe it. Dares not believe it, so he lies there with his hands still behind his back. Lies there until he's finally brave enough to pull them in front of him, turning and twisting them in the darkness. Slowly he rolls onto his stomach again, amazed at how easy it is when he is no longer bound.

He holds the knife in front of him; it's just a small kitchen knife with a red shaft, the kind you use to cut vegetables. In the context of his dirty prison, its ordinariness feels foreign.

Yassim gave him the opportunity to free his hands. But why?

So he lifts the plastic bag and beneath it he finds a single, folded piece of paper. It's too dark to read the penciled lines on it, so he stands up and walks to the window whose gray light is getting weaker every minute.

Just two lines, written in a hurry:

The window is open.

Be quick.

Jacob looks up at the black-painted window. He stops and listens but hears nothing outside the door. The window is just above eye level. He walks over to it and reaches for the handle. There is a keyhole on it, and on top of that someone has drilled loops into the window and window frames and connected them with a padlock. He feels whatever small hope he had evaporate again. It's not open: the lock is still sitting there.

But he's wrong. As he pulls on the padlock, it opens. Someone has forgotten to lock it. Or unlocked it.

He turns around, toward the darkness of the basement. Next to the door he sees the contours of an old armchair. Impatiently, eagerly, he grabs hold of it and pulls it out into the weak light, toward the window and freedom. It's heavy and makes a scraping sound as he drags it over the raw concrete. But he can't worry about that now: he has to get out of here, has to be quick. Has to escape.

He thinks he hears something outside the door. Another door opening, a creaking. Are they heading back down the stairs? For a moment he considers stopping what he's doing, pushing back the chair, closing the window, throwing himself onto the mattress again and pretending to be bound.

But it's now or never. This is his opportunity to get out of here alive.

He's up on the chair, looking out into an inner courtyard or an alley, just concrete and trash and trash cans.

He hears it clearly. Someone is heading down the stairs, toward his cell, and the terror claws at him, as he stretches an arm out through the window. He feels the damp, cold stone in the courtyard against his hands but can't get a grip. He can't go farther, can't get out. He just stands there, hanging in his cell, halfway out, still a prisoner.

His feet fumble, and he manages to get a foot onto the backrest of the chair, can hear it cracking, threatening to collapse beneath his weight. He continues to grope around the stones of the courtyard until he finally finds an edge to hang on to. Then he pulls himself out, first his upper body, then legs, then feet.

Suddenly he's lying in the courtyard. In a cold breeze that makes the skin on his arms turn to gooseflesh. He wants to cheer and laugh. He's free. But now he has to get away, keep moving.

He gets to his knees and lifts his eyes. There's only one exit, and it seems to lead to a normal city street. He sees a small kiosk or convenience store on the other side of the street.

He can barely believe a normal world still exists out there, as he stands up and takes a step toward the street.

But he doesn't make it farther before a dark figure appears in the opening to the inner courtyard, blocking his way.

NOVEMBER 24—BRUSSELS

GEORGE MANEUVERS HIS car into the traffic on Avenue Louise. Down into tunnels and up again. Just before the major transit route heads into Bois de la Cambre, he turns left toward Place Flagey, and the two small gray ponds known as the Ixelles Ponds. Klara looks at the gray buildings with flaking shutters and small Portuguese bistros.

"You're going to miss all this," she says.

George glances at her. "Brussels?" he says with a shrug. "Why do you think that?"

"You don't notice it until you leave," she says. "And maybe not even then. But you notice it when you come back. Everything that makes you so furious when you live here: the strikes and roadwork and the traffic and all the fucking hassle. Then you move and come back, and you see all the people sitting around drinking their Leffes at some outdoor café in November, and you forget about all the bullshit. We've been here too long. No other city will be like this one for us."

George nods and parks the car by the sidewalk next to one of the small ponds. The trees are bare and straggly; a cold drizzle hangs in the air.

"I won't miss being hunted by the goddamn Russians, that's for sure," he mutters, and jumps out of the car.

They order a coffee and sit down at Café Belga's outdoor seating area, despite the cold. Klara wraps one of the café's beige blankets around her shoulders and stares out over the small square and the tram tracks in front of them. She lights a cigarette and sips her cappuccino.

"At least we have a good vantage point here," she says, "if they track us down again."

George takes a Marlboro from Klara's pack and looks back over his shoulder toward the big, bright barroom where young students and freelancers are bent over laptops, phones, and croissants. He turns back to Klara again. His eyes are so different than she remembers them, so much less insecure and arrogant. There's a depth there now, something almost like caring. And something more, something bigger that makes her body tremble, and it's so strong and surprising that she doesn't know what to do with it, so she looks away.

"Are we gonna figure this out?" George says. "It could be just about anything. And the Russians? I don't like it."

She feels him hesitantly putting his hand over hers. It's as if he doesn't really know if it's appropriate, if he has permission, despite what happened yesterday and this morning.

She turns her palm upward so she can lace her fingers with his. She feels his cold thumb stroking her wrist. It feels so strange and confusing to touch him, to hold his hand. More intimate than lying naked beside him in his bed. And when she turns to him and meets his eyes again, it is as though a door opens inside her. For so long it's felt like she was stumbling around in a big gloomy room, a cave or a tomb, trapped inside memories, and she didn't know what to do. Memories and guilt. She got lost in that room, didn't know how to find a way out, didn't know where the door was, or if there even was one.

But now, here in the gray chill of Brussels, just days after Gabi's arrest and her grandfather's funeral, with George's hand in hers, it's as though she found it. As if she fumbled onto the door handle in the dark, as if she turned it and discovered the door was never locked.

She looks at George. Sees his blond hair, his slightly worried eyes, feels his fingers playing with her own. He's not the door, not the one who opened it. But maybe he's the one standing there when she cracks it open.

"Yes," she says. "We'll figure this out."

NOVEMBER 23—BRUSSELS

"HURRY UP!" SAYS the person blocking Jacob's way.

But the voice isn't threatening, just stressed, urgent, anxious. Jacob lifts his head and sees Yassim coming toward him.

"Come on!" he cries. "We have to get out of here now!"

It's like in a dream where everything is turned around without explanation or context. His friend is suddenly a monster, then a moment later he's transformed into a friend again.

He hears movements and voices through the open window. His jailers are on their way into the cell.

"Come on!" Yassim cries.

After so long in the dark, Jacob has to squint under the yellow lights of the Christmas decorations hanging across the street outside the gate. His whole body hurts as he runs. And when the first gunshot cuts through the gray evening air he jumps. He hears Yassim shouting in his ear. "Faster! Faster!"

Then more shots, more deafening explosions ringing in his ears, as Yassim points to a small green Volkswagen Polo parked just down the street.

They jump into the car, and Yassim has it started before Jacob even has time to blink. He speeds off down the uneven street so fast, Jacob is pressed back against his seat.

The car sits low, almost directly on the road, and it jumps and bounces, and somewhere another shot sounds, and cars honk all around them. Yassim grips the wheel in his right hand, his left is resting on his knee, as if it were loose or powerless.

A red spot is spreading near the collar of his jacket.

His friend is pale, his eyes glassy, as he takes the curve with one hand and soon they're out on a slightly bigger road.

"You've been shot," Jacob begins. "Yassim, you got hit in the shoulder."

Yassim doesn't look away from the road, but he moves his right hand quickly back and forth between the wheel and gear stick.

"Is anyone following us?" he says.

He slows but only enough to be able to take the next curve without flipping the car. Jacob turns around. He sees nothing at first, but as they swing left, a black car appears at the corner they just rounded. It's driving almost as fast and recklessly as them.

"A BMW," Jacob says. "They seem to be after us."

Yassim has already swung off the road, taking a ramp to an underground garage. He crosses between cars and finds an empty parking spot at the bottom of the stairwell.

"Out!" he says to Jacob.

He's already halfway out of the car. The garage is damp and smells like urine, and they take the stairs two steps at a time. They're on a landing now and it's just two more floors, then they'll be out on the streets of the city again.

Jacob can see the streetlights above. Somewhere in the distance he hears a siren. He takes the first two steps but then stops when he hears Yassim panting behind him.

"Wait!" his friend wheezes. "Wait a second."

Jacob turns around and sees Yassim leaning against the wall. His breathing is heavy and strained.

"What?" Jacob says. "They must be in the garage by now too."

But there's something in how Yassim leans, something in how he's breathing, that makes Jacob understand it's impossible.

"Come here," Yassim says instead. "I have something in my pocket, but"—he indicates his hanging arm—"but I can't get to it."

Jacob is at his side now, very close. Yassim's familiar scent in the midst of the stench of the stairwell.

"What's happening?" Jacob whispers.

But his friend doesn't answer. Jacob thinks he can make out a motor in the garage, but he can't be sure.

"I'm sorry," Yassim says, turning to him. "We have so little time."

He sinks against the wall, down onto the floor. Jacob leans over him and opens his jacket hesitantly to access the wound, but Yassim stops him. At the same time, in the garage, a car door is closing again, and there are footsteps on a concrete floor.

"Fuck it," he says. "Nothing you can do about that."

His voice is so weak now. He coughs and Jacob thinks he's going to spit blood, but he doesn't and that's a relief, in the midst of all this unspeakable terror.

"You have the chip, right?" he asks. "Somewhere? It's not still in Beirut?"

Jacob looks at him. How could he know that? Below them he hears the door of the stairwell opening. Several pairs of feet heading up the stairs.

"Who are you?" Jacob whispers as his panic grows. "First you helped them capture me, then you helped me escape? I don't understand anything. You're hurt and I . . . I . . . I . . ." He can't talk anymore. It's too much he doesn't know, too much he doesn't understand.

"You have to make sure that chip ends up with someone you can trust, someone independent, someone who's not in intelligence or the police. Do you know anyone?"

Jacob nods. "I believe so."

Yassim stretches out a trembling hand and caresses his cheek.

"I knew I could count on you. In my pocket there's a phone and a few hundred euros. Take them; you'll need them. Now you have to go."

"What about you?" Jacob says. "I can't leave you."

But he stretches down his hand and grabs the money and phone, puts them in his pocket. He already knows that he has no other alternative.

"I can handle it," Yassim says. "I have nine lives."

But he looks down the stairs, blinking. As if he can't quite gather the energy for this one last lie.

Jacob rises, he feels a lump in his throat that he can't do anything about. "You have to make it," he says. "You can't disappear now—we just met."

Yassim smiles. "You remember the roof terrace?"

Jacob nods, feeling tears welling up in his eyes. "How could I ever forget?"

Yassim reaches behind himself, to his lower back, and suddenly he's holding a big, heavy gun in his hand. He grimaces, and Jacob sees again how his left arm hangs uselessly at his side.

"You have to go now," he whispers. "You have to trust me."

Jacob swallows his tears and bends down and kisses him on the cheek. Then he turns around and heads up the stairs two steps at a time.

By the time the first shot rings out, he's already on the street.

NOVEMBER 24—BRUSSELS

TWO HOURS LEFT until Karl arrives for his meeting at the elevator outside the enormous courthouse, the Palais de Justice. Klara's sitting with George at the Häagen-Dazs café at Place Louise, just a few hundred yards from the meeting place.

She stares through the big windows at the chaotic roundabout, where the traffic seems to be standing still. Men out shopping in dark cashmere overcoats and women with Chanel bags mingle with tourists and Romanian beggars at the metro stop just outside the window. If she raises her eyes, she can see the more or less constant construction site around the dome of the courthouse, a renovation that never seems to be completed.

She glances at George. Not even a day has passed since she came to Brussels. Since she had a panic attack, was followed, had sex with George, and drugged a man. Now she's waiting to meet a mysterious person Gabriella was supposed to meet.

"What are you thinking about?" George asks, catching her eyes.

She shrugs. "It's been an eventful twenty-four hours."

She points to George's phone sitting in front of him on the table next to their coffee cups. "No news?"

It's been half an hour since he sent the license plate number of the Russian's car to Jean-Luc, a man George calls a fixer, who seems to be some kind of combination of private detective and administrative genius. The PR firm George is leaving apparently uses him to investigate various things within the jungles of Belgian bureaucracy.

I'm still technically employed there, George told her. *I'll just have him bill it to the Philip Morris account. No one ever checks the details on that one anyway.*

George shakes his head. "Not yet."

He glances at Klara, but she averts her gaze, looking back only when he's no longer looking at her. She shouldn't have room for such strong feelings. But something flutters inside her, knots up, when she allows her eyes to follow the clean lines of George's small, straight nose, clean-cut jaw, and high cheekbones. Or the hair that's curly and messy now. She remembers how he touched her, in the night, and at Café Belga earlier, and she can hardly sit still. Is this all in her head? Or does he feel the same?

She doesn't have time to explore her feelings any further before George's phone starts to buzz on the table in front of them. With a quick movement, he unlocks it. "Now we'll see," he murmurs.

Klara tries to wait a moment to let him read the message, but she can't stand it. "What does it say?" she asks.

George clears his throat. "Rental car."

Klara sighs. "Should have known. So we don't know anything."

George looks at her with amusement. "I don't think you really understand Jean-Luc," he says. "I wouldn't call him a genius if that were as far as he got."

"Okay . . ." Klara says. "This Jean-Luc can access the records of the car rental agency?"

George just smiles. "Here," he says. "Apparently, the car was rented by some guy named Phillippe Brouchard. That doesn't tell us much."

"The guy you drugged definitely was not named Phillippe Brouchard," Klara says dejectedly. "Of that I can be sure."

George nods. "Well, the interesting thing about Brouchard is that apparently he's a Belgian citizen employed by . . . wait for it . . ."

"For what?"

"The Russian embassy."

"You're kidding me," Klara shouts. She realizes she's raised her voice, so she leans over toward George and whispers instead. "That's fucked-up," she continues. "What in the hell did we get ourselves into?"

George shakes his head dejectedly but can't hide a small, tired smile at the corner of his mouth. "Same shit you always end up in, Klara."

"What do you mean?" she continues. "They're spies? I thought this Karl guy was some sort of Snowden. What does that have to do with Russia? And Syria? And how did Gabi get pulled into this?"

George puts his hand on hers and looks into her eyes. "I think the only way to know is if we meet Karl," he says. "Right?"

Klara drinks the last of her cold coffee. She grimaces and turns to George. "He probably won't come alone," she says.

George furrows his brow. "What do you mean?"

"If they've been keeping an eye on me, the risk is large that they've got one on him too." She falls silent and closes her eyes while massaging her temples. "Karl contacted Gabriella, who was probably arrested by Swedish cops. Before that, she was being followed by the Russians, most likely."

"Was it the day before yesterday they arrested Gabriella?" George asks.

Klara nods. "Tomorrow they'll have to charge her if they want to keep her any longer. A court has to decide, and the decision will be public. Then we'll find out why they're holding her, if she has a lawyer, and so on."

"If it's not classified," George says.

"We surely have to find out something," she says, frustrated.

He turns toward her, waits for a moment before gently putting his hand on hers again. Klara feels calm spreading from his hand into hers. A calm that spreads out over her grandpa's death, and Gabriella's imprisonment, over all the grief and weirdness and terror. Cautiously, she squeezes it. It feels so unexpected to have him at her side. She leans her head onto his shoulder and turns her nose to his neck and gently takes in his scent.

"What the hell should we do then?" she whispers. "What if he's also being followed? What happens then?"

George gently strokes her hair. "We'll come up with something, Klara," he whispers. "We always do."

We, Klara thinks.

What an unbelievably rare thing.

NOVEMBER 24—BRUSSELS

JACOB HAS BEEN sitting in a McDonald's all morning. He uses a map app to figure out that he's on Boulevard Anspach and that the dirty, stately building with the big, wide staircases on the other side of the street is the old stock exchange. Twenty-one minutes on foot to the meeting place, according to the app.

At three fifteen he stands up. Crumples his hamburger wrappers and throws them into the trash can on his way to the door.

Then thrusts a hand into the pocket of his newly purchased jacket, fingering the hard plastic of the memory card. Slowly he pulls out the card and looks at it again. It looks so small and insignificant.

Alexa saved his life when she took him to her doctor in Shatila. Had him roll it up in a condom and swallow it like a drug mule, then he fished it out of a toilet in McDonald's. He carefully puts the card back into his pocket again and walks out into the drizzle on unsteady legs.

He tries to keep up his pace, partly to keep warm and partly because he doesn't trust the map—he doesn't trust he'll be on time. He can't be late for this meeting.

Brussels is gray and gritty. Not exactly the type of city that impresses people right away. But all that gray is soon mingling with antiques stores and chocolate shops, small cafés, a square full of restaurants, and something that looks like it might soon turn into a Christmas market. Suddenly, a winding street opens up onto another small square, and there on the other side of it sits the massive Palais de Justice, as solid as a fort, a tangible reminder of the consequences of the law.

Brussels seems to be under siege. He saw it in the subway yesterday and down in the city earlier today. Military vehicles parked on the side streets, police and soldiers patrolling everywhere. It makes him nervous, but probably it's just related to what happened in Paris. He read about it before he flew here: all of Europe is on high alert.

But as he slows down and stares out over the small square, he freezes in his tracks. Two soldiers in red berets carrying heavy guns stand just outside the glass elevator, which connects the lower part of Brussels to the higher level, where the court is located.

He checks the time. Fifteen minutes to go. He looks at the soldiers again. They're chatting with each other, but he can sense their alertness. Should he simply walk by them?

He looks at the time again. Twelve minutes to go. If there are guards posted down here, what does it look like in front of the courthouse? Probably they've put extra resources everywhere.

"They're not looking for me," he whispers quietly to himself. "They don't know who I am."

Ten minutes to go. Had he arrived earlier, he might have been able to find an alternative route and avoid using the elevator, but now he has no choice. He hesitantly starts to move along the edge of the square toward the elevator, stress pounding his head.

The soldiers have moved to the center of the square, and he pulls his hat down over his ears and turns.

He reaches the platform where people climb on the elevator. Eight minutes. He quickly puts his phone back in his pocket and runs his fingers over the memory card, just to make sure it's there.

Behind Jacob, the elevator dings, and he turns slowly. The elevator is empty save for a man standing with his back to him, staring out through the elevator's glass wall. He's blond, his hair a bit tousled, and when he turns around Jacob can see he has tortoiseshell glasses and is about ten years his senior. Handsome, dressed simply in jeans and a dark-blue coat. On his wrist sits the most gigantic watch Jacob has ever seen.

The man quietly exits the elevator and stops when he catches sight of Jacob. For a moment, they look at each other. "Are you Karl?" he asks in Swedish, breaking eye contact.

Jacob feels his hopes start to rise. He wants to throw himself around the neck of this man, whoever he is. "Yes," he says. "I'm Karl."

The man seems to have barely heard him but just walks by quickly. As he does, he whispers something in Swedish, so quietly that Jacob almost doesn't catch it. "Follow me, twenty yards behind. Gabriella says hello."

Jacob turns around only after the man has made his way across the square. Carefully, tentatively, he takes a few steps in the man's direction.

It seems like the man's phone is ringing, and he takes it out of his pocket and stops. Something in his posture changes, Jacob can see that as he turns around. For a second, their eyes meet. The man seems to collect himself and then continues to cross the square, still with the phone to his ear.

Jacob looks around one last time and takes a deep breath. Then he starts to follow the man away from the elevator.

NOVEMBER 24—BRUSSELS

KLARA IS GRATEFUL it's just a quarter to four, so rush-hour traffic hasn't started clogging the streets yet. She pulls George's Audi out of its parking spot and maneuvers it onto the Boulevard de Waterloo, then down the slope toward Rue Haute, where she and George have agreed to meet.

Just fifteen minutes to go, and she has to struggle to keep her breathing normal. She wishes she hadn't let George go in her stead. She should be the one meeting Karl, like they'd planned from the beginning, since Karl was probably expecting a woman. But George insisted: if the Russians were in place, there was less risk he'd be recognized.

Slowly she turns up onto the narrow, one-way Rue Haute, past bakeries and dive bars, toward the antiques district, which she often strolled through on weekends when she lived here. That really was another life.

Six minutes to go now.

What is the worst-case scenario? That Karl never shows up but the Russians do? That Karl doesn't know anything about what happened to Gabriella or why they're being followed? What are they supposed to do then? They haven't even discussed that.

Four minutes.

Klara's almost at the square below the elevator now, and she allows the car to creep along the asphalt while she searches for somewhere to park. She can't go all the way to the square without risking discovery, so the plan is for George to lead Karl here.

That's when she sees it.

Just ten yards ahead of her, very close to the square, a black van with its engine idling. It has to be the Russians.

The lit clock on the dashboard reads 4:00 as she takes out her phone and calls George.

He answers on the third ring with a concentrated, resolute tone in his voice. "I think I have him," he says.

Klara feels the stress tearing inside him, inside her. "They're here," she says. "The Russians. You'll see the van when you turn around the corner onto Rue Haute."

"Damn," he whispers. "Are you sure?"

"No," she says. "Or yes. My gut is quite distinct on this point."

She hears George take a deep breath.

"Just take it easy," Klara says. "Continue walking toward the car like we agreed."

"How are we gonna get away from them?" he says.

Klara feels her blood pumping and pounding through her body. What she's about to suggest crosses all boundaries. But she didn't choose to be involved in this. They, whoever they are, will have to suffer the consequences.

She sees George coming around the corner farther down the street. "Wait," she says quietly. "Do you see the Russians' van?"

She can see him searching along the street. "Yes," he says. "I see it."

She takes a deep breath. "You brought the gun, right?" she says as quietly as she can.

NOVEMBER 24—BRUSSELS

HE'S ABOUT HALFWAY across the square when the shots ring out between the old, gray buildings. Jacob freezes, no place to hide in the middle of this square. At first he doesn't even make the connection. The sound's too loud and violent. But then there's another shot, and he hears screaming, slamming doors, footsteps running in all directions.

The man who met him is gone. Jacob is now almost at the street, standing there in a daze, as a shiny dark-blue Audi suddenly stops right in front of him with the man from the elevator hanging out the window, screaming at him.

But it's as if he can't hear him. As if he's behind a glass wall and reality can't penetrate, the world is just a silent movie.

He slowly turns his head and looks up the street, as if in slow motion he can see men in jeans and leather jackets jump out of a black van. It's only then that life returns to him, reality returns to color and sound, and he hears the man shouting from the car, right in front of him.

"Come on!" he screams in Swedish. "Get in the car now! Hurry up, for fuck's sake!"

Finally he obeys and takes a few steps toward the car, rips open the door, and falls into the back seat. Somehow he gets the door closed again, and the car almost leaps forward, with Jacob's face pressed against the cool leather of the seat. He hears the engine rev, and the man's stressed voice somewhere in front of him, but he doesn't have the strength to turn around, can't even take in where he is, who they are, what's happening around him.

Finally he lifts himself up onto an elbow.

"Take a right there!" the man shouts.

"Where? The next one?" says the person driving.

Jacob is almost sitting up now, and he sees it's a woman driving. Black hair, short, some kind of pixie cut, probably around thirty. She's holding on to the wheel so hard her knuckles are white.

"Next turn," the man says.

The man sounds calmer now, but it's hard-won, as if he's trying to tame something that's coursing inside him. The car turns and slows down.

"Damn it!" the woman shouts. "Damn, damn, damn!"

She drums her hands on the wheel, and Jacob realizes that they're stuck at a red light and the traffic is heavier here. He turns around and sees a queue forming behind them as well. Slowly the lights change, and they follow the traffic forward again.

The man turns to look through the rear window, maybe to check if they're being followed.

"Hi," he says hesitantly to Jacob. "I really hope you are who we think you are. Otherwise, I don't really know what to say."

"How does it look?" the woman asks grimly. "Do you see anything? Are they after us?"

She's driving calmly now, following the traffic down a wide street toward a roundabout with a statue in the middle. Buses and trams pass by in the opposite direction.

"I don't know," the man says. "Not that I can see."

"What . . ." Jacob begins. He wants to help them keep watch but doesn't know what to look for. "What happened?" he says.

"Klara here had the brilliant idea of shooting the tires on the Russians' van," the man says. "So they couldn't follow us when we picked you up."

Even after everything that's happened to him in recent months, this sounds very strange. He's just falling deeper and deeper into the rabbit's hole. "*Russians' van?*" he says hesitantly.

"*Yes*," the man says. "I feel like we have a lot to talk about." He turns back again, looking at Jacob. "Just so we're completely clear on things, you are Karl, right? And you did contact Gabriella Seichelmann?"

Karl. He'd almost forgotten that was the name he used. He nods. "My real name is Jacob," he says.

Klara follows the traffic to the right, between a park and something that looks like a dilapidated palace.

"The Royal Palace," says the man when he sees Jacob bending to look at it. "Shall we do a little sightseeing on our way out of town?"

"Do you think anyone saw us?" the woman asks. "Is someone following us? Not just the Russians. Anybody else? The police?"

The man shrugs and turns to her again. "I don't think anyone saw what happened. They definitely heard the shots, but I played the whole thing rather coolly if I do say so myself."

The woman throws a quick glance at him. "It was chaos, George. You don't shoot tires in the middle of a city without someone calling the cops. The question is whether they saw us or the car."

"Who are these Russians you're talking about?" Jacob asks.

The man turns around and looks at him attentively. "We hoped you could tell us. Please say you know what all this bullshit is about."

Jacob just shakes his head. "I don't know anything. I'll tell you what happened to me, but then I have to know who you are. I was supposed to meet Gabriella Seichelmann . . ."

"Yes," the woman behind the wheel says without looking away from the street and the traffic. "That's a reasonable request, I'd say."

They weave in and out through blocks full of office buildings, EU flags, and straight roads, while Klara and George tell their story. About how it started a few days ago when Gabriella Seichelmann was arrested in Stockholm and Klara received a letter from her about this meeting.

They don't seem to be a couple; in fact they make a point of telling him they're just old friends. But there's something about the way they talk to each other, look at each other, that makes Jacob wonder if maybe they haven't realized that they're in love.

They've entered a long tunnel, which ends as they finish their short story.

"So that's all we know," Klara says. "Which is to say basically nothing. Gabi has been arrested, and it seems like the Russians are mixed up in it."

"And that *you* probably have something to do with it," George says. "Now, we're hoping you can explain to us what the hell is going on. What happened to Gabriella."

Jacob takes a deep breath. "I don't know," he says. "I don't know what happened to Gabriella, but I can tell you what happened to me."

NOVEMBER 24—BRUSSELS

"BEFORE YOU BEGIN, Jacob," she says, turning to George. "Where are we headed? I'm just driving blindly here."

They're almost out on the ring road around Brussels. Out of old habit Klara is driving toward the airport, but their plan stretched no further than picking up Karl at the Palais de Justice.

George looks away from Jacob and back to her. "I don't know. Depends a little on what you say, Karl, or Jacob, or whatever your name is."

"I don't know where to start . . ." Jacob says. "I contacted Gabriella because . . ."

Slowly and quietly, almost hesitantly, the young man they have in the back seat starts to tell them a story. He starts from what he says is the beginning. An internship at the Swedish embassy. A rooftop in Beirut. A garden at a deserted palace. A mysterious man and an overwhelming and passionate love.

Then a young woman who claims to work for the Swedish intelligence service. And a memory card that's surgically inserted under his skin. A love that slowly turns to doubt. Here he falls silent. As if it's become too much, tears start to run down his cheeks.

"But he's dead now," he whispers. "Yassim is dead."

Klara lets go of the wheel with one hand and reaches back to touch his knee, to show she understands what it's like to lose someone in the way Jacob just lost Yassim.

George regards Jacob with suspicion. "What a fucking story," he says. "It sounds almost a little too dramatic."

"I want to remind you that you drugged a Russian spy this morning and shot the tires on a van like we're in a goddamn gangster movie," she says dryly. "You might not want to talk about what's a little too dramatic."

He flinches as if offended and turns to Jacob again. "I just mean it doesn't hurt to be a little critical," he mutters. "Who is this Yassim anyway?"

Jacob looks at him, annoyed. "I'm just telling you what happened."

"Don't mind him," Klara says. "George is a well-known asshole. But, Jacob?"

"Yes?" Jacob says weakly, and looks at her.

"What's on that memory card, and where do you have it now?"

"And you still haven't explained who these Russians are," George adds. "Or why you contacted Gabriella."

Jacob takes a deep breath and stares out at the dusk falling around them. "Yassim's part of a group that's been collecting information about drone strikes in Syria," he says. "About all the civilians who have been killed, all the war crimes. That's the information on the memory card. Myriam calls him a spy because the information is classified."

"So Yassim is the new Snowden?" Klara says. "Is that what you mean?"

He nods. "I guess so. And I guess Myriam is working on behalf of the Americans somehow. That's what Yassim says, that all the Western intelligence services are working together."

"What a jackpot for a brand-new embassy intern," George says, turning to him. "Straight into the thick of it?"

Jacob shrugs. "It wasn't my choice to end up here."

"But there's something that doesn't add up," George says.

Klara is silent for a moment, then she nods gently. "Yep, it doesn't explain the Russians. And it doesn't explain Gabi's arrest, which is the reason *we're* here."

"I don't know anything about any Russians," Jacob says quietly.

"Also your story doesn't account for the fact that your boyfriend kidnapped, then saved you. What the hell is that all about?"

"I told you I don't know." He lets his head fall forward again, into his hands, and it sounds like he's sobbing.

"The memory card," Klara says. "That's the key. Where is it?"

In the rearview mirror, she sees Jacob stick a hand into the pocket of his long parka. When he takes it out again, he's holding a small, insignificant piece of plastic.

"Is that it?" says George, almost sneering. "Why didn't your boyfriend just email it to whoever was going to take it?"

"Yassim said they never use email or computers connected to the Internet," Jacob says. "Everything is done face-to-face."

"And Gabriella?" Klara says. "Why did you contact her?"

He pauses before answering. Why *did* he contact her? "I read about her. She seemed tough, independent. And I didn't know what would happen when I got here. What if I flew to Brussels and Yassim never showed up? Should I go to the police after what I went through in Beirut? I thought I needed a backup. And I guess I was right."

The rain has started to fall harder and harder, and Klara adjusts the wipers.

"We're going home," she says quietly. "No sense in staying here. We're driving back to Sweden."

It feels good to make a decision, to have a goal, a direction, even if she has no idea what's waiting for them there either.

George types their destination into his GPS, and they follow the blue line on the digital map: Leuven, Cologne, Hamburg, Copenhagen.

"Ten hours to Malmö," he says. "Then we'll see where we go from there."

3

NOVEMBER 24—BELGIUM/GERMANY

It's getting dark by the time they pass Leuven, and by Liège, night has definitely fallen. Klara glances in the rearview mirror, but all she can see is a long line of headlights behind her.

"I wonder if someone's following us," she says. "I can't imagine that we got away that easily."

"Believe me," Jacob says from the back seat. "It wasn't that easy."

"One thing I still don't understand," George says. "You had the card under your skin until some shady doctor took it out. But you still have it, even though they imprisoned you in a fucking cellar? How did that work?"

Jacob looks out the window into the rainy darkness. "There are several ways to smuggle things inside the body," he says quietly.

"What do you mean?" George asks. "Did you stick it up your ass?"

Jacob turns and looks at him evenly. "It was Alexa's idea. She thought I should take control of my situation. She's smart." He falls silent, stares out the window again. As if he's still caught inside what's happened to him over the past weeks and is finding it hard to speak.

"She didn't know Yassim," he continues quietly. "She didn't know who he was, what we had. I guess she thought he was using me. So she arranged everything with the doctor. We got out the card and found a reader, Alexa has some friend who works with IT stuff. But the card was password protected, of course. The IT guy tried to break into it, but he couldn't. The encryption was too sophisticated."

"So you still don't know what's on the card?" George says, rolling his eyes.

But Jacob barely hears him. "Afterward, Alexa said she could keep it for me. But I promised Yassim I would bring it. How could I betray him? So she gave me a condom."

"She gave you a condom?" Klara says, looking curiously at him in the rearview mirror.

"I put the card in it before I left for the airport. Then I swallowed it."

"Like a drug mule," George says.

"Basically," Jacob says. "And I was able to get out of the cellar before, well . . . you know."

They stop for gas at a rest stop outside Duisburg. The rain is falling heavily now, but Klara needs air and a cigarette. She pulls her jacket tight around her and makes her way between parked semis to the edge of the parking lot.

The traffic on the autobahn whizzes by, and even if she can't see much in the darkness she knows the landscape here is flat, just asphalt and boggy fields, typical northern Europe.

She lights a cigarette and takes her phone out of her pocket, weighs it in her hand. She and George agreed to keep them off. Who knows who might be listening or following their movements via phone. She's been through too much in recent years to leave anything to chance. But it's been almost eight hours since she checked it last, and she just has to see if someone tried to reach her.

Gabriella's detention hearing was today. The first thing Klara plans to do tomorrow is to call around and find out where they're holding her and on what grounds.

So she turns on her phone. Just a quick peek to make sure nothing new has happened. But as soon as the phone finds a network, it vibrates in her hand. A text from a Swedish number she doesn't recognize. Just two short sentences:

Secret email. Check it.

NOVEMBER 24—DUISBURG

KLARA IS SITTING in the passenger seat, drumming her fingers restlessly on her phone, while George calmly steers his car out onto the autobahn again.

She glances over at him. How is he so calm? They've been on the run for several hours now, driven out of Belgium, are now making their way north through Germany. But how long will it last? They shot a gun in central Brussels at the very moment that terrorists from the Paris attack are being hunted down in Belgium. Of course somebody noticed. Is it just pure luck that they made it this far?

Her head starts to spin. Maybe they should have switched cars. Or just stopped somewhere and given Jacob's fucking memory card to the police. But would that even help? Somebody arrested Gabi, and they have to find out why and what's on that card before making any big decisions. Plus Gabi has now made contact.

"Gabi sent an email to my secret account," Klara says. "But I'm paranoid and don't dare log in on one of our phones."

"What do you mean a secret account?" George asks.

"We opened an anonymous account a few years ago," she says. "The first time we landed in a situation like this. So we would have a channel to communicate that wouldn't necessarily be intercepted. We haven't used those accounts for a very long time. I hope I remember the password."

George nods. His face looks almost terrifying in the cold light of the road and the dashboard.

Staring out the passenger-side window, Klara thinks she hears a helicopter. It could be a coincidence, could be anything, but it's clear that George hears it too. A sign indicating an exit in two kilometers for a rest stop appears.

"We have to get another car," she says. The rest stop looks like all other rest stops they passed by in the past few hours. A gas station and auto shop, a crummy restaurant, semis and continuous rain.

"Try to park somewhere so the car won't be immediately visible," Klara says.

They drive a few turns until George points to a garage.

"There," he says. "It's a self-service carwash. We'll rent it for an hour while we figure out what the hell we should do."

"We have to get out of here," Klara mutters. "That's what the hell we should do."

They park and jump out. Klara turns around and looks at Jacob. He's tall and skinny with blond hair and soft, almost fragile features. He looks a bit angular, with his high cheekbones and straight nose. But he's not ugly; on the contrary, there's something appealing, almost beautiful about his face. He also looks exhausted. Heavy bags under his eyes, a cracked lip covered by an ugly, black scab. His eyes are bloodshot and tired.

"You need to sleep," she says, putting a hand on his shoulder. "We'll just have to make sure you do. But first we have to get a ride."

She turns to George. "Take Jacob to the restaurant and get him some food. But be quick. I'll be back soon."

George's eyes turn warm. "You've made a comeback from your panic attack. Shifted to a whole other gear."

He winks and turns to Jacob. "Come on. Let's go get a burger or something."

Klara heads for the gas station, walks in between the candy and soda and car accessories. George is right. She hasn't even thought about it, but she feels like a different person today. She's full of energy and ideas despite this awful chaos. It's pointless to analyze it, better just to use it while it lasts.

At the checkout counter, she finds what she's looking for. "I want one of those prepaid phones," she says. "Does it include Internet?"

The man nods tiredly and puts it in a bag. "One gigabyte anywhere in Europe," he says. "Two hundred euros, please."

Klara pays. And when she steps out into the rain to go to the restaurant, she hears the helicopter blades clearly. "Fuck," she murmurs to herself as she starts to run across the parking lot. She'd hoped they'd have a few minutes. They're so close now.

George and Jacob are standing inside the door waiting, paper bags in their hands.

"We're in a big hurry," Klara tells them. "Get moving. The helicopter will be here soon."

"Where?" Jacob asks in panic. "We don't have anywhere to go."

Klara's already opened the door. "I said I'd take care of it," she says. "Come on!"

As George and Jacob rush behind her toward the trucks, they hear the sirens getting closer.

"Klara!" George shouts. "What the hell is going on?"

But Klara is already stopped in front of a huge, modern semi with Polish plates.

The rain is pouring down now, big heavy drops. The door of the truck opens from the inside, and she jumps into the cab as George and Jacob catch up to her. They hear her say in English, "Thank you so very much, you don't know what it means to us. We'll have to get the car towed tomorrow."

The driver, who is in his fifties, was the third one she spoke to. A colleague pointed him out in the store. He's headed north to Sweden. It could hardly be better. But when she asked him about a ride, he told her in his limited English that his employers didn't allow hitchhikers, and at the sound of the helicopter blades Klara felt her panic rising.

"But it's just me and my two friends," she said, and looked him straight in the eyes in a way she hoped was full of promise. "We won't be any trouble. Quite the opposite."

"Okay," he said in the end. "But you better be fast, I leave in five minutes."

"I might have given him the impression that you were girls," Klara says now over her shoulder to George, who's heading up the steps into the cabin behind her. "Just so you know."

She turns to the driver again and smiles. The cabin is modern and comfortable with two leather chairs and shining instruments. A crucifix is attached to the top of the instrument panel. The driver looks over Klara's shoulder and must see George's head appear; the disappointment in his eyes is obvious.

"Is that your friend?" he says.

Klara nods. "George is his name. He's very nice."

The driver sighs and draws back a curtain to a sleeping area behind the seats. A surprisingly comfortable-looking bed with a yellow bedspread is visible in the dim lights of the gas station.

"Your friends ride back there," he says. "You ride with me."

Klara nods eagerly. *This is going to work. He won't throw us out*, she thinks.

She turns to Jacob and George again. "Hurry up, for fuck's sake," she whispers urgently. "Before he changes his mind."

They've barely gotten into place behind the curtain when the blinking blue lights of the first police car appear on the highway. They drive past the gas station as more sirens start to blare.

"Better get going," she says in English. "Don't want the police to slow us down."

The driver turns to her with a questioning look. Is he starting to figure it out? Three people stuck at a gas station. A significant police presence. She feels George's gun, hard and heavy in her right pocket.

Please drive, she thinks. *Just drive. I don't want to have to use this.*

NOVEMBER 24—DUISBURG

THE SIRENS ARE everywhere. Jacob can hear Klara asking the truck driver to drive. George has crept over to the curtain of the sleeper cabin and is peeking out at the gas station. Jacob can see his foot bobbing nervously on the yellow bedspread. Cautiously, Jacob crawls over beside George and peeks through the drapes as well, just as the blue lights start to blink through the windshield of the truck.

Time stands still. Klara doesn't say a word, and when Jacob turns his head to see what she's doing, she looks almost unconcerned, keeping her eyes on the driver. But she's grinding her teeth; her legs are jittering, and she has a hand stuffed into her pocket.

Finally, the driver makes his decision. Without saying a word, he turns the ignition key. And before Jacob can really take in what's happening, the driver steers his truck between the blinking blue lights, past the parked cars, up onto the on-ramp that leads to the freeway. The rain streams down the windshield, and Jacob hears it clattering onto the roof. He pulls back into the sleeper cabin.

"Damn, that was close," George says next to him.

But the relative peace doesn't last for long. It is just a matter of minutes before they hear sirens again in the distance.

"What the fuck should we do?" he asks Klara through the drapes. "How did they find us?"

"They must have found the car and talked to the other truck drivers,"

Klara says with an unexpected, unaccountable calm. "Put the pieces together, guessed our only option was this truck."

Jacob sits up now, crawls over to the drapes. He looks out and sees the blue lights bouncing through the darkness in the cab. They make Klara's face seem ghostly. The driver turns to her with a question on his face, and Klara meets his eyes, unflustered.

"I'm gonna climb back there with the others," she says. "And you tell the police I asked you for a lift, but I never showed up."

Jacob sees her pull something halfway out of her pocket. Something that flashes in the blue light and looks surreal in her hand. Black metal. A gun.

The driver gives her a curious glance, and Klara keeps the gun out of his sight.

Jacob can barely breathe. "Klara, maybe it's best if we—"

But he stops. What happens if the police arrest them? What will happen to Klara and George? To him?

"We're not criminals," Klara says calmly in English to the driver. "I promise. The opposite. We have something we need to get to Sweden. It will all work out in the end, but if the police catch us, people will die. I'm not kidding about this."

Jacob sees her put the gun on the seat next to her. The police car behind them signals with a few loud honks, and the driver starts to slow so he can stop on the side of the road. He turns to Klara again with an expressionless face. Jacob sees her cocking the gun.

"Hide," the driver says. "I'll talk to the police."

They stare at each other silently. The truck has almost stopped moving now. Klara puts the gun in her pocket again, shoos Jacob and George out of the way so she can crawl behind the seats.

"Move, you two." She turns to the driver again. "I trust you," she says.

Then she slips behind the drapes and squeezes in between George and Jacob.

NOVEMBER 24—DUISBURG

IT TURNS STRANGELY quiet as the driver pulls the truck over onto the shoulder of the highway and turns off the engine. There's just the drumming of the rain on the roof, and the traffic swishing by.

It gets louder when the driver opens the door and hops out to meet the police.

"We're so fucked," George whispers.

Klara doesn't answer him. She's trying to listen, but all she can hear is the rain and the road.

"But they don't have anything on us," George continues.

"Just the shooting at the Palais de Justice," Klara mutters.

A few minutes go by before they hear the door of the cabin open again. All three of them hold their breath. Klara's hands are so sweaty she almost loses her grip on the gun. What is she planning to do with it anyway? Threaten the police? Shoot them? That would be insane, and not helpful at all.

She carefully raises the mattress and puts the gun beneath it. Better not to have it on her when the policemen arrest them. She should tell Jacob to hide the memory card as well.

Then she hears someone climbing the steps to the cabin. The door slams, the engine starts. The truck slowly starts rolling forward, then accelerating, and eventually joining the traffic on the highway.

Klara looks at George and raises her eyebrows.

He shrugs slightly, as if he can't believe it's true. They wait a couple of moments, as if to make sure.

Klara bends forward and looks through the gap in the drapes. The driver turns around and smiles at her. “Coast is clear,” he says. “Is that how you say?”

Klara furrows her brow and climbs up to the passenger seat. She turns to him. “Why did you protect us?” she says softly. “You really don’t know anything about me or the boys back there.”

He adjusts in his seat and puts his hand lower on the wheel. Klara can see tattoos peeking out from under his sleeve and on the back of his hand. Letters and symbols on his fingers and knuckles. He turns and smiles at her. “You remind me of my daughter,” he says. “Tough.”

Klara smiles back carefully. “How old is she?” she asks.

Without answering, he lets go of the wheel with one hand and removes a wallet from his trouser pocket. He fishes out a faded picture of a woman in her twenties.

“Old picture,” he says. “I haven’t seen her in ten years.”

“Ten years? Why so long?”

He puts the picture on the seat and knocks on his own head. “I’m stupid,” he says. “Prison. No good for her.”

He looks sad, then he turns and smiles at her again. “But I hate the police. So, good for you. I said you talked to me. But you wanted to go to Berlin.”

“Not so stupid, I’d say,” Klara says, and leans back in the chair. “Pretty smart, in fact. You surely bought us some time.”

Klara’s been sitting with the burner phone since they left the police, trying to gather her strength. Now she finally turns it on and it blinks to life. She takes a deep breath, opens the browser, and goes into her secret email account.

There’s only one new message, sent yesterday, and from a Hotmail address that consists of numbers. Yesterday? Did they release her yesterday?

Klara clicks on the message. Three sentences.

> We have to meet as soon as you come back from Brussels. Email me here to tell me you're okay, nowhere else. Don't contact the police before we meet.

The last sentence has been bolded. Klara looks up from the phone and stares into the darkness and the gushing rain. "What is this, Gabi?" she whispers. "What the hell is this?"

Then she turns to the truck driver. "Where in Sweden are you headed?" she asks.

"Gävle," he says, without looking away from the road.

"Can we go with you to Stockholm?"

He turns and looks at her with an amused expression. "You think I'd throw you out now? After I lied to the police for you?"

Klara smiles and shakes her head. "No," she says. "No, I don't."

NOVEMBER 25—MALMÖ

SOMEBODY IS SHAKING him gently, and Jacob rolls into a ball to protect himself. He's back in that damp basement; they're waking him up to assault him. Reluctantly he opens his eyes and around him is only blackness. The air is so stuffy he has to take a deep breath to get any oxygen at all into his lungs. But then he hears the sound of the engine, gets the unmistakable feeling of movement.

"Wake up, kid," George says, shaking him, more impatiently now. "You slept through Germany, sleepyhead."

Slowly Jacob sits up. A faint streak of blue light from the driver's cabin penetrates through the gap in the drapes. George whispers something to Klara. Then he turns back to Jacob again.

"Come and look," he says, pulling back the drapes. "Home."

Jacob crawls toward the opening and sees only night and asphalt. But part of the night is compact and bottomless, and he realizes that must be the sea, and beyond the sea are the lights of a city. And in front of them stands a high, sleek bridge, lit up like silver in the dark.

"Malmö," George says, pointing to the glittering lights. "Feel good to be home?"

Jacob can't believe it's true. For a moment he feels something almost like relief. Then he sees Yassim's face in front of him. His lifeless arm in the car. The blood spreading from his shoulder. The light in his eyes slowly going out.

He bends forward and looks at Klara under the cold lights of the lamps outside. She seems wide awake. Did she sleep at all? Her dark hair is a little messy. There's something sexy about her, Jacob thinks. That determined nose, those high cheekbones. There's something about her that makes him curious. She looks like somebody who's been through a lot and come out on the other side stronger for it.

"Did you eat some gape-soup?" she asks in a surprisingly broad, exaggerated Östergötland accent.

"Excuse me?" he says self-consciously. "I don't know what that means."

"Ah," she says, turning to him with a smile. "Just something we used to say in the archipelago where I grew up if someone stared at you."

As they drive across the bridge, the semi starts to slow and the driver turns to Klara with a troubled expression. "We have a problem," he says, pointing to the tollbooth.

Ahead of them a row of trucks is slowly inching forward. A few cars are doing the same thing in another line, but it's too early for commuters.

"What's going on?" Klara says.

"Border control," he says. "They're looking for something. Maybe refugees." He narrows his eyes at her. "Or maybe for you."

"They weren't supposed to start checking passports until after Christmas," George says.

The driver shrugs. "I guess they're looking for you, then?"

Klara meets his eyes calmly. "We got this far," she says. "Can you help us again?"

He sighs and rolls in slowly behind the last truck in the queue.

"You remember what I said?" he asks.

"That you hate cops?" Klara replies.

"That I'm stupid. Jump back with the others."

Slowly they roll forward and stop at what looks like a temporary blockage, right after the tollbooth. Jacob hears the driver open the door. "What's this?" he asks.

"Routine check," answers a female voice in English.

"What are you looking for?" the driver asks.

"Like I said, routine check. May I please see your passport and will you climb out of the vehicle."

"No," the driver says to Jacob's surprise. "If this is a routine check, I refuse to show my passport. Schengen Agreement. Routine checks at borders are prohibited. My shipping agent can sue you."

"What in . . ." says the woman. "Now you do what I say. Get out of the vehicle. And put down the phone."

"No," says the driver. "No, I won't. You said this is a routine check. That's illegal. So I'm recording this."

They can hear him pressing all his weight into his seat. Then the woman's radio crackles, and she says something they don't quite catch.

"I'm climbing in," she says. "And you don't move."

They hear the driver grunt something and then the cop climbing up. Through the little gap they can see her flashlight bobbing around.

"Move," the cop says.

"Tell me what the reason is for this inspection," the driver says. "Or I refuse."

"Put that down," says the officer harshly.

"My phone?" he asks. "I'm not going to do that. What you're doing is illegal."

The police officer sighs and hops down to the ground again. "Drive to the side of the road over there. We're not done here yet."

Jacob hears the driver pulling the door closed and slowly rolling down along the road. "Yes," he quietly mutters in English. "We sure are."

Then he accelerates, not toward the edge of the road, but up onto the highway as fast as his truck will go.

Klara has crept out of the sleeper cabin and back toward the seats again, and Jacob hears sirens behind them.

"I'm gonna stop at a parking lot," the driver says to Klara. "Someplace where you can disappear. Now, as soon as I can."

The truck careens off the highway. "Here," he says. "There's a McDonald's up there. You jump off there."

The sirens almost disappeared when they got on the highway, but now they're louder again.

"Okay." Klara nods. "We'll take it from here."

"You only have a few seconds," he says. "They're right behind us."

Jacob feels George pushing him forward into the cab of the truck. "Get ready," he says. "Now's not the time to fall into a coma."

The truck slows quickly. "In ten seconds," the driver says calmly. "As fast as you can. I'll stop so they can't see you as they come off the highway."

The truck stops and the driver shouts: "Now!"

Klara gets the door open and pushes Jacob out, and they tumble onto the wet asphalt, with George at their heels. They stumble toward the entrance as fast as they can. From the exit they can see the blue lights flashing, hear the sirens approaching.

Behind him, Jacob hears Klara's voice before closing the door of the truck: "I hope you contact your daughter," she says. "Ten years is too long, no matter what you've done. Believe me, I know."

NOVEMBER 25—MALMÖ

BLUE LIGHTS ON the other side of the truck, doors being thrown open and slammed shut, voices raised as Klara pushes Jacob in front of her, in among the parked trucks next to the gas station near the McDonald's.

George is somewhere near her—she knows she doesn't need to take care of him; he can take care of himself. In the midst of all the chaos she feels such unbelievable relief to have him there. Jacob, on the other hand, seems drugged or in shock and is barely able to make his way forward.

"Come on now!" she whispers, pushing him between two trailers. "You have to move, Jacob."

She sees George stop right ahead and peek out around one of the trucks, toward the blinking lights. He waves to them, and Klara drags Jacob.

"We can go straight across the parking lot and into McDonald's without them seeing us," he says. "Hide in plain sight, you know? They won't be expecting us to just sit down calmly in a McDonald's."

Perhaps he's right, it would be much worse if they were caught out here among the trucks without being able to explain how they got there. Maybe the restaurant is the best option. "Okay, let's go."

It's barely six o'clock in the morning, so there's no rush at McDonald's. Besides them, the room is almost empty; just three other people sit alone with hot coffee. Through the windows Klara sees the blue lights flashing, attracting the attention of the other guests who raise their eyes to see what's going on. Long, bright beams dance across the wet asphalt. Police officers search under and between the trucks with flashlights.

"Fuck," says Klara. "I don't have a good feeling about this."

George turns to her. "They seem to know what they're looking for."

Jacob has gone over to the counter and frozen midstep in terror. Klara goes to him and puts a hand on his shoulder. "Come on, Jacob," she says, stressed. "Let's go."

He points to a table where the first edition of the morning newspaper lies. The front page makes her almost lose her balance, and she grips Jacob's shoulder so as not to stumble. The page consists of three passport pictures in a row under the heading:

SWEDES WANTED FOR TERRORISM

The pictures are of Klara, Jacob, and George.

"Fuck," George whispers behind her. "We have to get out of here."

They stumble out and across the parking lot, with the semi and the blue lights at their back, half running, half sneaking, so as not to draw attention. When they manage to find cover behind a car wash, Klara glances back at the entrance to the McDonald's to see two cops heading inside.

"Just in the nick of time," she says. "Lucky we didn't sit down and drink a milkshake."

They head down a small slope of wet grass, toward an uneven road that passes between two flat, empty fields and darkness. Somewhere near the bottom they see a bridge. Klara takes out the phone she bought in Duisburg and opens the map app.

"We have to get out of here," she says. "I have no idea how much time we have. We don't know a fucking thing."

She checks where they are as they jog down toward the bridge. Maybe they can at least get some kind of cover there.

"What should we do?" George pants.

"Call a taxi," Klara says. "And pray the driver hasn't read the morning papers yet."

They're sheltered behind one of the columns beneath the bridge when they see the taxi approach.

"Come on," Klara says. "Let's try not to look like we're on the run."

They brush themselves off and walk down to the road just as the taxi stops. Klara gets into the front seat. She can feel the weight of the gun in her right pocket, and she sticks a hand inside and runs her fingers along cool metal. A last resort. Her hand closes around it.

But the driver seems tired, completely uninterested, and she gently releases her grip on the gun.

"Malmö Central Station," she says. "Our car broke down."

The driver nods quickly and rolls up the hill, back toward the rest stop where the truck dropped them off. As they pass by the exit, Klara sees two police cars, blue lights still flashing. The taxi driver turns his head to look, then speeds onto the highway.

"Malmö," he sighs. "Always some bullshit going on."

The central station is starting to fill up with morning commuters as they cross the departures hall, toward the ticket machines. Their faces are on the morning papers and on broadsides everywhere.

"This is surreal," George mutters. "Klara shows up in Brussels, and two days later I'm a wanted man in Malmö."

"We have to get out of here," Klara says. "We can't flounce around surrounded by pictures of ourselves."

George nods. "I'll take Jacob. He doesn't really seem to be able to handle himself right now."

They both glance over at Jacob walking beside them with his straggling hair and empty expression.

"You have to give me that memory card," Klara says. "Whatever it is, we have to make sure it doesn't disappear."

Jacob takes the card out of his pocket and puts it in Klara's outstretched hand, then takes his cell phone from his pocket. "I think I might have the solution," he says, holding the screen up to her.

His hand shakes as he holds the phone out, and Klara grabs hold of his wrist to steady it. A message is on the screen. A long line of numbers, letters, and symbols.

"Is that what I think it is?" Klara says.

Jacob blinks and looks around nervously. "How should I know?" he says. "But I got the phone from Yassim . . . it's his phone."

George pulls Jacob's hand closer to get a proper look at the screen. "The password," he says quietly. "Who sent that to you?"

"I don't know," Jacob says. "Blocked number."

"There's only one way to find out," Klara says.

"But we need a computer, and a card reader," George says.

"We can buy one when the stores open."

"How?" Klara says. "We can't exactly use our own cards . . . that won't work."

"Maybe we can use this?" Jacob holds up the credit card Yassim gave him.

They go back and forth about it for a while, but in the end they decide to use the credit card; no one has any cash and their own cards are most certainly being tracked.

Before leaving the station, they use the card to buy tickets to Stockholm from a ticketing machine. Klara will take the first train, just after eleven. George and Jacob will travel together an hour later.

They find a small café on a side street where the staff seems busy enough with early customers not to care who their guests are. Famished, they order grilled cheese and salami sandwiches and large coffees.

"I can honestly say this is the best thing I've ever eaten," Jacob says.

He's regained some color in his face. They shared hamburgers in the truck early yesterday evening, but Klara wonders how much he ate in the days before that.

"Enjoy it," George says. "Who knows what they'll feed you at Gitmo."

Klara puts her hand on Jacob's. "Ignore him. We're going to take care of all this. George and I have been through worse."

Suddenly time is running short, and George stands up. "Stay there," he says. "I'm gonna go buy a computer."

"That was fun," George says with a smile when he returns to the café a half hour later. "No matter the circumstances, I like buying stuff."

He puts a white Mac box on the table in front of them and what looks like an adapter; Jacob assumes it must be the card reader. He pulls a gray hoodie out of an H&M bag and throws a dark-blue hat to Klara. She pulls it over her head.

"Not the world's most advanced disguise," she says. "But better than nothing."

"That credit card is awesome," George says, looking at Jacob. "I'm keeping it. Feels good to go home with a brand-new computer and have no clue who's paying for it."

He's got the computer going now, and he clicks through the installation.

"Don't get on the Internet," Klara says. "Don't set up any networks."

George nods without looking up. "I'm not a complete idiot. I've learned a thing or two from all this bullshit. Give me the card, Jacob."

"Klara has it," Jacob says, and nods to her.

George messes around with the computer until an impatient Klara decides he's too slow and pulls it away from him. She pushes the card reader into the port. Its icon appears on the computer's empty desktop. She clicks the icon and a dialogue box asks for a password.

"Okay," she says to Jacob. "This is it. Read what you got on your phone."

Klara counts, checks the numbers, letters, and symbols. Sixteen on the phone. Sixteen on the screen. In the same order.

The slight murmur of the other guests. The clinking of the cups. The surreal normality of this morning.

She meets George's eyes, then Jacob's. "Okay," she says. "Here we go."

Without waiting for a response, she presses enter.

Immediately the dialogue box disappears from the screen and a folder pops up. Inside sit four documents with the names: Stockholm, Brussels, London, and Rome. Jacob and George lean closer so they too can see the screen. Klara glances at Jacob.

"It doesn't look like drone pictures," she says quietly.

He doesn't answer, but she can see his face blanch, notices his breath becoming shallow and labored.

"Open Stockholm," George says.

Klara takes a deep breath and double-clicks on the document. A regular PDF that takes a moment to open up and fill the screen.

"For fuck's sake," George says in frustration and stands up.

The document is in Arabic, with bolded headlines and bullet points and checkmarks beneath them. Like schedules and checklists of some kind.

Klara feels her spirits sink. She turns to Jacob. "But wait. Maybe you know Arabic? You were . . ."

But he just shakes his head. "I took a couple of semesters," he says.

"I can order coffee and ask about the weather. I know the alphabet and could spell my way through that, but I have no idea what it means."

Klara continues scrolling down in the document, and then she stops. "George, check this out."

"What?"

He hunches down next to her again, and she points to the screen where a map of a couple of blocks in central Stockholm has appeared. The castle, the water. And—with a circle around it—the opera. Below the map there are photos of the opera house from various angles. Entrance, ticket office, the foyer. Some of the pictures contain red, numbered arrows. They seem to match text in the document.

"What the hell is this?" George whispers.

Klara looks at his damp, frozen face. He already knows, but she says it anyway.

"This . . . is a plan for a terrorist attack."

NOVEMBER 25—MALMÖ

JACOB LEANS FORWARD toward the screen, as if getting closer would make it somehow easier to read Arabic.

A terror attack!

How could he have been so naive, so incredibly stupid? Allowed himself to be fooled so thoroughly.

But was he really? Or didn't he suspect this all along? Not a terrorist attack, but something more than what Yassim told him. And he decided not to care, to just allow it, whatever it is, whoever Yassim really is, to happen anyway. Beside him, he can hear Klara and George bent over the computer whispering to each other, visibly upset as they scroll through the other documents on the memory card. Jacob knows he can't escape this. He carried terrorist plans into Europe, and he allowed himself to be used.

"We have to take this to the police immediately," he whispers. "What are you waiting for?"

Klara turns her face to him, apparently confused. "Excuse me? Go to the police now?"

"Yes!" he says. "This isn't my fault! The police can't blame me! I was tricked into smuggling it!" He's struggling not to shout.

George puts an arm around his shoulder. "Calm down, buddy. We will contact the police, I promise. But there's too much shit mixed up in all this, believe me."

Jacob shakes himself free, can feel his whole body trembling. "What kind of shit? We just have to . . ."

"You brought this into Europe, Jacob," Klara says calmly. "My friend has been detained and seems to be in hiding now. We've been followed by Russians, and we're all wanted as terrorists."

She falls silent and looks at him, lets what she's saying sink in.

"Right now," she continues, "*giving this file to the police* just isn't an option. Not until we know what this is about."

"But how will we find out?" Jacob says bleakly. "It's in Arabic . . ." He throws his arms wide in despair, sinks back down into his chair. He's thinking about Myriam in Beirut, about the men who followed him until he escaped into Shatila, about the basement in Brussels, about Yassim on the stairs, about his own picture on the front pages. He knows they're right. The police are not an option until they know what they've landed in the middle of. He chose to let himself be used. If the police become involved, he'll never have any control over what's going to happen. He has to know more. And he promised Yassim he'd let someone he trusts help him.

Gabriella said she wants to meet. And she has experience with these kinds of things. Klara and George obviously do too. They've done so much for him over the past day, more than you could ever ask of someone.

"I have an idea," he says. "About how to find out what's in these documents."

NOVEMBER 25—BERGORT

Every seat is full by the time the train reaches Lund, and Klara can't decide if that's good or bad, if a packed car makes her more or less likely to be recognized. She pulls up her hood and sinks back into her seat. As the train rolls out of Lund, she takes out the phone she bought in Germany and opens her secret email.

Camp Nou, tonight 20:00, she writes to Gabriella.

Almost as soon as it's sent, a reply arrives.

Camp Nou?

Klara looks up from the phone. Damn! Gabi doesn't remember that's what the kids in the suburb of Bergort called their little artificial turf field. It's a perfect place to meet—far from any spots they might have under surveillance, like Gabi's apartment or office.

The Astroturf field in Bergort, she writes back. She wants to ask Gabi how she's doing, what happened. But she's afraid that they've already communicated too much over the phone, knows it's risky, even if she's using a secret email address and a burner phone. Better to meet face-to-face. The answer arrives immediately.

Okay. See you there.

She gets off the train at the Stockholm Central Station just after four o'clock in the afternoon and makes her way through the early-rush-hour traffic toward the subway. It's good that everyone is on the move, she thinks—no one is paying attention to her. She pulls her hoodie down as far as it will go, and the stocking cap beneath it.

It almost doesn't feel real to be back in the hustle and bustle of the subway. Klara takes a deep breath of that familiar and oxygen-deprived air. It smells like humanity and city and stone; it smells like Stockholm and, even though she's never lived here, that scent along with the clattering of the train and the crackling voice over the speakers somehow makes her feel like she's home.

The red line south. Klara looks around the subway car as it rattles and jumps farther and farther away from the inner city, and at each stop the number of blond, blue-eyed commuters becomes fewer. She's not riding this train to the end. Not yet. Just to the porous and ever-shifting border of gentrification.

The Skärholmen neighborhood is a mix of classic Swedish housing projects and a new, fresh shopping center and condominium development. There's also an open-air market just outside the subway: Asian tapas, junkies, and coffee chains. Genuine, but gentrified enough to have its sharpest edges rubbed off.

But Klara's not headed to one of the new condos with Miele kitchens, she's headed to the concrete block of rental apartments on Äspholmsvägen. She checks the address Jacob scribbled again, crosses the square, passing by the last few stalls in the market that haven't packed up for the evening yet.

She doesn't want to use the map on her phone; thankfully a helpful drunk outside the subway station points her in the right direction of the address after she declines his offer to personally guide her there.

It doesn't take long to find the right apartment building, and Klara grabs her phone to check the time. Just as she sees that it's just a few minutes past six, she hears a voice behind her.

"Are you waiting for someone?"

NOVEMBER 25—MALMÖ

GEORGE IS HUNCHED down next to Jacob. They're by the harbor now, where the wind is icy. The temperature's fallen since this morning.

They've been walking around Malmö for about an hour since they said goodbye to Klara. George wanted to keep them moving so nobody would have time to figure out who they were.

But why did they go down here to the harbor? Jacob is so cold he's shaking. When he lifts his eyes, he sees the gray, solid concrete of Øresund Bridge to his left and the dim, ghostly contours of Copenhagen on the horizon, straight ahead.

"We *will* go to the police," George insists. "We have to assume that if we have the plans, the terrorists can't carry them out. Klara just has to meet Gabi first, and we need to find out what the documents contain before we do anything else. Then we'll know what this means for you and for her. For all of us."

He stands up and stretches out a hand to Jacob, pulling him up. "Come on," he says. "We can't sit here; it's too cold."

He turns his wrist and looks at his huge watch. Several times Jacob has thought about asking to look at it; he's never seen anything more enticing, a concrete symbol of success and competence.

"Besides, we don't have long until our train leaves."

Jacob stands up and they walk in silence, past the newly built apartment buildings with a view of the sea and Copenhagen, past the spacious balconies of the comfortable bourgeoisie with a year's worth of salary in the bank and excellent credit. Past everything that will be out of reach for him now.

"I like your watch," Jacob says quietly. "It's . . . serious."

George looks at him with something like suspicion in his eyes. "Did you talk to Klara?" he asks.

"About your watch?" Jacob says.

"She thinks it's vulgar. But you know what?" George turns to Jacob and smiles easily. "Maybe it's okay to be a little vulgar."

Jacob shakes his head, feeling his panic rise again. They're in the middle of chaos, and they're walking around talking about watches.

"We could get caught anytime," he says, his voice hardly more than a whisper. "Maybe Klara got caught already."

"Anything can happen," George interrupts him. "At any time whatsoever. If there's one thing I've learned over the last few years it's that. All we can do is focus on the task at hand and do it as well as we can. We have to get to Stockholm. Then we'll figure out a way to solve this. We're taking the train, so the risk of being discovered will be much less than flying. Don't think about the big picture, the fucking terrorists and being wanted and all that other shit. You just take it one step at a time: We head to Stockholm, and we don't get caught. And then we solve this."

He looks at Jacob again. They're almost to the central station now.

"You follow me?" George continues. "Imagine this is a normal day, long before any of this happened. You're just taking the train to Stockholm to hang out with some friends. Nothing strange about that."

Jacob takes a deep breath and tries to smile. "Okay," he says. "Okay, let's go."

But almost as soon as the words leave his mouth, he sees two police cars parked outside the central station and a voice starts to scream: "There they are! There they are!"

Jacob twists his head to see a woman with a stroller screaming at the top of her lungs while simultaneously backing away, her eyes glued to them. She's no more than fifteen yards away.

Jacob stops, but he can feel George still pulling him along. "Oh fuck," he whispers in Jacob's ear. "Just when I was telling you to calm down. Ignore it, people think she's crazy, okay?"

But the people coming in and out of the departures hall turn toward the woman and then to where she's pointing.

Jacob stops and wrenches himself out of George's hand. Slowly he pulls his hood down and takes off his hat and turns to the woman.

"What the hell!" George shouts. "Come on, Jacob!"

But it's too late. Two police officers are on their way out of the arrivals hall. They see her, see where she's pointing. The people around them are screaming and jumping away from them in every direction.

"Come on!"

George tugs Jacob, drawing him into the crowd as if they were just part of the screaming, terrified masses. They stumble down the street; he can barely see straight, doesn't know if he's up, down, underwater.

"Stop!" he hears one of the police officers shout behind him. "Stop or I shoot!"

They're still hunched over, but Jacob feels George's arm loosen at his wrist. "No matter what happens . . ." George says, "stay calm."

From the corner of his eye, Jacob sees George start to raise his hands to show the cops he's unarmed. And at that very moment a gray car stops in front of them, and he hears a voice shouting in English from the driver's seat, sees the passenger-side door thrown open ahead of him.

A shot goes off from inside the car. Then another. Then he hears the screaming and the panic behind him. He feels it in his chest, his throat. He hasn't been hit. They weren't shooting at him.

He turns to George, who looks as shocked as Jacob feels—and just as unscathed. Jacob turns to the car again and sees the face leaning out of it. And before he knows it he's in the back seat, with George on top of him, and the car is speeding away, as surreal as a bullet or a dream.

NOVEMBER 25—BERGORT

At first, in the darkness, she sees only the silhouette of a man, but as he gets closer, she can make out his face in the dim light shining from inside the building. Jacob told her his old Arabic teacher is in his sixties, with thick, neatly trimmed gray hair, that he usually wore suits and carried a brown suitcase. The man in front of her fits that description perfectly.

"I'm looking for Hassan Aziz," she says.

The man looks at her for a moment, then passes by her, punches the code in, and opens the door.

"I don't know who that is," he says, stepping inside.

Before Klara can react, the door shuts behind him and the light in the staircase flickers on.

"Damn," she mutters, going over to the door where the lights are still on. She pushes her cheek against the glass and reads the names on the board in the stairwell. An Aziz is listed as residing on the second floor. She pushes on the door, but it's locked. She sighs and turns around. She settles against a bike rack opposite the door. Nothing to do but wait.

It takes no more than ten minutes until a woman with a stroller and some grocery bags approaches the front door. Klara takes a couple of quick steps toward her as she struggles to punch in the code while keeping her paper bags off the wet ground.

"Let me help you," Klara says, gently squeezing past her and pushing the door open just as the code has been accepted.

"Oh, thank you," the woman says. "I've got a lot on my hands right now."

"What floor?" Klara says. "I can carry the bags for you."

"Oh, that's so sweet," the woman says. "Thank you!"

Klara leaves the bags on the third floor and waits until the woman has closed the door to her apartment. She walks down the stairs to the next landing and looks at the names on the three doors. The door marked AZIZ is on the left. She takes a deep breath and rings the doorbell.

Nothing happens. She rings it again. And again. But with the same miserable results. Maybe the man she met in the entrance wasn't Aziz, after all.

She rings it again and again, almost desperate now. Then she bends down and pushes the letterbox open. The door is cool against her forehead as she leans into it.

"Hassan!" she shouts. "I really need to meet you. I'm supposed to tell you hello from Jacob Seger."

The slight echo of her words hangs in the air of the stairwell after she falls silent. But she hears something else, something from within the apartment. She puts her ear to the letterbox and can swear she hears someone on the other side of the door. Small, muffled movements. Breathing.

"Please!" she says. "Jacob Seger says hello!"

The door rams into her forehead before she has a chance to get away, a quick thud of pain. She takes a step back, rubbing her head. The man she saw downstairs is standing in the doorway.

"Hurry inside," he says. "You can't just stand there screaming."

Klara rubs her forehead as she steps into his apartment.

"Thank you," she says. "I need your help."

She takes off her shoes and follows Hassan into a small, tastefully decorated living room. He gestures to a low, brown leather sofa and settles himself into a matching armchair on the other side of the coffee table. Klara looks around. The walls are covered with neatly organized bookshelves, and there's not a trace of dust on the glass table. Hassan turns on a floor lamp in the corner and warm light falls onto a beautiful rug. There are two small lamps with green shades in the window overlooking the street, which contributes to the impression that this is an English gentlemen's club rather than an apartment in the suburbs. There's no doubt that Jacob's former teacher is a very proper sort of man.

"Thank you for listening to me," Klara begins. "We have—"

Hassan holds up a hand to interrupt her. "I trust Jacob," he says. His Swedish is perfect; Klara can detect only the slightest hint of Arabic in it. "But I've also read the newspapers. I've seen what they're writing about him. And about you, because you must be Klara Walldéen."

She nods. She talked to George and Jacob about it, about how they're pariahs now.

"I don't want to get involved in anything," he says. "I'm a simple man; I live a simple life. And I want to keep it that way. Do you understand?"

"Yes," she says. "I really do. Believe me. And I understand that it's selfish of us to try to pull you into something you haven't asked to be a part of. But Jacob is not a terrorist. I'm not a terrorist. I think you know that."

Hassan looks at her. Then he stands up and takes a few steps over to a cabinet inside one of the bookshelves. "Forgive me my rudeness," he says.

Klara catches a glimpse of mirrored glass and bottles when he opens the door.

"What can I offer you? I have most things, I'm afraid."

He glances at her with a slight smile. Klara feels a familiar urge, a kind of low-intensity euphoria awakening.

When he turns around he's holding a very nice bottle of malt whiskey and two glasses in his hand.

"I think this evening requires whiskey," he says, putting two coasters on the table before setting down the glasses.

Klara swallows deep and pulls her eyes away from the bottle. "Nothing for me, thank you," she says.

"No?" Hassan says, disappointed. "You don't like whiskey? I have other options to choose from."

Klara turns to him and looks straight into his eyes. "I like it too much," she says quietly. "Please don't offer it to me again. I'm not sure I can resist."

Without a word, Hassan collects the glasses and the bottle and puts them back into the cabinet.

"I'm sorry," Klara says. "I didn't mean you couldn't drink."

Hassan sits down in the chair again. "I should be the one apologizing. I didn't know."

She shakes her head. "How could you? I barely do myself. This is . . . I've had some hard years."

Hassan smiles. He doesn't need to say anything. Those eyes. Those dignified, gentlemanly eyes are proof enough that he knows more than a little about hard years. Maybe that's part of the reason he doesn't want to get pulled into all this trouble.

"Jacob is a climber," he says. "Is that what you call it?"

Klara nods.

"He wants to move forward, upward. I've seen more than a few in my days. They don't turn into terrorists. There's something else going on here, I think."

He rises and goes over to the bookshelf, pours a few fingers of whiskey into a glass after all. He takes a small gulp, turns around, and looks at her again.

"We're exposing you to risk," she says. "I know that."

"Yes. But it occurs to me that at my age a man should be grateful for any chance at risk. And I'm a curious person. I want to know what this is all about, what Jacob's done to make the powers that be so furious with him. Do you want to tell me?"

"I hoped that *you* might tell me," Klara says.

She takes out the computer they bought in Malmö from her bag, and sets it on the glass table. With a few quick clicks on the keyboard, she opens the folder where she saved the documents and slides the computer over to Hassan.

"It's a long story," she says. "Jacob met a man in Beirut who asked him to carry something out of the Middle East. It turned out the information wasn't what Jacob was led to believe; in fact it seems to be something much, much more serious. Something connected to what happened in Paris. Or a new Paris."

"And you don't want to go to the police because Jacob is in danger of getting hurt?"

"We know too little," Klara says. "We need to know what it's about first, and I think we do in broad terms, but the documents in front of you are in Arabic. We need your help to understand what they contain."

Hassan fishes a pair of reading glasses out of his front pocket and pulls the computer closer. Slowly he starts to scroll through the first document without saying a word. Klara can feel her legs twitching; it's so difficult to stay still with all this nervous energy coursing inside her. She glances at her phone. The time is half past six. One and a half hours until the meeting in Bergort.

Finally, Hassan looks away from the screen, takes off the glasses and meets Klara's eyes. His face is quite pale, his eyes wide and serious.

"This is a plan for a terrorist attack at the opera house," he says. "Detailed instructions. What weapons they should have, who they are, names, where to meet, all of it."

"Damn it," she says. "I knew it."

"Klara," Hassan says, looking away from the documents, turning them back to her. "They write about coordinated attacks. Are there any more documents?"

She nods. "Brussels, London, and Rome," she says quietly.

Hassan bends over the table toward her. "The plan is supposed to take place tomorrow evening," he says.

"Oh, Jesus."

Klara is overcome by dizziness, and she closes her eyes. "But they can't carry it out without these documents."

Hassan doesn't answer, and Klara opens her eyes.

"Right?" she says. "How can they attack without plans? That's the whole point."

"Maybe," Hassan says. "Unless each cell has a set of documents. Maybe Jacob's job was to get these to the Brussels cell? Maybe there's a Jacob for every cell."

The air stands still between them while this thought penetrates Klara's mind. Perhaps there are three more sets of documents, three cells getting ready out there.

"I have to hurry," she says, finally, standing up.

She walks lost in thought back toward the subway, through the darkness and under the yellow electric light, through the flurries of tiny snowflakes. There is so much at stake. She can't really comprehend the immensity of it. She needs Gabriella, her calm and clear guidance.

But there's still an hour left. In the meantime, something is eating at her, something that nags at her when she thinks about Gabriella. She's been so focused on the meeting with Hassan that she hasn't picked up the signs. A few snowflakes land on the screen of her phone in her hand.

The email from Gabriella.

She doesn't want to go back into the email again, afraid someone has it under surveillance. But she remembers what Gabriella wrote. And she knows there's something that just won't leave her alone. Gabi's memory is much better than Klara's, always has been. Gabi can still remember details about classes they took in Uppsala, when Klara barely remembers names or faces from that period.

Now that she thinks about it, Gabriella would never have forgotten the field in Bergort was called Camp Nou. So why did she ask? Was she trying to send a warning? Or is it not even Gabriella she's in contact with? And if it's not Gabriella, who is it? The Russians who are following them?

She feels her pulse start to race again. Is this meeting a trap?

She's at the square in front of the subway station now, at a little tobacco shop, where she buys the cheapest burner phone they have, then sends a text message to George's number, telling him that she's met Hassan and they should meet her at the field in Bergort but to have no contact until then.

She sits down on a damp park bench with the phone in her hand. The feeling that Gabriella's meeting is a trap won't go away. But maybe Gabi was just stressed and not thinking clearly when she responded, and maybe that's why she forgot what the kids called their soccer field.

She swallows and dials her number on the phone. It's a big risk. But she doesn't know what other options she has. It doesn't matter though, because it goes straight to voice mail.

Klara hangs up. What should she do now?

If Gabriella has been released from the detention and can meet her that means that she's no longer suspected of anything. Then she wouldn't have to hide or be afraid of the police. On the other hand, if it's the Russians Klara has been communicating with, she'll be in grave danger in Bergort.

A thought occurs to her. She goes through every option again, but ends up at the same conclusion. What does she have to lose?

She turns on the phone and looks up Säpo's number. It barely rings before an operator answers. "Security Service."

Klara clears her throat. "I'm looking for Anton Bronzelius," she says. "Can you connect me?"

"I'm sorry," the operator says. "I can't connect you with anyone. What's this concerning?"

Klara closes her eyes and leans back on the bench. "My name is Klara Walldéen. I'm wanted all over this country; my picture is on the front of every newspaper. Now, can you please connect me to Bronzelius?"

"One moment," says the operator, and Klara hears classical music.

It takes no more than a couple of seconds to be connected. "Hello, Klara," says Bronzelius's familiar voice. "I thought you might call."

NOVEMBER 25—MALMÖ

THEY'RE OUT ON a bigger street now, the inner city to their left, a park to their right, a casino, an intersection. They're driving at a normal speed, and Jacob was looking up, but now he pushes his head back against the seat again.

How is it possible? he wants to scream.

George, who is lying on top of him in the back seat, moves and sits up.

"Who the hell are you?" he screams in English to the driver.

Jacob also sits up and meets Yassim's eyes in the rearview mirror. His face is as pale as a sheet, heavy bags beneath his eyes.

But it's him. It's Yassim.

"How . . ." Jacob begins. "How . . . could you be here?"

"The phone," he says. "Why do you think I gave it to you? So I could find you, of course." Yassim presses out a smile and turns to the left, back toward the city again.

"I thought you were dead," Jacob says. "When I left you I thought . . ."

"I couldn't very well leave you yet," Yassim says. He gives him an exhausted and stoic look. "We just met."

They're back in the city center again, between shops and department stores and parked cars. Yassim drives with what seems like practiced calm through the streets. Jacob can see that he's following a route on the car's GPS. He's planned this.

Suddenly he stops and turns up toward a parking garage. He takes a ticket and a garage door opens to let them in. They drive in a spiral up and up until he turns off the ramp onto the third floor. It's so quiet in here, so unbelievably quiet.

"Come on," Yassim says.

He parks near an exit to an enclosed pedestrian bridge, which leads into a department store called Hansa. Yassim goes first; he makes his way bent and jerkily, his left hand inside his black bomber jacket.

They cross the bridge, pass by families having coffee, as if everything is normal. But the children press their faces against the large windows as sirens cut through regular traffic noise and drown out the quiet music streaming over the café's speakers. Blue lights flash down on the street, police cars drive by at high speed down below.

"Dad, look! So cool!" Jacob hears a little girl say in a Skåne accent.

Jacob turns around to look at her, a girl with long, dark hair, in jeans, a cap on her head, maybe six years old. She pulls her dad by the hand toward the window. Nothing unusual about the day in here. Just a family shopping together after school.

"Hats on and hoods up," Yassim says.

He leads them into the department store and down the escalators, past the shops and the people, out onto the street. The sirens shriek just a few blocks away, maybe not even that.

"They'll soon find the car," he says. "Follow me."

He turns left onto a side street by the department store and walks over to a dark-blue Japanese SUV. It's a bit beaten-up and seems to have at least ten years under its belt. The door is unlocked.

"One of you has to drive," he says. "I've been driving for ten hours with one arm."

George hesitates for a moment, then he crawls into the driver's seat. Yassim walks around the car and sits down in the passenger seat, and Jacob hesitantly gets into the back. Yassim bends down, fiddling with something under the steering wheel.

"Hold down the clutch," he says to George.

Then the engine starts running, and George calmly steers the car out onto the street. Behind them, the sirens are becoming ever more distant.

"Lucky I had time to prep an extra car," Yassim says.

"You stole this?" Jacob asks.

Yassim shrugs. "We can't exactly use a car with Belgian license plates. That would be a little too obvious."

Yassim turns to George now. "But who are you?" he says.

"I could ask you the same thing," George says. "But I think I already know."

They pass police cars as they make their way out of Malmö and up onto the highway to Helsingborg, but all the cars are headed in the opposite direction—no one is following them. They drive in silence at first, overcome by the moment, by the fact that they have actually escaped and that Yassim is here.

"I don't understand what's happening," Jacob says at last. "I don't understand anything."

He looks out through the window, to the water stretched out under the gray afternoon sky. In front of them sit the port and cranes in what must be Landskrona.

"First of all, I don't even understand how you could be alive."

But Yassim doesn't answer, and Jacob bends forward between the seats.

"I think he fell asleep," George says, glancing back quickly at Jacob. "Sorry, buddy."

Jacob exhales. It's no hurry, they have time. He hopes they have time.

"That's Yassim," he says.

"No shit," George says. "He's alive."

"I knew when I got the password," he says. "Who else would have sent it? Or I was hoping. But I never imagined he'd come after me. That he would search for me. Find me."

Jacob closes his eyes. It's dark outside now, but when he opens his eyes, he sees Yassim staring at him from between the front seats. His eyes are so tired, his face so dirty and grimy, and a cut runs from his temple and down under his eye.

"Hello," he says. "We're alive. Both of us." And then he smiles that smile that makes the whole galaxy stop, that makes the nights cease and time change direction, and Jacob leans forward between the seats and takes Yassim's face between his hands, and pulls it closer and kisses him gently, trying not to cause him any pain.

"What's going on?" he asks when he finally pulls back.

"Good question, and surely not a moment too soon to find out," George mutters from behind the wheel. "I, for one, am all ears."

"Where should I even start?" Yassim asks.

"How about from the beginning," George says. "I'm wanted by the police because of you." He glances at Yassim. "Nice of you to save us in Malmö, but honestly, it's pretty much your fault we landed in that situation to begin with."

"You told me I was carrying information about war crimes," Jacob says, leaning between the seats, "that I was smuggling it for you. But you lied."

Yassim nods calmly to Jacob. Outside, dark trees whiz by in the darkness—it almost feels like they're driving through a tunnel.

"Yes, that's true," Yassim sighs. "But you surely knew that."

"I guess," Jacob says. "Still, I trusted you."

They sit in silence for a while. Just the sound of the engine and the wind against the car.

"Do you know what Emni is?" Yassim asks finally.

Jacob shakes his head.

"It's the ISIS intelligence service, I guess you could say. They're behind many terrorist attacks in Europe."

Jacob says nothing.

"They were behind what happened in Paris. Or they developed the plan, coordinated it, local cells carried it out. The cells didn't know anything until a week before. Then someone took a flight with a little chip."

Jacob just looks at him.

"You," he says. "You were the one who came up with the plan."

"No," Yassim says. "I didn't carry the plan for Paris. That was someone else. If that had been my job, it never would have happened. I can promise you that. Just like the plan on the chip you carried is never going to happen.

"I've infiltrated Emni," Yassim says evenly. "I've been working with Russian intelligence for several years on it. Trying to make my way into the inner circles of ISIS, of Emni."

"Excuse me?" George says, glancing skeptically at Yassim. "Are you saying you're a Russian spy?"

Yassim turns and looks at him calmly. "I'm from Syria," he says. "It's a bit more complicated there, who's a spy, who's not. Everyone has their own agenda."

"And what is yours?" George asks, turning to stare straight into Yassim's eyes. "What is your agenda, Yassim?"

NOVEMBER 25—BERGORT

THE SUBWAY CAR emerges from the tunnel and into the autumn darkness between rusty fences, yellow grass, and concrete. The suburbs. Klara looks out at the lit windows of the concrete buildings and realizes she's never been here. She has never been to any of Stockholm's suburbs, even this summer when she was directly involved in what was going on out here.

When the train stops in Bergort, she exits onto a barren and windswept platform bathed in yellow electric light. She stops at one of the gray, graffitied pillars holding up the ceiling. There, behind layers of new graffiti and stickers, she sees it: a fist enclosed in a star. The riots of the summer have ended, but the symbol remains.

It's a quarter to eight, and she takes the stairs down from the platform, past the little grocery store where a few freezing kids are drinking Red Bulls and smoking, their puffy jackets buttoned all the way up and their hats pulled low. They look at her with interest as she walks by. She continues toward the small square, where she sees a pizzeria, an ICA, a pharmacy, a Middle Eastern food store. Otherwise, just gray concrete, brightly colored balconies of corrugated metal, Somali flags in the windows, a forest of satellite dishes and kick bikes thrown into the bushes.

She hunches slightly against the wind as she walks across the square. She's almost there now. At the end. They put the puzzle together, she and George, and have reached what might be the truth.

But she also knows that truth is only a small part of the story. That it's fragile and easy to manipulate. The manipulation that got Gabi arrested, got Jacob to smuggle terrorist plans to Europe. It's up to her now. And only her. She has to get the actual truth in order to break through everything else, so that the truth saves rather than destroys them.

Bergort feels completely deserted tonight. The weather has kept most of the kids indoors, in front of their computers and PlayStations. She thinks of Gabi and George. Of Grandma. Of Grandpa in his coffin. And for the first time in as long as she can remember, she feels up to the task at hand.

The buildings are lower near the edge of the small asphalt path that leads toward something that looks like a large square cage or enclosure. She can just make out one soccer goal, and as she gets closer she sees the other one. Camp Nou.

She stops and looks upward with a pounding heart, then slowly makes her way toward the fence. It takes a little while to find the entrance, but as soon as she does, she doesn't hesitate, just bends down so as not to hit her head and takes a few steps onto the coarse plastic surface.

The field is empty. She looks at the time on her phone. Just before eight. She turns around and listens, but all she hears is the wind whining through satellite dishes and rusty chicken wire. Slowly she walks into the darkness toward the center of the field and touches the artificial grass with fingers stiff from the cold.

Something rustles behind her and she freezes in place. Then she straightens and turns around. Someone has stepped through the opening in the fence. Not just one person, she realizes, but two.

And neither of them is Gabriella.

NOVEMBER 25—MALMÖ

Yassim turns to him again, and no matter how much Jacob wants to, he can't resist the warmth in those eyes. It's just like the garden in Beirut, like in that clinically cold apartment, or in the stairwell in Brussels.

"I told you about the bombing," he says. "The one that wiped out my family."

"You said it was a drone strike," Jacob says. "That's why you wanted to expose the US's war crimes."

Yassim nods. "Yes, that's what I said. That was my cover story, that I believed that. That I hated the Americans so much because they wiped out my family."

"But that was also a lie?" Jacob says calmly.

Yassim nods. "It's not a lie that my family was murdered," he says. "But they weren't murdered by the Americans. It was at the beginning of the war. Or before there even was a war, when it might, might still have been possible to save something. My father was powerful, a strong leader. He knew everyone important in Syria, and he invited them to my sister's wedding, because that's what you do, that's how you broker peace. The only ones who didn't come were the Islamists, Baghdadi Islamists. They didn't want peace; they wanted what we have now, war and misery and hell. So they placed a bomb at my sister's wedding to knock out their enemies. But the only thing they destroyed was my family."

He falls silent, stares quietly at Jacob. "You have to believe me," he says. "This is the truth."

"Why did you lie to me?" Jacob says. "Didn't you trust me?"

Yassim smiles crookedly. "I've been living under cover for five years, darling. I don't trust anybody."

Then he pauses, puts a hand on Jacob's knee.

"I mean I didn't trust anyone back then. We'd just met. In the beginning, the first year after the bomb, everyone thought the Americans were behind it. I mean this was in the Middle East; the Americans are behind a lot of shit. It was easy to believe that. I was already living in Beirut and working as a photographer. One evening at a bar in Gemmayzeh, a few months after the wedding, a Russian man offered me a few drinks. I thought he was coming on to me, and I was pretty self-destructive back then, open to anything really. But after we talked for a while, I realized he wasn't just a diplomat, like he said. And that he knew exactly who I was."

"He was a spy?" Jacob says.

"Gregorij Korolov is his name," Yassim continues. "That first evening, he invited me to his apartment in one of those new buildings just above the Corniche, not far from my apartment. Then he opened a bottle of vodka. Such a fucking cliché."

A slight smile and a glance out at the trees that stream by like water.

"He showed me pictures from the wedding, from some satellite or drone, and I could see how a waiter at the wedding brought in some boxes. Gregorij said they were full of explosives. He showed me documents and a video of interviews with infiltrators they had in Baghdadi's circle, who described the plan. Gregorij even had calculations that proved the bomb couldn't have come from the air, had to have been placed under the buffet table at the party. There was no doubt. The Islamists were behind it. And he asked me if I wanted revenge."

"But why you?" George asks, looking skeptically at Yassim. "You didn't have any connections with them."

"That wasn't hard to explain—they were expanding at that point, in need of good people. And I think I understood that I would be seen as valuable. I lived in Beirut and might be called westernized, had been in the United States, was a photographer. More or less openly homosexual, something I had to tone down with the Islamists. Although they knew, and that was one of the reasons they wanted me. It made me less suspicious, if you know what I mean. Why would a gay guy be working for ISIS? Gregorij had other infiltrators in Baghdadi's outer circle. There were people who could vouch for me and pave my way. I started as a courier for small stuff, driving cars, carrying small items and messages between Tripoli and Aleppo. Slowly I worked my way up and in. They started to trust me, and in the end I became a courier for Emni. And through it all I reported to Gregorij. Often, I didn't know what was in the messages I was sending. But I could tell who they were sent between, and where their leaders were located. My work yielded results. The Russians were able to map out the leadership, how they communicated, and I got closer to the core of the terror machine itself. But then Paris started to be planned, and this plan we're in the middle of right now."

"Did you know about Paris?" Jacob whispers. "Did you know it was going to happen?"

It's as if the air in the car is suddenly too heavy to breathe, there is so much hanging in that question.

"I knew something was going to happen in Paris that week," Yassim says. "I knew who was planning it and who was carrying the information. I even knew who would be receiving the information in Brussels, because that's where they met the courier."

"But why didn't you say anything?" Jacob asks. "Why did you let it happen?"

Yassim stares at him intensely. "I told all of that to Gregorij," he says. "And I told him it was something on a whole new level. Several independent cells. Concurrent attacks. I told him everything, and I can prove it. I recorded all our meetings with that phone and saved them."

"Then why did it happen?" George interrupts. "If they knew everything except the exact date? Why didn't they grab the courier or his contact in Brussels? This story doesn't really feel like it adds—"

Yassim turns to George, with cold indifference in his eyes, and George's eyes return to the dark road in front of him.

"Because the Russians let it happen," he says slowly. "Because the Russians benefit from the instability that resulted from a terrorist attack in central Paris. The Russians fight ISIS in Syria because they're allied with Assad. But it also serves their purposes to have ISIS seen as a threat in Europe. Nothing is black-and-white, no matter how hard you try to make it. You can play for both teams at the same time. But I have no excuse. I should have known better, and I'll have to live with the fact that I trusted Gregorij and the Russians. The people who died in Paris died because of my naivety."

The car is silent again. What Yassim has told them is too big for the limited space inside this car, and Jacob wants to open a window just to burst the intensity of this bubble.

"Are they really that fucking cold?" George says. "They let Paris happen when they could have prevented it?"

Yassim shrugs. "I think they're desperate," he says. "Or maybe not desperate, but they see themselves as under attack from the West, as if the West distrusts everything they do. Like a cold war I guess. Just somewhat less intense."

"So what Myriam said was true," Jacob says quietly. "She thought you were a terrorist. The only thing she didn't know was that you were working for the Russians.

"Why didn't you tell her about this new attack? I could have just given the information to her. Why did I have to smuggle it?"

"Do you trust her?" Yassim asks, still calm. "Are you even sure she's a Swedish spy?"

Jacob thinks about the ambassador's car and what happened at the bathhouse, Myriam's blackmail and ruthlessness. He shakes his head. "I don't know," he whispers. "I don't know what I trust."

They sit in silence for a while.

"So what you're saying is that the Russians want these terrorist attacks to be carried out," George says.

"Look at it this way," Yassim says. "Several terrorist attacks in Europe at once, just a few weeks after the massacre in Paris. Coordinated with military precision. It would push Europe into greater involvement in the war against ISIS in Syria, and it would help those forces in Europe that want to take a more aggressive stance on immigration. There's nothing that irritates the Russians more than a Europe with open borders. These attacks mean calls for the opposite. For the Russians it's a win-win. A few hundred people are an acceptable price to pay."

"But why not go to the media yourself?" George says. "Why pull Jacob into this?"

"I had the chip," Yassim says quietly. "I had the plan, but I didn't have the password. I knew it involved multiple coordinated attacks. But I had no details. And I trusted the Russians before Paris. But after that, when I realized how ruthless they were . . . I realized that if I gave the cell in Brussels the chip everything would be over, they'd have the information and I would lose control. And the Russians wouldn't stop them. Jacob offered to do it that very evening."

Yassim turns around and looks at him.

"I didn't want to at first. The thought had occurred to me, but I couldn't pull you into this. I definitely couldn't suggest it. But when you brought it up . . ." He shakes his head slightly. "I knew it was an opportunity. It was dangerous, of course, but it gave me a few days to find the password and then pick you up at the airport. But they were suspicious and insisted on meeting you themselves. I had no alternative so I had to agree, then try to improvise. It was just dumb luck that you were smart enough to remove the chip, Jacob. Even though in the moment I was afraid they were going to shoot us both. It was close—I think I got you out at the very last second."

"But how did you get the password?" Jacob asks. "If you tried so long . . . ?"

"How do you think?" he says, staring coolly into Jacob's eyes.

"You forced them?" Jacob says. "Somehow?"

"Somehow," Yassim says, turning his gaze back to the forest and darkness outside.

NOVEMBER 25—BERGORT

TWO MEN HAVE entered the soccer field and they're coming toward her unhurriedly with their hands at their sides. One is dressed in a long, dark coat, bareheaded. His well-trimmed gray hair is styled in a way that doesn't seem to be affected by wind or snow. In the dark, Klara can just make out that he seems tan, with deep wrinkles on his forehead.

The other man, walking right behind him, is very large and wears some kind of Gore-Tex jacket, with a hat pulled low on his forehead.

He has a gun in his hand, but it's pointed down toward the artificial turf.

They stop about five yards from Klara without saying a word. She throws a glance over her shoulder, toward the other end of the field, and sees another man there.

She's surrounded. It's a trap, just as she thought, and now it's time. Time to drive this story to its end. Her mouth is very dry, but she feels strangely focused, strangely calm. Despite the men coming toward her.

"I know you're waiting for someone else," the man in the coat says in excellent English that's not quite free of Slavic diphthongs. "I apologize for the fact that we had to hack your friend's email and be so—how shall I put this?—mysterious."

"Who are you?" Klara says. "Where is Gabriella?"

"Gabriella is, as far as we know, still in jail," he says coolly. "The evidence against her is apparently quite damning."

"What kind of evidence?"

Klara takes a slow step back when the man steps toward her.

"This is not your fight," he says, holding up his hands as if to calm her. "You were pulled in by chance when a project of ours in Syria took an unexpected turn."

He stops, maybe trying not to scare Klara any further.

"Someone contacted your friend Gabriella. A person we had eyes on and who had access to sensitive information. Something we could not allow him to share. We thought it would be enough if we had our Swedish colleagues put a lasso around Gabriella so we could take care of it in Brussels. But, but . . . We didn't account for you. Or that this Jacob would end up being so resourceful. Or that our man would fall in love with him. Or . . ."

The Russian looks disappointed as he throws his arms wide.

"Nine out of ten projects are so predictable," he says. "But the tenth? The tenth defies all description. Unfortunately, you've landed in the tenth."

He starts to walk toward her again, purposefully.

"But now it's time to take care of all this. You have something we need. A memory card."

"No," Klara says, shaking her head. "I don't have it."

The man looks disappointed and cocks his head.

"We are on the same side here," he says. "I give you my word that we'll get your friend out of detention. The evidence against her could quickly prove to be thin as air. Do you understand? And if you're worried about letting something happen, I'll give you my word on that too. Do you think we're beasts?"

"I don't know," Klara says, looking straight into his eyes. "How should I know what you're capable of? I don't even know who you are."

He stares at her with such coldness that Klara almost has to look away. But only almost.

"What do you know about making this kind of decision?" he asks. "What do you know about the world, Klara Walldéen?"

She sees the man in Gore-Tex moving toward her now, something intentional in his eyes, the gun in both hands. There are a lot of things that could go wrong here. That insight goes off inside her head like a bomb. She thought she was in control, but anything can happen now. Anything at all.

Her knees start to tremble but she pushes away her growing panic.

"You or one of your friends have the card," the man in the coat says. "It's in everyone's best interest to make sure we get it."

Klara shakes her head. How long will she be able to handle this?

"I know what's going to happen," she says. "I've seen the information. I know there are supposed to be coordinated terrorist attacks tomorrow. As long as we have the information, they can't carry them out."

If he's surprised Klara knows what's on the chip, his face doesn't show it. "Are you really so naive?" the man says. "What you have is the information for *one* of the cells we managed to infiltrate. We have reason to believe there are several. And that all the cells got the same information. Terrorists don't let a plan this carefully arranged rest on just one person's shoulders. Surely you understand that?"

"Did you know about Paris too?" she says without looking away.

He stares at her with those colorless eyes. "You don't understand what this is about," he continues. "You don't know what's at stake. We have spent years analyzing ISIS, their leadership, how they communicate. Do you think we'd let the biggest terrorist attack since September 11 be ruined by a couple of self-righteous Swedish women? Do you seriously think you can stop the wave of history?"

But Klara can see he's self-conscious after her mention of Paris, and no longer calm. He considers her beneath his dignity. This whole fiasco, a bunch of gays and women, all beneath his dignity. He nods to the man in Gore-Tex, who takes a step toward Klara and raises the gun.

"You and your friends are completely alone," the man says. "The

Swedish police think you're working with a terrorist, which you are. You have nowhere else to go. Not you, not Gabriella, and not your friends. All you have is me."

"And what can you do?" Klara whispers.

She's backed all the way up to the fence now. There's no way out.

"You can cooperate, and I'll explain to my friends in the Swedish intelligence service that there's been a big mistake," he says. "Or I could kill you here. And then hunt down your friends one by one. Your choice."

The man in Gore-Tex takes one more step forward, pushes the cold gun against her head. The world freezes around her. How could she have been so stupid? How could it all go so wrong?

"No," she whispers. "Please."

Then a shot rings out, and the world flashes to white.

NOVEMBER 25—BERGORT

IT'S HALF PAST eight by the time they drive past Södertälje, above water and rocks and trees, and then in among the warehouses, office complexes, and gray, dreary industrial areas that start popping up more and more frequently. Small pieces of ice beat ever more intensely against the windshield as Jacob opens his eyes.

"How long did I sleep?" he asks.

"On and off since Vättern," George says, looking at him in the rearview mirror.

How can he still hold his eyes open? The first night they were in the truck and then he drove basically without stopping from Malmö. He looks a little pale, but otherwise unfazed.

"Almost there," George says. "I just wish I knew what the hell was happening. All I know is that she wants to meet in some goddamn depressing suburb where she got some help from your Arabic teacher. And now she's turned off her phone."

Jacob bends forward to look at Yassim. His head is resting against the window, his mouth half-open.

"Is he alive?" he asks worriedly.

George throws a glance at Yassim. "He doesn't seem easy to kill," George says. "Besides, he's spent more time awake on this trip than you have."

George has turned off the highway now and slowed down. They drive by wholesalers and car washes, bare trees and empty streets; ten-story apartment buildings rise up like towers on the horizon.

"That's our destination," George says. He appears to shiver. "This trip just keeps getting more and more depressing."

Yassim wakes up as they slowly roll into the mix of aging concrete apartment buildings and playgrounds, bare bushes with white berries, all lit by yellow streetlights waving in the wind. Jacob can see his eyes light up when they look at each other in the rearview mirror, but he grimaces as he turns toward him.

"You're in pain," Jacob says. "I'm worried about you." Jacob leans forward and puts his hand on an unexpectedly warm cheek. "You have a fever. We need someone to look at your wound."

Yassim smiles weakly. "It's fine. We have more important things to think about now."

"I think we're there," George says. "Or as close as we can get."

They park the car by a school. Low buildings in yellow brick, like barracks, a playground with broken swings, basketball courts without a net, a dark, empty parking lot.

Yassim grimaces as he gets out of the car, but won't let Jacob support him. Instead, he gently pats his cheek and stares into his eyes. "I can handle it, Jacob. You don't have to take care of me."

He doesn't get further than that before the muffled sound of an engine revving reaches their ears, and they turn to the entrance of the parking lot where two black, unmarked vans roll in with their headlights off.

"What the hell is it now?" George whispers.

They are in the middle of the parking lot.

The vans stop about twenty yards away, their long sides facing them. From the corner of his eye, Jacob sees Yassim put his working hand inside his jacket, down to the small of his back where he grabs his gun. He glances at Jacob. "Our only hope now is your friend," he says.

Then he squats down, without ever looking away from the vans, and lays his gun on the ground. He kicks it a few yards beyond their reach. "Do not resist," Yassim says. "But say nothing. Not a sound. Whatever they threaten you with, you can't trust anything they say." He looks at Jacob with desperation in his eyes. "You got back the chip in Malmö," he says. "You have it, right?"

Jacob puts his hand in his pocket. His sweaty hands slippery on the memory card as he fumbles for it. He nods.

"That's all they want," Yassim says. "But if we give it to them, it's over. Do you understand? Then we have nothing."

"Who are they?" Jacob asks. "Russians?"

"We should have stayed away from here," George whispers. "I should have known better."

As if in slow motion, Jacob takes the card out of his pocket with trembling fingers. He looks at Yassim, who nods calmly, and Jacob raises his fingers to his mouth. He puts the card as far back as he can, closes his lips, and swallows.

They can hear the side doors being pulled open. Then everything happens so fast that Jacob can hardly register it. A number of men in civilian clothes jump out of the van, wide-chested, ski masks over their heads, small, effective automatic weapons in their hands. Everything happens so fast, everything is violence, the threat of violence, and Jacob feels like he might vomit.

"Lie down!" the men scream in Swedish. *"Lie down!"*

Weapons raised and aimed at them, low center of gravity and short, quick steps toward them.

"Do as they say," Yassim says next to him, as he falls down to his knees with his hands up.

Jacob follows his example, but they're already there and someone pushes so hard on his back that he falls forward. He feels the asphalt against his face, feels it scraping his cheek, feels blood in his mouth.

"Who are you?" Jacob screams. "What are you doing?"

"I said lie down," someone says in a remarkably deep voice behind him.

It feels like they should be screaming more loudly, like they're holding back. But now Jacob's hands are pulled behind his head and something hard and cold is wrapped around them. He can hear George nearby. "Jesus Christ!" he screams. "I'm not fucking resisting!"

"Keep your mouth shut," says one of the faceless men, and he pushes a foot into his back, pressing him down next to Jacob.

Voices all around him, still deep, strangely low. "It looks like the two plus one more," says a voice.

Then somebody lifts Jacob or maybe drags him by his arms up to his feet, someone shoves him, and he turns his head and sees them doing the same thing to George and Yassim, pushing them all toward the vans.

"Who are you?" George shouts now. "What the hell are you doing? What right do you have to detain me?"

"I'm serious," one of the men in black says. "Shut your mouth now."

When they get to the van someone opens the door. They push Yassim up the steps and then George.

Jacob has just put his foot onto the step when a shot rings out through the frozen darkness, and he stops short. The men in black do too. Then they turn in the direction the shot came from and see the whole sky illuminated by white, electric light.

NOVEMBER 25—BERGORT

When Klara opens her eyes, Camp Nou is bathed in light. The man who was holding the gun is stretched out flat and unmoving on his back in front of her. The gray-haired man looks around in confusion, blinking under the sudden bright light, while backing away from Klara and his lifeless colleague.

"What the hell . . ." he says.

Then they start streaming in, through the low entrance to the field. A SWAT team dressed in black with helmets on their heads and weapons in their hands.

"Police!" they scream. "Get on the ground! Lie down!"

From the corner of her eye, Klara can see that the other man who was standing guard has already been overpowered and is lying with his face against the field. Two more police officers are bent over the man who was aiming his gun at Klara.

"He's wearing a flak jacket," one officer says. "Turn him over and cuff him."

She falls down to her knees, holds her hands above her head and looks at the man in the coat. He's also on his knees, with his hands on his head.

"I have diplomatic immunity," he screams. "You cannot arrest me."

Suddenly Klara is lying on the turf with a knee in her back, someone pulling her hands behind her, and she can feel cold steel as her hands are cuffed.

All around her, legs and weapons move under bright and merciless light. Somebody grabs hold of her arms and lifts her brusquely to her feet, leads her away from the light, down a slope and toward a dark, almost deserted parking lot.

They've made it about halfway across when two black vehicles roll in, plus an ambulance with no sirens or blue flashing lights. In the darkness by the school, Klara can see two unmarked vans along with some kind of prison transport.

It is strangely quiet. It's almost impossible to imagine that what just happened on the soccer field really happened. Klara turns to the police officer who's leading her forward.

"Why am I being arrested?" she asks. "What am I wanted for?"

The police officer doesn't react, as if he doesn't hear; he just pushes her forward toward the parked transport.

"You can't let that Russian go," she continues. "You know that, right?"

Fifty yards to her left she sees the passenger door of one of two black Volvo SUVs sliding open. Somebody jumps down onto the asphalt and heads in her direction. It's not until he's just a few yards away that she sees who it is.

Anton Bronzelius turns to the black-clad police officer with a firm grip on Klara's arm. "I'll take it from here. Säpo." He holds up his badge to the faceless man.

The officer nods and releases her arm.

Over by the vans, Klara sees doors open and two people in civilian clothes and flak jackets and stocking caps start to move toward them. Bronzelius grabs hold of her arm firmly and leads her quickly to the parked Volvo. "Get in," he says.

He pushes Klara into the back seat and gets in on the other side. She hears shouting from outside just as Bronzelius pulls the door closed again, maybe one of the two people in civilian clothes. Without having to say a word, the car starts driving across the parking lot. Klara turns around and looks out the back window, her heart pounding.

"What the hell is going on?" she asks. "Are you kidnapping me?"

"I guess you could call it that," Bronzelius says.

Klara turns to him and looks at his gray face, at his blue, straightforward eyes. There's something in his eyes, something in that naive calm that makes something suddenly quite clear to her.

"You have no idea what this is about," she says. "Not when you arrested Gabi. Not now."

He looks at her without changing his expression. "For someone whose life I just saved you sure aren't very thankful," he says.

Now she looks at him, quite composed again. "You're just a cop. A good cop. But you don't understand what this is about. Do you?"

She knows she should be grateful. Without Bronzelius she'd be dead now. But she can't resist the feeling that if it weren't for him she and Gabi wouldn't have landed in this mess either.

She turns around and sees one of the vans from the parking lot following them. They're driving fast now, up the on-ramp to the highway. She knows that she shouldn't give in to the impulse, but it is growing like a balloon inside her. "You got played. You all got played," she says. She shakes her head. "The Russians tricked you into arresting Gabriella. Did you seriously believe she was involved in a fucking terrorist attack? I thought Säpo's job was to protect us from Russian spies. Not do their bidding."

He looks calmly at her. "It was good that you called," he says. "For everyone's sake."

The anger she feels is mixed with something else, the feeling that she too doesn't really know what's going on.

"Who's after us?" she asks and feels her anxiety come back with full force. "Where are my friends?"

NOVEMBER 25—BROMMA AIRPORT

THEY'VE BEEN DRIVING for about half an hour when the van finally slows. Yassim is lying on Jacob's lap and his feverish, damp forehead shines whenever the occasional headlight flashes through the high, latticed window. Yassim wavers on the edge of consciousness and Jacob's panic feels ever tighter in his chest. George somehow succeeds in getting up onto his feet, and he starts kicking and pounding on the wall to the cab. But the wall is solid, and it's clear that nobody will hear them.

"He'll soon lose consciousness completely," Jacob whispers. "What the hell should we do then? They can't just let him die."

Jacob can see Yassim's lips moving, and he leans over him. Yassim's voice is so weak, Jacob can barely make out what he's saying. But at the very moment the van stops and the door slides open again, he hears: "Tell them nothing."

When the door opens, Jacob sees a pair of dark and familiar eyes.

"Lookee here," Myriam Awad says. "Have you missed me?"

There are probably five or six other people. They're all burly and bearded, wearing flak jackets and black guns in the holsters over their jeans.

"Up and out," says one of them. "Get outta the van."

"This man is injured," George says. "He's lost consciousness and needs help immediately."

The bearded men look at him with disinterest. "He's a terrorist," says one of them. "That's the price he pays."

Two of them step into the van and lift Yassim roughly, carry him out together. Jacob stands up, but his hands are bound behind him, and he can't do a thing.

"Help him!" Jacob screams at the top of his lungs. "He needs help!"

Myriam stands in front of him and slaps him across the face.

"Shut the fuck up," she says.

Then someone pulls a hood over his head, and everything goes black.

Jacob blinks under intense fluorescent lights when the hood is pulled off. He's sitting in a cell or interrogation room. Perhaps it's just a storage closet. Concrete floors and brick walls. Hands cuffed to a stainless-steel table. There is no window, only a steel door, and Myriam is standing in front of it, staring at him impassively. There's something close to pity in her eyes.

"I'll take it from here," she says to the man in a Kevlar vest who's just jerked Jacob's hood off.

The man exits and Jacob can hear the door being locked behind him. The room is so cold he shivers, and it looks like smoke coming out of his mouth whenever he takes a quick, terrified breath.

"Yassim," he says. "Where is he?"

"You think Yassim is some kind of Snowden," she says. "He gathered information about some unnamed war crimes. And helping him makes you a hero."

Jacob blinks, doing all he can not to give anything else away. Could it really be possible that's all she knows?

"But you're swimming in some deep fucking water," she continues. "And there's no going back for you now, Jacob."

Somewhere outside his cell, he hears engines. Enormous engines revving up, and then becoming ever more distant. He recognizes that sound—it's an airplane lifting off.

Why are they at an airport? Myriam also hears the sound of the plane, doesn't speak until it's gone. Then she sits down in front of him.

"You have *one* chance," she says. "One chance to save yourself and your beloved Yassim now. Tell me where that chip is."

"I want a lawyer," Jacob says.

Why did he say that? Because he's seen it in movies. Because he can't stand to be alone in this room with her.

Myriam just looks at him as if he's speaking in some incomprehensible language. "Excuse me?" she says. "Do you think you've been arrested?"

She leans forward, staring at him, her eyes completely cold now.

"We aren't the police, you little pussy," she says. "This is an intelligence operation. We're in the shadows now. There are no courts or lawyers here. Nobody knows where you are, nobody knows where you're heading."

She squats down next to him. Hopelessness burns inside him.

"You can't do this," he whispers. "There are rules, there are processes. . . ."

But Myriam just shakes her head. "Jacob," she begins. "I don't think you understand how deeply mixed up in this you are now. Why didn't you just listen to me in Beirut?" She points over her shoulder, to the wall and whatever's behind it. "In twenty minutes, I'm putting Yassim on a plane to Egypt," she says quietly. "He'll be handed over to their intelligence service, and he'll have to answer their questions. We know he has knowledge of a very large terrorist attack taking place in Europe in the very near future. It's up to you if you and your friend George end up on that plane or not. The Egyptians are adept at making people talk. Unfortunately, they're not as good at keeping people alive."

"Are you threatening me?" Jacob whispers.

"Am I threatening you?" she says. "Yes, Jacob. Yes, I am."

NOVEMBER 25—BROMMA AIRPORT

THEY'RE ON THE highway headed toward Stockholm when Bronzelius's phone rings. His answers are short, and he asks no questions: "I understand. . . . Yes. . . . That's understood."

After he hangs up he turns to Klara and meets her eyes.

"That was my boss," he says. "MUST, military intelligence, wants you in Bromma. My guess is that your friends are already there."

"But you're not going to do what he says," Klara says. "Why not?"

"Maybe I'm tired of being a good cop?" he says. "Maybe I'm tired of sneaking around and letting the wrong people end up hurt."

"Like last summer," Klara says.

"Do you know who you were talking to on the soccer field?" he asks.

Klara shakes her head. "A Russian?" she says. "We've had them after us this whole time. I suspect they're behind the evidence against Gabriella."

"Gregorij Korolov is his name," Bronzelius says. "He arrived in Sweden this afternoon. I know because he's a major player. The kind Säpo keeps an eye on whenever he's around. But he's a professional, so he managed to evade our surveillance team almost immediately. And because he has a diplomatic passport, there's nothing we can do other than throw him out. But I would love to know what this is about, why you were standing on a soccer field in Bergort with a well-known Russian spy. Why did military intelligence take an embassy intern to Bromma Airport? Why do they want you there?"

Klara can't make heads or tails of him or his motives. This summer he threatened her and allowed ruthless Russian interests to foment riots in the suburbs of Stockholm just to gain some advantage in an endless spy war. Now he says he's willing to help her.

"I don't trust you," she says. "It must have felt good to arrest Gabi."

He looks at her neutrally. "I arrested Gabriella because we have convincing evidence she was connected to Jacob Seger and through him, a terrorist organization in Syria. But that I would think for a moment that either of you were terrorists is laughable. I was annoyed at you this summer. You ended up in the middle of one of our operations, which despite everything did end up successful. I would much rather you'd kept quiet, no doubt. But that's just how the game is played. I'm not driven by revenge, Klara. Quite the opposite."

She turns away and stares out into the darkness. She knows it's true—that's why she called him, because she knew somehow he'd do the right thing, despite what happened.

"If I tell you," she says, "will you promise to let us go? Do you promise to let Gabriella go?"

She thinks of the terrorist attacks barely a day away. She can't let them happen. But she has to save her friends too.

"Turn your back to me," he says.

Klara does, and he uncuffs her.

"I promise," he says, stretching out a hand. "Same team?"

"Same team," Klara says, taking his hand.

They take a detour through the expensive neighborhoods of Bromma with their nineteenth-century wooden houses and apple trees, while Klara tells Bronzelius everything. All she knows. About Jacob and Yassim. The journey from Brussels, the rest stop in Germany, and that Yassim showed up in Malmö.

Here, Bronzelius nods. "Quite a scene at the central station there this afternoon. Shots fired. But what the hell, it's Malmö. What I don't understand is the Russian involvement."

He falls silent and looks out the window at the idyllic neighborhood around them, then he turns back to Klara again.

"And you're right about Gabriella," he says. "Someone was listening to her, but it wasn't us. Can't imagine it was MUST or the National Defence Radio Establishment either—they don't have the resources, and a Swedish lawyer wouldn't be interesting to us or them, no matter how irritating she might be."

"The Russians," Klara says with a shiver.

The thought of Gabi being bugged all through the autumn, maybe even since this summer, is genuinely unnerving.

"It was the Russians who really lost out after what you all did this summer," Bronzelius says. "Their whole apparatus was destroyed when you discovered what they were up to. It's not unthinkable that they might want to fight back, mainly against Gabriella because she's been the public face. They've gotten a hell of a lot more aggressive lately."

"So when Jacob called her from Beirut, they picked up the trail," Klara says. "Maybe they're trying to stop a terrorist attack, just like us?"

Bronzelius shrugs. "Maybe. But I'm pretty sure there's more to it than that."

The car has stopped at the small hill in front of the airport, just behind the taxis and the gates.

"They're at hangar four," Bronzelius says.

Klara turns toward him. "Well then," she says. "Time to finish this. But there's one thing I'd like to show you first."

NOVEMBER 25—BROMMA AIRPORT

A NEW SOUND IS audible just outside the cell Jacob is sitting in. The rumble of engines.

"Your plane," says Myriam serenely. "That's what you're hearing out there. We've arrived at your last chance now."

Jacob has laid his head on the table, too exhausted to even sit upright, but he straightens and looks at Myriam. She's moved over by the door, her eyes still on him.

"You're bluffing," he says. "You can't send a Swedish citizen to Egypt."

"Is your experience with me thus far that I bluff?"

His head is spinning now. "I don't have the chip," he says. "But I know where the terror attacks are going to take place. And I know when."

He can't sacrifice Yassim or risk himself.

"I'll tell you if you promise to hand us over to the police instead of sending us away," he whispers.

Myriam walks slowly over to the table, sits down opposite him. "It's a start," she says. "You can stay if you tell me."

He tells her everything he knows about the attacks against the opera house in Stockholm, Gare du Midi in Brussels, the airport in Rome, and Harrods in London. It's not much. Just the places and time, 19:00 on November 26, tomorrow. That's all Klara wrote in her text when they were on their way to Stockholm.

Myriam writes it down in her notebook and looks at him when he falls silent.

"Is that it?" she asks. "Is that really all you have? No names or details? Nothing more?"

"That's it," he says. "I swear that's all I have now. I can get you the rest, I promise. But surely that has to be enough for you to prevent it, put in extra guards, keep people away from those places, whatever you have to do."

She looks at him indifferently. Then she stands up, walks around the table, unlocks his handcuffs before pulling him onto his feet and fastening his hands behind his back.

"Time to go," she says, pulling him through the steel door to a big hangar where a small, white aircraft is waiting with its engines running.

One of the bearded men comes toward her. "Not a sound," he says, shouting over the noise of the engines. "He's a clam. Also, barely conscious. That George Lööw won't say anything either, just keeps demanding a lawyer and shit like that. I don't think he really understands the situation."

"Get them on board," Myriam says. "I have what we need right now, the rest we can figure out."

The man nods hesitantly. "You sure?" he says.

She narrows her eyes at him. "Do I look unsure?"

He shakes his head, takes a small radio off his belt. "Get them on board," he says calmly.

"What the fuck?" Jacob screams, trying to tear himself out of her grip. "You swore you wouldn't send us away! That was the only reason—"

Myriam punches him hard in the solar plexus, and he collapses onto his haunches, silenced, still with his hands behind his back. She leans over him.

"You smuggled terrorist plans," she says. "Together with your terrorist boyfriend. These are the consequences for that. Why didn't you listen to me in Beirut if you didn't want to play this game?"

Jacob lifts his eyes and sees two of Myriam's men leading Yassim out of a room and farther into the hangar. He has handcuffs on and a black hood over his head; it takes two men to support him.

"Yassim!" he screams. "Yassim!"

From the corner of his eye, he sees a man heading in through the open hangar doors, a small automatic weapon bouncing at his hip. Jacob turns instinctively toward him.

"We have a problem," the man shouts. "A big fucking problem."

In the next second, Jacob can hear sirens blaring somewhere, and they're getting closer and closer. Suddenly, the hangar is full of blinking blue lights and police officers with weapons drawn and ambulances.

He falls down onto the concrete floor, completely still, completely exhausted.

NOVEMBER 25—BROMMA AIRPORT

KLARA AND BRONZELIUS are sitting in the car outside the terminal, and she takes out the computer and shows him what's on it. He turns pale.

"Can we get an interpreter here now?" he screams to a uniformed police officer, who immediately runs off.

They finally find a young police officer fluent in Arabic, and he squeezes into the back seat next to Klara. Not exactly an interpreter, but at least someone who can confirm what Klara already knows. The officer's eyes widen as he takes in what's in front of him, and he summarizes it quickly for Bronzelius. Translates the information in the documents, the coordinated terrorist attacks on four European cities.

Bronzelius leans back in his seat and stares straight up at the ceiling. "Jesus fucking Christ," he says. "It's insane."

"What should we do?" Klara says.

Bronzelius turns to her and stares straight into her eyes. "I'm gonna have to take care of this gigantic mess."

Then he gets out his phone, and it seems to take only a couple of minutes before an armada of police vehicles appear around them.

A police officer in civilian clothes opens Klara's door and tears the computer from her hands. Another police officer tries to force her out of the car.

"No," Bronzelius says. "She's riding with me, and she should in no way be considered a suspect in connection with this."

Then he jumps out of the car and confers with the uniformed police officers. All she hears is something about a "kidnapping" and "possible hostage situation," and then they leave.

"I didn't mention to my colleagues that we are probably chasing rogue government officials here," he tells Klara when he gets back into the car. "Better to have this sorted out before my bosses get any other instructions or understand what's going on. People with a higher pay grade than me can figure out the legal details later. No time to lose."

They roll past the commercial terminals quickly, through a gate that a security guard opens as soon as he sees the procession of police cars with flashing blue lights and screaming sirens.

Now they're on the other side of the airport, in front of a large hangar with vaulted ceilings.

"I thought Säpo and MUST were on the same side," Klara says. "And I certainly didn't think that one of the organizations kidnapped citizens."

"Well," Bronzelius says. "We both want to keep Sweden safe, if that's what you mean. But our methods . . . differ slightly. We're just cops, like you said. We want to see people arrested and convicted and democracy defended. It sounds silly maybe, but I really do believe in it."

"A little pompous perhaps," she says. "But I understand what you mean."

"MUST likes to work in the shadows," Bronzelius continues. "Everything is just one long game for them. The exchange of information between countries, shifting alliances. The secrets themselves are the goal, not revealing them. That's where we differ. I work in the darkness, but I want to bring it into the light. They just want to go further in."

"What happens when we drive into the hangar?" Klara says. "Who has the right to arrest whom?"

Bronzelius looks at her with an eyebrow raised. "Who has the right to arrest whom?" he repeats. "I thought you were a lawyer, Klara. Who has a monopoly on force within Sweden's borders?"

"The police," she says. "But is it really that simple?"

"Is MUST the police?" Bronzelius asks rhetorically.

"They're military, I suppose."

"Exactly," Bronzelius says. "They can think what they want, but what they're up to is illegal. I'm with the police. It's my duty to arrest them for kidnapping if that's what they're doing."

There's something reassuring about Bronzelius's old-school attitude. She sees him hold up a hand and point to the closed-off area in front of them.

"This is where government planes usually land," he says. "And they're sending people to be tortured in dictatorships from here."

He turns toward her. "But we're fucking done with that."

She nods calmly. "Yes, we are," she says.

She hears aircraft engines above the sirens. Through the windshield, she sees several armed guards in civilian clothing approaching the police cars and then being waved back to their car.

Bronzelius rolls down the window and holds up his badge. "We have a report of a kidnapping situation," he says briefly. "Open the gates."

The guard barely looks at his badge, staring at Bronzelius with confused, icy-blue eyes. "There is no kidnapping here," he says. "However, the security of this nation is depending on this operation. I can't let you in, and I think you already know that."

Without looking away from the guard, Bronzelius lifts his radio to his mouth. "Force the gate," he says. "Now."

They drive forward so fast the guard is forced to jump aside. Klara sees other guards streaming in through the gate, uncertain what's required here or permitted. They finger their weapons but don't raise them.

The doors to the hangar open, and several SWAT vehicles drive in at full speed, and police officers jump out with automatic weapons. Armed men like the one at the gate, and with ski masks over their faces, look up in confusion, but in the end they lower their weapons and raise their hands.

The situation is confusing at first, a chaotic mix of flashing lights, cars, people with guns and a rumbling plane in the middle of it all.

Klara scans the hangar as she follows Bronzelius out of the car. A man in a black hood is lying on the floor. He was being guarded by two of the men in the hangar, but now there are two police officers at his side, and they're waving over the EMTs.

She also sees Jacob lying on the floor with his hands bound behind his back, his face pressed into the concrete, and a police officer leaning over him.

"Is there anyone here who considers themselves responsible for this goddamn circus?" Bronzelius roars.

His voice manages to be heard even above the roar of the engines. Klara turns to him. He seems so unimaginably stable, almost like a father figure, in his leather jacket, his jeans, his sturdy boots.

"Can somebody turn off that goddamn plane?" he roars. "Now!"

It takes a moment, but soon the sound is muffled.

"Again," he says. "Who the hell is in charge of what's going on in here?"

A woman, just a few years older than Klara, with dark hair and eyes, takes a step forward and is restrained by the police. She looks furious, at her breaking point. "What in the hell is this?" she yells. "Do you have any idea what you're doing?"

Bronzelius walks over to her. "So you're the one who's responsible here?" he asks. "Who are you, first of all?"

"Myriam Awad," she seethes. "The Office for Special Acquisition. I suggest that you turn around and leave immediately."

If it wasn't for the uniformed police officer standing between them, she would probably launch herself at Bronzelius. There's no doubt that she would win that fight.

"This is far above your skill set," she continues. "Calmly back away and call your boss. If you're lucky, you might still be able to save your fucking mediocre career."

Bronzelius looks at her curiously. "I'll be damned," he says. "They're just getting younger and younger." He turns to the police officer standing next to her. "Cuff them all and take them in."

"You're gonna regret this," Myriam Awad fumes. "Of that I'm one hundred percent sure."

"Without a doubt," Bronzelius sighs. "Without a doubt."

One after another, the plainclothes agents are handcuffed and led to a police bus, which quietly drives away.

Klara looks around and sees Jacob standing up but being held back by two police officers.

"Where are you taking him?" Jacob screams, pointing to Yassim. "He's almost unconscious!"

Klara goes over to Jacob and puts a hand on his shoulder, but it's pushed away by the police.

"He's wanted by the police, and he's being arrested," the policeman says. "We have orders to take him to the detention center."

"Klara," Jacob says desperately. "Where are they taking Yassim?"

She assumes Yassim must be the man in the black hood she saw being led into an ambulance.

"He'll receive medical attention," she says quietly, looking into Jacob's eyes. "I'll make sure of it, I promise."

He looks at her with something wild and almost crazed in his eyes. "What's going to happen to him?"

"I don't know, Jacob," she says. "I don't know."

The police push him into the back seat of a police car, and Klara turns around and scans the hangar. In all that chaos, she must have missed George. She finds Bronzelius among the uniformed police officers and approaches him.

"Someone is missing," she says.

Bronzelius turns to her with a questioning expression.

"George Lööw," she says.

Bronzelius sends away the transports full of the detained and gives instructions to keep them isolated until further notice. Then he turns to the twenty or so police still there.

"We're missing somebody," he says calmly. "Start looking."

The police officers spread out across the hangar, starting to search everywhere, inside the airplane, the office, the storage room, the cleaning closet and toilets.

Finally, Klara is the one who finds him. She's sitting in the back seat of one of the police cars with a blanket wrapped around her shoulders. But she can't sit still, so she gets up and goes out to the hangar floor to help out. When she peeks into the back seat of a parked black Volvo she sees him.

"Here!" she shouts. "Here he is!"

Through the window, she can make out George rolled up in the fetal position on his back, the hat he bought at H&M in Malmö still pulled low on his forehead, down over his eyes. "George! George!" she cries, pounding on the window.

And Bronzelius is beside her, holding her shoulders and pulling her away from the car. One of the police officers motions for an ambulance.

She hears the heavy car shatter on the concrete as the police beat their way in to George, then she sees only the blinking blue lights and the stretcher and feels arms around her, hears voices saying everything will work out okay, even though she knows that's not true.

Nothing ever works out in the end.

NOVEMBER 26—STOCKHOLM

THEY ARRIVE AT Söder Hospital, snow whirling around the car in the yellow lights of the emergency exit. The police car stops behind the ambulance to give the emergency room staff space. There's already a team in green and white waiting for the ambulance to arrive.

Klara starts to pull at the car door. She has to get out, get to George's lifeless body.

"Wait," says the police officer in the front seat. "You don't want to disturb them now. Let them do their job first."

She knows he's right, knows it's futile, knows the door is locked; still she can't stop pulling on it. Can't stop trying to prick this bubble, end this nightmare.

The young police officer stays with her in the waiting room even though his shift is over.

"I can't leave you here alone," he says. "Not after everything you've been through."

She turns to him and stares into his dark eyes, at his short black beard. He looks Iranian, or Middle Eastern—she hadn't noticed before, hadn't noticed anything. Except George, and now nothing else matters anymore.

"Thank you," she says.

Then a doctor is standing in front of them, just inside the door. She's in her fifties, dark hair in braids, looks like she hasn't slept for a week, with dry, deep bags beneath her eyes.

"Are you with the patient who arrived in the ambulance about half an hour ago?" she asks, still standing in the doorway.

Klara nods; her voice no longer works. The lump in her throat feels so large nothing will ever get by it again.

"We don't have a name for him," the doctor says. "Do you know who he is?"

Klara nods again, but it is as if she has lost her voice and she can't even get George's name out.

"George Lööw," the policeman says in a calm voice. "His name is George Lööw. How serious are his injuries?"

The doctor shakes her head slowly, as if she's not sure she heard correctly. "Injuries?" she says. "Doesn't have any that I know of. He's unconscious, definitely. But we think he's been drugged or anesthetized. All of his vitals are completely normal. We've sent him up to a hospital room and we're waiting for him to wake up."

Klara sits down on a chair beside George's bed and looks at him. At his smooth, calm face and ruffled blond hair which she brushes away from his cool forehead. It's over now. She feels a relief bordering on euphoria but at the same time the new possibilities scare her. What will happen when he wakes up?

"He gave you a good scare."

She jumps and turns around. Bronzelius is leaning against the doorframe. Behind him, she catches a glimpse of the two uniformed police officers who showed up as soon as they moved George to this ward. Klara doesn't know if they're here to protect or guard them.

"Hello," she says. "God, what a day. What a bunch of fucking days."

Bronzelius enters the room and sits down on a chair next to her.

"Do you have time to be here?" she asks. "Don't you have people to interview to try to figure out what the hell this is all about?"

"We are already making the arrests," he says calmly. "Everyone in the Swedish cell you had on your computer has been arrested. We have most of the London, Brussels, and Rome cells, too."

Enormous relief washes over her. "Oh, God."

"The English found the same plans in London when they made their crackdown, so at least one courier was able to smuggle the information into Europe. It seems like they'd realized that Yassim was a traitor and the plans in Brussels were abandoned after what happened there. They were still planning to carry out the attacks in London and Rome, but in the morning instead of waiting for the evening."

"It's so insane," Klara says. "It would have been a bloodbath. Oh, Jesus."

"Almost too much to fathom," Bronzelius says. "After Paris? So fucking awful."

"What happens now?" Klara says, looking at him. "Where do we stand in all this?"

"First of all," he begins, "your friend will be released." He sighs. "Unfortunately. Lord knows she made life tough for us this summer and autumn."

"Gabi?" Klara says.

"Yes," he says, falling silent for a while. "All the information we had was generated by Myriam Awad's team, and she received it from the Russians. MUST apparently recruited Jacob Seger in Beirut, but he was a bit too independent for them."

Klara nods and smiles. "Yes," she says. "Love is inconvenient."

"The real mystery is Yassim," Bronzelius says. "He's just a few wards away from here. He's the real reason I'm here. Felt like the natural place to start, to interview him. And I'm sure he has quite a story to tell. He was recruited by Korolov in Beirut, when his family was murdered. Then he infiltrated ISIS and became a courier. He even informed the Russians about what was going to happen in Paris. . . ."

"Do you believe that?" Klara says.

Bronzelius shrugs. "It's the only thing that makes any sense if you consider what happened to the rest of you. It explains why the Russians were after you, right? They got Gabriella arrested so that she wouldn't get hold of the information Jacob had. But they hadn't reckoned on you and George. And Myriam's wild bunch."

"But why didn't they work with you?" Klara says. "Why did they go their own way?"

"You have to remember they thought Yassim was a terrorist," he says. "And best case, Jacob was naive; at worst, an accomplice. And it got out of hand. They lost control and direction. Apparently they intended to send at least Yassim to Egypt."

He shakes his head.

"Their spy craft looks a little different than my mediocre cop work, or whatever it is she called it. But there are still rules that even they are supposed to follow. At the same time, it's not entirely unproblematic to storm in like we did. There will be quite a bit to untangle. But the terror attacks have been averted. People have been arrested throughout Europe. This ended up being quite a success, even if the road here was messy. Especially for you and your friends."

"Sorry I was so angry with you before," Klara says. "I was still furious from this summer."

Bronzelius smiles at her. "No problem. I've been through considerably worse. And no matter how it ends up, it was good we got hold of that little cell of Myriam's. Who knows how many people they've sent to be interrogated in Egypt or Yemen or God knows where? But it's over now, I can promise you that."

"The rule of law has been restored," Klara says. "Who would have thought we'd do it together a couple of months ago?"

He smiles again. "It was goddamn good luck that you showed up," he says. "Otherwise, the Russians would have taken Jacob in Brussels and we'd be a few hours away from one of the worst terrorist attacks in European history."

Klara turns to the bed again and sees George starting to move his head. She stands up. Bronzelius does as well.

"You're no longer suspects," he says. "Just so you know. The police are just here for some added security. I'll have to interview you, so don't leave Stockholm before I have the chance to do that, okay? But otherwise I can only say: thank you."

"And Yassim?" she says.

"Who knows?" he says. "We'll interview him too and try to figure out his story. It's not likely that the Russians will want him back after this." He falls silent and looks out through the window.

"So what will happen to him?" Klara asks quietly.

Bronzelius shrugs and turns to her again. "If we can't prove he's committed any crime then he'll be deported," he says.

Klara nods. "Without him, we never would have been able to do this," she says. "Don't forget that."

"Life isn't fair," he says.

Klara hesitates for a moment and then takes a step toward him and gives him a hug. "Thank you," she says. "For listening to me, even after all that happened this summer."

"Klara?" She hears a faint voice coming from the bed. "Where the hell am I now?"

Bronzelius pats her on the shoulder. "Take care of him," he says. "Talk to you later."

She turns around and leans down over George, kisses him on the cheek.

"You're with me," she whispers.

NOVEMBER 26—STOCKHOLM

IT'S STILL DARK when Klara exits the Rådhuset subway station on Kungsholmen. She's freezing in the frosty morning air and clutches the coffee she bought at Pressbyrån tightly in both hands. She takes a right on Bergsgatan, toward the police station and Kronoberg jail.

It's strange that she's not more tired—she only slept for an hour, curled up in the hospital bed next to George. A nurse offered to let her sleep in another room, but leaving George felt impossible. They lay with their faces so close their noses touched, so close that their lips almost touched, and George told her everything that happened to him, Jacob, and Yassim.

"But why did they drug you?" she asked. "The other two were conscious."

"I didn't have anything they needed," George replied. "I think I was just ballast for them. I don't remember anything from that hangar you're talking about. Perhaps they didn't want me to know what they were doing with Yassim and Jacob. To avoid any witnesses."

Now she's sitting on a bench just outside the entrance of the detention center and taking small sips of coffee. A few snowflakes float down into the white light of the lamps near the gates and behind her she can hear the noise of the city's morning traffic. It's just a minute after eight when the gates of the jail open from inside.

Gabriella looks the same, though her curly red hair is bigger and wilder than usual, and she has no makeup on, which is unusual for her. When she sees Klara she stops and flings open her arms, a smile spreading on her lips. Klara gets up and walks toward her. They hug each other without saying anything at first. Then Klara pushes her best friend away from her and looks into her eyes.

"I can't believe it's only been four days," she whispers. "So much has happened."

Gabriella laughs and shakes her head. "Has it?" she says. "As far as I'm concerned the world stood still."

Gabriella takes a sip of her coffee and groans with satisfaction as they slowly walk down toward Norr Mälarstrand.

Klara starts to tell her everything, and Gabriella just stares at her with increasingly wide eyes.

"This is insane," she says. "I can barely take it in."

"Me neither," Klara says. "I still don't understand why they arrested you. On what grounds?"

"First they told me it was the conversation with Jacob, as you call him. They had information that was super top secret that pointed to him being a terrorist or collaborating with terrorists. Like you said."

"Myriam and her gang," Klara says. "Yes, that much I understood. But it was enough?"

"They confiscated my computer and phone, of course, claimed there was a bunch of communication between me and Jacob via email. That we had decided I would help him smuggle this into Sweden along with two other people."

"What?" Klara says. "But . . ."

"Yes, completely fabricated of course. That was clear from the start. Not even the Swedish in the messages was correct; I realized when I finally saw them. Some Russian wrote fake messages between my address and a fake Gmail account. The whole thing was surreal. Seeing things sent from your own account that you absolutely did not write or know were there. And the judge yesterday just heard the word *terrorism* and that was enough for him—he granted the detention and didn't listen at all to what we said about hacking or whatever. But then the prosecutor canceled the detention last night, just a few hours afterward, after you revealed what was up."

Klara shivers. "So disgusting," she says. "They hacked your secret Gmail account as well, the one we used before. But I figured out it wasn't you. Do you want to know how?"

Gabriella nods.

"What is Camp Nou?"

"The soccer field in Bergort?" Gabriella replies without a moment's hesitation.

Klara nods. "Exactly."

Gabriella throws her empty coffee cup into a trash can and walks to the quay, right down to the water. She turns to Klara. "Thank you," she says steadily. "For not giving up on me."

They continue toward the city while the sun rises slowly, and the world goes from black to a gentle gray; the sky is the same color as the water next to them, the same color as the dock and the cars. Klara clears her throat.

"But it doesn't end there," she says carefully. "There's one more thing."

She tells her about George. About how something has taken root in her, something she didn't even think she could feel anymore. Something arrived so suddenly that she didn't realize it and now it won't leave her for a second.

Klara feels her cheeks turning hot.

"You're blushing!" Gabriella laughs. "Well, I'm not surprised. You were already babbling about him on our way to Stockholm. But who would have thought it would blow up in the middle of all this too?"

They stop and look out at the island of Söder towering up on the other side of the water, where Gabi's apartment is located.

"I like your neighbor," Klara says. "She's quite a woman."

Gabi laughs. "Maria? Yes, she's fabulous. I can't believe she gave you Rohypnol." Then Gabi turns to her. "You don't know how happy I am about this thing with George," she says. "It's time for you to move forward. Finally."

Klara faces the water, watching as the sky turns pink in those first rays of the sun.

"Yes," she says steadily. "At some point you have to start living again."

NOVEMBER 26–28—STOCKHOLM/ESKILSTUNA

JACOB WAKES UP to someone gently shaking his shoulder and he opens his eyes. Gray hair in gray light. A face he recognizes from yesterday—or earlier today? He no longer knows what day it is. Or where he is.

"I don't know if I introduced myself," the man says. "Anton Bronzelius is the name. I'm with Säpo."

Jacob nods and struggles onto an elbow, blinks in the bleak yellow lights of the room. Bronzelius. He was Klara's contact at Säpo; he understood that much in yesterday's chaos.

"Where am I?" he says. His voice is hoarse and creaky, and he clears his throat. Bronzelius is already on his feet.

"Söder Hospital," he says. "They're holding you for observation. It seems like you've been through a lot lately."

Jacob looks around—it's definitely a hospital room; shiny floors, big beds, tubes and a TV hanging from the ceiling. A vague memory of police cars and an ambulance taking him here.

"Am I a prisoner?" he says. It feels like the wrong word, but his brain is neither quick nor clear enough. Bronzelius just shakes his head.

"We have a lot of questions," he says. "But you're not suspected of any crime. Even if your role in all this is still far from clear. But we have time to talk about that later." He gestures to the door. "We're in a bit of a hurry," he says. "I think there's somebody you'd like to see before it's too late."

Jacob's body aches as he follows Bronzelius through the desolate corridor of the hospital. His shoulder, knees, head. It feels as if he's just been pulled out of the rubble, as if he survived an earthquake. Maybe that's what he's done.

The silence and tranquility of the hospital is confusing; he can hardly believe that after everything, he's safe now, or something like it. He's not going to die. Whatever happens, he's going to live.

Bronzelius stops in front of a door that a police officer is guarding. They exchange a few words, but Jacob is so exhausted and drowsy he doesn't really process what they're saying. The door opens and Bronzelius pushes him gently through it.

"You have five minutes," he says. "I'm sorry, but that's all I can give you."

In the bed in this small room, Yassim is lying on his back on white sheets. His head rests against the pillow, his eyes are closed, and an overwhelming tenderness sneaks over Jacob. He hurries to the bed, leans over it. An IV in Yassim's arm, a white, freshly dressed bandage on his chest. Yassim turns his head and opens his eyes.

"You're here," he whispers faintly.

Jacob nods and takes Yassim's face between his hands, gently kisses those dry lips. Something rattles at the edge of the bed, and Jacob turns and sees that Yassim is handcuffed to the bed frame.

"I think they'll be keeping me a while," he says.

"What are they going to do to you?" Jacob says. "What's going on?"

He turns around and sees Bronzelius's face in the dim light at the door. "I'm afraid your friend will have to stay with us," he says. "He's been connected to ISIS. Acted as courier."

"He was exposing them!" Jacob bursts out.

He stands up, turns completely toward Bronzelius with his hands at his sides. The insight hits him ever more fully and leaves him with a paralyzing sense of powerlessness. Someone is going to have to pay, someone will be made responsible. And they've decided that's Yassim.

"You have three minutes left," Bronzelius says dryly. "It's up to you what you do with them."

Jacob can feel he's shaking now, but he turns back to Yassim, leans over him again, sinks down beside him, places his head so they're side by side.

"I'm so sorry," he whispers. "I . . ."

"Shhh, shhh," Yassim whispers. "I'm not sorry. We did the right thing, darling."

Jacob feels tears welling up behind his eyes, feels his throat burning and the lump there growing. Yassim's skin against his lips.

"You can't disappear," he whispers. "We just met."

When the train stops at Eskilstuna, Jacob takes a deep breath and squeezes the armrest. He closes his eyes. It's been two days since he left Yassim at the hospital. A day since Bronzelius let him leave the police station.

"We'll have to talk to you again," Bronzelius told him. "Don't go too far."

Jacob has already told them everything they wanted to know. Answered every question in the most minute detail as best he could. All in the hope that Bronzelius would answer just one of his own: "What is going to happen to Yassim?"

But besides those five minutes at the hospital that Bronzelius stole for him, he refused to give an inch. No promises, no information, nothing.

"Focus on yourself," Bronzelius said. "That's my only advice."

But there was something about the way he said it. Something in his eyes, his expression when he looked at Jacob, which seemed to open a door rather than close it.

"But he's not going to disappear?" Jacob asked. "You won't make him disappear?"

Bronzelius just shook his head, almost imperceptibly. "No," he muttered. "This is Sweden. People don't disappear here."

And that was all. That was all he got, the only straw he has to cling to.

As soon as he gets off the train and steps down onto the platform, it feels like a mistake to have gone back to Eskilstuna. It feels like too much, too soon. He swore he'd never, ever return. Just keep moving forward and upward and never ever look back. That was the promise he made to himself. The promise that allowed him to survive his home and school and everything he swore never to think about or share with anyone.

When he opens his eyes he sees a light, cold rain falling in the lights of the station.

But he knows it won't work anymore. He knows that Myriam was right when she found him in Beirut. It was an illusion from the beginning. You can't hide from who you are.

It's just a few minutes' walk from the station to the yellow brick buildings, the white balconies, the vodka bottles, the cigarette butts. His childhood. He still had the key in a small box in his room in Uppsala. He couldn't quite let go of it during his studies, no matter how much he wanted to, and now he's holding it in his sweaty hand as he opens the door to the apartment building.

But he stops there, unable to take another step. Then he feels Yassim's hand in his, feels him gently pulling him up the echoing stairwell, hears Yassim's voice whispering in his ear: "Don't be afraid, Jacob. Don't be afraid anymore."

She doesn't answer when he rings the doorbell, but he didn't expect she would. He carefully puts the key in the lock and turns it. It's been so long since he opened this door, still he remembers the exact movement, how the lock slides and clicks. He remembers the vacuum suck as he pulls open the heavy door of a musty apartment and the stench of smoke and alcohol and closed windows with curtains drawn.

His mother is lying on the stained couch. On the coffee table are some leaflets and a half-eaten chocolate cake, an empty pack of cigarettes, a full ashtray, an empty bottle of gin, a couple of beer cans. He turns around to see where Yassim went—he felt so real just a moment ago, there in the stairs. But he's disappeared again. It's just Jacob and his mother here now, and he goes over to the window, finds the handle and opens it. A cold wind swirls into the apartment, making the dirty curtains flutter.

He turns to his mother just as she's opening her eyes and starts to sit up on the couch.

"Matti?" she says. "Matti, is that you?"

Jacob goes over to the couch and squats down beside her. She looks at him with cloudy, tired eyes, her skin gray, her hair thin.

"Yes," he says. "It's me."

ACKNOWLEDGMENTS

THANK YOU TO:

My wonderful American and English publishers, Jennifer Barth and Laura Palmer

My excellent translator, Liz Clark Wessel

My Swedish publisher, Helene Atterling

My friend and agent, Astri von Arbin Ahlander

My careful, smart, and patient Swedish editor, Jacob Swedberg

My German publisher, Nina Grabe, who pushed me forward

My friend Tobias Almborg for the trip to Beirut, without which there would be no book

My brother, Daniel Zander, 26–28, for all the tips and contacts in Beirut

My guide to Beirut from a distance, Professor Leif Stenberg

My invaluable contact at American University in Beirut, Rami Khouri

My guide into the heart of young, political Beirut, Dima Tannir

My friend Johan Jarnvik, like always

My parents for all the security and help

My Moa for everything

ABOUT THE AUTHOR

JOAKIM ZANDER WAS born in Stockholm, has lived in Syria and Israel, and graduated from high school in the United States. He earned a PhD in law from Maastricht University in the Netherlands and has worked as a lawyer for the European Union in Brussels and Helsinki. Rights to his debut novel, *The Swimmer,* were sold in thirty countries. *The Friend* completes the trilogy begun by *The Swimmer* and continued in *The Believer.* Zander lives and works in southern Sweden with his family.

ALSO BY
JOAKIM ZANDER

THE SWIMMER
A NOVEL

"A terrific globe-trotting page-turner, rich with complex conflicts and a big, meaty, chillingly credible conspiracy."

—Chris Pavone, author of *The Expats* and *The Accident*

A deep-cover CIA agent races across Europe to save the daughter he never knew in this electrifying debut thriller—an international sensation billed as "*Homeland* meets Stieg Larsson" that heralds the arrival of a new master sure to follow in the footsteps of Larsson, John Le Carré, and Graham Greene.

THE BELIEVER
A NOVEL

"Zander has written another compelling, timely, and character-centered thriller, and many readers will look forward to what he does next."

—*Booklist*, starred review

An intricately plotted and brilliantly conceived stand-alone sequel to the international bestseller *The Swimmer* that turns the hottest political topics of our times into a complex, resonant thriller. With *The Believer*, Joakim Zander delivers another "page-turning" (*Entertainment Weekly*) novel of suspense that is as sophisticated and timely as it is compelling.